**Jessica Duchen** writes for and about music. She was a journalist and critic for the *Independent* from 2004 to 2016, and her work has appeared in the *Guardian*, the *Sunday Times* and *BBC Music Magazine*, among others. Her output includes fiction, biographies (Fauré and Korngold), stage works and librettos.

Among her recent novels is *Ghost Variations* (Unbound, 2016), based on the true story of the Schumann Violin Concerto's rediscovery in the 1930s. It was chosen by John Suchet as his Best Read of 2016 for the *Daily Mail*'s Christmas Books selection and was Book of the Month in *BBC Music Magazine*. Jessica often narrates concert versions of her novels, which have been heard at the Wigmore Hall, The Sage Gateshead, Kings Place and numerous music societies and festivals.

Her librettos include *Silver Birch* for composer Roxanna Panufnik, commissioned by Garsington Opera and shortlisted for a 2018 International Opera Award.

Jessica was born within the sound of Bow Bells, read music at Cambridge and lives in London with her violinist husband and two cats.

*Immortal*

# Immortal

*A novel inspired by real events*

Jessica Duchen

*[signature: Jessica Duchen]*

*For darling Camilla, with lots of love! [signature] xx x*

**unbound**

This edition first published in 2020

Unbound

TC Group, Level 1, Devonshire House, One Mayfair Place, London,
W1J 8AJ

www.unbound.com

ISBN (eBook): 978-1-78965-116-4

ISBN (Paperback): 978-1-78965-115-7

Cover design by Mecob

Printed and bound in Great Britain by Clays Ltd, Elcograf S.p.A.

*For Eric, with love and thanks*

Rodolphe Olard

Rebeca Omordia

Birgit Pappers

Lev Parikian

Duncan Parsons

Norman Perryman

Adam Philp

Joanna Pieters

Caroline Potter

Nazrin Rashidova

Mary C Rodriguez

Neysun Rouhani

Anne Serina Lynch

Susan Sinclair

Jon Smalldon

Eleanor Stanier

Gillian Stern

Kathryn Stott

Brent Straughan

Helen E Sunderland

Peter Thompson

Madelyn Travis

Barbara Urban

Errollyn Wallen

Ruth Waterton

Timothy Weir

Ken Woods

Katherine Youn

The following people helped to make this book possible by sponsoring a character.

*Julie Guicciardi* is kindly sponsored by Judith Barnard.

*Therese Brunsvik* is kindly sponsored by Harry Hyman.

*Ludwig van Beethoven* is kindly sponsored by Ivo Stankov.

*Franz Brunsvik* is kindly sponsored by Shelley von Strunckel.

*Josephine Brunsvik* is kindly sponsored by Lars Vogt.

# The Letter

After Ludwig van Beethoven's death in March 1827, a hidden drawer was discovered in his apartment. It contained items of intense personal significance, including a love letter, either returned or unsent, its recipient addressed only as 'my Immortal Beloved'.

*6 July, morning*

*My angel, my all, my own self – only a few words today, and those in pencil (with yours) – my lodging is definitely fixed only until tomorrow. What an abominable waste of time – dealing with necessities amid such desperate grief?*

*Can our love continue except through sacrifice, through not demanding everything? Can you change the fact that you are not entirely mine, I not entirely yours? Oh, God, gaze at the beauties of Nature and prepare yourself for the inevitable. Love demands everything and rightly so, and thus it is for me with you, for you with me – only you forget so easily that I must live for you as well as for myself – were we wholly united, you would notice this anguish as little as I should.*

*My journey was terrible. I arrived here only at 4 o'clock yes-*

terday morning, because they lacked horses ... at the penultimate station they warned me against travelling overnight, made me afraid of the forest, but that only provoked me – but I was wrong, of course the coach broke down on the dreadful road ... still, I again found some pleasure as I always do when I am fortunate to survive something.

Now quickly from the external to the internal, we shall probably see each other soon, and today I cannot tell you those observations about my life that I have made during these days – were we always close together, I would not need to do so. My heart is full, with much to tell you – sometimes I find words are no good at all. Be cheerful – remain my true and only darling, my all, as I do to you. The gods must send what must and shall be for us.

Your faithful

Ludwig


*Monday evening, 6 July*


You are suffering, you, my dearest creature. I have just noticed that letters must be posted first thing early on Mondays – Thursdays – the only days when the post goes from here to K. You suffer – oh! Wherever I am, you are with me, I talk to myself and to you – arrange that I may live with you. What a life!

So! Without you – pursued by people's kindness here and there ... I deserve it so little, and do not wish to deserve it ... it pains me – and when I see myself in connection with the Universe, what I am, and what he is – whom one calls the Greatest – and yet – again there lies herein the divine essence of humanity. I weep when I think you will probably receive the first news from me only on Saturday – as much as you love me – I love you even more strongly – but never hide yourself from me.

*Good night – as I am taking the waters, I must go to bed. Oh God – so near! so far! Is it not a true citadel of heaven, our love – and as strong as the firmament –*

*Good morning, on 7 July*

*In bed my thoughts already rush to you, my Immortal Beloved, sometimes joyfully, other times sadly, waiting to see whether Fate will listen to us. I can only live with you either completely, or not at all. Yes, I have decided to wander far and wide until I can fly into your arms and call myself entirely at home with you, and send my soul enveloped by yours into the realm of spirits – yes, regrettably it must be so. You will recover more easily as you know I am faithful to you; never can another own my heart, never – never! O God, why must one leave somebody one loves so much, and still my life in W[Vienna] is a miserable one at the moment. Your love made me at once the happiest and unhappiest of men. At my current age I need some continuity, some stability in life – can that exist in our circumstances? Angel, I have just heard that the post goes every day – and therefore must close, so that you will receive the letter at once. Be calm – only through calm consideration of our existence can we achieve our goal of living together – be patient – love me – today – yesterday.*

*What longing in tears for you – you – my love – my all – farewell – oh, keep on loving me – never doubt the most faithful heart of your beloved*

*L*
*Ever thine.*
*Ever mine.*
*Ever us.*

# Overture

'Mariam Tenger, Madam.'

The maid stood back to admit my guest. I knew her at once. She was not 'Mariam Tenger' at all.

Those smiling, innocent eyes had scarcely changed since her childhood. She used to hide behind my skirts when she was six years old, too shy to show her face in front of visitors. We grow older, we grow up – well, some do – but I have seen enough children progress from infanthood to some measure of maturity to know that in essence we stay the same. The years roll back and I am once more in our Ofen house, high above the Danube, with little Marie, the first school I founded of forty girls, and my ever-grumbling mother.

'Marie Hrussoczy!' I held out my arms. My visitor crossed the room in a rustle of silk.

'I thought you would have forgotten me.'

'I have changed a lot more than you have. Sit down, my dear, and tell me everything.'

Marie settled herself on the velvet sofa. She was in her late thirties, blooming with health. Her dress was well tailored, but practical and she wore no wedding ring.

'I had to come and see you, Countess Therese. I was so excited when I heard you would be passing through Vienna. Everything I am, everything I do now, I owe to you.' Her gaze brushed the old, silver-tipped walking stick propped against the side of my chair. She would be wondering whether a lady of my years should be travelling at all. Indeed I should.

'I am spending some time with my nieces – Blanka has had a difficult decade and she is leaving for Paris to build a new life. We have been too much apart and will be again. Soon we are going to Dresden, but I had once more to see my dear Vienna…' I knew it might be for the last time.

'Blanka *Teleki*?' Marie's eyebrows lifted.

'At last she is released. Terrible, terrible, what has happened to her. My dear, there is no limit to the cruelty in this world, yet no limit, either, to its wonders.'

Marie gave an earnest nod. She had a writer's eyes. Eyes that notice: alert to atmospheres, the unseen, the unspoken.

She would be perfect.

An autumn chill was upon us. The maid came in to replenish the ceramic stove; Marie extended her hands towards it for warmth. I don't feel the cold.

I am in reasonably good condition. The curve in my spine has grown more pronounced, but I give thanks each day that my sight and hearing still work. A distorted back is not the worst problem one could have at eighty-four. I can still play music, write and enjoy seeing friends or courting supporters for my schools and the associations. I spend my days as I have for years: correspondence in the morning, a light meal at lunchtime – I do not need to eat much – and for two hours every afternoon I practise the piano.

Korompa, with profound gratitude, from your pupil, "Mariam Tenger".'

I smiled. 'At least you have not taken a male pseudonym.'

'I might try that. It could sell more copies.'

'And your next project?'

I guessed what was coming. 'Actually, I am planning a book about Ludwig van Beethoven.'

'Any particular aspect of our great Master's life?'

'You know about the letter? The mysterious, unaddressed letter to someone he calls his "Immortal Beloved"? They found it in his apartment after he died.'

I closed my eyes: there he was. I could feel his presence. He always seemed to fill a space when he entered it, as if his body became as sizeable as his spirit – despite that terrible old blue coat of his. The length of his stride, the tilt of his head as though facing into the north wind...

Marie was looking at me with concern. I must stop drifting off when people are talking to me, or they will think I am about to die.

'You've found out who she was?'

'I was hoping that... perhaps I can be the one who does. Oh, Countess Therese, you knew him well. *You* must have some idea?'

'Have you seen the letter itself? Is it genuine?' I said. Anton Schindler, Beethoven's bumptious secretary, had published it in his book about the Master back in 1840. Waves were made.

'I visited Schindler. He showed me the original.'

He used to totter about declaring himself the Master's closest associate and spreading lies. To make matters worse, he often tottered about at our family home at Martonvásár. My late brother Franz was far too good to him.

'I wondered if it was a forgery,' I admitted.

'It is Beethoven's writing – there's no doubting its veracity.'

'Schindler the Swindler... Forgive me, dear, for speaking ill thoughts – but Luigi van Beethoven couldn't stand him!'

'Luigi?'

'Ludwig, Louis, Luigi, it was all the same then. What did Schindler say?'

'He says it's Giulietta Guicciardi, and that your brother confirmed it. She was your cousin?'

Good brother, Franz. Well spoken. We had no reason either to like or to protect 'Countess Vanity'. Anyway, they are all gone now. 'Her real name was Julie. So why ask me?'

'Because I don't believe it.'

Not so good. I leaned back in my chair. Time, perhaps, to introduce a little bit more confusion.

'It's funny you should say that.'

'Tell me?' She was holding her breath.

'Because, my dear, I myself was his Immortal Beloved. And if you would like to tell the world about it in your new book, it will be not before time. I can swear, with hand on heart, that the only man I have ever loved was Ludwig.'

There you are, Marie: the coup of which you dreamed is all yours. What a shame for you that it is not true.

Though tears were now quivering in her eyes, Marie was a professional. In no time her notebook and pencil were in her hands, poised and ready.

'I first met the Master,' I began, 'not half a mile from this room. The year was 1799...'

# 1

My dear niece,

For many years I have put off the moment when I must write you this letter. I am old now, and around me there is gossip, excessive chatter that ventures too close to territory that I, personally, hold sacred. Perhaps Marie Hrussoczy will write her book; if she does, I can wait no longer. The story I shall tell will take longer than one session of *Kaffee und Kuchen*, and you, the person closest to my heart, deserve to know the whole truth. More than that, you are the only one who has an absolute right to it. May I suggest you find a quiet, private place to read and absorb what follows.

The year was not 1799. Our tale begins much earlier, with my grandfather's purchase of a huge sweep of puszta, the Hungarian plain that spreads beyond the line of land and sky southwest of Ofen and Pest. It was useless: marshy and full of mosquitoes. A few peasants and shepherds lived in desultory huts, working any cultivable land and tending the animals. Nothing much had existed here since the Ottoman occupation flattened the place, though they had been gone – and little lamented – since 1686.

We owned several town-houses on the hills of Ofen, the higgledy-piggledy royal town filled with the ring of hooves on cobbles and everywhere the strains of Gypsy violinists playing on the corners for money from passers-by. Below lay the mighty Danube, which separated Ofen with its palace from the busier city of Pest. About two hours' ride into the countryside was the hamlet of Martonvásár, and beyond it Martonvásár Castle which, when I was a girl of ten, my father built to be our true home.

How I wish you could have met my father. Few men could match him for kindness and sincerity, brilliance and intellect, strength and honour, or the quest to inculcate his four children with the curiosity of mind that attended us from earliest childhood. I can still picture the wry kink in his smile, the generous beam of his wide-set blue eyes, the way he would grumble about his wig's scratchiness and the heat of it in warm weather. Anton Brunsvik von Korompa! A joyous father, the visionary maker of an ideal life, a 'paradise', he called it, for his beloved family.

Martonvásár Castle melded with its serene landscape. Among the trees, its image reflecting in the still waters of the lake, it seemed lost in contemplation unless some eager visitor came galloping in after a ride across meadows of scarlet poppies, and tethered his horse, planning to join the young inhabitants for a card game or some music-making. This haven was our base for two-thirds of the year; the four winter months we spent in the city.

Our mother, born Baroness Anna von Seeberg, was as different from Anton as winter is from summer, yet they married for love. Her family opposed the match, for they were high-ranking enough in the aristocracy to send their daughter to be one of Empress Maria Theresa's ladies-in-waiting, while Father's family was nowhere near so grand. After a courtship lasting three years, the empress herself intervened. She instructed the elder Anton Brunsvik that his son *must* marry the young baroness; neither he nor the Seebergs could disobey. Upon the marriage, she elevated our grandfather to the status of count, 'of Korompa', our other family estate. I, the eldest daughter, am named Maria Theresa in gratitude. My godmother was the empress herself.

My mother clung to the notion of nobility in the same way anyone predisposed to nostalgia insists everything in the past was better than anything in the present. She could never quite escape the sense that since her husband's family had been ennobled, the snobbish circles around the Habsburg and later the Habsburg-Lorraine courts looked down upon our family as not '*geboren*' but '*geworfen*' – not born into the nobility, but 'whelped'. Sometimes, when we four whelps let off excess energy in the grounds, and there'd be games, horse riding or rowing on the lake, I'd spot Mother staring at us from a window as if she were one of the dead watching the living without envy.

Pepi was younger than me by four years. Her real name was Josepha, but this became the prettier-sounding Josephine, and thence the affectionate Pepi. Our youngest sister Charlotte's real name was Caroline, but we dubbed her Lotti, or sometimes Roxelane for her dusky colouring, after the concubine of Suleyman the Magnificent, sultan of the Ottoman Empire.

Franz, our brother, was less than two years my junior. He took after Father: bright blue eyes set in a broad face, with a wide if laconic smile to match. I could recognise his strong, light step almost from the other side of the house. He had the puffed-up confidence of a boy who thought himself in charge of a brood of sisters who required only to be married off to suitable men they did not dislike too much (we begged to disagree). We all – his parents, three sisters and two dogs, silky-haired Hungarian Vizslas – adored him. However infuriating he was, however much his pastimes worried us, it did not matter. Franz needed no nickname.

Neither did I, beyond the obvious 'Tesi' – until life presented us with unexpected roles in which private allusion was helpful. But I am as I am. I am as you see me. I am not an onion, with hidden layers to uncover. If you are a multifaceted person, you can carry many names, but not if you are me.

Besides, we have enough trouble spelling our surname. There are as many different versions as there are Brunsviks, or Brunswicks, or Brunszviks to wield them. Today in 1859, as my homeland's identity surges forth after long years under the Habsburg yoke, I have switched to the authentic Hungarian spelling: Brunszvík. I learned Hungarian when I was seventy, and if I can absorb such a language at that age, one new spelling should present no great challenge.

'What are you reading?' Pepi's bright eyes peered round the chair's wing and over my shoulder. In the library at Martonvásár I had curled up with a volume acquired with persistence from an Ofen book dealer, who had ordered it for me from London. To my side was a small table bearing a glass oil lamp; beside that sat an English dictionary.

'*The – Vicar – Of – Wakefield.*' Pepi read the embossed title. 'What's that?'

'A vicar is a type of English priest. Wakefield is a town in northern England.'

She grabbed the book. 'You don't read English.'

'I do now.' I patted my friend the dictionary. 'Haven't you

been listening to Father's lessons?' He was trying to instruct us in the language.

'But we have all of French and German literature, and Italian, here in the library. Why do we have to do English too?'

'*I* want to, Pips. I want to learn. I want to read Shakespeare, Milton, Chaucer and Mary Wollstonecraft. It's not the same in translation. And American democracy – how am I to understand that if not in its own tongue?' Father believed that electing a president was an advanced ideal, an Enlightenment principle that left our empire floundering in the dark ages.

'It's too difficult!' Pepi whined. 'They have these ridiculous words that are spelled differently and mean different things but sound the same.'

'Willpower, Pips, is everything. If you apply yourself, nothing is impossible. We don't give up. Never forget that.'

My sister tossed my precious book back to me. 'I'll bet you anything that you don't read beyond halfway through.'

'I don't make bets. I'm not Franz.' I rifled for my lost place.

'I was joking. Franz and Lotti want to go on the lake – come on!' She seized my hand and pulled me after her.


Minutes later the four of us were clambering into the wooden boat beside the jetty. Franz sprang ahead and grabbed the oars, rocking us in the shallow water near the trailing willows; Pepi climbed over to the prow, and Lotti, who was ten and small for her age, took the stern. I was longing to pull the oars. 'Let me have a go,' I pleaded.

'Girls can't row,' Franz declared, motioning me after Lotti

and untying the rope. Then with a creak, a clonk and a swish of spray we were waterborne.

I love the quietness of the water. Casting off into the lake, the real world becomes distant – the barking of dogs, the shouts of peasants as they scythe the fields, clopping hooves and clanking wheels from the nearby road; you are insulated from it all by the lapping ripples and the dip and sigh of the oars. On the shore the lindens, alders and oaks, dry after the hot summer, were turning russet. Franz was an expert rower; we made rapid progress towards the island at the centre. Some ducks flapped aside, looking most offended. Pepi leaned out towards a group of white geese.

'Don't pat them, Pips – they bite,' Franz advised.

'Can't we go closer?'

He manoeuvred the boat through a half-moon and towards the birds, which honked and rustled. As Pepi reached out, the sun cast a bright outline around her profile, her broad forehead and delicate nose under her sun-hat. My little sister was growing into a beauty, with slender neck, deep brown eyes and chestnut curls, which were escaping her hat to cascade over her pale shoulders.

In a flash of feathers, the world tilted, the trees spun to the diagonal and there was a shout, a scream and a splash. 'I told you!' shouted Franz. He dropped the oars and leapt into the water after her. The geese took to the air. Breathless with fright, I glimpsed Pepi's white dress below the surface. Her hat had come off and was bobbing away towards the reeds. In a split second, all the promise of her adolescent beauty might be wiped out.

'Lotti, hold my shoes,' I directed, and without stopping to think, I was in, plunging down. I just had time to hear Lotti shout, 'Tesi, you can't swim!'

No matter – I'd watched Franz often enough. When I was

able to raise my head and gasp for air, I found I could paddle with my feet, swirl the surface with my arms and stay upright. The lake, like God, was my friend and held me up, as long as I allowed it. And Pepi –

Pepi had learned to swim. I had not been permitted because of my curved spine, but she had benefitted from lessons in the Pest hot springs with our governess in her pantaloons – yet she was out of control, flailing and splashing, and when she broke through the surface, she used the air to scream rather than breathe. Keeping one's head in a frightening situation seemed worth ten swimming lessons.

I grabbed her waist, but my waterlogged skirts were threatening to drag me down. Water rushed into my mouth and I felt the threat of physical panic. Fighting it, I supported Pepi under the armpits. The wooden prow of the boat rose ahead; Franz was beside me and between us we managed to hoist our sister upwards. She seemed too much in shock to help herself.

'Grab the top and pull yourself up,' Franz ordered.

'You can do it,' I encouraged her, spluttering, and a moment later she was aboard. Franz hauled himself after her, then reached down to pull me out.

We were all shaking. I tried to laugh.

'Weren't you scared?' said Lotti, whose sobs were subsiding.

'Yes,' said Pepi.

'No,' said I.

'Stupid girls,' grunted Franz.


Once we had changed into dry clothes, Mother lined us up and told us off. 'Therese, I'm ashamed of you. Why didn't you take better care of them? You're the eldest, you should set a responsible example.'

'She did!' Lotti cut in. 'It wasn't Tesi's fault.'

'Don't answer back. And Pepi – you were trying to pat the geese? What possessed you, girl?'

'I did say she shouldn't,' Franz said. 'They can be absolute buggers—' Then he remembered he shouldn't use the schoolboy language of his friends in front of his mother. We tried to stifle our giggles, without success.

'Go to your rooms, all of you, and don't let me hear a squeak out of you for two hours.' Mother turned her back.

I had found escape in the pages of *The Vicar of Wakefield* – where Squire Thornhill was building up Mrs Primrose's expectations for her daughters beyond all reason – when Father returned from the estate office, heard about our adventure and dashed up the stairs, two at a time. He provided embraces, anxiety, a caress for my unfortunate backbone.

'You shouldn't take such risks, not with your condition.' That was as gentle a scold as a slightly misshapen seventeen-year-old could hope for.

'Though my spine lacks a sound form, my spirit does not,' I told him, chin raised. 'I wasn't thinking. I just wanted to save Pepi.'

'Oh, Tesi... You're good by nature and virtuous by instinct, but you must remember to look after yourself as well as you look after other people.'

'Is Mother still angry?'

'Furious.' He grinned. 'But *I* couldn't be prouder of you if you were to marry the emperor himself.'

The incident bonded the four of us even more closely. I had read Plato's *The Republic* and while I was transfixed by its explorations of justice, government, reason versus passion and the place of art in society, its structure provided equal fascination. These discussions between educated individuals who raise each other's spirits through equal and elevated discourse: why should this exist only in the pages of an ancient philosopher's writings? In the spirit of the Enlightenment, building a world upon divine reason, why should we not do likewise?

I proposed that we should form a Social Republic of Exquisite People. Franz jumped at it, and our sisters, though puzzled, agreed. We chose for our meetings a crossing of paths in the grounds, where four linden trees marked the directions of the compass. 'This one is mine,' I said, claiming the western tree, 'looking towards America, like Father.'

'Mine will be the south,' Pepi decided, 'for Italy, the Alps and the sea.' In landlocked Hungary, seeing the sea remained a distant dream. Franz took the north, for the Rhine and the prosperity of Prussia. Little Lotti had to accept the east, but was enchanted by the notion of the Carpathian Mountains and the ancient towns and villages of Siebenbürgen. Here, at the intersection of pathways and progress, we would become ourselves at the best we could be.

'As a democracy, we have to *elect* the leader,' Franz pointed out. 'I shall stand.'

'So will I,' I announced. 'Lotti and Pepi, now you must vote.' Unlike the ancient Greeks, we could set our own rules and allow everyone a say, whether male or female. My sisters both voted for me.

Sometimes, we decided, we might allow others to join us, but they must earn the right. When our cousin Julie came to stay, we told her nothing. We strolled with her past the lindens, chattering about something else.

Julie was the daughter of Aunt Susanna, our father's sister, who had married an Italian count and settled in fashionable Trieste. Now, though no older than Lotti, Julie did not so much walk as parade through the gardens, speaking loud French with an affected Italian slant.

'You should come and visit us,' she remarked, casting a critical eye over our faded dresses and thence towards the dusty countryside. 'We have excellent couturiers in Trieste.'

Julie might be the apple of her parents' eye, but she would never be admitted to our republic.


The weather turned. The wind galloped across the puszta, where there was nothing to stop it; the peasants fought its gusts in the fields; and Lotti was in bed with a cold after the boating accident, despite having been the only one who didn't get wet. Her fright had had a worse effect than our drenchings. Franz was grounded as punishment, though he had done his best to help. Pepi and I took turns at the fortepiano, playing to one another. Pepi was working on a piece by Joseph Haydn; I was struggling with a sonata by Wolfgang Amadeus Mozart. The finale needed a fancy instrument with special percussion effects in order to sound Turkish. Ours had none. As for the state of its keyboard –

'Nothing would make this sound even unless you took it to bits and rebuilt it,' I grumbled. 'We should buy a decent piano. A Stein or a Streicher, with more notes.' We had a mere five octaves; the standard was becoming six, and composers were keeping up with the trend.

'Try some decent music,' quipped Franz, who was playing a card game with Father at the other end of the room.

'This is *Mozart!*' To me, Mozart was holy. On hearing of his death I'd cried for a week.

'Turkish Rondo indeed. Nikolaus Zmeskall in Vienna just wrote to me about a friend of his who's been studying with Haydn. Apparently the old boy was having difficulty taming him. He improvises, Zmeskall says, like some kind of devil, or maybe an angel if angels do such things. He says he makes Mozart look like an old—'

'*Franz!* Don't you dare!'

'Has he written anything? Can we play it?' Pepi asked.

'I'll get Zmeskall to send something. Your turn, Father.'

'My turn will be to buy my children a new piano.' He cast a wink towards me. Over her embroidery Mother, thinking of the cost, uttered a quiet snort. While Father loved to collect, build and give, Mother offset his generosity by fussing over every last forint.

Two weeks later, the post coach stopped at Martonvásár with a parcel for Franz. On the volume within, a decorative frame of flowers and cupids surrounded words in Gothic script.

### LUDWIG VAN BEETHOVEN
### 24 VARIATIONS ON 'VENNI
### AMORE' BY RIGHINI

Franz took a paper knife and slashed open the pages. We clustered round to see what lay inside.

We had learned as small children to read a score like a book, hearing the music in our heads. I could tell that from these pages arose something resembling a sonic tongue of flame. Extremes were everywhere, in rhythm, dynamics, pitch – top and bottom of the range, sometimes at once. Yet the little theme by Righini, whoever he was, could not have been simpler. Alongside many fast, virtuosic variations – one demanded scales that flashed almost from end to end of the keyboard – there came a long, florid *adagio sostenuto*. Then a fast coda, and a soft ending. Mastering this piece would keep Pepi and me busy for weeks. No wonder Haydn was having trouble 'taming' his pupil.

'Come on. One each. I'll start.' Franz grabbed the music and – except for Lotti, who was a few years behind us – we took turns sight-reading. Pepi was gifted at the piano; Franz was competent, but preferred his cello. I had played a piano concerto with an orchestra for the first time when I was six years old, and though I have scant recollection of it, Father said I complained afterwards that it was too easy.

Pepi, who was a strong sight-reader, took the adagio. While its tender melody unfolded, wonder crossed her face. 'This is incredible,' she breathed. 'He's not writing for the keyboard, but some extraordinary thing that doesn't exist...'

'He must be an idealist,' I divined. 'Someone with the highest aims and strongest principles.'

'They say he's a cantankerous German bastard with a frightful temper,' Franz said. 'I can't wait to meet him.'

Before we could even consider a means to do so, our lives were overtaken by a calamity from which I thought I might never recover.

We were packing for the winter of 1792, ready to return to Ofen, where Mother had plans to open our gallery to the public as an experiment. We had several hundred paintings there, so we could make money from it, she decided; besides, there was something wrong, something selfish, about keeping the beauty of Raphael and Rembrandt for ourselves alone. Father came in one evening, coughing. His forehead was hot, but he joked about the contrast of warm skin and cold air and insisted he would be fine after a hot toddy and an early night. Mother was anxious; he had been prone to chest complaints for years, his general health left vulnerable by his army experiences. Occasionally he would cough up blood.

By morning he was running a high fever. He pleaded with Mother not to fuss; he had had them often enough before. By the second evening the illness held him in its talons, spreading its dark wings around his body. Mother was silent, her face expressionless and her hands icy. Lotti and Pepi were trying to stifle tears; Franz shut himself in his room to hide his anxiety. I sat by Father, cooling his face with a soft cloth, wiping the sweat from the sinews that tautened in his neck with every attack. I'd read him Homer once when he was ill – but now even that could not calm his raging cough; he told me to stop, because he could not hear me. Instead I held his hand and tried not to look at the stains of fresh blood that built on the handkerchiefs beside him with every spasm.

'We must call the doctor,' I pleaded. But storm clouds were building, while the trees bent low under the gale.

'We can't ask him to ride out from town in this,' Mother said; and Father, between coughs, insisted there was no point. What could a doctor do, he protested. They'd put leeches on you, and how that was supposed to clear phlegm and reduce fever, goodness knows – perhaps the pain was meant to serve as a distraction. As for the potions, they put you to sleep, which was all very well, but he would sleep anyway.

Dusk was enveloping the castle when he whispered my name. He beckoned me closer and with one unsteady finger wiped a tear from my cheek. 'Don't cry, my darling. Listen. Promise me something.'

'Father, don't talk like that. You're going to get well. I'm going to *make* you get well.'

'Promise you'll look after your mother and your brother and sisters. Duty is crucial. But after that, remember: you also have a duty to look after yourself. Promise that too.'

I could not pretend I did not understand what was happening. On his bedside cabinet lay a Bible; I took it up. I did not want Mother to witness this action, or the way my voice was shaking. 'I will make a vow for you.'

Father watched through fever-dimmed eyes while I placed my hand on the leather binding and spoke: 'I, Therese Brunsvik von Korompa, do solemnly swear that my first duty is to my family. And after that, to my calling. So help me God.'

'That's my girl.' He lay back on his pillow. 'You will achieve great things, Tesi. I'm proud to have been your father.'

'Papa—' I began to panic.

'Go now, and let me rest.'

'I won't leave you,' I wept. 'I'll never leave you.'

Mother slid into the room and, for once, pressed my shoulder with some tenderness before taking up her vigil on his other side. Later that evening, he fell asleep and did not wake again.


I opened my eyes at first light in the chair by his bed and found there the husk of the body that his great spirit had inhabited. The air seemed as empty as the face, stone grey against the sweat-blotched pillowcase. The hand within mine was cold as a frozen lake. Mother, slumbering in her chair, had only a few minutes more of blessed unconsciousness before she must awaken to our loss.

I was too numb for tears. I trailed over to the window and stared out towards the brightening sky, grey-gold above the parkland where he and I had walked so often.

My world, the idyll I had taken for granted, overnight had slipped behind a curtain that would never draw open again. We are all mortal; we must all go. But, oh God, why Father, why so soon? He was not yet fifty; he could have had ten or even twenty years more of a fine life. I said a prayer: peace for his spirit – and for mine, enough courage to face the future without him.

Although that memory is as clear to me as yesterday – indeed, clearer – I find it difficult to remember the time that followed. I know that even as I plaited Lotti's hair and played piano duets with Pepi and cello sonatas with Franz, I was acting. I felt as if my body and soul had parted company; the latter had gone away with Father.

'We will pray together,' said Mother. Wrapped in woollen shawls, we knelt on hard red prayer stools in the palace chapel, where the cross loomed above us like a Sword of Damocles. I longed for it to fall and crush me. Every morning I would open my eyes to two seconds of peace before the memory burst through the dam of sleep to flood me with fresh despair. Mother must have been experiencing her own agonies; prayer was her solution. I was too swamped by my grief to be much use to her.

Pepi noticed; she knew it was not like me to lose my strength. She comforted me with silent walks together in the grounds and a tactful word to Lotti and Franz; they all acknowledged my primary closeness to Father. Our brother, though just fifteen, now became Martonvásár's joint owner, along with Mother; we three daughters counted for naught in this part of the will. And so Pepi went to him, her charm and natural grace serving her well even within her family.

'You could perhaps help Tesi,' she said, as she later told me, 'by allowing her part of the garden to plan to her taste. It might distract and cheer her.' Franz was surprised, but agreed at once.

He placed in front of me at breakfast a plan of the grounds, with a circle around a section of the wooded area close to the lake, where he knew I loved to sit and read on summer afternoons. 'TESI-LAND' was scribbled beside it. 'You are to have this for your own and turn it into anything you desire.'

I must have smiled properly for the first time since Father's death. Franz's affable young face, new to such power, turned pink and proud at my delight.


I had set aside some savings from my allowance, and over the winter I built up enough to commission a memorial to Father. One of my favourite walks passed through a glade where sunbeams danced between the beech leaves. Here we cleared enough undergrowth to erect the monument, in red marble with my engraved dedication:

> *In Memory of the Finest Father*
> *from his Daughter*
> *Therese Brunsvik*

I would spend solitary hours beside it in contemplation, holding silent conversations with him, hoping his answers would come to me. On summer evenings at dinner I stopped eating when my mind began – as sometimes it would – to dissolve in great dark patches. Sometimes now I could forget for a day or two that Father was no more, but I had no way of controlling the rush of remembrance and the pain it brought. Mother, who understood this better than she understood other things, allowed me to go.

I ran out over the grass, past the lake and into the trees, and did not stop until I reached my domain. Here I took refuge to watch the moon rising into a clear June sky, hearing around me the songs of crickets and distant nightingales. I sat on the bare grass at the foot of the memorial, my back against the marble, the sap-scented night drying my tears.

Be honest, Tesi, the air whispered. You cannot pretend before the All-Seeing.

Father, help me! I am nearly eighteen. I have many advantages of mind, intellect and spirit, but my spine is curved and may worsen. My sisters have the prospect of good marriages, but even if I did – and with my physique, it is unlikely – I fear I would not want the outcome. How am I to love, respect or even accept being tied to a man who is not the equal of my Father? Who could ever be that equal? What shall I do? Where shall I go?

I listened for the response – perhaps from Father's spirit in the breeze, or from the space in my inner self that one must be still and silent to access.

You can do and become anything, Father had told me many times, as long as you have sufficient insight, determination, will and perseverance. 'My dear daughter, if you had been a man, what could you not have achieved? You will need to work twice as hard, because people are reluctant to accept that a woman has such intelligence, let alone a real capacity to apply herself. But that does not mean you cannot do it.'

The nightingale's song rose in the darkness; my heart lifted. Might music be my world? I could play the piano, but... No, came the whisper within. You have facility – music, writing, languages and painting – but no appetite for public display. That accursed curve. Why should a misshapen spine affect my state of mind?

I decided: I shall not give in. Life is bestowed by God, but I can choose what to do with it. I will know my calling when it comes to me. I will never marry. I will be no lamb-bearing ewe for any ram. I shall cede my independence to nobody. I will be a Priestess of Truth: whether through teaching, charitable work or cultivating my spirit to the highest realms. Now, dear Lord, I entrust my fate to Thee. Whatever You decree, I am ready.

Beyond the silhouetted trees the full moon hung above the lake, sending a pathway towards me, flickering gold on the indigo water. I knelt by Father's memorial and placed my right palm on the cool stone. To the Father, Son and Holy Ghost, to the muses and their sisters, to my own Order of Truth, I, Therese Brunsvik von Korompa, consecrate myself forever.

## 2

My dear niece,

I turned twenty-three on 27 July 1798: a woman in my own right. Yet rarely had I felt less optimistic. Since making my private vow I had turned, with Mother's support, in the direction of God and a cloister, but it seemed I could not even be admitted there. I approached the Institute of the Blessed Virgin Mary – founded by an Englishwoman named Mary Ward, hence known as the Englische Fräulein – which appealed because they were devoted to teaching. To join them, though, I would have to be submissive. I love God as much as any; I can be disciplined and follow rules; but I prefer to make those rules myself.

Instead, Mother asked me to help administer the estate, since Franz was frightful at it. His talent was for planning the gardens, continuing to create the 'paradise' Father had envisioned, but he puzzled over paperwork.

'Two thousand florins,' he mumbled, chewing the end of his pencil. 'Why is there a minus sign?'

'Because that, Franz, is loss, not profit…'

Mother's parsimonious hold on the bank account tightened: Father's generosity had left a fearsome trail of debts.

We were aghast when she told us we could not have new dresses that year. Yet Franz, the popular young master of Martonvásár, spent most evenings out drinking with his friends and playing cards, cards and more cards. There, too, he had not learned many lessons about profit and loss.

One day, a letter arrived from our Aunt Susanna Guicciardi in Trieste. They were to rent a house in Vienna for several months, since there was a prospect that her husband, our Uncle Francesco, would be recalled there soon in his capacity as court councillor. Would not Anna consider bringing her daughters there for a few weeks? It was the perfect opportunity to launch us into society. '*Therese is so talented; Josephine, at twenty, need only pass a young man in the street for her beauty to set him walking into a wall; and Lotti, just seventeen, is the dearest, sweetest girl, the same age as darling Julie…*'

Darling Julie might be Lotti's age, but she had the looks, bearing and confidence of a woman ten years older. 'I don't know about Julie,' Mother grunted, 'but Lotti is far too young. She and Franz will stay at home.'

I can't say Pepi and I were eager to go. It meant a long journey, strange people, and having to behave ourselves. Moreover, I had spent one school year in Vienna at an establishment for girls and remembered little but oppressive walls, vain and spoiled classmates, and the cruelty of that vile posture-straightening contraption, the backboard.

Mother was cleverer than I had credited her for. 'Why do we not take this opportunity for you both to study the piano with someone special?' she said. 'For example, that young man whose music you so admire, Ludwig van Beethoven? Zmeskall says he is the best pianist in the world.'

We arrived late in the afternoon at the hotel Zum goldenen Greif after three arduous days in the stagecoach. During the journey we had stayed overnight at staging inns where Mother tried to keep costs down by insisting that Pepi and I share a bed. 'Nose to tail,' I suggested. But my memory of crossing the Danube and passing through the high ramparts at the Stubentor into Vienna is tinted with dizzy exhaustion and the image of my sister's pale toes flailing into my face, to say nothing of the bruises I had sustained en route on the bumpy roads.

The hotel was on the Kärthnerstrasse – No. 31, an ancient mansion full of spacious rooms, updated from the four-teenth-century original to all the modernity and elegance of the eighteenth. Some actual lavatories had been built and as a result one could smell the flowers in the vases by the front door. We waited behind another group of guests to sign the registration book and be given our keys. The innkeeper was in no hurry, and even Mother's announcement of herself as Countess Anna Brunsvik von Korompa seemed to impress him little.

'I hope you have a pleasant suite for us. We have requested a sitting room and two bedrooms, one of which my daugh-ters will share,' Mother instructed, 'and of course we are hir-ing a fortepiano for the duration of our stay, as my girls are here to study with the city's finest musician.' I admired her confidence, for we had no guarantee the 'city's finest musi-cian' would accept us as pupils.

The innkeeper sucked on his teeth. 'That could be dif-ficult, Madame. We do not usually permit musical instru-ments in the hotel.'

Pepi and I glanced at each other. When Mother played her nobility card, doors tended to open fast. Here, though, everybody seemed to be a count, a baron, a prince or a relation of one.

'But why? The arrangement is already fixed, with Madame Nanette Streicher,' Mother protested. 'I have made a down payment and there are letters to prove it, including one from your good self.'

She motioned us backwards – we thought for a minute that we would have to walk out in protest – but no doubt she did not want us to witness this exchange. It appeared to end with a note being drawn up, which she signed. I wondered how much extra she had to pay him for the privilege of re-agreeing the agreement. At last he ushered us towards the stairs with an obsequious little bow: 'Welcome to Vienna, my ladies.'

That evening, just before we left for the party the Guicciardis were holding to welcome us, Mother summoned Pepi with a jerk of the head. From a velvet box deep inside our trunk she extracted a glittering string of jewels which she fastened around my sister's neck. Small diamonds; a ruby the size and shade of a wild strawberry. 'This was mine for my wedding, a gift from the empress. It suits you very well.'

Pepi, disbelieving, raised her hands to her throat, caressing the stone. 'It's so beautiful... but should Tesi not have it, as she is the eldest?'

'Josephine, it has been designated yours.' Mother's tone would have been better suited to estate management than the handing on of an heirloom.

'Mother is right, Pepi – you look wonderful,' I said. I would not want to wear anything that drew attention to the shape of my neck and shoulders; my preferred necklace consisted of plain white pearls, natural and without ostentation.

The Guicciardis had rented a modest palace until the end of the season. I can still see Julie sweeping down its marble staircase, ready to meet the country cousins (us). Rose and lilac silks set off her raven's-wing hair and deep blue eyes, inherited diamonds from her father's family were shining against her throat, and the expressions of the first guests lit up with unconcealed admiration. Trailing after her like dowdy pigeons flapping behind a peacock, Pepi and I were wearing our old white silk dresses, some years behind the fashion. We had brought nothing else with us, for we had little else. Mother would spend what money there was on the most careful of targets – yes to a good hotel, no to excess frocks.

A sizeable team of servants were taking cloaks from the arriving guests, then relaying names to a footman who announced them to the ballroom upstairs. Face after new pasty face peered down into ours. 'Ah, the guests of honour! What a joy to meet you, Countess, and your charming daughter... oh, daughters plural!' Admiring exclamations attended Pepi, who curtsied and laughed. I watched those strangers, especially the men, glance straight past me and settle like bumblebees upon my sister's honey-sweet smile. On the landing I took an extra breath before following Mother and Pepi forward into the throng, where I, an old maid at twenty-three, expected to disappear at once.

How difficult it is to hear well in such an environment. Voices blend under the soaring ceilings and bounce off the mirrors and the gilded mouldings around them; the musicians in the corner swirl more complexity into the atmosphere; and the names, even when I can catch them, exit my memory the moment they enter it. Baron von Thing, the

Count Whatsit von Somewherestrange, Baronin von Howdoyouspellit, her daughter Girlie von Howdoyouspellit...

At dinner I found myself on the Guicciardis' first table;
Mother was to my right, with Pepi on her far side, and Julie
opposite. Thank goodness, I was in one corner; thus posi-
tioned I had breathing space and could relax out of the mor-
bid self-consciousness about my shoulders while our hosts
pointed out to us a number of supposedly eligible officers. I
divined that in this parade, I had been cast as maiden aunt-
to-be; Pepi was the prize heifer, with the ruby as her rosette.

I managed to stay awake through dinner, working out
with Mother's tactful help (a cuff with one foot beneath the
table) which silver utensils belonged to which course. Sharp
prongs for oysters from Trieste; a flat knife to slice the fine
flesh of the Danube trout ('I *love* the fish here,' Julie declared,
taking meagre little mouthfuls); and a weightier knife and
fork to tackle the Bohemian partridge. I was not used to such
excess, such decadence; faced with a fifth course, a knot of
heartburn coalesced in my stomach.

As we rose from the table, a young officer some years
my junior offered me his arm while we moved on for the
evening's highlight: a recital in the salon, where more gold-
framed mirrors and myriad candles in Venetian glass chandeliers cast creamy light across the inlaid wood floor. Julie
sidled into a place beside 'my' officer, whose name I could
not even remember, fluttering her eyelashes at him. Alongside Pepi and Mother, we perched on tapestried chairs, their
wooden backs carved into swanlike curves. Across the room
an inebriated gentleman, his chest glinting with military
medals, sat down too heavily and tipped his seat over.

There ensued some music played by a pudgy yet excellent
violinist and at the fortepiano, to my surprise, a graceful
woman of advancing years, dressed in pewter-grey silk.

Their playing enchanted me, despite the tempting prospect of closing my eyes while they performed.

Pepi nudged me in the ribs. 'Tesi, don't fall asleep – you don't want to miss this.' Her whole form was tilted forward towards the musicians in rapt attention.

'Who are they?' I asked Julie at the end, while we applauded.

'Ignaz Schuppanzigh and Marianna Martines,' came her answer, filled with pride.

'Ha – and I thought we had the best musicians in Ofen,' Pepi remarked.

I had thought we also had the best palaces, food and fashions. I was wrong.

Julie laughed, the candles flattering the silkiness of her exposed décolletage. 'They are wonderful, but wait until you hear Beethoven.'

'We want to hear Beethoven more than anybody,' Pepi told her. 'Where can we find him?'

'And what's he really like?' I added.

Julie beamed. 'He's an *animal*.'

'Oh, Julie, won't you introduce us, please?' Pepi begged.

'Well... I've not met him properly... at least, not yet...'

'This violinist must know him,' I said.

'Let's go and talk to him,' said Julie. 'Oh, and remember, the Viennese like to use titles.'

While the breeze of conversation began to rise, Pepi, Julie and I, equipped with tulip glasses of Sekt, navigated around the gathering to approach Schuppanzigh. He was about my age, though several times my girth, tucking in with glee to the ice cream that was now being served. I noticed Pepi glance at his premature paunch. He bent to kiss Julie's bejewelled wrist, a crystal dessert bowl still poised in his left hand.

'Countess Giulietta, you look more lovely than ever. Do introduce me to your charming companions?' He sized up Pepi. '*Very* charming…'

Music lessons, indeed! We were here to be married off. Or Pepi was. I was too plain, too bent and too old. Perhaps Mother only wanted me there for propriety's sake as the eldest, or as handy chaperone? Or else she was more of an optimist than I thought regarding my prospects. An accomplished young lady, pupil of the famous Beethoven – how good that would sound to some hypothetical suitor…

'These are my cousins from Ofen, two of the young Countesses Brunsvik von Korompa – Therese and Josephine.'

'My dear Countesses, I am dazzled beyond bedazzlement!'

'As we are by your playing, Herr Doktor Professor Schuppanzigh,' I assured him. 'We are keen musicians, though amateur in such company.'

A stumbling motion close to the tall windows suggested that somebody had perhaps overindulged in Sekt. 'You see our merry friend?' The violinist beckoned us closer and spoke low. 'With the turquoise coat and strange gait? Imagine him, if you will, dressed in a costume of feathers from head to foot, carrying a birdcage.'

'Oh my goodness – not Schikaneder?'

'The very same. Mozart's librettist for *Die Zauberflöte*. An impresario nowadays, of sorts. You must meet him, of course… but maybe another time,' he added, as the gentleman in question, carolling to himself and anyone nearby, snaked his way towards the grand entrance, where a manservant grabbed his arm to guide him out.

The evening was acquiring a dreamlike, fairy-tale air, as if it had been dipped in icing sugar. Perhaps I would wake up and find I had never been there at all. This ballroom might be full of Rococo embellishments, marble statues of naked cupids and semi-nude goddesses adorned the staircase and landings, and those opulent chandeliers hung in each one of the interlocking rooms that stretched out before you through portal after portal, but this was just one, somewhat modest, palace within a crammed city centre composed almost entirely of palaces, many of which were a great deal bigger. I had never seen a place that shouted about such unimaginable wealth from every Grecian portico, nor a room in which so many throats were wound with fine gems, or torsos clad in so many shades of silk, or so many military coats and court uniforms sported medals galore. Moreover, I had never before been in the same room as someone who had eaten, drunk, joked and above all worked with Wolfgang Amadeus Mozart. My dreams and the real world were colliding and becoming one at last.

Father had always told me I could excel at anything, given the determination, but in Martonvásár and even in Ofen, there was little to fit this handy directive. Here in Vienna everything took on a new colour, as if a tinted glass had slipped in front of my eyes. Here in Vienna we were at the centre of the world. Here in Vienna anything was possible.

'Do you know Herr Beethoven?' I asked Schuppanzigh. 'Could you perhaps introduce us to him? We have written to him via our friend Zmeskall, but as yet heard nothing back.'

He gave us a shrewd once-over. 'He is like a brother to me – he came to me for violin lessons. But, er, you do know he hates teaching?'

'You are right,' said the diplomatic Pepi, 'in thinking we would like to play to him. My sister is particularly talented and we have both been learning his works. But really, we would love to *meet* him. Our brother says everyone here talks of Beethoven as the successor to Mozart.'

'Everyone except Haydn,' Schuppanzigh mumbled, through his ice cream. 'I think there is a type of explosive in Beethoven's mind. Given half a chance, that young man will plant dynamite under the finest institutions of this city. He is ambitious, but he does not want to play the game. This is a difficult combination, if you know what I mean.'

I knew exactly what he meant. 'I am rather like that too,' I said, thinking of my polite letter from the nuns. Pepi and Julie caught each other's eyes and smirked.

'Well, then,' Schuppanzigh said, 'I will introduce you. How long are you in Vienna?'

We had only two and a half weeks. We were not to know, as the dancing began and Julie dashed off for a minuet with a fresh-faced young officer, that these scant eighteen days were where our lives would begin in earnest. Schuppanzigh offered Pepi his hand and took her to the ballroom floor. I watched my sister bend and twirl with the poise of a linden and the flexibility of a willow. The violinist strutted about as best he could – he did not take himself too seriously – but Pepi's dancing was drawing every eye to her graceful form despite her outmoded dress. Julie, for all her finery, was casting sharp glances in her direction.

'There is something magical in your sister,' Madame Martines said to me. 'She is radiant, without knowing it – like a blossom just beginning to unfurl.'

The pianist had come over upon seeing us in conversation with her duo partner. Past fifty, she was still striking in appearance: I was fascinated by the intelligence in her eyes and her expressive way of speaking. I could not help agreeing about Pepi, but I had other things to ask this splendid musician.

'What was that last piece you played? I had not heard it before – it was full of spirit and invention.'

'Oh, a little something of my own.' She gave me a conspiratorial smile. 'People in Vienna love good music – until they learn it was written by a woman. Did you know that Maria Anna Mozart was just as talented as Wolfgang Amadeus?' Madame Martines described her: the girl who had travelled and performed with her brother around the imperial courts of Europe, yet since her marriage had been confined to her home by a lake outside Salzburg, playing to four walls and her dog.

We found a quiet spot to sit two rooms away and spent an hour discussing music and literature and what one could do to persuade men that female musicians were not prostitutes, or courtesans, or bad mothers, or unattractive to the opposite sex, or daughters of Sappho, but people whose gifts deserved a chance to shine. I felt grateful that here in Vienna I had, on my first day, found a soulmate of sorts.

'Good luck with the young lion,' she said to us when, sometime after two in the morning, we took our leave.

# 3

Dearest niece,

I don't know what Schuppanzigh told Beethoven about us, but it must have been tempting. Not two days later Mother received a scrawled note in deep-pressed, long-tailed handwriting. We were to go to Beethoven's apartment in Petersplatz at noon and take some music to play. Franz's friend Nikolaus Zmeskall von Domanovecz, who worked at the Hungarian Court Chancellery in Vienna, had already warned us never to expect Beethoven to come to us. 'He won't take a fee,' he advised, 'as he doesn't have much clue what money is for – but take him a present, preferably a useful one, as a token of your esteem.' Aunt Susanna hurried to the rescue, directing Mother to her favourite linen merchant.

'Yes, Susi,' said Mother, who looked cornered.

Beethoven's apartment was a short walk away, past the giant Stephansdom with its steep, bright-tiled roof, and through the Graben, dodging market stalls, delivery carts and treacherous cellar entrances. Peering down into one of the latter, we could not even see the bottom. 'They dig five storeys down sometimes,' Mother explained, 'because, as you can see, there is no space in Vienna to build anywhere else.' A group of whores with garish painted lipstick and exposed ankles were draping themselves around a part-gilded monument to the Viennese killed by plague two centuries earlier; they watched us with open contempt while we tried not to stare in return. All around us seethed the aroma of cooking sausages, wooden boxes of the first fresh fruits growing warm in the spring sun, the lure of ice cream, and confectionary shops that presented a tempting array of pink, green and yellow marzipan along with the darkest of chocolate.

'Perhaps we should take him an *edible* token of our esteem.' Pepi gazed with huge eyes at an interior where curved glass display cases were laden with delights.

'We are taking him plenty,' Mother snapped.

The copper-domed Peterskirche squatted like a fat melon in a basket of narrow streets, just off the Graben. Opposite, Beethoven lived three floors high, above the dust and din of carriages passing between houses and church wall. A stone staircase twisted up towards his door, from behind which came the sound of a fortepiano being played with a firm touch. Mother climbed the stairs ahead of us. Pepi and I joined hands for courage. We each carried a book of his music. Pepi had brought the Variations and I the Op. 1 trios, to the publication of which we had subscribed; we could show him our names on the list of supporters.

Mother knocked four times. The music stopped. I could feel Pepi's pulse in her wrist rising to meet the headlong pace of my own.

The door opened and a shabby-looking servant motioned us inside with impassive expression. And then Beethoven was there, in front of us. I had imagined him fair or even ruddy-haired, like the lion everyone said he was, but no: he was as dark as a Spaniard, as dark as our own sister; not tall, but broad, imposing, confident, hair swept back above his collar. His eyes were eager and curious, under low-set brows that threatened to meet in the middle. His neck was wide and short, his jawline squared, with a cleft chin that made him more determined in aspect; high cheekbones brought refinement to this unusual visage. His grey morning jacket looked as if he had slept in it. He was younger than I had expected, not yet thirty. My hands were sweating. I had no idea how I could make them play this man's music.

'Good morning, Herr van Beethoven. I am Countess Anna Brunsvik von Korompa,' Mother said, nothing daunted, 'and these are my daughters, the pianists: Therese and Josephine.'

When he took my hand to kiss it, I sensed in his grasp a startling energy and warmth. Then I watched as Beethoven's gaze and Pepi's met.

'Dear Countesses...' His Rhineland accent was quite different from the Viennese twangs to which we were becoming accustomed. 'Please. Make yourselves at home, and please excuse the mess.'

The apartment was pokey, furnished with a frugal minimum of necessities. Most of the main room was occupied by the fortepiano. On the wooden dining table sat his breakfast plate, but the desk too was scattered with crumbs; he must have begun work while eating. Some papers sketched with freshly scribbled music – bar lines drawn and awaiting the next phrase – bore a splatter of coffee and a smear of honey. A book of poetry by Friedrich Schiller lay open next to them; squinting at it, I detected the title *An die Freude*. Beside the desk sat a large stringed instrument case, perhaps a viola; a violin hung on a peg on the wall above, its bow beside it. In the far corner, I spotted a flicker of movement: a mouse scurrying to safety.

The clatter of carriages and horses' hooves rose up through the open casement; street air mingled with the apartment's aromas of coffee and perspiration; and in a shaft of sunlight, Beethoven surveyed us with a penetrating stare. The church bells struck midday – Mother was nothing if not punctual – and the apartment walls vibrated with every chime.

'Good,' he said. 'Who would like to go first?'

Mother and Pepi sat on the narrow sofa while I went to the piano, shaking as if I were still in the carriage from Hungary. He must have understood my terror and at once put me at my ease. 'The E flat trio? I'm glad someone thinks it worthwhile,' he joked.

I took a breath, lifted my hands and began, singing the violin line while I played. The piano was a Streicher, its touch light and even beneath my fingers: this pleasant surprise took my mind off the attentive presence watching my every move, his right hand discreetly beating time. After the opening section he stopped me: 'Excellent. You play very well. So...' And we began to work: he would stand behind me, watching, then tip me off the chair to take my place and demonstrate.

'Look – this theme' – he played the first punchy motif – 'is related to this one' – the second subject – 'but now it becomes lyrical, its meaning is turned inside out... and then' – the closing theme – 'it has been tamed, or so we think...'

When the room shook again with the sounding of one o'clock, we had dissected barely two pages. He gave a shrug; on we went. His main theme was made of just three notes – yet what could he not do with them?

Two o'clock passed. Mother's eyes had closed. Pepi was

still paying attention, coughing occasionally, but absorbed far beyond her usual capacity for patience. My head was throbbing. Did Beethoven not need to eat? Did he not ever have to, well, relieve himself? Our morning coffee had caught up with me and I was far from sure what I was meant to do about it.

Finally he seemed to remember that Pepi, too, was supposed to play to him. We had a break – five minutes for the necessaries – then switched places. A little way into Pepi's Variations I nudged Mother awake.

I don't think our host had noticed her nodding off. He corrected Pepi's posture – 'Do not lift the shoulder because the tension will affect your wrist and ultimately your sound' – but then praised her sense of rhythm, the flow of her phrasing... He was praising *everything*, letting her fly, making his music her own. As she began the adagio, my stomach rumbled audibly.

At five o'clock, Beethoven, who had been leaning over to write instructions on Pepi's music, must have noticed that his valiant pupil was developing shadows under her eyes and a slight tremor in her hands. Nobody had eaten since breakfast.

'Shall we have a rest?' he suggested.

Mother explained that we had to go back soon to dress for a party at the young Prince Kinsky's palace – and now reality encroached, bringing with it laughter, incredulity at the hour, and the suggestion of the same time again tomorrow.

'Where are you staying?' he asked. 'Do you have an instrument? I can come to you – it might be pleasanter for you than this mouse-ridden house.'

We had little expected such an honour. Mother's gaze was drifting to the parcel of linen she had placed on the table, beside the remains of Beethoven's breakfast.

'Don't worry about *that*,' he said. 'It is a pleasure to find two such talented pupils. And if you can put up with me…'

Pepi was still at the piano, her smile unreserved as she gazed up at our new Master. She looked different: older, radiant, comfortable.

'Well, then,' said Mother. 'I suppose… we will see you tomorrow.'

That night we set off for our second Viennese party, floating, or else light-headed through lack of food. Julie, chattering about the new gown in the latest high-waisted style that was being sewn for her by the empress's own dressmaker, found us distracted and uninterested; Pepi and I, talking non-stop as we went through to the colonnaded courtyard and inside by the main door on the right, were still taking apart our lesson with the Master.

We were briefly dumbstruck, nevertheless, by the sight before us. Every inch of marble seemed to be carved into a figure from Greek mythology making gestures full of motion; vast sheets of mirror glinted on the walls above crimson carpets and beside Prince Kinsky's chandeliers those in the Guicciardis' temporary home would look like scullery lamps. The prince, who was younger than Pepi, had a year earlier lost his father and gained his title. He had begun at once to make himself known to the court and its entourage through holding the most lavish of functions.

I tried not to eat too much at dinner, because now I knew that dancing on a full stomach is an uncomfortable business. Soon the ballroom's expanse of parquet was as stuffed with music and eager dancers as the dinner table had been with caviar, quail's eggs, fish soup, soufflé, venison, mountain cheeses, grapes, apricots, almond pastries and chocolate fancies. Officers regaled us with tales of military exploits while we pranced to the strains of polkas, mazurkas and the latest, outrageous invention of this louche city.

'It's easy,' the prince himself enthused, claiming Pepi for this new dance. 'My arm round your waist; your hand on my shoulder; keep counting three and keep turning as we go.' Pepi, more accustomed to the arm's-length minuet, was flustered but, on return, rather thrilled.

'Your palace is wonderful,' she remarked, fanning herself.

Kinsky gave a rueful smile. 'You know, I would give every last candle of it to have my father back again.'

Mother cast a knowing glance at Pepi's rose-tinted cheeks and the brightness of her eyes. The ruby was gleaming carmine at her throat. 'You must keep an eye on your sister,' she hissed at me. 'She's enjoying this too much.'

'The dance? Or the prince?'

'This dance is improper. One must stand far too close to one's partner – it is virtually an embrace. My empress would have been scandalised to see such a thing.'

'I don't see the harm, Mother.'

'You wouldn't. But look at Pepi. That one will sin against God, given half a chance.'

'On the other hand,' I noted, 'she might marry a prince.'

To our disappointment, we learned a few minutes later, from the gossip around us, that the prince was already engaged and much enamoured of his intended bride, Caroline Maria, Baroness von Kerpen. Later we enjoyed a warm conversation with this enchanting girl, then watched them hopping about in a polka, their gazes locked in mutual delight.

I had sat out the unfamiliar dance – it was named a 'waltz' – but soon found myself cornered by a middle-aged officer who had been in Paris during the Revolution and what followed. He had seen the king guillotined. He brought me a fresh glass of wine, then related everything in gory detail, perhaps in the hope of impressing me. It did not.

Another officer had met Napoleon Bonaparte: 'A pugnacious, jumped-up little temper tantrum on stumps,' he opined, 'who would turn himself into a dictator if he had half a chance.' There will be war soon, a silver-whiskered general told Mother, who was not happy. Father had sustained injuries in the battles of the Austro-Turkish War; she blamed that for his vulnerability to the disease that killed him. Pepi and I ignored such dire predictions. We were dancing on air: not because we were among princes – and making friends with Kinsky's fiancée, Caroline – but because we were now Beethoven's pupils and would see him again in just a few hours.

We were back at the hotel and preparing for bed when Pepi's eyes lit up with an idea. The same thing had crossed my mind, though I'd hesitated to mention it lest it seem improper. The day after tomorrow we were invited for a picnic in the Vienna Woods. Could we not ask our Master to join us? His company would be worth ten of the military types. 'A hundred,' said Pepi. And he was of the right class: a 'von'.

'Don't be silly,' said Mother.

'Isn't "van" just the Flemish version of "von"?' Pepi demanded.

Mother admitted she was not certain. 'His family has been in Germany for several generations, according to your brother. Besides, he could not possibly be a nobleman.'

I agreed: 'He is far too intelligent and cultured for that.'

'He has a *profession*. Noblemen do not have professions.'

'Most of them are too stupid.'

'Tesi, shush. You are speaking against your own class.'

'But how do you know that he's not simply the first nobleman in his family to have a profession?' I needled her.

'The Beethovens have always been musicians. Everyone knows this. It just does not happen, Tesi.'

'But *how* do you know? *Why* are you sure?'

Pepi's foot brushed against mine. She knew I had a perverse enjoyment of sparring with Mother, using the latter's favoured techniques.

'Because,' Mother scowled, taking the bait, '*everyone – knows*. You cannot keep a secret among the aristocracy. Especially not here. I learned this in my time at court. So, my girls, watch out. You are not to fall in love with a musician.'

'Oh, Mother,' I groaned. 'Why not? What's the worst that could happen if one of us *did* want to marry Beethoven, his piano and his mouse?'

'Listen.' Mother flapped a hand towards the chairs to make us sit down. 'As women, you take your husband's name – so if you marry a commoner, in one stroke you lose your status and title. Moreover, should you marry a musician, you would never know where the next meal is coming from. Musicians are dangerous, because while in public they may move with ease among different social circles, in private they are poverty-stricken, vice-laden wastrels. Your celebrated music master will be no different, you mark my words.'

I laughed aloud. Pepi kicked me, but said nothing.

'Girls, girls,' Mother said, 'have you not met any young men these past evenings who appeal to you?' We had received calling cards from several. I had been asked for twice; Pepi five times. '*Why* don't you like them?'

'They are so dull, Mother,' Pepi yawned. 'Either they do

nothing except hunt, eat and spend, or they push papers around, or they are soldiers and kill people.'

'I have taken a vow never to marry,' I reminded them.

'Don't be silly, Tesi,' Mother snapped. 'And remember, opportunities do not grow like plentiful blossoms on the branches.'

Nevertheless, I had made my vow. To fulfil my calling, when I found it, I would need complete independence. Whatever it took to defy Mother, I must and would prevail.

On the morning of the picnic I awoke with a headache, feeling not a bit rested; Mother and Pepi went along without me. But later, free to spend the morning as I wished, I had no doubt what to do: I went to call upon Marianna Martines, musician, composer, salon hostess and my new friend. She lived with her sister, Antonia, in their old family house on the corner of the Michaelerplatz, beside the Burgtheater and the Hofburg.

'Beethoven?' She stirred a splash of orange flower water into our coffee before pouring in some warm milk. 'An *aristocrat*? Good heavens, my dear – his name means "beetroot field" in Flemish.'

'He's not Flemish, though.'

'I fear many Viennese will always see him as an outsider. Some assume he has a distant noble background, but I doubt it – he is known to be a great admirer of Napoleon. Which, as you can imagine, would be a little bit awkward at court. They even say – not that I wish to spread gossip, but I'd rather you heard this from me than from someone else…' She leaned forward, eyes bright. 'There are rumours, malicious no doubt, that his swarthy colouring may be the result of some mixing of the blood. You know that Flanders gained some Moorish influences from its century and a half under Spanish rule.'

I gasped. 'He may be unrefined in demeanour, but the music is that of a genius.'

'My dear,' said Marianna, 'I would never say that someone with African origins cannot produce music of genius.'

I had never thought about this before.

'Take Alexander Pushkin – Russia's finest poet. And did you hear of the Chevalier de Saint-Georges, his father French and his mother Caribbean? A legend in Paris before the queen who favoured him was guillotined... Anyway, in Beethoven's case we do not know and we never will. Another rumour has it that he's the illegitimate son of the King of Prussia, which is palpable rubbish. His grandfather was Kapellmeister at the court in Bonn, and I know our young Ludwig is proud of that – if less so of his own father.'

'Tell me more?'

Marianna began to explain – and I listened, star-struck.

She knew Beethoven well, through his teacher, Joseph Haydn, who was one of her oldest friends. As a boy Haydn had lodged in the attic of this very house after his voice broke and the Stephansdom choir threw him out; her earliest memories were of the silvery sound of his harpsichord through the ceiling. She had been friends with Mozart as well and used to play two-piano works with him. Beethoven often performed at her weekly salon. He would whirl in in everyday, modern garb that was common in the Rhineland, his curls forming a wild halo above his blue tailcoat and yellow waistcoat; the elder Viennese audience raised their eyebrows, observing this chaotic appearance from within their powdered wigs, old-fashioned frock coats and silk stockings.

'He's the eldest of three brothers, sons of the musician Johann van Beethoven, who was a drunkard and used to beat them,' Marianna said. 'He seemed out of luck for a long time – he came to Vienna to study with Mozart, but received word that his mother was on her deathbed and went straight back to Bonn to be with her. The family was troubled thereafter; he was unable to leave for five years. In the meantime poor Mozart fell ill and died. Beethoven had pinned all his hopes on his instruction.'

'So the glorious Haydn was actually second-best?'

'Count Waldstein found an excellent way to persuade him. When Beethoven finally set out for Vienna, Waldstein arranged for him to lodge in Prince Lichnowsky's attic, and told him he would be "receiving the spirit of Mozart from the hands of Haydn". Who could ask for better?'

If anyone dared to, I suspected, it would be our Master. His mind did not seem to know the usual limits. There would be no stopping him.


When my mother and sister returned from the picnic, they had news for me: Beethoven had been there after all. No matter 'von' or 'van'. 'An artist is an artist,' Pepi sparkled. 'They can go anywhere, do anything, socialise with anybody from any strata – because of their art.'

'Who said that? Aunt Susanna?'

'No, *he* did. I have been talking to him all day.'

She excused herself to lie down for a while, with shutters and curtains closed.

Before our fourth afternoon at the piano with Beethoven, Pepi and I cornered Mother in our rooms. 'You have to invite him to dinner,' we chorused. 'Please? We will do anything, go anywhere, obey you without question, but you must invite him! We will cry all night otherwise. We will lie down and die.'

'Girls, *honestly...*' Poor Mother. Having targeted our favourite musician for the value his name as teacher would lend our eligibility as 'accomplished' marriageable women, she was now out of her depth amid the social confusion. Yet it was the perfect opportunity; tonight we were dining in our hotel. Aunt Susanna had a headache, Julie had been throwing tantrums about the late delivery of her new gown, and we were all feeling the effects of our intense schedule. In short, we needed an evening in.

He went home to dress for dinner. Watching from the window, we spotted him returning to us: humming aloud, waving a hand as if conducting, oblivious to the startled glances of those he passed, or to the occasional whinny of a disconcerted horse. He seemed so much in his own world that I thought he was going to stride straight past the inn. Just beyond the entrance, he pulled up short; there was a quick reversal and soon the door sprang open and he was with us, all apologies and smiles and the charm that he could turn on if and when he wished to.

As the sole male amid a brood of adoring countesses, he did wish to. Hands were kissed, praises lavished upon us, before we settled at a table in the quietest corner, furthest from the window. Even Mother was flustered – her face displaying a pink blotchiness that she always developed when worked up – when she realised other diners were noticing our guest with approval, some greeting him and thanking him for his music as they passed by.

Beethoven sat at the head, with Pepi to his left and Mother and me to his right. First he wanted to show us some music he had just fetched from home: three recently published sonatas, his Op. 10. I read the first pages, entranced: they were packed with striking ideas and new challenges. 'Tomorrow,' he suggested, 'let's try them.'

Mother wanted to know about his plans for the future, his prospects, his sources of income ('But *why* don't you want a Kapellmeister post?'). Beethoven began to talk. He had everything worked out: the nearest thing to a long-term plan for a business that I have heard a musician utter. The trios and sonatas were going well; next, he must write a symphony, similar to Haydn's, but with his own stamp upon it. Then another, soon, to consolidate his achievement. Audiences loved his improvisations, so he would always include some in any concert. He longed to set to music the Schiller poem I'd spotted on his desk, the bizarre Bacchanalian *An die Freude* – Ode to Joy – but it had resisted all his well-intentioned attempts thus far. He had just written a new finale for his first, or first official, piano concerto in B flat major and had completed another, in C major – and there must be more chamber music to win favour with patrons who liked to play stringed instruments.

'Our brother is a fine cellist,' Pepi exclaimed. 'You must write something for him!'

Mother cast her a sharp look; no doubt she worried that Pepi's words might make him assume we would pay for a commission, even though he was teaching us without further fee than that first bundle of household linen.

Dinner arrived: Mother feasted on Hungarian goulash smothered in cream, Beethoven and I both chose trout (I have never enjoyed heavy, rich food) and Pepi picked a dish apparently imported from Italy, a veal escalope coated in breadcrumbs. While she and I tried to emulate Julie's table manners, taking small forkfuls and dabbing our lips with the tip of our napkins, Beethoven dined with the gusto of a mountain lion and talked on while picking fish bones out of his teeth. We ordered a second carafe of wine; he had most of it, and not slowly.

Everyone expected an opera from him, he said, but it had to be the right subject. He wasn't interested in the royal intrigues that had formed the substance of many before Mozart. Nor was he in the business of providing show-off material for some self-obsessed prima donna. He needed a good libretto. Most were dross. Mozart's work with first Lorenzo da Ponte, then Schikaneder had been a story apart; and for all the excellence of da Ponte's writing, Beethoven considered *Die Zauberflöte* the best.

'*The Magic Flute*? A crazy fairy tale?' I interrupted, haunted by the image of Schikaneder bumbling his inebriated way out of the Guicciardis' party.

Beethoven stared. 'Oh no, this work holds the very heart of the Enlightenment. It has everything: wisdom, wit, a quest, a triumph over darkness, and above all a heroine whose noble spirit is never sacrificed to her sex.'

I noticed Pepi coughing, small chiming sounds that she muffled in her napkin.

'Who is your ideal heroine?' I asked him.

'She is strong and true. She is virtuous, exalted of mind and spirit, and courageous beyond the level of any man. There is no length to which she will not go for the sake of her true love and she will never betray him or refuse the challenges that love demands of her.'

'That is *very* ideal,' Pepi remarked, having banished her cough with some water. 'Where would you ever find such a woman?'

'On stage in an opera, for no such person exists beyond it,' I tried to joke. Beethoven and Pepi were not listening. The look passing between them made me grateful that Mother just then was speaking to the waiter. For a moment I wondered if I were imagining that gaze of connection, and if I were not, what turn of events it could presage.

After we had finished a third carafe of wine, plus some excellent strudel and coffee, Beethoven pushed back his chair, relaxed and ruddy-faced, with a white-toothed grin almost the width of the table. 'Supposing we go upstairs and I improvise for you?' he said. We sat open-mouthed; everyone said that Beethoven could never be prevailed upon to play. Then again, they reckoned without the charms of a twenty-year-old Hungarian countess to spur him on.

We repaired to our rooms, lit the candles and arranged three chairs near the piano. Beethoven tossed his hat up to the top of the cupboard beside the door. While we settled down, he sat at the keyboard, playing some figurations, testing the instrument's possibilities.

A moment of silence: then, through the deepening May twilight and the golden glow of the candles, there emerged the sounds of Beethoven's spontaneous imagination. At first this music was low and mysterious, then it broke into a propulsive new motif. He punched it out towards us, turned it upside down and back to front, carrying it through modulation after startling modulation; he transformed it into phrases that could have become first an operatic aria and then a duet; and after a tremendous build-up, the first theme was back, joyous as it overcame adversity.

Just when we thought he was going to stop, he played the motif again, now as a single line answered by another at a suitable interval: our theme was transformed into a fugue. How anybody improvises a fugue I have no idea, so intricate is the notion. All my willpower was dissolving in this sudden music, this outpouring of a giant soul. My breath was fragmenting as my tears formed; perhaps he was conjuring the spirits of air, water, earth and fire, willing them to obey his command. The fugue reached its climax and subsided into a simple coda that seemed to cradle some profound, unspoken truth; and now he transformed our motif one last time. Into, of all things, a minuet.

A delighted laugh escaped Pepi: this was her favourite dance. I fancied that Beethoven was glancing at her – why would he not? – and that the minuet's poised triple-metre progress was designed to capture her graceful movements. Or was I imagining it? Two chords: the simplest, most innocent cadence. And silence.

Beethoven stayed where he was, arms lowered, head bowed. We sat motionless: we dared not interrupt this atmosphere, because it would be gone forever, together with the music. How would he ever get it back? Could he remember it all and write it down? Or should we not seek to recapture such magic? How can something so perfect be so transitory?

Before we could break the spell, it was shattered by a commotion outside. Shouts of fury, a slamming door, the wheedling of the innkeeper and thumping as servants carried something heavy down the stairs. The noise continued in the street beneath. Through the window we glimpsed the gentleman from the rooms next to ours, his wife and young son cowering behind him near their luggage: he was yelling at the innkeeper. 'Stop the music! There is no let-up! All afternoon, every day, nothing but piano, piano, piano – and now in the evening too, when the child is trying to sleep? We are off! We are leaving! We will tell all our friends never to stay in your godforsaken hotel again. It is inhabited by the devil himself.'

Beethoven burst out laughing, as if he were indeed a demon. We joined in, released from our rapture, and Pepi rushed to his right side and I to his left, and nothing in the world could have stopped us from taking his hands and kissing them. If Mother were shocked, she said nothing; perhaps beneath her frosty exterior she longed to join in.

'Look at you, all tearful!' he teased us. 'Come along, dear Countesses – it's a beautiful May night and the stars are out. Let's go to the Graben and I will treat you to ice cream.'

'Ice cream? At this hour?' Mother said.

In the street, our Master grabbed our arms, one on each side, with Mother clucking and tutting behind, and soon we were feasting on the best ice cream in Vienna. And if I remember him chasing Pepi round the towering gilded plague monument, then leaping onto its base to imitate the statues while we half screamed in hilarity, and Pepi scrambling up behind him, and him taking her hand to help her and pointing out the figures whose poses to strike, and the two of them up there, looking like Zeus and Aphrodite, ready to cast blessings across a city sozzled and choking on its own wealth, perhaps I am imagining some of it from a great distance, but perhaps I am not.

# 4

My dear niece,

I saw dawn the next morning break blue and gold over the city's steep red rooftops. The birds sang in ecstasy outside our windows: the only music that could supersede Beethoven's. Who could sleep after such an experience – except Mother?

After scant dozing through the small hours I noticed Pepi's bed was empty. I rose, put on a shawl and went through to our living room.

She was there, sitting at the piano without touching the keys, reading Beethoven's new sonatas and humming to herself as she did so. One look at her face, when she lifted her gaze towards me, told me all I needed to know.

'Pips, you're in love.'

'Isn't it sad?' she said. 'I don't know how I can ever look at another man after yesterday… Tesi, not you too?'

'It's you he loves.'

'It's impossible. I am making a resolution. I know you are good at those.'

'I've made a few.' I went across and hugged her. I have always been capable of keeping a cool head in a crisis. 'We're just dazzled by his playing. It doesn't mean he would be a good husband for you.' (Or indeed for me.) 'He would be a difficult man to live with.'

'I don't care.' Pepi's eyes were red, whether with tears, exhilaration or exhaustion. 'I'd do anything for him. Obviously Mother will never hear of it. A commoner. A musician.'

'Has *he* said anything to you?'

'When would he? There is no opportunity. And he will know it's hopeless, as I do.'

I stopped myself from telling Pepi what I really thought: that such matters should not be left to one's mother, and especially not ours. What good would it do to encourage my sister to rebel? I sought words of consolation instead.

'Pips, remember: it's not the man that we love. It is the *musician* – and that is fine. We can love his music always, without fear of repercussion.'

'I will add that to my resolution, which is to be his pupil, his friend, his supporter if I can, but never to long for more.'

With that she gave a smile – not happy, but resigned. Perhaps it was safest to stay on either side of those barbed divides: master and pupil; aristocrat and artist.


Our afternoon lesson passed, rather to my disappointment, as if nothing had changed. We worked on the D major Sonata, Op. 10, No. 3. The slow movement left us both marvelling; we knew of nothing so tragic and despairing in all of Mozart or Haydn.

Marianna had told me about Beethoven's difficult background – but didn't everyone have a difficult background to some degree? I responded to the tragedy of Father's death by building a memorial, taking a vow, and determining to devote myself to good works that would make him proud. Perhaps Beethoven could react to whatever had befallen him – his father's drunkenness, the tragedy of his mother's death – by sublimating emotion into music.

I tried to ask how his music came to him. 'It's what I hear in my heart,' was all he said.

'But the improvisations?' Pepi demanded. 'How do you *do* it?'

Beethoven broke into one of his most magnificent smiles. He couldn't look at Pepi without doing so. 'I don't know,' he said. 'I find it within myself, and it must *out*.'


We had a musical salon to attend that evening at Prince Lobkowitz's palace, and an early morning ahead: we must rise at 4 a.m. to travel to another picnic in the countryside, and the chances were that we would not have more than two hours' sleep. 'We need air and exercise,' Mother decided, once Beethoven had taken his leave. 'You girls have done nothing today but sit at Beethoven's feet, and dream of doing so when you are not. We shall go for a walk and improve our minds by visiting a museum.'

Pepi gave a sigh of anticipated boredom, but I found a way to enliven the prospect: we could ask Marianna Martines to join us, if she were free.

Instead of writing an acceptance, she arrived in person with our messenger. After warm embraces for us all, she suggested we visit an unusual museum near the Red Tower. 'Waxworks,' she said. 'The most extraordinary likenesses, fashioned by Herr Müller and his colleague. It is worth a look if you like something a little bit ghoulish. We can spend an hour there before closing time.' The 'Müllersches

Gebäude' was a five-minute walk from the Stephansdom towards the Donaukanal.

'Goulash last night, ghoulish today,' I tried to joke. Mother rolled her eyes, but Marianna laughed and tucked my arm through hers as we made our way up the bustling Rotenturmstrasse, dodging horse dung in the road and groups of students who were jostling each other and might jostle a group of unescorted ladies too – though the withering look Mother gave them would have silenced a pack of hounds.

'You were lucky he played for you,' Marianna said, when I told her of the previous evening's marvels. 'I advise you not to fall in love with him!'

'We are both his slaves forever,' I declared. 'But is he not in love, or contemplating marriage?'

'I hear that he is always with one mistress or another, but soon tires of them. They say seven months at most. The trouble is that he is so intelligent: he needs a wife who can match his mind as well as his body. He has made, er, *conquests* that surprised those who learned of them. But those women cultivated enough for him tend to be aristocrats, hence out of his reach in marriageable terms.'

An image sprang into my mind of Beethoven in bed with some pink-nosed chambermaid, or a whore from the Graben. I tried to banish it. 'It's ridiculous. The idea that people who match each other's souls should be kept apart just because one is an aristocrat and the other is a commoner – it's not even as if being of noble birth means you're rich…'

'Tesi, *shush*,' came from Mother. 'Madame Martines does not need to hear us grumble.'

We had arrived at the city wall and the arched gateway of the Rotenturmtor. Just before it stood a long, bland, three-storey building of light-grey stone, tucked behind the

ramparts at an awkward angle. 'This used to be the toll station for the Rotenturmtor. Müller bought and remodelled
it in the 1770s,' Marianna recounted. It boasted a porti-
coed entrance topped with stone eagles, but had no room
for a proper courtyard. An engraved notice declared that
the Imperial and Royal Copper Storeroom was located here
too. 'Müller keeps the storerooms downstairs, has the gallery
upstairs, lives in his own quarters and lets out the other
rooms,' Marianna explained.

At the main entrance, shadowed by the city wall, which
kept this northeast-facing corner colder and darker than the
rest of the city, we allowed the attendants to take our shawls
to the cloakroom. We made our way up one of Vienna's less
fussy staircases and through a tall mahogany door to the left
of the landing into the museum. Mother tutted over the otherwise modest price of our tickets.

This cavernous gallery belied its harmless exterior. Under
gleaming candelabras, the space seemed airless despite its
size; people had been milling through it all day. We had
arrived late and now most visitors were leaving; we had
the impression of swimming upstream as we approached the
exhibits, which were as bizarre as Marianna had intimated.
Waxworks? To me they looked like dead bodies.

One statue showed the naked form of a pregnant woman,
the anatomy delineated so that visitors could view the place-
ment of the infant in her womb. In another case, a mechanical canary opened its mouth to release a sound that, even if
not a perfect imitation of the bird's song, seemed to emanate
from within it. Then I found myself face to face with a dis-
embodied head that loomed in front of me in the late afternoon light.

My eyes met its glass ones. A bust of King Ferdinand IV
of Naples, down to his chest but minus his arms, made by

Joseph Müller and Leonhard Posch. It wore a military uniform with high collar, sash and medals, and its lips and jowls were so lifelike that one imagined they would move and speak. 'I'd like to get out of here,' I confessed to my friend. 'I feel a bit nauseous.'

'It's all right, my dear, it's only a gallery,' she said. 'You must look instead at the Etruscan vases – he has a hundred and fifty or so…' Then something behind me caught her eye.

'Frau Martines, what a delightful surprise.'

'Herr Müller! The delight is all ours.'

We turned. A bulky-shouldered man in a frock coat as dark as his features was approaching, with an outstretched hand. His eyes darted from me to Mother to Pepi.

'This is Herr Müller, "Hofstatuarius", artist and creator of this gallery,' Marianna said. Mother made magnanimous countess sounds of greeting. His face filled with ill-concealed wonder when he lit upon my sister's wide-set eyes, soft round cheeks and tiny waist.

'This is no coincidence,' said Müller. 'I spotted you arriving and I confess I have been following you ever since! I understand you are from Ofen, Countess Brunsvik. How are you enjoying Vienna?' He offered Mother his arm. Threads of silver laced his temples and on his broad hands the veins were pronounced. I wondered for a moment if it might be Mother upon whom his designs were focused.

While we strolled through the rooms, Müller was eager to explain his techniques. The wax in which Ferdinand IV had been cast was a new formula, he said. 'The closest approximation to actual flesh that you can hope to see.' On that, I had to agree.

He had travelled across Europe, plying his trade for royalty; he spent two years in Naples and Rome, making sculptures of the imperial family for their Viennese cousins. 'And here is the emperor himself.' He indicated a waxen horse with its imposing master on its back. 'The size is true to life.' We marvelled politely at his skill, the sheen of the animal's flank and the warrior-like gaze of its rider. Those terrifying glass eyes again.

'Now, come over here – this is very special, in the Cabinet.' Müller's delight in his art produced a gleeful impishness in him, to which I somewhat warmed.

To his creation I warmed less. It was a life-size waxen model occupying a small room of its own. A beautiful young girl, quite naked, reclined on a couch, her head tipped back, her hair flowing golden, her pale arms in an open attitude; around her draped silken curtains, while alabaster jars sheltered the candles that lit the scene. Music was playing across this image, resembling the eerie strains of a harmonium. Close by stood another statue, one with the perfect proportions of a Greek goddess: an exquisite female form raising the drape of her dress and gazing back and down over one shoulder at her own exposed backside. Three mirrors created the illusion that there were in fact four of her. 'We are entering the Bedroom of the Graces,' Müller explained in a low voice. 'Our Fair Sleeper is observed, as you see, by the Aphrodite Kallipygos, who is transformed by the mirrors also into the Three Graces.'

'It's from an actual Greek statue, isn't it?' Marianna asked.

'Indeed, though it is a copy that is preserved in the museum in Naples. Queen Maria Carolina kindly allowed me to take a plaster cast of this remarkable piece, thence to make my wax replica.'

'Queen Maria Carolina?' said Mother.

'What does "Kallipygos" mean?' Pepi asked.

Müller burst out laughing, as if embarrassed, then assessed

the two older ladies and chose Marianna as the person who should convey his answer. She whispered it to me and I in turn to Pepi.

Ancient Greek is such a poetic language. Nothing sounds quite as good in German, or even in French. The expression translates as 'Aphrodite of the Beautiful Buttocks'.

'I need some air,' said Pepi.

'Come, then, and let me take you to my pride and joy.' Müller offered her his arm. 'It's a short walk away and being outside will do you good.'

Pepi glanced up into Müller's face and returned his smile.

By the door the footman arrived with our wraps. He approached Herr Müller: 'Would your Excellency like to help the ladies with the shawls himself?'

'Thank you, Schmidt.' Müller took each garment in turn and placed them over our various shoulders. He lingered for a moment over Pepi. Mother's eyes had taken on a new gleam. Müller was an 'Excellency'?


We gulped the welcome air as Müller – if Müller he was – paced ahead up the busy streets. Dust-caked workmen were making for the taverns at the end of a long day; bewigged officials sauntered from their offices while street urchins dashed around them to clamour for stray coins or, I suspected, to pick their pockets; horses' hooves flicked up dust, mud, dung and straw as they trotted by. All of life was charging onward, builders and aristocrats united under the Stephansdom bells ringing out for Mass. Upon the first chime, a flock of dark birds broke free from the vast cathedral tower into the evening sky.

It was not life, however, that was celebrated in Müller's 'pride and joy'. This turned out to be a mausoleum dedicated to General Laudon, specially built within a grand house on the Himmelpfortgasse.

Marianna hesitated in the doorway.

'My dear,' she said, 'I promised to meet my sister to attend Mass. Would you mind if I take my leave now, and we can meet tomorrow after your lesson?'

Seeing her pace, quick and light, over the road towards the Stephansdom, I experienced the unsettling impression that a sympathetic spirit had peered into our burgeoning world, made an assessment and decided it belonged elsewhere. For a moment I considered dashing after her. Instead, with Pepi and Mother, I had to turn and walk into Müller's monument to death.

Müller led us up three flights of stairs and through a tall doorway, greeting with a wave the woman charged with selling tickets and souvenir prints. Within, the monument was brightly illuminated. Now I began to see and hear what Müller was trying to do.

The mausoleum was a waxen cenotaph, the figures as well crafted as if chiselled from Italian marble. At the centre lay a glass coffin, containing an effigy of the general himself. A small temple encased this, its four pillars topped by a façade bearing a clock and a set of flagpoles. Before it stood the figures of three men in suits of armour and two women in attitudes of mourning.

On the stroke of the hour, music began to emerge from an invisible source, some kind of mechanical organ. 'We vary the music week by week. Each piece lasts eight minutes,' Müller said. 'There are three. I commissioned them. Can you guess who this is by?' There was something sublime in this music, despite its odd mechanical nature.

'We give up,' said Pepi.

'Wolfgang Amadeus Mozart.'

'Mozart agreed to write for an automaton?' I was incredulous.

'Mozart and his charming wife needed the money. Most artists will work for you if you pay them enough, because not many people do. Frau Mozart was ill; she needed to go to Baden for a cure, and he had to pay her way. Those operas were not going to provide the necessaries. My commission did so instead.'

'You commissioned Mozart...' Pepi marvelled.

'Not only that. I myself made his death mask.'

'I have always wondered how these are done,' said Mother. 'Do tell us, Herr Müller?'

'The principle is the same as our Aphrodite. I take a plaster cast of the face – as soon as possible after cessation of life, so that the image has an aspect akin to sleep rather than rigor mortis. It is fashioned into a mould, which is then filled with molten bronze.'

This man had handled the dead body of Mozart. I imagined those broad-tipped fingers pushing plaster over the deceased composer's forehead, the pale nose, the closed eyelids, with Frau Constanze weeping beside the bed and the stillness of the departed soul freezing the room, as Father's had at Martonvásár. How could Müller endure this profession, let alone take pride in it?

Mass was finishing when we emerged. I scanned the throngs of departing worshippers for any sign of Marianna and Antonia, in vain. I pictured them sipping orange flower water coffee and laughing with their friends as they observed the absurdities of Viennese society.

'Herr Müller, we must be going,' said Mother, 'but I cannot thank you enough for your kind attention and fascinating exhibits today.'

Now, of course, he would invite us for *Kaffee und Kuchen* the next afternoon... Had I been directing this ensemble, I could have cued him in. 'Please will you come to me for *Kaffee und Kuchen* tomorrow, once your tuition for the day is complete? I would invite you tonight, were I not aware of your prior engagement.'

Mother explained that we would be picnicking in the woods the next day – but the one after would suit, if that were convenient. And so we took our leave, promising to meet him at the museum after Beethoven had left us.

'Beethoven,' reflected Müller as we parted. 'Now, there is someone I would love to commission...'

After an evening of string quartets in the affable young Prince Lobkowitz's high-ceilinged, bronze-hued music room, we found ourselves – somewhat disconcertingly under the circumstances – at his dining table opposite Constanze Mozart herself. It only took a few gentle questions before the down-to-earth widow rewarded us with a diatribe, delivered *sotto voce*, about how Prince Lichnowsky had sued her husband and won, to their impossible cost, only a short while before Wolfgang died.

Guess who else was there? Lichnowsky himself: a broad-chested forty-something with raised eyebrow and supercilious tilt to the nose. We spotted him looking every young woman up and down, like a farmer assessing ripe peaches in an orchard; our sympathies gravitated towards his long-suffering wife, Princess Christiane. Constanze Mozart, her eyes unfathomable with memories, acknowledged the prince with a slight nod, then pretended he was not there.

'I'm going to speak to him,' I decided after dinner.

'Tesi, be careful!' Pepi pleaded. 'He's Beethoven's biggest supporter.'

'He's drunk. He won't remember a thing about it tomorrow.' I polished my best smile and went up to our host, whom I liked much more, to ask him to introduce me.

The deed done – and Lichnowsky's impassive expression suggesting he was unimpressed with my own appearance – I challenged him about my beloved Mozart's debt. Any topic can be made to seem civilised if uttered with amiable tone and the corners of the mouth turned upwards.

'He owed me money.' The prince shrugged. 'What was I supposed to do? You lend a man 1,400 florins and then he defaults?'

'But *Mozart*! The greatest of musicians – who had *nothing*.'

'No man is different from any other by virtue of talent. I was within my rights.'

'He died only a few months later.'

'Dear Countess, I sincerely hope you are not accusing me of killing Mozart?' Lichnowsky laughed, kissing my hand.

'If men do not differ from one another by virtue of talent, how should they differ by virtue of anything else, such as wealth? Does *that* exempt a man from moral judgment, or from the need for goodness, generosity and consideration?'

'The two concerns, talent and wealth, must cancel one another out.' Lichnowsky's gaze strayed to a glimpse of ankle provided by a passing young baroness. 'Please excuse me, I must just say hello to someone...'

By the time we were back in our hotel in the small hours

and disrobing in our room, our minds were in too much of a ferment to permit even the thought of slumber.

'Müller's a creep,' I said.

'He's rather fascinating,' said Pepi. 'But yes, a bit creepy.'

'He's in love with death.'

'Nonsense. He's an artist.'

'He's not who he says he is.'

'That's possible.' Pepi stood by our washstand, wiping her teeth with her cloth.

'He can't be. Because everyone calls him Herr Müller, which must be the commonest name in Austria, yet his servants address him as "your Excellency". And didn't Mother notice!'

'Perhaps he maintains delusions of grandeur with the servants.' Pepi sounded as if she had delusions of grandeur herself.

'But think, Pepi. Think of Beethoven – a real artist.'

'You were positively impolite to Herr Müller. He practises a very unusual and respectable craft.'

'I don't see anything to respect. Look, when you have one chance of life and one chance to develop your artistry, why would you choose to do *that*?'

Pepi took a sip of water and rinsed her mouth. She was paying sudden attention to the freshness of her breath. 'Tesi, who are we to judge? Everyone approaches these matters in different ways.'

'Why are you defending him? You don't *like* him, do you?'

'I don't *dislike* him. Not the way you seem to. And Frau Mozart spoke well of him tonight.'

'She would, wouldn't she? Come on, Pips, let's get some sleep.' If this conversation went on, Pepi would start hinting that I hated Müller because I was jealous of the attention he was paying her. I could not deal with that degree of idiocy at two o'clock in the morning.

When I opened my eyes from a yawn, she was standing by the mirror, still in one layer of petticoat. She had picked up the hem, holding it high above her head, and was peering backwards over her shoulder towards her own exposed buttocks.

## 5

The picnic left us no time for a piano lesson, but the day after, we were back at the instrument with our Master, trying out his Sonata Op. 7. Pepi surprised me by asking if she could play first; usually I had begun. Initially I believed this was because she had such affection for the piece. Its vigour and brilliance suited her; and we both loved its golden-hued key of E flat major, one of intimacy, love and devotion, in which Mozart had centred *Die Zauberflöte*. Beethoven praised her skill at the repeated notes, melodious legato and treacherous leaps. I hoped that by losing herself in the music, she might forget about the waxworks museum and its proprietor.

When Beethoven suggested I take the slow movement, Pepi did not settle in the listener's chair. While I played, she slipped out; I heard the soft tap of her shoes on the stairs. Beethoven stared after her.

Pepi had noticed something from the window: a carriage depositing a single gentleman caller. Müller had not waited for us to come to him. He had arrived to lurk here until we were ready. Mother, of course, was ready at once.

I could have wept. After the evening of Beethoven's

improvisation, our sleepless night, the enchanted dawn – to turn her back upon him and his music? How could she? My anger and sorrow invaded my hands, making my fingers press to the bottom of the keyboard. A deeper, richer sound began to emerge.

'Splendid,' said Beethoven. 'That's just the tone I want.'

At the end, he cast around and asked what had become of Pepi.

'I think Mother has a guest...'

'Your mother's guest is more important to her than her own?' I sensed the heat rising. 'It is clear enough.'

With one broad paw, he closed the piano lid, then grabbed his hat from the top of the cupboard – and before I could utter another word he had vanished. Paralysed by misery and embarrassment, I thought of running after him. Surely Mother and Pepi would stop him in the entrance?

A slam – the front door – and there he went, striding away from us, head bowed, hands behind his back.

I retreated to my bed to stifle in its pillow my tears of shame.


Fifteen minutes later I righted my appearance and made my way downstairs. At the café table where we had dined with Beethoven only a few days earlier sat Mother, Pepi and Herr Müller. Across the room, filled with guests taking coffee and reading the *Wiener Zeitung*, the waiters wielding trays laden with porcelain cups and glass tankards of beer, I could see Müller holding forth with lavish gestures, while Mother and Pepi listened as if entranced. Pepi spotted me; she waved before I could turn and go upstairs again.

'Tesi, listen,' she said, when I slid into my place beside her. 'Herr Müller is not Herr Müller at all.'

Our visitor inclined his head in a bow to me. 'Count Joseph Deym von Střítež, at your service.'

'You'll have to explain all over again,' I tried to joke.

'Our friend the "Hofstatuarius" is a count with family origins in Bohemia,' Mother announced.

He took up the tale. 'An unfortunate incident some thirty years ago sent my very young self perforce into exile. I took the opportunity to hone my craft and build my collection. When I came back ten years later I took the name "Müller" and opened my first museum – and so you find me now.'

'What "unfortunate incident"?'

'Tesi, shush,' said Mother.

'I can keep no secrets from you, worthy Therese.' Deym rose to my demand, palms upturned. 'Alas, I killed a man. We duelled – a matter of honour. In such a situation, had he not fallen, it would have been me. I had aimed to miss, but...'

Pepi let out an actual giggle.

I did not know at whom to glare hardest: Deym for his murder, Mother for her sycophancy or my sister for what was beginning to seem like a serious lack of judgment.

Did I really know my sister at all? We had never been in such a situation before, experiencing life in a new city, changing our level and joining the circles of artists and aristocrats: a good way, it seemed, to learn the truth about those one thought closest. Silently I instructed myself as I would a schoolroom: whatever happens, extrapolate information, store it, understand its processes – and thus good may be drawn from anything. May it not?

While Deym remarked that his fate had been liberating, having enriched his life with travel and art, Pepi touched my wrist under the table. 'Where's Beethoven?'

People send me newfangled pieces – my youngest niece, who lives here in Vienna as companion to Countess Bánffy, is a fine musician, has met Franz Liszt and presented me with copies of some of his works. But I always return to my volumes of Beethoven. Their spines are almost as bent as my own. Sometimes pages fall out, taking the Master's handwritten annotations with them. I mend those precious books as tenderly as I would bandage a child's injured hand.

My visitors may come either before lunch or after 3 p.m. for *Kaffee und Kuchen*. The maid placed a three-layered silver stand on the table and stood poised with the cake slice, waiting for Marie to choose.

'Don't pretend you don't want the Sachertorte,' I encouraged her.

'A traditional Viennese cake!' Here in Vienna, things become 'traditional' rather fast.

Near the door a mahogany clock was grinding towards the half hour. Clocks are a comfort to me. We should not forget how little time we have left. To live is to be awake. Every morning since our arrival, either the maid or Blanka has woken me at my desk, where I've fallen asleep in the small hours.

'Countess?'

'Sorry, my dear, I'm rambling.' She had finished her cake while I was gabbling on. 'Tell me things,' I said. 'A writer's life is a strange one. Why do you write?'

'It's ridiculous, perhaps, but I want to feel I'm producing something that will give people pleasure for a long time. A legacy, of sorts. I've brought you a copy...' Marie extracted from her holdall a small leather-bound book, which she placed in my hands. It was the first part of a three-volume novel, entitled *Drei Cassetten*. On the flyleaf she had inscribed: 'For dear Countess Therese Brunsvik von

I mimicked walking away, with two fingers of my right hand. For a second, a shadow crossed her face.

Towards the end of our Vienna sojourn, matters came to a head.

Beethoven continued to teach us. Watching the marketing of my sister to the first be-titled bidder, I sought solace in music. I took the brand-new Op. 13, the 'Pathétique' ('my publisher's title, not mine,' the composer complained), as my own: the slow movement, noble and dignified, could help me rise above my fury. Pepi had chosen Op. 10, No. 3, with its exceptional largo, full of deep personal tragedy.

'Very beautiful,' Beethoven encouraged her. 'Now, let's work on your sound quality.' He demonstrated, his hand beside hers on the keyboard. His palms were generous, with long, straight thumbs; his fingers, though plump, were fine-tipped, like substantial quills with sharpened nibs. I remembered the surge of anger that had enabled me to produce the sound he wanted. If Pepi could let out that emotion...

She tried again. 'Relax the arm, let the feeling travel from the heart into the piano. Don't worry about wrong notes, but do not play without feeling. That alone is unforgivable... Good... Now, the melody... imagine you're a singer...'

He pulled his chair level with hers at the keyboard, playing the left-hand part with his right, in duet with her while she played the upper line. I experienced the peculiar illusion that I was listening not to two people playing, but one; not a broad-bodied Rhinelander and a petite girl of twenty, but one soul.

I couldn't explain this bizarre magic, but I knew that were I to take Pepi's place, the effect would be quite different.

Was there something more malleable and empathetic within my sister? She could adapt herself; she could send out her soul to meet another's. I could never release my inner self to such a degree. Was Pepi wax to my marble? Or was this duet something else – a unity of spirit she had found with our Master that I could never match?

The largo came to an end. I was so far away that I almost missed the tremor in Pepi's hand as she withdrew it from the keys.

'You know we must go home soon. Will you come to us in Hungary?' I entreated Beethoven when he finally pulled down his hat from the cupboard's top.

'Try and stop me,' he said. 'I'm writing a duet for you to play and sing together and I shall need to have you perform it to me. It's on a poem by Goethe: "Ich denke dein".'

We went downstairs with him to say goodbye, then watched his familiar stocky figure marching away at speed. Pepi continued to stare after him long after he had vanished into the stream of anonymous passers-by on the Kärthner-strasse.

*Ich denke dein.* I think of you.

I think that was the last carefree afternoon of Pepi's life.


Mother had gone out; we thought she was visiting Aunt Susanna. When she returned, she was unsmiling, her flustered flush skirting her nose and mouth.

'Tesi,' she began, 'let me have a moment alone with Pepi, please.'

Pepi must have guessed what was coming. She protested: 'Tesi and I tell each other everything. Let her stay?'

'Very well. It does affect us all. Now…' She motioned the pale Pepi to a chair. 'My child, you have the chance to make your whole family very proud. I have seen Count Deym this afternoon and, to cut a long story short, he declares himself so much in love with you that he went down on one knee to *me* to request your hand in marriage. Now, what do you say?'

Pepi stayed silent, biting her lip.

'Must she decide on something so momentous right away?'

'Tesi, shush. Let Pepi speak for herself.'

I refused to shush. 'What will it mean for her life, for *our* lives? Where will they live? *How* will they live?'

'Oh, Tesi – you see why I wanted Pepi on her own… Well, one presumes they would be here in Vienna, at the Palais Deym, at least during the season.'

'The house is called the "Müllersches Gebäude",' I corrected her. 'It's dark and miserable.'

'He is even now setting about reclaiming his title,' Mother stated. 'So, Pepi, you will have access to all the music and culture you could desire. And I imagine you could have lessons with Beethoven whenever you like.'

Pepi's mouth opened slightly.

'Have you questioned him enough, Mother?' I interrupted. 'What is his financial situation?'

'Tesi,' Mother snapped, 'he's a *count*. The Bohemian aristocrats are the crème de la crème and he is from one of the greatest families in the Empire. Pepi, what am I to tell him?'

I could sense Pepi trembling in her chair as she gave a tiny nod and said: 'Yes.'

Mother bustled about our suite, moving our laundry into a muslin bag in the trunk and piling our books and music alongside. Now that she had achieved her aim, she was ready to go home.

'As for *you*, I despair.' She glared at me. 'You need to keep your opinions to yourself, Tesi. Nobody wants to marry a shrewish, sniping, bossy girl who looks every gift horse in the mouth.'

'Somebody has to take care of the detail,' I retorted. 'You can't rush into things without checking first. Besides, I don't want to get married. I took a vow.'

'I will add to the list: mulish and stupid.'

'Stupid? I speak five languages.'

'That means nothing.'

'In which language?' I crossed the room, kissed her on the cheek and grabbed my bonnet and shawl.

'And where do you think you're off to? Gadding about on your own again? Do you think this makes us look like a respectable family?'

'I'm going to see Marianna Martines. It's a five-minute walk. Four if I go fast.' I made my escape – and soon, in Marianna's drawing room, I was offloading my concerns to a more sympathetic ear.


Pepi walked around with head held high all evening. At about three o'clock in the morning I woke from a fitful sleep to the sound of sobs. In a patch of blue-silver moonlight, she was lying face down, pressing the pillow over her ears, and her nose and mouth into the mattress to muffle the noise.

'Darling, don't cry,' I pleaded.

'Oh, Tesi. What have I done?'

'The best that you can.'

'Mother has been telling me... things.' She sat up, hunting for a handkerchief on the bedside cabinet.

'About marriage?'

'Tesi, has she told *you*?'

I knew enough. I had witnessed Lotti's birth, peering through the bedroom keyhole unnoticed by the busy midwife. A distant compartment in my memory still held the horror: Mother's screams tearing my ears, the hideous distension between her splayed legs, my seven-year-old self's blind terror that she was about to die, and the revulsion when a slimy, squalling mass of scarlet-wet flesh and mucus came slithering out of her body. My father must have heard me whimpering; he caught me there, scooped me up and carried me off. When I finally met my baby sister – clean, warm, swaddled in a woollen blanket and cradled in our mother's arms – it was difficult to relate her to what I had observed. Meanwhile I could not help but see what rams did with their ewes on our estate, and overhear with disgust the conversations of Franz and his friends when they thought themselves only among men. The notion of a man touching my body, pushing me through whatever it took to reduce a woman to that screeching, mindless mess –

'If you really believe it is a mistake, is it not better to say so now, rather than go through with it?'

'It's too late. I gave my word.'

'You are being good, Pepi – to everyone except yourself. You hardly know him! Is it sensible to rush into this?'

'But someone must marry him, because he's a wealthy aristocrat… Tesi, can't *you* marry him?'

I bit my tongue. 'He is in love with you. He fell in love with you on first sight.' I could have added that he had not changed his mind even when we wore the same old white silk dresses every day.

'Well… if I'm in Vienna… I can still have music lessons.' Pepi allowed a smile to cross her face.

I had to break the news to our Master the next day, for Pepi, Mother and Deym now had other matters to attend to. I had refused to forgo my lesson.

For two seconds I thought he would strangle me. Instead, he turned away and sat at the piano, shoulders sagging. 'Just because he's a count,' he said.

'He's infatuated. He loves her.'

'He scarcely *knows* her!' He improvised quiet musical strands, doodles, experiments on the keyboard, as if trying to calm himself. 'Therese, you "wise young judge". Are you happy about this?'

'It's not up to me. But I'm glad you like Shakespeare.'

Now, though, I knew Beethoven trusted me to tell him the truth. From then on, I felt I could speak to him of anything – and his confidences would likewise be safe in my keeping. For a fortnight we had been master and pupil, genius and admirer. Today we were becoming friends.

'I have also known her for only two weeks,' he said. 'But I *do* know your sister. I know her very well. See if I'm right?'

'Tell me.'

'Pepi is like a Viennese chocolate – dark and smooth on the outside, with all manner of colour and flavour beneath. The silken veneer conceals great imagination, exceptional sensitivity, tremendous stubbornness and a sensuality she is too innocent to understand. She has a capacity, I believe, to put herself in the place of others and experience their emotions by imagining them within herself. And you Hungarians are so different from these slimy, slippery Viennese types. You and Pepi are both full of that fire and pride that your nation absorbs from its folk music and its Gypsies. You say what you mean, and you speak out every time.'

'You are right, in every last detail.'

'Her strengths are too many to list,' he mused. 'Charm, grace, intellect, breadth of interest. Were she a man, she would be a musician, a poet or a swordsman. And her weaknesses? She is too beautiful for her own good...'

I let out a chuckle. Beethoven smiled, more to himself than to me: 'I know how that must sound, but there is some truth in it.'

Though I would never speak against my sister, I could have added that Pepi had many more weaknesses. She could be spoilt, haughty and bossy; and while I distrusted luxury, I feared her taste of it here would leave her craving more.

'Whatever happens, we must still be friends,' I pleaded. 'Come to Hungary whenever you wish. You must and will be our treasured guest.'

'I shall.' His word was given. I knew he would keep it.


Mother and Pepi talked matters of marriage all the way back to Martonvásár. I tried to read, but it was difficult in a cramped stagecoach on frightful roads. I had to stop every few pages to rest my queasy stomach; then I would doze off into dreams of our two and a half weeks among the Viennese, the surprise encounters, the moments that were about to change all our lives. Marianna Martines, twinkle-eyed and independent, hiding her frustration by making music every day. Aunt Susanna, fussing over her vain, precocious daughter (now Julie wanted lessons with Beethoven too). Ferdinand IV and his glass eyes in the bleak museum that was to be Pepi's new home...

'We don't have to stay there,' she said. 'He could sell it and we could buy a castle out among the vineyards...'

'You must be in the city during the season, dear,' said

Mother. 'You will be moving in the highest echelons of Viennese society.'

A malingering unease had possessed me since the engagement became official. Graceful Pepi, musician, poet or swordsman, pupil of Ludwig van Beethoven, was being married off to a man we had known for less than a fortnight, more than twice her age (he was forty-seven, as was Mother), who had a disturbing fascination for effigies of the dead and – despite a certain charm, to which Pepi was clearly not immune – had little to recommend him other than an aristocratic title. I allowed myself, for a second, to imagine that she was instead marrying Beethoven: oh, how much more easily she – and I – would have breathed.

On 29 July, two days after my twenty-fourth birthday, I sat in the front pew of the Martonvásár chapel, staring at my sister's back. She knelt at the altar. Her head was bowed, her hands pressed together in prayer. Her bridegroom was beside her, in the same pose. Latin words were intoned over them; a ring was placed upon her finger to indicate that now she belonged to Deym. Mother, to my left, was sobbing into a linen handkerchief; Franz, to my right, was misty-eyed; Lotti, still trying to grasp the speed with which all this had happened, was clinging onto Mother's hand.

On Franz's other side was Deym's sister, Countess Victoria Golz. Close family, all of a sudden – met for the first time a few days before, when her carriage arrived in our park, from her country home in Nemischl. It was a lengthy journey, but she was determined not to miss the wedding, and eager to discover us. Dark and tall like her brother, she lacked his obsequiousness, replacing it with good humour. She greeted us with warmth and praise, and extended her arms to Pepi for an enthusiastic embrace. 'You must come and stay in Prague whenever you like,' she assured everyone, then shuddered at the mention of the museum, making us laugh. She was a widow, an independent and happy one; she had married into stratospheric Bohemian aristocracy whose marzipan-pink baroque palace on Prague's old town square had been bought by no less a family than the Kinskys. These days she held a musical salon at home every Thursday and had a box at the opera house where Mozart had premiered *Don Giovanni.*

Pepi bounced for joy. 'Come, dear new sister, let me show you around.' They linked arms and set off for a tour of the castle. I didn't want to remind Pepi that she was marrying Deym, not Victoria.

Deym had gone upstairs to dress for dinner. After a while, I wandered up to make sure all was well. I found him examining some cracks in the wall above the library door, and looking with a quizzical expression at our somewhat rustic wooden furniture.

'We live simply,' I told him, 'but our riches are of the soul. Have you seen my late father's library?'

It seemed to impress him: myriad topics, many languages. He took down book after book – few had been left uncut and unread – and asked which my favourites were. I showed him Mary Wollstonecraft's *Vindication of the Rights of Woman*, in translation by Salzmann. It was but a small revenge, and in any case I suspected his mind was elsewhere. Perhaps he could only think about the wedding night ahead. The notion left me miserable on Pepi's behalf.

There was another issue, which Mother showed me later. A crucial piece of paper, bearing her signature and Deym's. A marriage contract, with terms and conditions.

I sat down to read it. Then I read it again, twice. Mother had agreed to pay Deym a dowry for Pepi of 25,000 florins.

'Can we afford that?'

'No,' said Mother. 'Why would you think we could?'

'What are we to do? Sell a painting? Even a Raphael won't fetch that much.'

'Tesi, we're *not going to* pay it.'

'What?'

'They're marrying. It's not a financial transaction.'

'Oh, Mother, of course it is… Do you mean you've signed a contract to pay an amount you can't afford and don't intend to raise, so you've broken your word before your daughter has even left your house?'

'He needn't know for a while.'

It was just as I had feared. Mother was so keen to marry Pepi off to a count that she hadn't checked his financial status; and he was so eager to marry a beautiful countess that he hadn't checked hers either. For all the talk of high society, family estates, exhibition visitors and rent at the Müllersches Gebäude, he was probably as impecunious as we were. Sometime he would realise that between us we had not a bean. I wondered if my sister's beautiful buttocks would make up for that, once all was… revealed.

A storm was billowing on the flat horizon when we stood outside the castle, saying farewell. The servants were loading Pepi's trunks onto the carriage and the stable boy had filled the trough to give the horses a good drink of water. Victoria Golz had already left for Nemischl. The humidity was intense, and growing. That storm would come our way. Mother wiped beads of sweat from her neck and Franz stroked his dogs' silky ears to reassure them; the two Vizslas could tell something was afoot.

Pepi put her arms around me and held on. 'I'm frightened,' she whispered.

I wanted to tell her everything was going to be fine, but I was by no means sure it would. 'Courage, darling. If you need me, send word and I'll come to you straight away.'

'Come anyway. As soon as possible.'

'Don't forget to practise the piano. There's always a world waiting for you there.'

Pepi's grasp slid from mine; Deym took her lace-gloved hand to help her into the carriage. My last glimpse of my sister for many months was as she leaned out of the window waving to us, her handkerchief flapping like a trapped butterfly.

'I hope they can make it to the good road before the rain starts,' Franz remarked.

'It's an ill omen,' I said. 'Seeing them set out with a storm ahead.'

'Why are you such a misery, Tesi?' Mother snapped.

Cassandra's fate was that her predictions were always right, but nobody ever believed them. I, a Cassandra of the puszta, prepared to escape into my ultimate refuge: music.

## 6

My dear niece,

It is 1801. He is in his shirtsleeves, with his old blue coat serving as his rug on the long grass, resting his back against my red marble monument to my father. In the shade of new leaves in the Martonvásár park, he is sketching a stave in his notebook, humming and sometimes singing, oblivious to his own volume. I stop in my tracks, watching him. In my hands is a silver tray: a pottery jug of lemonade, six glasses – for him, myself, Franz, Pepi, Lotti and Julie – and a bowl of chippings from the ice box. The air is sweet; the birds are praising God and springtime. I am loath to interrupt either the creator or the Creator.

Pepi and Julie, walking arm in arm, are some distance behind me. Julie is nineteen and gorgeous, and knows it. Pepi is heavily pregnant, blooming like the earth itself. This will be her second child. Her first – named after not her own sister, but Deym's, Victoire – is in the house with Mother, who has been transformed by grandmotherhood into a benevolent creature helpless with love, singing baby songs and helping big-eyed little Viky, eleven months old, to try rising onto her tiny feet.

Beethoven's gaze lifts. Though he doesn't move, a change comes over him. I glance round and see what he sees. Two young women in the sun, their hair and skirts dancing in the breeze, their shoulders adorned with white lace: the perfect image of joy and promise. He lifts a hand to greet them and, as an afterthought, me. Then turns straight back to his pencil and paper. He had neither seen nor heard me approaching before that. I assume he has focused so much on his inner sounds that outer ones count for nothing. I hesitate a moment longer, then go forward with the lemonade. Even Beethoven needs a cool drink in the sunshine.

Beethoven had arrived at Martonvásár a few days before Julie; we took care to make the most of our time before Countess Vanity descended.

'These four lindens,' I said, while we walked through the grounds with him, 'signify our Republic of Exquisite People.'

'We would like to add you to this republic,' Franz declared, with a click of his heels.

'Thank you – I'm honoured. What must I do?' he asked.

'Choose a tree – north, south, east or west – and it will represent you,' I told him. 'We can address it then as if we are speaking to you, and we will hear you reply through its branches.'

He rested a hand the size of a beefsteak against the trunk of the northernmost linden; above him, a red squirrel scuttled, curving, through the leaves. 'North, for my hometown,' he said. 'I miss it. I miss the Rhine. You must all come with me to see it, one day.'

'The Danube takes some surpassing,' Franz challenged.

'To me, the Rhine surpasses all. And you would enjoy the

wine. It's very special, somewhat aromatic.' He could not obtain Rhineland wine in Vienna, and we in Hungary had never sampled it. 'Tell me, which tree belongs to Julie?'

We exchanged glances. Lotti suppressed a giggle.


Several days after Julie had arrived, I awoke with the dawn chorus, which had sprouted some strange descants. A whistle. Franz's two Vizslas, Silver and Balász, barking. Purposeful steps on the gravel beneath my window: two sets of them. Franz and Beethoven had become the closest of friends when first they met, at Pepi's Vienna home where the composer had organised a performance of his Septet. Franz adored that piece, as did everyone, including Deym. Now they were in harmony as two men rarely can be, whether walking the dogs, visiting the taverns or playing a cello sonata together.

'Wake up, girls! We're going for a walk!'

Julie burst into my room, still in her nightgown. 'Tesi! What's going on? Are we having an excursion?'

'Looks like it,' I muttered from the wash-stand, splashing cold water on my face. It was not yet six o'clock.

We went down to the courtyard to find Franz suggesting to the kitchen maids a better way to pack the picnic, our moustachioed coachman Takács harnessing the two chestnut mares and the Vizslas jumping with excitement on their leashes. I bent to pat Silver; his tongue rasped against my temple.

Julie, lace shawl over shoulders, chasséd towards Beethoven. '*Buongiorno, Luigi!*' she declaimed.

'*Buongiorno, mia bella Giulietta.*' He swept into a bow, then offered her his arm.

One could not blame him for having his head turned.

Pepi, whom he so admired, was busy with her child and imminent new arrival. She was happy. She was radiant. She was unavailable. And so, with Julie gazing into his eyes, tossing her lavish dark curls, exposing from under her skirt an extra glint of ankle – a man would have to be resistant in the extreme to manage his reaction. In that respect he was no different from anybody else.

Pepi appeared at the door, still half asleep, her hair blowing across her eyes. 'Enjoy yourselves,' she said. 'I wish I could go with you.'

Beethoven acknowledged her, then turned back to 'Giulietta'.

'I thought we were going for a walk.' I looked at the carriage and the long-suffering but affectionate face of Takács, who had been with us for twenty years and ruled us with a will of iron. His daughter, Magda, was now Pepi's personal chambermaid.

'Lake Balaton,' said Franz. 'Takács says we can get there in six hours, picnic and walk for another six, then be home for midnight.'

'You could have warned me.' I dashed back inside to hunt for boots in which I could manage a lengthy hike. Lotti had already buttoned up her strongest pair. Julie had donned pink silk ones with pointed toes.

Packed into the carriage, we had a to-do about the roof. Julie – whom Beethoven continued to call Giulietta, while she called him Luigi – begged to lower it. Franz insisted the ladies should not be exposed to the sun. Lotti backed Julie, I backed Franz. Takács lost patience, resolving it in his furious Hungarian accent: 'We can reach Balaton by midday or we can open the roof, but not both. If your hats blow off, I shall not stop to retrieve them!'

I started pondering the sense, and potential danger, of a situation in which the servants spoke among themselves a different language from their employers. We could scarcely understand a word of their tongue – the true Hungarian that the nobility had long been trained to reject in favour of German and French.

Julie, having engineered a place beside Beethoven, gave a theatrical yawn and nodded off to 'sleep', letting her head rest as if by accident on the Master's shoulder. 'Do as we say, Lotti, not as Julie does,' I warned our little sister, but she, like Franz, was trying not to laugh.

Near Balaton, the landscape transformed from puszta to vineyard. Flat-tipped hills and a conical mountain – a dormant volcano – dotted our line of vision and at last the lake spread before us, its milky and sulphurous water jade green under the morning sun.

'We could swim,' said Franz.

'I'd rather walk,' said Beethoven.

Between the vineyards and the shore, Takács slowed the coach, then turned onto an expanse of meadow. He was from this area; it was his recommendation that we picnic here, then walk to a famous landmark nearby: a group of natural basalt columns that, if you were brave enough to climb their steep path, afforded a spectacular view across the great lake. He, meanwhile, would take a nap and let the horses feast on a wildflower lunch.

While Julie stood and watched, Beethoven and Franz carried the picnic baskets and spread out the rugs; Lotti and I took charge of arranging crockery and unpacking fresh bread, goats' cheese, preserved peppers, some cold fish left from last night's dinner and a basket of apples from the cellar. How Pepi would love this…

Beethoven threw himself flat on the grass, one arm shielding his eyes from the sun. It was as if he offered all his being to the earth, while nature filled his heart with – one hoped – fresh music. Julie swooped down beside him and teased him, holding an apple above his mouth. He raised his head to bite into it, but she pulled it away, leaving his powerful jaw snapping into thin air.

'Minx,' scolded Franz, while 'Luigi' gave a roar of laughter and with one paw swiped the fruit from his pupil's hand. Julie had finally got her music lessons, after months of nagging at Aunt Susanna.

'But soft, what light through yonder apple breaks,' Beethoven intoned. 'It is the east and Giulietta is the sun…'

'What's that?' Julie asked.

I rolled my eyes: was my cousin so preoccupied with fashion and flirting that she knew nothing of theatre?

'You don't know *Romeo and Juliet*, and you a Juliet yourself?' Beethoven said. 'Be careful, or I'll recite the whole play.'

'Give us a speech, Luigi,' Franz encouraged him.

He put down the apple. On his back, gazing up into Julie's deep blue eyes, he recited in fine if accented English:

> '*O, speak again, bright angel! for thou art*
> *As glorious to this night, being o'er my*
> *head*
> *As is a winged messenger of heaven*
> *Unto the white-upturned wondering eyes*
> *Of mortals…*'

'Bravo,' Julie said, 'but what a funny language.'

I knew every word of that speech. Pepi would have understood most of it, if some with her heart more than her brain. But Julie: nothing. Could Beethoven not see through her? Wretched empty-headed girl, determined to make a man fall in love with her, when she knew she could never marry him because her parents would object to his 'inferior social class'. Besides, it struck me that she was flirting with Beethoven in order to make *Franz* jealous. Oh God – Julie as my sister-in-law? My appetite for the picnic was fading fast.

'How can you remember it?' she asked Luigi, once the speech was suitably translated.

'How could I not?' said Beethoven. 'If we can find some violinists, Franz, let's play the girls the quartet…' Beethoven could play violin or viola, but preferred the latter.

'Quartet?' Julie yawned.

'The first of my set. The slow movement depicts the tomb scene, or its atmosphere – when Juliet awakens in the crypt after her simulated death and…' He looked for a reaction and received none. Julie did not even know the story.

Suitably fuelled, we set off for the columns. Beethoven and Franz powered ahead up the rocky pathway, while we earthbound women had to clamber along, held back by pinching shoes and long skirts. Who invented the petticoat, I grumbled to Lotti. She looked horrified – it had never occurred to her that one might survive without these hideous garments.

After walking for half an hour amid long grass, juniper bushes and golden alyssum, Lotti and Julie were pleading for a rest and some water. Beethoven, though, seemed as cool and unbothered as if he were strolling through Vienna to give a countess a piano lesson.

'Isn't this wonderful?' he said. 'The air's so different from Vienna…'

'What's different, Luigi? What can you smell?' Julie asked.

Between us we began to assemble the scents of a spring afternoon. The distant lakewater, pungent with sulphur and minerals. Juniper and herbs releasing essences underfoot. Woodsmoke from the village by the shore; horse dung from the road. Does the sun have a scent? That day, we could believe that every sunbeam held a droplet of its own.

'And the sounds?' suggested Franz. The twigs crackling beneath our feet, the dogs' paws pattering along, the whirring of birds' wings above us, and in the distance, a thread of melody from a shepherd's pipe.

Beethoven stayed quiet.

'Luigi?' I tapped his elbow. 'You're miles away.'

He started at my touch, then forced a laugh. 'I was thinking about sounds we *cannot* hear.'

'You're writing music as we go,' Julie suggested.

'Not quite.' He changed the subject abruptly: 'Have you ever seen an Aeolian harp?'

While we walked, he explained he had found a fascinating magazine article about this contraption. Its strings are sounded by the wind. You hang it up to catch the breeze, but when it resonates, what exactly is playing it? 'The article suggests it's the spirits of the outcast, the dispossessed, the lovers who have died without fulfilment.'

'Like Romeo and Juliet?' I asked.

'Exactly – this is how they return to keep their memory alive, in the sorrow of their songs.'

'That is fanciful.'

'Of course, but beautiful, no? They are called the "Children of Moonlight".'

'The music is in the poetry of the concept,' said Franz.

A final push brought us to the pillars' feet among the trees. Sharp against the bright sky, they formed a forest in their own right, like the pipes of a great organ: the plateau above them was tempting to any who crave grand views, alarming to those who do not. Beethoven was already leaping up the narrow, muddy slope that was well trodden by intrepid visitors.

'Be careful, Luigi!' cried Julie. Trying to watch his sturdy figure and strong limbs making swift progress upward, I found the sunlight glaring into my eyes. He might have been ascending a path into the heavens.

From the top there came his shout of triumph. Franz, who was not fond of heights, took a breath and set off after him. We three women looked at the slope, our shoes and our skirts.

'I'm not going up there,' said Lotti.

Julie agreed. 'How would we get down again?'

'You could always jump,' called Franz from above. Evidently he was losing whatever patience he had had for Julie. To think Aunt Susanna had sent her to stay in order to charm him into marrying her…

We had travelled six hours by coach, picked our way among rocks, thorns and probably wild animals for two more hours, we'd still have to walk back, yet we women would be forced to miss the whole point of the trip because of our clothes?

'As you say, we can't do it in these skirts.' I marched off to a thicket and began to fiddle with ribbons and buttons beneath my dress.

'Tesi! What are you doing?' Lotti cried.

The girls looked on in horror as I emerged and dumped my petticoats on their outstretched arms.

'Tesi!' Franz shouted down, 'are you insane?'

'I was, before this moment.' Now, despite my long skirt, I could move. You sometimes forget the sheer weight of clothes until you are free of them. The climb, though precarious, seemed to my liberated limbs the easiest part of the entire walk. At the top, my brother had no choice but to grab my hand and guide me up the last few steps. Beethoven stood close to the plateau's edge, drinking in the view like the wine of his homeland.

We could see for miles across a jade and lavender landscape, under the shadows of passing clouds, and watch the patterns of colour in the lake shifting moment by moment. The quietude was as pleasurable as music. Above us, three huge birds of prey crossed the sprawl of sky. The sun's touch was tender upon my skin. I alone, of all us females, could stand on top of the world beside Luigi van Beethoven.

'Amazing,' I breathed.

'Perfect,' said Franz.

Beethoven was silent. Again, I found myself wondering if he had even heard us.

Finally the girls' anxious voices called up to us, along with the barking of Silver and Balász.

'We should go,' Franz said. The path, such as it was, was too narrow for more than one at a time.

'I'll go first, I'm the fastest,' said Beethoven.

The moment he had disappeared, Franz began to scold me. How dared I disrobe like that? How immodest! And without any beauty to show off!

'I'd rather be ugly and see the view than look like every Greek Aphrodite rolled into one,' I snapped.

'All right,' came Beethoven's call. 'I am down. Now you, Tesi.'

'Come along, let's get you started,' said Franz. I shook him away.

On the precarious gradient, my hand against the rocks to steady myself, I found my dress slowing my progress more than it had on the ascent. I did not want to look down for fear of vertigo, but the voices below were growing nearer.

I was a few steps from the ground when my foot caught in my hem. Rock scraped the skin from my arm and my body struggled in vain to right itself; I heard my sister and cousin cry out as I slid downward, the view somersaulting before my eyes.

A second later, someone with unshakeable grip was grasping both my hands, helping me up. At first I was too dazed to realise who it was. When I turn to his music in times of trouble, I feel again that iron-strong certainty which for a few moments makes sure that I am safe.

'It's all right, Tesi,' he said. 'Lean on me. Try and stand.'

I did so; a bolt of pain flashed through my ankle. The sprain was swelling, a tender agony against my boot. My sister helped me struggle back into my petticoats, but a long walk awaited. 'Luigi and I will carry you on our backs, in turn,' Franz offered.

'I can walk.' My pride and my injury were nevertheless in considerable conflict.

The sun was sinking as we made slow progress; night could fall too soon. In the woods dwelt lynx and possibly bears. It was not the first time I thanked God for giving us a sensible and bossy coachman: we heard approaching hooves and Takács arrived astride one of the horses, worried and looking for us. With profound gratitude I let him hoist me onto the saddle and lead us back at last.

My foot on a cushion, a muslin ice pack over the sprain, I was unable to join the fun the next day. Pepi came to keep me company with Viky, who climbed all over me, bouncing and hugging. Isn't it extraordinary, the instinct that a tiny child, not even one year old, has for affection? I thought of my first sight of my sister in radiant new motherhood: sitting up in bed suckling her baby, suffused with a new, overwhelming love. Visits to Vienna, though, would never be the same again. Pepi's formerly light-hearted conversation was always interrupted by children's concerns – and I feared for her piano practice, though she insisted she would never let it slip.

Here was a rare chance for us to talk, for her husband had not come to Martonvásár, pleading too much work at the museum and the Palais Deym (as we were now supposed to call the place). 'Tell me things, Pips,' I said. 'Your life. All the details.'

She sat back. 'Well, after the fuss last summer...'

It had taken a whole year, and the birth of a child, for the truth about Deym to emerge. It was as I had feared – and I'd had to bite my tongue to prevent myself saying so and making everything worse. I am not sure who was angriest: the count when he discovered we did not have the 25,000 florins stipulated in his contract, or Mother when she found that neither did he. Meanwhile, debts were continually incurred by the museum's upkeep, never mind the aristocratic lifestyle he and Pepi liked to maintain, brightening their spartan living quarters with the velvet, brocade, tapestry and glassware that my magpie sister loved.

When Mother and I went to Vienna after Viky was born,

the whole story came tumbling out. Mother screamed at Pepi – as if it were her fault she had been married off in haste to the first man who asked.

'Leave him! He married you under false pretences!' she yelled. 'Annul the marriage.'

'I married him to please *you*,' Pepi said. 'You didn't check his affairs, even though Tesi said you should.'

'You ought to be glad to be rid of him.'

'I shall never leave him.' Pepi set her jaw. 'I vowed to be his wife for better or for worse, he is the father of my child, and his wife I shall remain.'

I don't know why Mother thought they could 'annul' a marriage that had already produced an infant. And if Pepi's beauty were blossoming with motherhood, so was her character. I could tell, even if Mother could not, that a genuine bond kept her with Deym. In her own way, she loved the man.

'You are content with him, despite all?' I asked her now.

'He's wonderful,' said Pepi. 'I don't know what I'd do without him.'

I did not understand how she could possibly have fallen in love with him; she being my little sister, I told her so. I avoided mentioning the tenderness that had been growing between her and Beethoven before we walked into the wax-works museum.

'Tesi...' She seemed to be measuring her words. 'Listen. You know what Mother told me about the facts of marriage? There is so much more. You have... no idea.'

That was true enough.

Seeing me baffled and curious, she talked on – telling me of ways that he knew to touch her, and places in her body that she had not known existed. 'I lose myself, I lose control, and there is nothing in the world but feeling – and while he desires me, I hunger for him, for his physical self, for more and more… Tesi, *this* is love, *this* is how a child is sparked to life. What could be more wondrous?'

I took in her words. Then I asked, 'What about the money?'

Pepi deflated. 'With the museum and renting out the rooms, we manage. We're not extravagant.'

Oh, my sweet sister, how easily you deceived yourself. Not extravagant? While I was in Vienna after Viky's birth, you insisted on buying me three new ball-dresses in the latest fashions, promising I should wear them all. One was pure white, the second boasted a silver tunic, and the third offset yellow silk with a purple sash. Your letters over the season described royal receptions and balls; dancing through Carnival with masks and white gloves, amid diamonds that glittered like ice; salon concerts and premieres at Prince Lobkowitz's, Prince Lichnowsky's, Prince Kinsky's and Count Pálffy's palaces with Beethoven, Beethoven and more Beethoven.

'But I never see anyone,' she protested. 'We live in seclusion.'

Seclusion? When you are off to celebrate the arrival of the tsar's daughter, waltzing the night away in the Hofburg's ballrooms, or going to Beethoven's Burgtheater concert to hear his first symphony as a guest of honour? Seclusion, when you are taking *Kaffee und Kuchen* with *my* friend Marianna, and playing chamber music with Schuppanzigh at Zmeskall's house – and when you perform Beethoven's music everyone gasps at your technique and your beauty alike? And would you indeed object to seclusion when you and your husband have plenty to do alone together in the bedroom?

'Nobody comes to see *us*,' Pepi explained. 'We can't afford to hold parties like the princes, some people are still uncomfortable about... what happened to Joseph, that duel years ago... and he doesn't like me having visitors. He's so jealous – he wants me all to himself. Yes, we go out. Yes, I know my playing is admired and when we promenade people compliment us and say I am fit to paint. But...'

'Then what do you do all the time?' I asked.

'Card games. Endless whist.' Pepi rolled her eyes. 'It's *so* boring. He is friendly with a couple, the Sauers, who come round twice a week to play and I can't stand them. They don't like music.'

'You must find useful occupation, then, beyond whist, motherhood and the act of love. You could give more performances – you spend long enough at the piano. And we must think, too, about how best to educate your children. How I wish you would let me teach them.'

Pepi looked astounded. 'Really?'

'I'm stuck here, Pips. Beyond the estate and my own studies, I want to be doing something useful and I know I could teach. I can *see* it.' I held the image in my mind's eye: myself, authoritative yet gentle, directing my guidance of wisdom, culture and godliness to a group of little girls sitting silent at their small desks to learn, from me, their way forward.

'You didn't much like that school in Vienna that Father sent you to,' Pepi said.

'Mine would be – will be – different.'

In that scant year, I was twelve years old, and even if the place had not been cruel and oppressive, it was too late to make much difference. By then, one's character is set. The Institute of Mary opened a school for girls in Vác, near Pest, back in the 1770s; more followed. Rejected by that parent institution, I was pondering how I might create one of my own. Ideally, I would take children in at three or four years old, when they can learn patterns of excellence that will stay with them for life. Through my adored niece, I was discovering a capacity for loving children that perhaps I could extend to all of them. The question was how to bring this about.

'I consult books on education when I can,' Pepi said. 'Joseph does not like me to read. He thinks it does strange things to women's brains.'

'Oh, for heaven's sake!'

'He uses *you* as a case in point.'

I flushed with anger. 'You mustn't put up with that.'

'I… find ways.'

'So, you never see anybody, but you're out every night. You're not allowed to read, but you manage this or that. What about music? If nobody visits the house, what about your lessons?'

'Oh, that's different. Beethoven comes every three days to teach me. Did he not tell you?'

'You mean… your husband is jealous and won't let you have visitors, but he lets you have *Beethoven*?' I hoped the irony was not lost on her. Perhaps his crush on Julie was strong enough for him to have forgotten his embryonic feelings for my sister. He was a vigorous man of thirty, sought after throughout Vienna; he would not keep his whole heart for a woman he could never have.

'For piano lessons.' Pepi was faking her old, innocent, wide-eyed self. She had changed, immutably. 'Isn't that all right?'

'Very much so,' I muttered.

'And he's written a piece for the mausoleum, for the mechanical organ. Joseph commissioned him and gave him a massive silver candlestick to say thank you. So everyone's happy.'

Music reached us: exploratory, restless, ranging across the piano from one extreme to the other. Beethoven himself was in the music room, playing. After a minute, Pepi took my hands to help me up. Leaning on her to take the pressure off my sprain, I hobbled down the back stairs towards the sound.

Beethoven gave us a glance of greeting. Then he switched from his improvisation into something new. A minuet, in E flat major. On the window seat, we listened together, enchanted, to this most serene yet intimate dance.

'You like it, Pepi?' he said.

These four words were enough. He scarcely knew I was there. Forget Pepi? Beethoven, forget Pepi?

She went across to examine the manuscript paper on the piano.

'Part of a new sonata. It's for you, but don't tell. I know you love to dance a minuet.'

Pepi played a fragment of the theme – a falling figure with a dotted note on the upbeat – then laughed aloud. 'That's my name! "Jo-se-*phin*-e..."'

'Lie-be *Pips,* Jo-se-*phin*-e,' sang Beethoven, extending the melody from the beginning. Then he played the theme of the duet he had written for us, *Ich denke dein*. Its rhythm was different – in four beats, not three – yet the melodic shape, even if not a precise match, seemed to rhyme: a variation of sorts.

'Where's the rest of the sonata?' I asked.

'On the way. And its companions. It is a set of three...'

He had been writing a ferment of sonatas. The A flat major, Op. 26, two in experimental form, marked 'quasi una fantasia', and one in 'pastoral' mode. Now three more, and we could study them at the piano for as long as we liked. A symphonic score would be heard only in an occasional performance – which might be poorly played – unless someone created a piano version. He had to weigh public expectation against practicality and sales: symphonies and, someday, an opera for the first, then sonatas for the second. 'Don't forget, dear Countesses,' he growled, 'that I do not hold a post and don't wish to, but I have to make a living. The kind Lichnowsky is giving me a stipend every year, but it rankles to be dependent on a prince. Therefore I must also sell some music.'

After dinner, Franz and Beethoven saddled the horses and rode out over the plain to the nearest tavern. I watched them go. Our guest was an inexperienced rider – and the recalcitrant mare knew it and kept stopping to munch the bushes. Beethoven had bought himself a horse once, because he fancied learning to ride. Franz never tired of laughing at the topsy-turvy nature of this move and the tales of the bruises that inevitably occurred. 'First I will teach you,' our brother roared, 'and *then* you can buy a mount…'

Upstairs, Pepi put Viky to bed and sang her a lullaby, surrounded by adoring aunts and cousin. Julie was restive.

'You should come to Vienna. We have shops,' she said, yawning. 'There's nothing to do here.'

Not much in Martonvásár could compare with late-night ice cream on the Graben.

'Wherever Beethoven is, that is the most exciting place,' Pepi sang, improvising. Viky snuggled down in her cot.

'He's in love with me, you know.' Julie preened. 'He's preoccupied with that play about the girl who has my name.'

'He loves Shakespeare,' I said. 'I doubt it's only about you.'

Julie looked satisfactorily outraged. 'He's dedicating a piano sonata to me, in print. He told me so himself.'

He had never dedicated a sonata to either of us.

'He said he was writing one for *me*,' Pepi ventured, stroking her sleepy daughter's cheek.

'No, Pepi, this is an actual, *printed* dedication. Oh, I love him so much – but he's such an angry man. He's so difficult. He's so clueless about worldly matters. He's going to propose – I know it. But Mama and Papa want me to marry a count.'

I hoped Franz had made it clear this count would not be him. He was far too sensible to lose his heart to a girl who did not deserve it – wasn't he? I was less sure about 'Luigi'.

The next day my sprain was much reduced and I could make my own way to the library after lunch. Hearing a familiar strong step under the window, I limped across to open the casement.

'Luigi!' He was off for his afternoon walk. How good it was to be on nickname terms with him – he was one of us now.

He swerved off the path and stepped up onto a plant pot beneath my window, the better to talk. 'How's the ankle?'

'Mending.' There were things I had not been able to ask him at lunch. 'Luigi, is it true you're dedicating a sonata to Julie?'

'Sorry?' He must be too far down to hear. I repeated myself, louder, hoping Julie was well out of earshot. She did not frequent the library.

'Yes… it is…' He stood on tiptoe. 'But there are reasons. Your kindest of aunts… I do not ask payment for Julie's lessons, so she gave me a rather excessive gift of linen, which she'd stitched herself, and I wrote her a letter that was also excessive, saying it was too much to accept, so we have to smooth the waters. Meanwhile, they have bought a new piano, among the best I've seen. There is a particular effect I wanted to try in that piece – it's to do with the Aeolian harp I mentioned – which I think this instrument will make possible. And so: a dedication to "Giulietta".'

'But the sonata for Pepi—'

'—is the one we played yesterday. The whole set is for Pepi… Tesi, don't you see? I can't put her name on them, or her big boss will be jealous. I don't want to cause her trouble. She knows, I know and now you know, too.'

I watched him stride away up the drive. Back in my armchair, I found myself wondering, not for the first time, what was to become of us all. I imagined a tranquil future: Pepi and Deym surrounded by their growing family, Beethoven teaching the children the piano, for they would all be sensationally gifted, while I became their governess – and Julie would marry some long-suffering aristocrat who would take it as a compliment when she flirted with others. Maybe Franz would find a nice girl to be his wife, and Lotti a fine husband. We could all live together in Vienna – except Julie… Imagine: three happy households, a music master and a governess-cum-household manager, joining forces, raising everyone's children, with no division of status or of sex.

A bizarre instruction from the Master: keep the dampers raised throughout the first movement. The sounds resonate, surreal, mixing new sonic formulae like molten wax. A solemn song is intoned, perhaps a funeral march. Beethoven seemed obsessed with funeral marches then; in his sonata Op. 26 he devoted a whole movement to one. The sonata dedicated to Julie is Op. 27, No. 2, in C sharp minor. 'Quasi una fantasia' – as if a fantasia: a term that blows apart any preconception of what a sonata was, is or 'should' be. The triplets evoke the sound of aerial strings whispering under the touch of long-departed spirits. Some critic invoked a poetic image involving Lake Lucerne by night and now everybody calls it the 'Moonlight' Sonata. It has nothing to do with moonlight – unless it be Luigi's vision of the Aeolian harp and its 'children of moonlight'.

It was not a love gift, not even secretly, unless Luigi neglected to admit it. He had, after all, become infatuated with our cousin, Countess Vanity. He even proposed to her. We enjoyed a proxy revenge, courtesy of her father, our Uncle Francesco. Making clear that Julie could forget any notion of accepting, he did not shout at her. He simply laughed.

Franz was having none of her, so she was married off a year or two afterwards to Count Wenzel Gallenberg, a young man who considered himself a composer, but only wrote ballet music – yes, an aristocrat with a profession! – and in the end became an impresario. They had a gigantic wedding at the Stephansdom, then departed together to live the high life. Julie's beauty was soon famed across the continent. Luigi, we surmised, was merely another for her collection of broken hearts.

Years later, though, he told me a different tale altogether. After Julie had been married for a matter of weeks, she encountered him at a salon concert, managed to coax him to a back room out of everyone's earshot, then ran up to him and burst into tears. She loved him much more than her husband, she declared, but she had had to marry the count for her family's sake and now when he touched her she wanted to scream. Couldn't Beethoven... help her?

I had thought, by that time, that nothing could shock me. 'What did you say?'

'That I could not.'

This exquisite young countess, his ex-pupil to whom he had once been in thrall? Most other men of my acquaintance would have locked the door at once and set about unbuttoning.

'Within moments,' he said, 'I lost all my admiration, attraction and even my liking for her. I cannot love a woman I do not respect, and if she is prepared to prostitute herself into marriage for the sake of money and status, then readily deceive her husband, while moreover expecting her lover not to mind taking second place – she is not for me. I swore to myself then that I shall never have an affair with any married woman.' The remembered fury in his eyes and his voice made me shudder for its likely impact upon my humiliated cousin.

Nevertheless, I admired him for this assertion and told him so. 'I fear your ideals are so strong that you may never find someone who matches them,' I said.

'And you, Tesi? Will you ever find someone who matches yours?'

My ideal was my father. No – nobody could ever match him. I held Luigi's gaze and shook my head.

That summer of 1801 we were still lost in our idyll. We had no idea, as we practised Beethoven's sonatas, played with little Viky and supported Pepi as she laboured to bring her first son into the world, that within a few short years the smooth lawn upon which we stood would begin to heat, shrivel, then burn beneath our feet.

## 7

My dear niece,

My advice to you is never to take anything for granted. Looking back from beyond three revolutions in my lifetime, it is strange to remember that we used to question nothing. I note with shame that as a young woman my chief concern about the French Revolution was its effect on my immediate family.

Paris seemed a long way from Ofen. Yet the guillotined queen, Marie Antoinette – formerly Maria Antonia – was the daughter of my own godmother, Empress Maria Theresa. I was five years old when the empress died; eighteen when Marie Antoinette was murdered. Were our people to follow the French example, we could be next – for there was no shortage of grievances, given the entrenched and closely guarded privileges of our aristocracy.

Have you ever checked, my dear, what it took to be recognised as a member of the nobility in the Holy Roman Empire? We never thought to do so until Beethoven, to our anxiety, let slip that he still held Napoleon Bonaparte in the highest esteem. After that, Franz and I began to quiz Mother at length. Her preoccupation with the court – which I suspect she had always missed – made her a communicative interviewee.

We spent long winter evenings in Ofen talking together in the living room. Mother seemed surprised we should suddenly take an interest, but we found her revelations sobering. 'These differences are *legally* determined,' she said. Aristocrats' and commoners' disputes were settled by separate organisations with differing laws: the Landrecht for the former, the Magistracy for the rest.

'And do they also decide who is accepted into the royal court?' I asked.

'No, no – what happens then is that special examiners in the office of the head chamberlain, the *Oberstkämmerer*, will actively trace your ancestry. You have to demonstrate direct descent from sixteen full members of the nobility. No deviation is acceptable closer than a great-great-grandparent, and even there a marriage to someone of the middle classes or a lesser *Gesellschaft* will raise eyebrows. If you marry beneath your *Gesellschaft*, you will be ostracised, and worse, you ruin the chances of your children and their descendants ever holding noble status again.'

'It's not actually illegal to marry a commoner?'

'No,' Mother acknowledged, with some distaste, 'but it is ill-advised, especially for a girl, because you will lose your title. Conversely, the daughter of a wealthy merchant, for example, could marry a baron and hence become a "Baronin" – I have seen a few such instances. A woman's status, as you know, is determined by that of her husband.'

'And we,' I said, 'can trace our own noble ancestry from…?'

Mother simmered. 'My family is high-born enough for court, but your father…'

Franz's bright eyes dimmed slightly.

'How silly. Father would have thought so too,' I said.

Our grandfather's status had been 'elevated' by the empress to that of count; the snobbery he encountered had helped to inspire Father's praise for the newly independent United States of America.

'That is the way it is.' Mother's thin lips twitched into something resembling a smile.

'So we are… trapped?'

'Basically,' said Franz, 'yes.'

We could not struggle out of this corset ourselves; indeed, we fell between possibilities, too grand for the commoners, not grand enough for the upper nobility.

'I cannot stress strongly enough the hold that these traditions have,' Mother declared. 'We are talking about centuries of practice. Moreover, if you think yourselves corseted now, you should have seen how it was in my empress's day.'

Should one have wished to bend some rules for love, my godmother had introduced a secret morality police to keep everybody in line. Empress Maria Theresa's purity drive extended from the censoring of books, theatre and opera to spies who would follow and challenge any young girl walking on her own. Police raids upon brothels little deterred them from business, though, and we were lucky that by the time Franz was of age, the 'purity police' was long disbanded; he went often enough to sample those wares.

'Let's be grateful for some progress.' Franz had the grace to look self-conscious. 'I must go and do some cello practice…'

My godmother's puritanical systems could be slackened, but the divided legal system, and the strict bloodline that it supported, could not. Therefore, making Beethoven 'one of us' could have seemed, to some, a cruel mistake. We regarded this great musician as better than royalty. Worse, he agreed. With his peculiar awareness of his own genius, his high-minded personal standards and a rapier-sharp eye for non-sense, he refused to value noble status more than he valued his God-given art. Unfortunately, that was not how every-body else saw it.

Many accepted him simply for his talent, virtuosity and increasing fame; his middle-class origins could be ignored thanks to the convenient ambiguity of his 'van'. His circles included serious aristocracy – Count Waldstein, Archduke Rudolph, the Princes Kinsky, Lichnowsky and Lobkowitz – but also lawyers, doctors and artists: his oldest friends from Bonn were the musician Ferdinand Ries, the physician Franz Wegeler and Stephan von Breuning, a lawyer whose father had been an invaluable support to Beethoven as a youngster. Artists were once servants; Haydn had worn liv-ery as the Esterházy princes' Kapellmeister. Now, instead, it seemed they belonged everywhere and nowhere, at least when they were practising their art. Beethoven could give a prince a piano lesson in which he was the master and the exalted one the pupil. But should he ever try to cross the line, trouble would result.

Too often, people have said to me that Beethoven's egal-itarian spirit and love of liberty must have come about because he fell in love with aristocratic women above his sta-tion, which left him loathing that social rift. I think the truth was the opposite: Beethoven's idealistic soul refused from the outset to accept those artificial rules; thus he saw no harm in courting a countess.

I have observed the revolutions of 1789, 1830 and finally 1848, in which dear Blanka participated and for which she has been cruelly punished, and I can promise you that more are guaranteed: the question is merely when, where and how. When will the time come, Beethoven used to muse, when these divisions of class will disappear and there are only *people*? It is sadly far away.

Thus I came to understand something of how and why Luigi would admire Napoleon Bonaparte: an anti-monarchist leader, sweeping away the structures of bygone days, with the repute, if not the actuality, of a self-made Titan. You might think that when in 1794 Napoleon's forces occupied Bonn, Beethoven's birthplace, it would have entrenched the young composer against him. Yet Luigi followed his progress with enthusiasm. Italy, Egypt, Palestine: the general became a hero and thence 'First Consul' in France. Austria lost to him at Marengo, but although Beethoven was by now an adopted Viennese star, he still found Bonaparte's success inspiring.

I mention this, my dear, because I wish you to remember it during what follows. Every part of our lives is bound up with the state of our politics, economics, education and society; this social volcano, galvanised by the sulphurous heat of Bonaparte's ambitions, affected all aspects of our fate.

All except one.


In autumn, Pepi wrote to me from Vienna. 'Tesi, have you heard from Beethoven? I ask because I have not. He has disappeared.'

I dispatched a letter to his latest lodging at once. It was returned. *Gone away. Address not known.*

Franz was frantic, unable to settle to cello practice or office work. 'Something must have happened,' he said. 'It's a precarious livelihood, performance nerves can be fearful, and

Luigi has no grounded home life – it's only a step to destitution or madness or both.'

I'd thought his strength indomitable. 'What are you going to do?'

'All I can.'

The next day he set off on horseback for Vienna to look for his friend.

How cruel can God be – the same God who gave us music, art and nature? What more heinous fate could He conceive for His servant whose music could bring solace to all who heard it?

I had never seen my brother depressed. He could be angry, outspoken or sorrowful, but when he returned after many days' absence, something had left him blank with misery. He came to find me in the library and slumped down at the table, head in hands, quoting Goethe: '"My peace is gone, my heart is heavy, I shall never find it again".'

First, he reported, he discovered Pepi desperate with worry; she could not let Deym see this, because she was pregnant again and he would be angry if her state of mind were unfit to support her condition. Deym, for his part, insisted Luigi would be back any minute; at worst he'd be having an illicit love affair.

The Guicciardis had not seen him either. Julie was just married and away on her honeymoon with Gallenberg. Mutual friends – Zmeskall, Schuppanzigh, Wegeler – were also anxious. Zmeskall told Franz that Beethoven had two brothers, Johann and Kasper Karl, both living in Vienna. Franz sought out Johann's place and discovered, with surprise, that it was a pharmacy which this younger Beethoven managed.

'I'm not sure that that was all,' Franz said. 'He has a num-

ber of different establishments and I think he knows a thing
or two about making dosh.'

'What's he like? Does he resemble Luigi?'

'Not beyond the temper. Red in hair and face, choleric,
unhelpful and, over Luigi's music, downright scornful. He
says that if his brother earned a decent living, that would be
fine, but he does not. Johann thinks he lives as if in another
world, clueless about money, carrying insane expectations
that others would tolerate this on behalf of his oh-so-pre-
cious art! He declared that a comeuppance would be long
overdue. I was not best pleased and there seemed little point
in prolonging the conversation. Off we went, my steed and
I, clip-clopping our way to the other brother, Kasper Karl's.'

'More edifying?'

'Less. He is not scornful of his brother. He is *jealous*.' Franz
gave a bitter laugh. 'He, too, wants to be a composer! He
earns a crust – nothing more – by giving piano lessons, and
he has published a few pieces, which he was eager to show
me, rather to my distress. Now he's trying to be Luigi's business manager.'

'He had heard from him?'

'As far as he'd admit, not a squeak. Business manager,
indeed! Tesi, I do feel I've had some insight into Luigi. He
is the one solid element of that family. The brothers are no-
good drunkards both – much like their father.'

Luigi was fond of his drink too, I noted, and his temper
could be both rapid and terrifying.

'You know what I did in the end?' Franz continued. 'I
remembered I was in Vienna, so I simply bribed his old
landlord. Turned out Luigi was spending the summer in
the countryside, on medical advice, and might still be there.
Possibly Heiligenstadt.'

A tiny square beside the church, three taverns and two

streets, one heading downhill towards the brook, the other leading upwards and out: that, said Franz, was the sum total of Heiligenstadt. He tethered his horse in the field behind the church, then plodded up the muddy lane from house to house, asking after Beethoven.

He soon determined that Luigi was there, and had been since April. A delivery boy said he often dropped off boxes of sausages, fish, cheese and wine for the musician gentleman who lived behind the bakery. He had become a familiar figure, striding daily through the woods beside the stream, hands behind his back. There'd been great excitement, the lad remarked, when a bloke arrived to visit, likely his brother – they had the same scowl – but some disagreement had taken place and they came to blows in the street, providing the villagers with some spectacular entertainment. 'So Kasper Karl *had* seen him – he just didn't want to tell me,' Franz said.

Autumn set in, but an alarming change came with it. When Franz called at the bakery, the proprietor, Beethoven's landlord, said that the gentleman upstairs nowadays rarely came out except for his afternoon walk. He could hear him clomping up and down, up and down, sometimes long into the night. He was anxious for the man, but didn't know what to do.

With his help, Franz stormed the apartment door, up the stairs to the right of the little courtyard – and found Luigi: unwashed, unshaven, pacing from edge to edge like a captive bear. He even kept on when they came in and tried to calm him. At last my brother, through speaking of me and Pepi, managed to gain his attention: the news that Pepi was worried precipitated him into a storm of despair. Why? He thought his life might be over. He was losing his hearing.

No doctor had yet found the cause. One thought it might

be the result of a peculiar seizure a few years earlier, or the long-term effects of an infectious illness, perhaps typhus. Another opined that if this were so, it should improve with time, but nothing could be done to speed the progress. A third said that if the condition were related to the ossification of the bones inside the ear, it would grow worse and nothing could be done to slow it.

When Franz pressed him, horrified, the truth emerged: this was not new. The symptoms had begun to plague Luigi even before he met us. Now he must face up to all it implied. If he seemed absorbed in his own world, it was because the sounds of our sphere could not reach him. The day we went to Lake Balaton and counted the noises, he did not join in because he could not hear the birds' wings, or the crackling twigs, or the distant shepherd's pipe. He felt this absence as a body blow, a humiliation; how could he admit to such a malady? He, a sociable and generous soul, now preferred to avoid company rather than allow his disability to be seen. The art for which he lived, the concert career on which he depended, the lessons he could give, the chamber music he could play: all was in jeopardy. Even if he could hear now, if less well than before, a day would come when he could not. He was a musician and nothing else. He had considered taking his own life.

'You hear your music *within*,' Franz said. 'That will never change.'

'My art is all that binds me to the world,' Luigi responded. 'There is so much that I feel charged to bring forth. But for that, by now I would have found peace.'

Franz, alarm blocking his throat, went to stand by the window, head bowed. He was not too overcome to use his sorrowful guise to scan the place for rope, knife or gun. Thankfully, none were obvious.

'It's as if Luigi feels a duty to his music,' Franz said to me. 'As if some inner contract exists between him and God, or Nature. Here is life: use it for art. Music that nobody else can create. Music that can change the world. You cannot leave until you have fulfilled this vocation.'

No suffering would be too great for its sake. He would live like a hermit if he had to. His social life and his prospects for marriage could be ruined by deafness, but always he would stay true to his art. We Brunsviks were among the few who might understand.

Luigi stood bathed in sunlight, turning his face away from his anxious visitor. 'I shall not give in,' he promised. 'I shall seize fate by the throat; it will not wholly overcome me. How beautiful it is to be alive – to live a thousand times!'

Franz embraced him. He could not save Luigi, but he knew that music would.

'Is he working? Surely he can't write if he is suffering so?' I asked.

'Of course he's working.' Franz sounded as if I must be insane to consider otherwise. 'He showed me. A second symphony, a third piano concerto and three violin sonatas for the Tsar of Russia. I think Pepi introduced him to the tsarevna when she was in Vienna.'

'I hope he is being well paid.'

'So does he.'

'But... still, it is horrific – whatever will he do?'

'Luigi isn't afraid he won't be able to compose. It is more that he is angry with God for making everything so bloody difficult. For him, the biggest defiance, the most gigantic shake of the fist, is *to keep on composing*. He will not be deflected. I asked if his second symphony would be an outlet for all his feelings, but he laughed in my face and declared it one of the sunniest pieces he has ever written.'

'But *you* are depressed?'

'I want to help him, but I feel powerless. He's so changed from when we first met, at the Septet at Pepi's house… I can't bear to see him like this. I swore to remain his friend for life. But that is no substitute for good health and clear senses, and we both know it.'

Soon after this, I set off for Vienna myself: a long visit to the Deyms, bringing a selection of books about the education of small children. Every morning I awoke in my room at the back of the house to hear, in the distance, the telltale sounds of my poor sister succumbing to morning sickness. I fussed over her, brewing herbal concoctions to soothe her stomach, and encouraging her to play piano duets. 'Let's do *Ich denke dein* for old time's sake.'

'Not that again,' Deym grumbled.

'We haven't played it since last winter, dear,' Pepi pointed out, 'and I can perform it with none but Tesi.'

I could see Deym glaring as we left him behind on the way to the music room, where we warbled through Beethoven's song about thinking of us, or at least of Pepi.

Luigi had returned to town and at once resumed his twice-weekly visits to give Pepi her piano lesson. I ran to meet him with some anxiety – quickly replaced by joy. To my astonishment, he seemed his old self, as if nothing could trouble him as long as he was in Pepi's home. His manner was formal and respectful, raising no objection from Deym, who liked him and the discussions they enjoyed together about politics.

Nor did Luigi hold against Deym the fact that the count had married the woman Luigi most desired. After the musical session ended, Deym would summon a decanter of

Moravian wine and the two men held forth over it, Deym aghast at Luigi's praise for Napoleon.

'Look at what he's achieved,' Luigi protested. 'The Revolution seemed the Apocalypse itself, but now there's stability. There's hope. People need hope: there's an energy it brings that nothing can match.'

'You are surmising, dear fellow,' Deym pointed out. 'You haven't been to France yourself to experience the reality.'

'He's brought in a Legion of Honour, to recognise the highest achievements in the land. An education system to benefit everybody.' Luigi accepted another glass. 'These are all measures that can build *hope* in the people's hearts.'

'Education for all is a fine development,' I offered, from my window seat.

Luigi leaned his left ear – the better one – in my direction. I flushed and spoke louder. Nobody mentioned his ailment.

'No good will come of Bonaparte. You wait and see,' Deym countered. 'And you, Beethoven, be careful. We don't want to find you're spouting treason. I'd keep it within these four walls if I were you. Now, where on earth is Pepi?'

'He's not an enemy.' Beethoven would not let it drop. 'He's an example. A self-made man, powered by strength of character and true, high ideals.'

Deym shook his head in despair. '*Musicians…*'

Pepi came back from the nursery just then; she had been saying goodnight to the children. Luigi switched away from politics. He was preparing a huge quantity of music for publication, he told us: the Symphony No. 2, the Piano Concerto No. 3 and an oratorio, *Christ on the Mount of Olives*. He intended to put on a concert at Schikaneder's new opera house, the Theater an der Wien, that would include them all. In another few weeks he could firm everything up. I dared not ask how much he could hear of the orchestra if he were conducting. Schikaneder had appointed him 'composer in residence'; he had moved into a flat in the theatre building, where he could step out of his door and be in the stalls in half a minute. His appointed task there was to write an opera for the place, with Schikaneder's libretto. While he spoke of his plans, much as he had at our first dinner together in Vienna, you would never think this walking firework had recently been so deep in crisis that he had considered suicide.

'Perhaps he is a good actor,' Deym suggested, after Luigi had left.

'Perhaps,' I said. 'But I don't think so.' All the time we had known him, Beethoven had never pretended to be other than he was, unlike most of Vienna; this was partly what drew him to us, for we too were forthright foreigners with a low tolerance for pretension and hypocrisy. Glancing at the bulky shoulders and slight stoop of my brother-in-law while his gaze drifted after Pepi, I suspected he was a good actor himself.


Beethoven had left some proofs on Pepi's piano, as if by accident. I pounced on them. Piano sonatas. Three, brand new. Deym, seeing the inevitable about to happen, sloped away with a shrug.

Pepi and I took turns, reading at sight, if with difficulty – for Luigi ambushed us on every page. Still, having played fifteen other piano sonatas of his, and much of the chamber music, I expected surprise: no two of his pieces were alike. Each matched concept, structure and expression in a new, unique way.

In the first of these sonatas, he made a musical joke, writing as if the pianist's two hands were uncoordinated. Since plenty of pianists played like this, and Luigi loathed it, the effect amused us. I gravitated nevertheless to the second sonata, in D minor: mysterious, twilit and stormy by turns, creating some astonishing effects with the sustaining pedal. Keep the dampers raised and spin one skein of music, like an operatic recitative; out comes a voice from another world, under the sea or beyond the mountains. The second movement was a deep meditation, and the finale with its interlocking swirls of triplets conjured in my mind the earth circling the sun, the moon circling the earth, the planets circling in their orbits, everything circling in a limitless firmament, mirrored within the human heart.

Pepi turned the page to the final sonata, in E flat major, only to burst out laughing. 'He's done it again! Look. "*Jo*-se-phin-e*! Jo*-se-phin-e*!*"'

'Pepi, you're seeing things,' I protested. 'Last time it was "Jo-se-*phin*-e". What makes you think Beethoven is setting your name to music?'

She flipped several pages forward – and pointed in triumph to the minuet. Sure enough, it was the same one he had played us when I'd sprained my ankle.

This sonata was intimate and tricksy, as if Beethoven were flirting with his pianist, teasing her with moments of suspense and great flights across the keyboard. The second movement, with a bouncy, bubbling bassline, was all pianistic sleight of hand, its snapping rhythms positively itching to trip you up; its ticking staccatos reminded me of some of the automatons in Deym's museum. Then the minuet, and a precipitous finale – a tarantella? Or galloping over the open puszta towards Martonvásár, filled with joy and anticipation?

'These are for you?' I watched Pepi's face light up with happiness as she played. 'There's no dedication.'

'Then they are *definitely* for me,' she declared, without stopping.

I remembered Beethoven's words about not wanting to cause Pepi trouble by making her 'big boss' jealous: these must be the pieces he meant. Wasn't he too self-centred to write music inspired by anything but God, nature or his own inner world? But this sonata was all about human feeling. Anything lofty had gone into the D minor work, yet it was the palpable joy that flowed uninhibited from the E flat major sonata that felt truly celestial.

Pepi was playing the minuet again, almost in tears. 'This is— everything. You feel… as if you could travel a thousand miles side by side, sharing this music. It's a perfect balance, so simple – just to *be*.'

The music twisted: one note of longing, vanishing into the distance. What were these two being denied in life, one trapped by her family, the other by double dint of his malady and his social class? Could this music transmute their perfect companionship and immortalise it? Then they need never lose it again.

Pepi's third child was born – a son, whom they named Carl – and she and Deym rapidly set about conceiving a fourth. I went back to my duties in Hungary: the estate, the Ofen gallery and Mother, who had been writing to me repeatedly asking, 'But *why* can't you come home?' There, helping her stage some soirées, musical performances and, inevitably, card games, I listened every day for the post coach, bereft without my sister, my Vienna friends and above all, the children. Little Viky was already mine in spirit. I could see in this tiny girl the same determination and intelligence that graces all the Brunsvik women. Perhaps someday we would work together, founding a school, and I would hand on to her all that I had learned. Telling her baby stories while she fell asleep at twilight, cosy in her little cot, I had tried not to think about how much I loved her, let alone how much I would miss her.

In Luigi's tiny apartment inside the Theater an der Wien, a new symphony, his third, was undergoing a birth more complex than that of Pepi's third baby. Our Master was redoubling his energy. He wished to jettison his old methods, to find a new path for his music. The Revolution and Napoleon had shown him that structures could overturn and new ideals be built on their ruins. As in politics, so in art.

Then, without warning, the foundations of our world – but Pepi's in particular – collapsed.

## 8

My dear niece,

In 1803, Pepi and her husband decided to spend the winter in Prague. Victoria Golz was eager to host them and certain bridges remained to be built with their brother, Count Casimir Deym von Střítež, treasurer, privy councillor and supreme court master of the Kingdom of Bohemia. Viennese society was not happy at the prospect of Pepi's absence: all the countesses, baronesses and musical cognoscenti, notably Marianna, wanted her in their salons, playing Beethoven's music. 'The exquisite Countess Deym' was developing a name as a performer, despite her own best efforts not to. Deym would shake his head as invitation after invitation arrived. 'Not in your condition,' he pleaded, powerless against the recognition that if he loved Pepi, so did everybody else.

'I have never felt better,' she insisted.

Removing Pepi from this circuit would not keep her away from Beethoven; he was planning to go to Prague himself. But she protested when I tried to blame her husband's jealousy. Prague would be wonderful. They could spend valuable time with Victoria, go to the opera, walk by the Vltava and enjoy the city's beauty at their leisure – and Prague had plenty of salons of its own. Besides, it would be nice for the children to get to know their well-connected Bohemian aunt and uncle. I tried not to take this personally.

It was decided that Fritz and Carl would stay with us in Ofen while Deym and Pepi went ahead with Viky to settle in at Victoria's. This would give Pepi breathing space from dealing with three tinies while her pregnancy advanced. Then Deym would come back to fetch the boys.

The distance from Ofen to Prague is about five hundred and sixty kilometres. In winter, it seems further. With heavy snow, the carriage slowed by slush and mud, one could never be certain how long it would take. The coaches were freezing, overnight travel could be dangerous because of highwaymen, and Deym would have to keep his toddler sons warm and safe as they trundled along the Danube to Pressburg and Brünn, then northwest through the Bohemian countryside. By the time they reached his sister's door, Deym would have undertaken this trip three times in rapid succession. He was not a young man – he was past fifty – and if he were concerned about Pepi's condition, she showed equal anxiety about his.

Deym arrived at our house one dank evening, blowing in from the cobbled hill with snowflakes on his coat. He had an uncontrollable cough, which flung me into memories of Father. But Fritz came charging out of the nursery on hearing his voice, the wet-nurse brought Carl to say hello, and Deym was so happy to see the children that all else was forgotten in the flurry of greetings, news and curative hot drinks. Pepi had sent word that we must equip him well with food, medicine and blankets for his return journey; she would pay any costs we incurred. '*If he loved us less, he would think of himself more,*' she wrote.

By bedtime, Mother was as worried as we were. 'You must stay a few days and regain your health.'

'There's no need, truly. It's just a winter cough. Pepi's time is near and I can't bear being away from her.'

'But *why*?' Mother demanded. Deym, less accustomed to Mother's quirks than we were, simply shook his head.

He ate little, then retired to sleep. We four conferred. 'I fear his constitution was spoilt by the balmy climate of Naples,' Mother opined. 'I don't know why he had to stay *there* so long.'

'Mother, it's not his fault that he's ill,' Lotti reminded her.

'He's crazy,' Franz said. 'This whole Prague malarkey is a terrible idea. Typical Pepi, if you ask me.'

By morning, the clouds had dispersed, leaving an overcoat of snow across the city from the Danube up to Ofen Castle; beyond the river Pest was glittering like a sugar-cake. Fritz woke me at sunrise, jumping on my bed and shaking me as only an overexcited toddler can. I wrapped us both up in several layers and took him into the courtyard to build a snowman.

We came back, red-nosed and flushed with exercise, to find Deym at the dining table with Mother, Franz and Lotti. He had eaten scarcely half his breakfast. 'I've no appetite,' he said, trying to suppress his cough.

I looked at his eyes, then pressed a hand to his forehead. 'Joseph, go back to bed. You're ill.'

'I'll be fine. We are off in an hour.'

Unable to sway him from his purpose, I gave Carl's wet-nurse instructions for dosing Deym with medicine en route – I had assembled a goodly chest of potions, rubs and remedies. 'If you are worried, find a doctor as soon as you reach Pressburg,' I told her.

If I thought myself lucky to be at home in a warm, well-built Hungarian house, it was not to last. Nobody was surprised when a letter arrived from Pepi. Deym had a serious chest infection; the doctors held out scant hope. She was at her wits' end. Once I had told her that should she need me, I would come to her. Would I come to Prague now?

A good maxim for efficient journeys: travel light and travel alone. Taking as little as I could, I booked a place on the stagecoach and bade my family farewell.

Prague was just as Pepi had described it. Through the frosty air, cafés emitted tempting aromas of fresh bread and chocolate, flights of ancient stairs led down into cavernous beer cellars, and the famous astronomical clock, the Orloj, on the medieval Old Town Hall, sounded out as the hour arrived: its mechanical apostles shunted through their turrets, alongside the stalking skeleton of Death. I had neither time nor heart to stop and watch. Past Prince Kinsky's pink palace, bought from Victoria's in-laws, and then through the back streets, I pulled my small trunk on its wooden wheels, following Pepi's directions beyond the Black Horse Inn.

Victoria's home was a compact palace on the corner of the Neue Allee and the Nikolandergasse. Like our Ofen house, it was built around a central courtyard, sheltered from the street behind a carriage gate. Victoria, pallid and anxious, came hurrying down to meet me. Inside, I could hear the children playing upstairs, out of the way.

Deym was in bed, sitting up because his cough would not let him lie down. He was almost incoherent with fever. Pepi sat close by, holding a cool flannel to his brow; she spoke to him in a low, soothing tone, but when she dipped the cloth into cold water her hand was trembling.

'The doctor says we must call a priest,' Victoria told me, tears in her eyes.

'Lawyer,' Deym pleaded. 'Must make my will.'

What? He had no will? I ran downstairs and found Deym's manservant to dispatch him in haste to the lawyer's office before Victoria could catch him first and send him to the church. If Deym were to die intestate, Pepi would lose everything.

In the bedroom doorway, Pepi clung to me like a drowning woman.

'Come downstairs, get your breath,' I suggested.

She shook her head. 'I won't leave him, not for a moment.'


Within the hour the servant returned, bringing the lawyer. It was as I had feared: Deym had to stipulate that Pepi would have custody of the children, for otherwise she would not retain that right; and for the same reason he made over the museum and its building to her. Should she remarry, the lawyer added, ownership would pass instead to Deym's children. She and Count von Sauer he appointed as joint administrators. No sooner had the lawyer left than the priest arrived to administer the last rites. My brother-in-law was barely strong enough to kiss the cross.

Pepi cradled him in her arms, resting his head against her belly. The last sound he heard would be their unborn child's heartbeat. Before the sun could set, his spirit slipped away into the beyond.

She stayed calm until all was still, the body had been laid out like one of his own waxen effigies, and the equipment of illness – the cloths, bowls and sweat-drenched garments – had been taken away to be cleaned or burned. Then she accepted my arms and gave way to grief.

An extra pair of hands and a cool, well-organised mind proved assets in the sorry weeks that followed. Victoria and I together arranged the necessary notifications, a grand funeral and a reception afterwards. Pepi wept, held her children close and wept some more.

The boys were much too young to understand what had happened to their Papa. So, we thought, was Viky. 'His soul has gone to heaven,' I told her.

'What's a soul?' she asked.

'It is the spirit, darling, that *lives in* our body, but is not *part of* the body. It feels and thinks and loves. It is immortal. And when our body is worn out and must cease to live, our soul goes back to God, where it came from.'

'Oh,' said Viky, that astonishing child. 'Yes, I know.'

Now they must return to Vienna, where the reckoning would happen. The activities of the Palais continued and Pepi herself must take over the management of all its piecemeal, complicated affairs.

You may have gathered that Pepi was not born to be a businesswoman.

'Tesi, come with me?' she pleaded. Of course I would, and I wrote at once to Franz asking – instructing – him to come to Prague and help us take Pepi and the children home.

Our journey seemed to age the fresh-faced Franz by several years. Prague was much closer to Vienna than to Ofen, but with the February roads it took four days even in his own carriage driven by the voluble Takács, and seemed longer with three squalling children whose distress at their father's sudden demise was becoming evident. Pepi's bulge was moving ever lower down her torso. About halfway through the journey, she admitted she was nine months pregnant: labour could begin at any moment. She had not told us this before. Franz and I could take scant sleep. On the box, Takács uttered ferocious Hungarian expletives.

At the Palais, we arrived unannounced in the middle of the night, half petrified with cold. We had to rouse the servants to warm the rooms and find us food and milk for the children; worse, we must break the terrible news to them. There was a rush of concern for Pepi, to whom the staff were devoted; her maid Magda and I helped her upstairs to the bed that she would never again share with Deym. She was on the verge of collapse, and it was no surprise that early in the morning I awoke to urgent calls: her labour pangs had begun.

'I've never known a night and day like this,' confessed the terrified Magda as we dispatched a messenger to find a midwife.

Giving birth took Pepi's mind temporarily off her bereavement. It was, thank heavens, straightforward: by sunset, she was holding in her arms the tiny daughter Deym would never see.

'If it was a boy, I would have named him Joseph after his father,' she said, through her tears.

'Then call her Josepha, or Josephine, like you. She can be Sephine for short.'

I fetched the children to meet their new sister, and at the sight of Viky standing on tiptoe to kiss Sephine's forehead, my fortitude crumbled and I had to excuse myself to do some private crying of my own. Franz fled from all this emotion, saying he must head home in the morning.

I pulled myself together by writing letters to all who needed to know. Aunt Susanna, Julie and her husband in Italy, and certain others.

The next afternoon there came a tactful servant's cough in my doorway: 'Excuse me, Madame: Countess Deym has stipulated no visitors, but there is a gentleman downstairs who absolutely insists upon being admitted. Please would you talk to him?'

At the foot of the stairs stood Beethoven, his eyes full of anxiety and his arms filled with flowers.

After a death, when your world must rearrange itself, two things offer solace. First: hard work. Then: music. Fortunately, we had both.

Pepi roused herself at the sound of Luigi's voice. Magda begged her not to try to get up, but she had no trouble standing and moving around. She emerged in a silken dressing gown almost as beautiful as a ball-dress; and after soft, concerned words – he leaned his ear towards her, the better to hear her speak – he offered to play for her. He could do little else to help, but he could be a spiritual doctor for a bruised soul.

Pepi stretched out on a sofa in the music room; Beethoven – who had already tossed his hat up onto the cupboard nearest the door – accepted some coffee, then went to the piano.

In my heightened state, I paused in the hallway. I fancied that the improvisation he began was a message to Pepi, straight from his heart, and it was as if nobody else should hear it, myself included. I slunk away to Deym's study, its bookshelves lined with giant filing boxes, and began to hunt through the desk.

The accounts ledger was easy to find, and simple to

understand. To check its figures, I sought in the files the necessary letters and statements from his bank. These were unambiguous. My Cassandra fate was upon me. I had warned Pepi about rushing into marriage with a man she barely knew. Nobody had listened.

A widow at twenty-four, a mother of three infants and a newborn, Pepi must now learn that Deym had saddled her with debts at least five times greater than she had expected. The man had nothing. When he fled his homeland and changed his identity, he had forfeited any rights to monies from the family estate in Bohemia. He had reclaimed his title, but nothing more. His income had been adequate to maintain his lifestyle as a bachelor, but not to support a noble-born wife and four children. This situation could fast become desperate.

I wandered along the landing to the darkened gallery. The sound of Beethoven's playing faded into the distance and the chemical smell of wax filled my nostrils. There stood our old friends, cloaked in shadow: the Fair Sleeper with her thrice-reflected Aphrodite; the mechanical canary, silenced; the ghoul of Ferdinand IV with his glass eyes. I raised an arm – and stopped myself, for if I were to smash Ferdinand, unleashing such violence might lead me to smash the rest of the vile contents as well, and it would achieve nothing. Poor Pepi needed all the income she could get from this little lot.

Out on the deserted stairs I sat down, praying for the answers God or my father's spirit might provide.

Beethoven was no longer improvising. He was playing Pepi something strange, something that burst the bounds of her little piano. E flat major, triple metre, a simple pattern rising and falling until it was no longer simple at all. The scale of this expression was immeasurable, yet expanding further all the time. I slipped back in to listen.

I had always been convinced that music is not 'about' anything but itself. Now Beethoven scotched that idea.

'I have been working on this for two years,' he said, between movements. 'It is a symphony called *Bonaparte*.'

Vienna was teeming with soldiers: army uniforms mingled with the fashionable cognoscenti along the Graben, the sound of military music was more often heard than folk singers and zithers in the streets, and the talk in every salon turned sooner or later to the likelihood of renewed war with the French. Beethoven had picked this time to write a heroic work about Napoleon?

Pepi, exhausted, went to lie down, but I moved my chair closer to the piano. 'Tell me more?'

'It's not about politics. It's the new against the old. The nineteenth century against the eighteenth. The open against the closed. Liberty against tyranny. Freedom against—'

'Luigi, we are *in Vienna*.' Here he could soon find himself at odds with the very people he depended on for his livelihood – princes like Lichnowsky, Lobkowitz and Kinsky. It is awkward to ask for financial help from royal patrons while praising someone who might annihilate them and their way of life the moment opportunity arose.

'I loathe the place,' he said. 'I am moving to Paris.'

I swallowed my shock. 'So your Bonaparte reference has a job to do?' I hesitated to say 'currying favour'.

He ignored me, lost in his own world. 'I don't see why one needs words and voices to expound philosophical ideas. A symphony's structure and orchestra can accomplish that without them. Look, this is man as hero. Not God, but man. The first movement develops all the time. It never stands still. It is *about* becoming; the act of a hero's self-creation through free will. The second movement reflects on mortality, a funeral march in the French style. The scherzo celebrates life returning and the finale reawakens my Prometheus.'

He had taken a theme from his music for *The Creatures of Prometheus* – a ballet score which I would not have liked to dance to – and based on it a gigantic set of variations in which the theme emerged from its skeletal outline, then grew to the heights of sophistication and ultimate triumph. From the Prometheus germ he had built the material for the entire symphony: Prometheus, the Titan who stole the fire of the gods to create out of clay humankind itself.

'We will sell it to Simrock to publish. Ries has already told him that Prince Lobkowitz wants it exclusively for half a year in return for his payment, so only after that will it be printed and take its title.'

Would Lobkowitz not feel his support had been flung back in his face if the title *Bonaparte* appeared on *his* precious symphony? 'Isn't it dangerous? Won't the police be suspicious?'

Luigi gave a shrug. 'Perhaps, if I were glorifying the idea of guillotining the monarchy – but I'm not. I am calling for no revolution but a musical one. I am celebrating self-made heroism in a self-made symphony.'

I suspected he might be deceiving himself on a grand scale, but I lacked the energy to argue with him, which was impossible at the best of times.

'So perhaps it is not about his heroism, but yours,' I divined. 'What does Pepi think?'

'She is too tired to think anything. I haven't yet told her I am leaving.'


Early March in Vienna: icy winds from the hills beginning to soften, blessed by the aroma of hot spiced wine, the stirring of the first green and bronze buds on the trees, and in every drawing room the light of myriad lamps and the making of music. I could not think of returning home. Pepi was struggling to regain her strength, the museum had to reopen because she was desperate for the income, and the rest of the building's plentiful rooms must be prepared to rent out if she were to make ends meet. Since she was in no state to do this herself, and her co-administrator Sauer had limited time, somebody else had to step in – which of course meant me.

'Go to the emperor and ask for financial help,' Mother directed Pepi from Ofen. 'He is a relative. I was lady-in-waiting to his grandmother, and Therese is her god-daughter. Why would he not accept your petition?' We applied for an audience via the Office of the Grand Master and awaited notification of an appointment – which, rather to my surprise, soon arrived.

I readied Pepi for her visit to the Hofburg with black silk widow's gown and veil, plus sombre clothes for the children. What could tug at the Holy Roman Emperor's heartstrings more than sad-faced toddlers in mourning? If he were moved to help, Pepi's problems could be solved forever.

When they returned, the children were wide-eyed – they had never seen such a palace, with rooms as expansive as fields and everywhere the brilliance of crystal sparkling and gold shining and silken wall drapes seducing. Pepi could not contain her happiness.

'He will help us! He will!'

They sank at his feet, she recounted, with baby Sephine in her arms and the little ones clasping each other's hands; and she, relating her full, terrible story, fortunately burst into tears. The emperor took her hand in both of his and said: 'Do not cry. Your children are my children.'

'That wasn't the emperor,' grumbled Viky. 'He wasn't wearing emperoring clothes and he didn't have a crown on.'

'Darling, it *was* him,' said Pepi, 'and he will help us, as he said. You heard him yourself, didn't you?'

I was less convinced. *'Do not cry. Your children are my children'* was a comforting statement, but to my mind – more practical and less poetic than Pepi's – it mentioned neither money nor a promise of any. For once, I stayed silent. The energy of hope has a value all its own.

While I fought the necessary battles at the Palais, Pepi decided she and the children should move somewhere quieter. Hietzing, in the countryside by Schönbrunn Palace, was popular with the Viennese middle class and minor aristocracy; it would be perfect. The bereaved Pepi needed rest; the children needed stability and fresh air, and they loved to visit an extraordinary innovation in the Schönbrunn park: a menagerie that housed animals from all over the world, including elephants from Africa and a group of Australian wallabies.

When we arrived to house-hunt, the village was thrumming with construction work. Pepi, who could be surprisingly decisive, the same day agreed to rent a new-built, small yet elegant villa, with a sizeable garden where the children could run about.

'Oh, and Tesi, I'm asking Lotti to come and live here with us, since you'll be busy in Vienna,' she said, her back to me while she examined some shelving.

'What?' I had been envisaging our tranquil new life here.

'Darling, it's not that I don't want you around, but Lotti has never had the Viennese advantages we enjoyed and it is time she should. We might even find her a suitable husband. You can visit any time, and stay over, sometimes, if you like.'

Smarting with rejection, I had my suspicions. Lotti was altogether a gentler person than I was. My days were structured to the last second and I was sometimes aware of Pepi's dark eyes hardening into a glare when I tried to exhort her, too, into useful activity. Aware of the brevity of life, determined never to waste time, I spent every minute on something productive, whether paperwork, painting, reading, writing or practising, and I cannot deny that if others around me inclined towards indolence, I could sometimes be short-tempered. The occasional snipe from my sister about 'maiden aunts' did nothing to prevent that, for an aunt is neither a servant nor an inferior to her siblings – at least, not to my mind.

Once the little family had made their move, Lotti duly arrived, thrilled to be away from Mother's censorious eye and to have, instead, the company of delightful children bent only on having as much fun per day as possible. There they settled to await the emperor's 'promised' assistance, Lotti minding the little ones while Pepi refused all visitors and spent much time in bed. I agreed – having little choice – to divide my time between Mother in Ofen and the Palais. Before long I began to know the stagecoach journey between our Danube cities well enough to recognise every inn and virtually every linden tree along the bending road.

Then, in my Palais office, I was surprised to receive a note from Beethoven, inviting me for coffee at his apartment in the Theater an der Wien.

Open a pass door to any theatre's backstage area from the auditorium and you understand at once that the public magnificence is designed to immerse you in fantastical illusion. The five blue, gold and white balconies, the giant chandeliers, the gilded sculptures, the crimson velvet stage curtains with their golden ropes and tassels, are but a fictional world. Go behind the scenes and you are in chaos, tripping over pieces of painted scenery, ropes, pulleys, props, cups, nervous performers and, worst of all, lights – no wonder theatres often burn down, with so many flames exposed to mishap.

This theatre, only two years old, was a grand construction set high on the left bank of the Vienna River in Mariahilf, a short walk from the city centre and the Palais Deym. One critic declared that Schikaneder could have made a fortune by charging people to look at the building, without having to stage a single performance. My eyes feasting upon its luxury, I agreed.

I found Beethoven waiting for me outside, ready to give me a tour. He pointed at a statue over the main entrance, showing Schikaneder himself as Papageno in Mozart's *Die Zauberflöte*, attended by the opera's three cherubs. 'This is the *Papagenotor*.'

'Modest, isn't he?' I noted. 'Luigi, tell me – what news of your opera? Have you found a story?'

Beethoven leaned towards me and asked me to repeat the question, a little louder. I wanted to dissolve with shame.

'I have,' he said. 'It has the advantage of being true.'

Pacing at speed around the theatre's exterior and in through the courtyard from the side entrance, he told me about it. During the French Revolution, news had emerged of a woman who set out to save her husband from imprisonment and execution by his political opponents. She, the spirit of love and devotion, disguised herself as a man, came to the prison asking for a job and was hired. Having ingratiated herself with the head jailer, she found her way to the deepest, furthest cell in the dungeons and there, at last, discovered her husband in chains. The prison governor arrived, intending to kill the man with his own hands. The valiant woman flung herself in front of him and cried: 'First kill his wife!' A play based upon this, by Jean-Nicolas Bouilly, would form the skeleton of his opera.

'Did they kill her?'

'No. The evil was revealed, the dictator fell and the couple were freed to live in peace.'

'How far through are you?'

'I'm not.' He gave a scowl. 'I am writing another first. It's called *Vestas Feuer*, it's set in ancient Rome and it will go nowhere unless Schikaneder does something about his text. I've told him to rewrite it, but it's only fit for washerwomen... Tesi, how is Pepi? Will she accept visitors yet? And – would you give her something from me?'

This, then, was why he had summoned me: for her, not for myself. As ever.

He ushered me through to his apartment, in which there was scarcely room to turn round: the usual muddle of books and music everywhere, a precarious inkwell and a pot of well-used quills poised on a scratched wooden desk, and on the floor a wine bottle sat half empty – or maybe, for him, half full. His bed was on one side of the room, his piano on the other. He furnished me with eye-wateringly strong coffee, which he made himself, having spent some of the generous annual stipend he received from Prince Lichnowsky on an expensive grinder. He counted the beans before placing them in the machine, sixty per cup. While I sipped with some caution, he handed me a large envelope filled with sheets of handwritten music.

It was a piano piece in F major, in a graceful, Pepi-like

triple metre. Indeed, it reminded me of the minuet to which Pepi, laughing, had sung her own name.

Luigi watched me read it. 'Not a minuet, but an andante.'

'Jo-se-*phin*-e, Jo-se-*phin*-e,' the piece's melody sang to me. I blinked. Was I hallucinating?

'Why an isolated, stand-alone andante?'

'Worthy Therese, you've spotted the truth: I wrote it first for a sonata, but it doesn't fit. It's a different concept.'

'How do you mean?'

'If you have a minute, I'll demonstrate.'

He went to his piano. A moment later the whole theatre seemed to be shaking with the force of a hurricane as the sonata's first movement cracked open. Then came a slow transition, which led straight into a rondo: a simple, clear melody, its textures soon garlanded with trills and cascades that seemed to conjure the pealing of bells. Different episodes unfolded with wild contrasts, gales of triplets, thorn-trees of octaves, but it returned always to its sublime centre.

At the end, Luigi turned, saw me and laughed his loudest, mocking his music's effect upon my hapless self. 'It's for Count Waldstein, my old patron,' he said. 'I need to give him something good – it's long overdue – so the finale is based on a Rhenish song as a tribute. Do you think the Andante would have made a good slow movement for this?'

I hesitated – did he really want *my* opinion? 'You're right... it doesn't fit at all. The sonata is perfect as it is. Just... perfect.'

'And you will give Pepi the Andante?'

'I will take it to her in Hietzing tomorrow.'

\*\*\*

At Pepi's villa the devoted Magda opened the door. I took one look at her eyes. 'What's wrong? What's going on?'

'Oh, Countess Therese, Madame is not at all well…'

I ran up to Pepi's bedroom. She was lying still under several layers of blankets. For a moment I thought she was unconscious. Then the sound of a deep sob reached my ears.

I sat with her for hours. She was sweating, feverish, coughing and beset by uncontrollable weeping. The doctor, Magda told me, had said my sister was suffering from 'a nervous fever'. I took this diagnosis with some cynicism. Could Pepi not mourn her husband without running a fever? Why should a woman of her fragile nature suffer from such a thing, yet when I had my time of grief after Father's death, my temperature remained stable? Nobody would think *me* likely to experience a 'nervous fever'. I suspected we had the same affliction, a natural response to a devastating loss – but Pepi had also contracted something else.

Thinking of Father's illness, I wondered if it were one of those conditions that passes along successive generations of the same family. Pepi's cheeks were not pale but scarlet, and her eyes, when she opened them, too bright. It was all too familiar.

I clasped her hand and said a silent prayer. Then – 'Darling Pips, look what I've brought you from our Master.'

Calming a little through curiosity, Pepi found the strength to prop herself against her pillows and draw out of the package the manuscript of the piece that we now call the *Andante favori*. '*Here*,' wrote Luigi in a gushing accompanying letter, '*is your* – your – *Andante.*'

It was several months since Deym's death – in mourning terms, no time at all. Traditionally, one allows the bereaved a year's grace before attempting to draw them back into life and perhaps towards love. I believe that still longer is needed before the shattered soul can reconstitute itself.

'He was going to Prague,' Pepi remembered, gazing at the music. 'Is he still going?'

Of course not. He had only planned to go because she was. As for Paris, that idea had gone quiet too. I did not doubt that Luigi's summer lodgings this year would be, instead, somewhere near Hietzing.


I left Pepi to rest and made my way towards the sound of conversation in the drawing room. Lotti – and an unfamiliar male voice, speaking French. I saw them before they saw me: my little sister sparkling at a stranger, a dark young man of fascinating aspect, with a thin face and an impressive moustache; he wore a high-collared black jacket with elaborate golden fastenings, the garb of Hungarian nobility.

'This is my eldest sister, Therese.' Lotti gave the widest smile I had seen from her in years. 'Tesi, this is Count Emerich Teleki. We met the other day at a reception in Schönbrunn. He is from Siebenbürgen and we have been speaking endlessly of home! He is just embarking upon his grand tour, which is why he's in Vienna, and then he plans to study in Göttingen...'

Teleki stood, kissed my hand and clicked his heels. I had not a moment's doubt that this tall youth would someday become my brother-in-law. I trust first impressions, and now as I looked into his face I wished that I could read him at once, as I could my brother Franz or for that matter Beethoven. Describing his travel plans, he struck me as having strange depths: inscrutable, fervent, haunted; a strong character – if only I could detect what kind of strength.

Tiny green leaves were venturing forth in the garden; golden daffodils laced the borders and the birds were relishing the sun on their wings. Nature was gathering her energy for the months of blossoming, melding and producing – and as spring deepened our Master was spotted in nearby Hetzendorf, exploring apartments to rent for the months ahead. But spring brought Pepi renewed anguish, for at just twenty-five, her life of love and fertility seemed to have died with Deym. Her fever would not go away.

'I need to give her hope,' I told Beethoven a few days later, when I visited to report on Pepi's health. 'Hope is the only chance. The Andante will certainly aid her recovery when she's well enough to play it.'

'I thought, two years ago, that hope was dead,' he mused. 'I was close to taking my own life. But look at the wonders of nature, Tesi; take heart. Be calm. I would not have imagined that hope could return to me – yet it has, through sheer endurance. Your sister may find the same relief, if she can muster the strength. When may I see her?'

'Soon, Luigi – I hope. But not yet.'

It was not long afterwards that I experienced the truth and the pain of my prattlings about hope. In short, I fell in love.

## 9

Dearest niece,

We knew little of the war Napoleon had been waging against Britain – beyond the evidence, from reading and discussions, that it was a grand-scale mess. The British objected to Napoleon's increasing power, as well they might; and his insistence that this parochial island should have no voice in ordering the affairs of Europe was made worse by the fact that their king, George III, was German by descent and an elector of the Holy Roman Empire.

We were facing our own battles: Pepi's illness, some awkward religious convolutions in Lotti's romance – with horror we learned that Emy Teleki's mother was a Calvinist – and endless funds were required to keep the Palais and its blasted waxworks museum running. Still, as summer progressed and Pepi began to go for short walks, play with the children and accept occasional callers – notably her piano professor – we did not believe we could be directly affected by Bonaparte's aggression.

Our military remained uninvolved yet restive. The regiments were kicking their heels in the capital; sometimes they would turn up at the theatre. The Guicciardis had a private box at Beethoven's opera house home and, once Pepi and family had moved back to the Palais and the theatres were open for the autumn season, Aunt Susanna often invited us to join them, or to use the box in their absence. Together Lotti, Pepi and I went to a performance of Salieri's opera *La cifra*. 'How strange,' I said after Act One, 'that this anodyne style can coexist alongside Luigi's.' We had heard him on that stage barely a year and a half earlier, playing his own Piano Concerto No. 3.

Pepi nodded. 'It's a little like Mozart without the knives...'

The auditorium, for all its splendour, could be rancid, given the number of human beings crammed together under the flames of countless candles; seeking fresh air in the interval was a welcome relief. In the loggia foyer, though, there was a commotion: the cannonball that was Beethoven, flying up the stairs two at a time, dodging round groups of gossiping operagoers to reach Pepi's side. She lifted her gaze to his, open and shining with surprise.

Watching them, I nearly missed my footing at the top of the lengthy stone staircase, on which the carpeting was only partial. It was neither Pepi nor Beethoven who rushed to my aid.

'Allow me,' came an unfamiliar voice. It was my turn to look up into an attentive pair of eyes – deep green and bright with sparkles. I noticed he was in military uniform, but I had difficulty regaining my balance, because my head had begun to spin.

'Please, Madame, come and sit down,' he said. 'Are you feeling unwell?'

I allowed him to take my arm and escort me to a bench by the foyer wall. Under the warmth of his large hand, my elbow seemed to turn to rubber.

By the end of the interval he not only knew my name and various addresses in Vienna and Ofen, but also that we were fellow Hungarians, that I was with my sisters – hence implicitly unmarried – and that we were countesses. I knew that he was a baron and an officer, that he loved the military life as long as no actual war was involved, and that his family came from the south of Hungary. And I knew his name: Anton. 'My late father's name, too,' I told him.

A handbell sounded for the end of the interval. I wondered if Salieri would miss me if I did not return.

Lotti, Pepi and Luigi came up to us, saucer-eyed upon seeing me with a tall and handsome stranger. I introduced them.

'Call me Toni,' said he.


When I awoke early the next morning, the world had turned green. The coverlet on the bed was of sea-green silk. I had not noticed this before. Green was everywhere. It lit up the early dawn sky, shot through the curtains, bounced back at me from my mirror, which reflected my green-hazel pupils with their somewhat puzzled gaze. I went downstairs; I could not imagine I would ever sleep again. I assured the kitchen maid – who arrived, rubbing her eyes – that I could make my own coffee and that she should go back to bed. I drank three cups of Beethovenian strength, fast, trying to jolt myself back into my own mind. What was happening to me?

Pepi came down and stared at me as if I were a stranger.

'I can explain everything,' I began, and did so.

'Tesi, darling,' she cried, through her hilarity, 'you're in love!'

'Is this what it feels like?' I flushed with humiliation.

'Oh darling, have you never—? How old are you – twenty-eight?'

'Twenty-nine.'

'Not even for Luigi?'

'Pepi, *no.*' That was the make-believe love of a star-struck little girl; I could no more imagine touching Beethoven than I would if he were Pepi's husband.

'But can you imagine touching Toni?' Pepi sparkled, when I had given a tactfully edited version of these thoughts.

'Pepi, don't. I'll faint.'

Her laugh was so loud that Viky came pattering in to see what the fun was. At least my predicament had cheered up my sister.

'Viky, your auntie has met a lovely man,' Pepi told her. 'Now we have to make sure she marries him!'

'I've met him *once.*'

'That is enough. Now, Tesi, the Guicciardis are holding a ball next week. I'll make certain they invite Toni, and you shall have a beautiful dress in which to dance with him.'

'We would be an odd couple – he is twice my height.'

'Auntie Tesi, your face is purple!' Viky was laughing as much as her mother.

This was impossible. Such things did not happen to me. I had vowed never to marry. Perhaps this did not protect me against mishaps of the heart.

Mishaps? I felt as if I were seeing the world for the first time. As if everything until then had been upside down and inside out. Imagine that you have always thought God a figure extraneous to Earth, looking down and shaking his white beard in disapproval. And the stage curtain swishes aside and now God is within, not without; God is the mystery of life. And the mystery of life is love. Rip the world like a veil; beyond it, there's a mountain range.

'Tesi, pull yourself together,' I instructed. 'It's all in my mind. It's all imaginary. I hardly know the man...'

Marriage? Sleeping beside him, always with him, dependent on his kindness – dependent? Me? Yet if you love someone, how can you not depend on them? How, then, could so many women enter into such a relationship with someone for whom they had no liking or sympathy, let alone love, just for financial or dynastic advantage? Julie, married to Gallenberg; Pepi, married within weeks to Deym. How could we have done that to her? At least that marriage had turned out well, while he lived. But then I would see the music room door slightly ajar and hear the piano music dancing in there and, with it, the laughter of our Master and my sister, returning to life as if his presence were the green embrace of summer.

Toni called upon me two days later – to make sure, he said, that I was feeling well again. He smiled down into my eyes; he possessed that slight stoop of tall men who have the grace to be embarrassed about their height.

'Put me next to Napoleon,' he joked. 'Just imagine!'

Over coffee, I explained my somewhat itinerant existence. 'I must return to our estate in Hungary soon to keep my mother company. I divide my time between there and here.'

'Then I will visit again, if I may, before you go?'

Every day for a week we took *Kaffee und Kuchen* together in the Palais drawing room. 'You'd have a wonderful view over the water if only they'd knock down the city wall,' he said, not the first to make this observation. I showed him the museum, explaining Pepi's situation, Franz and his friendship with Beethoven, the way I had played a concerto in public aged six and it was much too easy for me. As his company began to be familiar, then comfortable, I found myself telling him more of my hopes – my dream school, the potential for girls' development if only they could enjoy equal education. On the eighth day I wondered if I must have talked too much, for it seemed no time before Toni glanced at the clock and declared that he must go.

The next day he sent a note; he had hoped to visit and invite me to a concert at the university, but was detained due to his mother's health. He would try to come tomorrow, or perhaps the day after.

I had one week left. Each morning I woke to find the house slightly darker and the air slightly cooler; each day I made sure coffee was ready at the stove; each evening came and went, bringing no Toni.

'He'll come and say goodbye.' Pepi hugged me, her eyes full of sympathy – she could sense how upset I was, despite my silence.

When my last case was loaded onto the stagecoach, the driver gave me his hand to help me up. No Toni. I kissed the children goodbye, took a last gaze up and down the street, then found my seat alongside a garrulous middle-aged couple and their three energetic dogs and let the door shut beside me, ready for the return of winter.

'*Dear Tesi,*' wrote Lotti. '*Emy has asked me to marry him. He says "May I hope?" What shall I do?*'

The reason she hesitated was that none of us much liked the sound of Countess Teleki. Her conversion to Calvinism could only spell problems for Lotti as a Catholic, and she wanted to make the pair wait longer before marriage: not because they were young, not because Emy had not finished his university course, but because she wanted in a puritanical way to test poor little Lotti's love for her precious son.

I was with our sharp-tongued parent at Martonvásár at the time; the inscrutable Emerich would also be taking on a difficult and demanding mother-in-law. Mother and I had, I cannot deny, some happy times despite all. The best were when we rode together to the estate's managerial office: our horses trotting side by side across the quiet plain, the skies spreading limitless above us, we would be at peace with one another, the world and ourselves. In Mother's set jaw and proud bearing, I could see the fire that my father had loved – and sometimes I could see myself, or what I might one day become.

Franz was spending a year in England to study its farming practices. He hoped its approach to managing a soggy climate and innumerable sheep would offer useful lessons for the Martonvásár estate. Besides measuring fields and exploring sheep-shearing techniques – oblivious to all Napoleonic battles – he had been in London, playing chamber music with a great friend of Beethoven's named George Bridgetower: a remarkable violinist who was half African. Beethoven was writing him a sonata.

I wrote to Franz asking what he thought about Lotti and Emy. 'She has a chance,' came his answer. 'She had better take it.'

That meant we would have to pay her dowry.


The next time I went to Vienna, I noticed that Pepi's mahogany display cabinets were less crowded than before.

'Your wedding presents. Your silverware. Are you in that much trouble?'

'It's Lotti. I wrote to Victoria about the situation and she agreed I should do what I must with these objects, however prized.'

'You sold your wedding silver to pay Lotti's dowry?'

'I'm not having her go through the humiliation I suffered. Still, I hope she's doing the right thing. I find Teleki a strange boy, Tesi – do you?'

'She says she loves him.'

'But the castle is in the middle of nowhere. I'm afraid for her, flinging herself into a new life so far from us.'

'Then we will make sure she visits us often, and if she can't, we will go to her. But Pips, what about you? Will you consider a new husband?'

The Vienna rumour mill was bound to link her name with one nobleman or another, but she had shown scant interest in any of them. There was, I had observed, another issue, one that was absorbing all her attention, both at and away from the piano.

'I shall live for my children and manage alone,' she insisted.

'And Beethoven? He's here all the time. Sometimes every day!'

'It isn't a problem, Tesi,' Pepi insisted, faking innocence even to herself. 'Having lessons motivates me and I enjoy his company. Truly, it isn't a problem.'


It's odd that one of the hardest things for anyone to do is admit making a mistake. Nobody likes to be wrong, and especially not to learn that a deep belief is based on, if not quite a lie, then an unexpected falsity. 'Blind faith' must be reserved for God alone. It certainly should not be pinned onto a living being – neither an army officer, nor a royal, political or military leader.

When Napoleon declared himself Emperor of France in 1804, Luigi flew into a rage as violent as if he had suffered a personal attack on his artistic integrity. Bonaparte was holding his own coronation in Notre-Dame Cathedral, with his queen Josephine beside him. Franz, who had stopped in Paris on his way to England, was there to watch. 'After the imperial crown was held above his diminutive head – not placed on it, because he was already wearing a golden laurel wreath – he took it himself and set it upon Josephine's,' he told us afterwards. 'You'd think he'd have remembered he was supposed to put on a crown before using the laurels.'

Beethoven had come to give Pepi her lesson as usual, but could not settle; he was pacing up and down the music room as if he were back in Heiligenstadt. 'It's a betrayal of everyone who believed in him. Now he's no better than the executed king. There is no *égalité* in making oneself emperor and no *liberté* implied for his subjects, and as for *fraternité*, it's only a matter of time until that comes to mean "jobs and cash for one's own brothers".'

'He was always going to do that,' I said. 'And with so much public support behind him, why would he not?'

Luigi had spent years pouring his best artistic efforts into a gigantic, iconoclastic piece of music that celebrated Bonaparte in person. 'To hell with it! You know what I have done?'

'Luigi, no!' Pepi cried, anticipating horrors.

'It's all right. It's only the dedication.' His voice softened as he spoke to her – but the event itself had been less gentle. He had scratched out the dedication so hard that he left a hole in the paper that could be matched only by the one in his hopes. In his place, I'd have done likewise.

Fortunately he was sane enough not to allow the symphony to go the same way. It has always irritated me when people suggest that he was crazy. In many ways, Beethoven was the sanest person I have ever known, and more perceptive than most who have full use of their hearing. His enemy – though I learned this only over time – was sometimes his own idealism; more often, the demons of his vicious upbringing, the drunken beatings from his father that left him with his own propensity for temper and alcohol; but above all, the class system of the Holy Roman Empire, which was not holy, scarcely Roman and empirically sent into meltdown by Napoleon himself.

Pepi wrote to me and Mother in the spring of 1805: '*Beethoven has written me a beautiful song.*' He had set a poem by Christoph August Tiedge called *An die Hoffnung* – To Hope – especially for her.

It portrayed the agony of longing. The sufferer senses an angel counting his tears; then raises his eyes to lament his fate, and observes the glow of sunset on the hem of a cloud. It is hope resurgent.

'May I hope?' was a phrase we had heard before: from Deym to Pepi, and from Emy Teleki to Lotti. It meant only one thing from a man to a woman and the message was not subtle. Pepi, lost in the song's beauty, seemed little to consider its implications at first – or pretended as much.

The storm broke a little while later. Beethoven was preparing to send *An die Hoffnung* to his publisher and, tidiness never having been his forte, happened to leave the manuscript on his desk when Prince Lichnowsky came to call. There in the dedication lay Pepi's name, ready for any prying visitor to note.

By then I had returned to the Palais. The first I knew of the unfurling crisis was when Magda shot past me on the back stairs, clutching a small bottle of smelling salts. I followed her. Pepi was face down on her bed, beside herself with fury, fear and despair: 'How could he? How could he do that to me?' Beside her I found a note in familiar writing, explaining briefly what had happened and reassuring her that everything was, truly, absolutely fine.

It was Luigi's carelessness that had upset her: the idea that he had so little consideration for her well-being that he did not trouble to hide this virtually public declaration from judgmental eyes at such a sensitive stage. Worse still was that it was Lichnowsky who saw it.

Prince Karl Lichnowsky was, on the surface, the most magnanimous of wealthy men. When Luigi first came to Vienna, Lichnowsky and his wife, Princess Christiane, gave him lodgings in their own home, premieres at their Friday salon and introductions to all the great and good. Unfortunately their reasonable enough demands for formal dress and punctuality at meals were not exactly how Luigi liked to function and some magnificent arguments no doubt ensued. But five years later, in 1800, Lichnowsky agreed to give Beethoven that stipend of 600 florins per annum so that he need never have to worry about money.

Our encounter with Constanze Mozart had shown us the other side of the prince: he could be high-handed over what he expected in recompense for his support. He appeared, moreover, to have a warped sense of humour. He persuaded the unfortunate Ferdinand Ries to play the *Andante favori* – of all things – to Luigi after announcing it as Ries's own brand-new composition. God alone knows why. Luigi took furious exception and blamed Ries, a fine composer and close friend.

But for Pepi, the problem was Lichnowsky's wagging tongue. He used to trot along to every party in town, leaving in his wake a trail of seductions, woman after compliant woman. With such a preoccupation always uppermost in his mind, he would light upon Beethoven's song dedication – and the news would be all over Vienna before you could say 'Schikaneder'.

This was so unlike Beethoven that speculation would be intense. Often his dedications were to his patrons, or if to a woman, then a bejewelled matron with a long-established marriage (or in Julie's case, a pupil whose mother needed placating). To dedicate a song about hope to a beautiful young widow – telling the world 'This is the woman I love and for whom I wait' – didn't bear thinking about.

Pepi had come to rely on Beethoven to care for her – goodness knows she needed caring for – yet now I could see that the potential for damage betrayed, ironically, the very *hope* that she needed. For fear of 'compromise', Luigi had not placed her name on the Op. 31 sonatas, which we understood were for her, nor on the *Andante favori*, which we knew from his letter *was* for her, and which he had taken to performing in every salon. But now?

He gave way; he could do nothing else. *An die Hoffnung* was published, without the dedication. Nevertheless, I knew Pepi's panic had another cause besides: the recognition that his love for her had grown so palpable that he could hold it back no longer.

He should have been at home, writing his opera. Yet when the weather warmed up and we all decamped to Hietzing, he would walk there to find us and work, supposedly, on Pepi's piano playing. How many more symphonies could he have written, how many more sonatas for us all, if he had not been spending every hour he could with my sister?

When they were not at the piano, they would walk together. Luigi insisted it would benefit Pepi's health, which remained fragile: 'You must build up your strength – it will help you to withstand illness.' If she needed to rest on the way, they would settle in a sunny patch by a brook, or under an ancient tree, where Beethoven might scribble a phrase, motif or concept for a piece, and Pepi would sketch a bird or the outline of the hills, or simply close her eyes for a few minutes to let the powers of nature restore her.

I can see them now, strolling together alongside tidy vineyards and through deep forests of oak, beech and linden. Feet on the earth, arms in the air, head in the sun, Luigi drank deep of this verdant joy. Pepi did her best to keep up. I would go too, for the sake of propriety, and they would encourage my presence; but it would not take a philosopher to note that I was an optional extra.

I am sure that at times the rain fell on them, and the wind worried at their ears and the trees of the Vienna Woods dripped moisture and linden blossom over them, yet when I remember them there, pacing in step, the scene is always drenched with the green-gold light of the afternoon sun. The composer powering forward, swerving back and forth, pointing to a buzzard high above, or pulling off his hat and lifting his lion head to feel the sunshine on his nose. The slender woman beside him, her curls gleaming chestnut under her straw hat, one hand grasping her skirts to keep them clear of the mud, her laugh rising in response to her companion, who leaned closer to hear it. Their movements harmonised as if their dance had been choreographed in a set pattern for centuries. It was not that Pepi had not loved Deym. She had enjoyed a sensual closeness with him which took her by surprise, but took her nonetheless; yet they never had that shared spirit, that instinct for mutual understanding. How strange that society should insist two people as much in sympathy as these must have a third to keep them apart – even when they walked in an earthly garden of Eden.

I challenged Pepi only when this enchanted summer had drawn to a close and we were back at the Palais. Months had gone by; this delicate state of courtship existed in such precarious equilibrium that one misplaced prod could fling the balance as wide as *An die Hoffnung* had. Yet it was dangerous for Pepi not to acknowledge its implications simply because she was enjoying it too much. Even the children now assumed Beethoven was family; Viky and Fritz would run to hug him when he arrived.

A conversation with Marianna spurred me into speaking up.

'How is it going,' she said, 'between Beethoven and your sister?'

'What do you mean? Is there gossip?'

'My dear, there's always gossip. There's also gossip that your sister is to marry a Count Something von Whatsit.'

'She isn't.'

'But Beethoven? He scarcely tries to hide it. He plays that Andante everywhere, in all the salons, but it's not his best piece – there must be a reason he is so attached to it. Anybody with half a mind can hear her name in its melody.'

'Surely not?' I had fondly imagined this to be private.

'Pepi must bolster herself and be sensible. His emotion is genuine – Beethoven is never one to dissemble. So she must be careful, Tesi, or there will be a compromising situation. Of course, if she does intend to marry him…'

'Mother and Franz will never hear of it.'

'I thought Franz was his best friend?' She raised an eyebrow.

'He is. But he's under Mother's thumb.'

Marianna gave a wry smile. 'The usual story, then. Friendship between aristocrat and commoner is fine. More is not.'

I steeled myself to broach this impossible subject. I should have done it months ago. Yet who could see such a rare and delicate bird visiting their garden and willingly disturb it?

Returning from Marianna's, I was just in time to glimpse my sister bidding Beethoven himself a tender farewell at the door. She turned back into the house, her cheeks flushed with emotion. Upstairs I took her arm and steered her to a chair.

'Pepi, listen. That man loves you with all his heart. This has been going on for more than a year. What are you going to do?'

## 10

My dear niece,

Your uncle Franz was back in Hungary, glad to be home. He had brought us all presents of fine Paisley shawls. In England, he said, he had felt dragged down by fog, rain, damp and draughty houses ('as if they think it's unmanly to mind draughts,' he fumed), plus appalling food which left him craving our local cherries and apricots, good beef goulash and fresh Danube fish. 'They're so provincial,' he grumbled, wolfing down second helpings, 'yet they think themselves masters of the world. It would be laughable if it were not so pathetic.'

'I hope you learned something useful?' I said.

'Oh yes. I learned plenty.' Franz had his mouth full.

I took the opportunity to explain to him a little more of the situation we as a family were facing, given the relationship between our sister and Franz's prized friend.

'It's serious. But what can we do about it?' 'It' was fast becoming the code-name for 'Beethoven-and-Pepi'.

'She's risking being compromised,' he said. 'It's not as if they are nobodies. Pepi is a widowed countess and Beethoven is the most famous composer in Vienna.'

'I think I knew that already.'

Franz glared. 'My point is, it will rebound on her.'

'Even though it's *his* fault.'

'Do you think he is... pressuring her?'

I had not considered this enough. Pepi had blossomed in Deym's embrace. Physical love suited her, and she it. To live without it now must be onerous, especially when she was so close to a man who thought himself her soulmate. My brief, hopeless experience of uncontrollable attraction had left me more sympathetic to this idea than I might have been a few years earlier.

Lotti, now married to Emerich and living some six hundred kilometres away to the east, contributed to our debate via letter. '*She must be careful not to be alone with him,*' she instructed. She said little of her own situation – which should have worried me more, were I not so preoccupied with Pepi.

'What's the worst that can happen?' I mused.

'Needless to say, it would shame us all if she were to...' Franz made a gesture indicating a swelling pregnancy; he could not bring himself to say the words. 'But actually the worst is that Deym's children could be taken away from her.'

'What? Even if she marries him?'

'Especially so. Obviously she'd lose her title, so the children would be sent to a guardian appointed by the Deyms, to preserve their status.'

Beyond a brief insight when the dying Deym made his will, I had never yet had serious reason to worry about this. 'But couldn't I adopt the children, or you could, or Lotti and Emy, so they stay in *our* noble family? I could take them, I could teach them...'

'Tesi, widows don't have any rights to speak of, and the Deyms are higher placed than we are. I'd bet that behind our backs his oh-so-distinguished brother Casimir regards us as *geworfen* upstarts.'

The term stung, the idea even more so.

'And by the way,' Franz continued, 'they can already challenge Pepi's guardianship any time they like if they happen to hear something dubious about her morality. They're a very powerful family, Tesi, even if our Joseph was its black sheep. And just think what it would do to Pepi. She may *love* Beethoven, for all I know, but she *lives* for those children, and she knows, full well, what would happen.'

'Even the lovely Victoria Golz? Pepi adores her.'

'Victoria Golz will always do the right thing, as she sees it. That may not be the same as how you see it.'

That explained, then, the extremity of Pepi's reaction to the *An die Hoffnung* dedication. It had seemed exaggerated and over-precious to me. But with such an appalling outcome a real possibility, how could anyone blame her?

'Well, then,' I said, 'Pepi must find it in her heart to say no.'

Beethoven's opera *Leonore* would soon be ready for premiere. I suspected Luigi had a plan. The long-awaited performance would arrive; the opera would triumph; Vienna would crown him emperor of composers and at last, knowing himself worthy of her, he would propose and crown his Josephine, Pepi, to reign alongside him.

This was impossible. Even if she returned all his feelings, Pepi would never place her children in jeopardy. To reject him now – after the walks, the talks, the lessons, the blissful hours of unsullied companionship – would be like a second bereavement. Yet do it she must.

We could all see by late summer that 1805 was not going

according to plan. No sooner had I returned to Vienna for the autumn, while Pepi stayed longer in Hietzing, than Marianna reported that Beethoven had held a playthrough of *Leonore*, at his apartment, and I had missed it. 'He sent Ries out of the room!' she recounted. 'He was still stewing about the *Andante favori* incident. His trust is hard-won, and tough to regain.'

I was in no doubt as to why he was so sensitive about that piece.

'Otherwise,' said Marianna, 'I can promise you the opera is a masterpiece. The run-through bodes well.'

True – until the censors banned it.


Someday, my dear, the very concept of censorship will – I hope – be consigned to the furthermost privy of history where it can stink away to itself while its targets try to forget what it did to them. In the dying days of the Holy Roman Empire, though, its control held our artists in chains.

Luigi had called upon Joseph Sonnleithner to translate and adapt Bouilly's play for his purposes. Sonnleithner was a capable writer, lawyer, music publisher and artistic director of the Theater an der Wien; after the place was sold, the new owner had sacked Schikaneder and appointed Sonnleithner in his place. Beethoven's contract as composer-in-residence was nevertheless in shreds. He had had to move out, going to live first with Stephan von Breuning, who deserved unlimited medals for putting up with him, and later – after that all went wrong – in another apartment in the same block.

You'd think, given his connections, Sonnleithner would have been well versed in matters of censorship, with a nose for likely problems. Still, I sometimes wonder how artistic directors are chosen. The censors decreed that in all artistic work that involved words or images, there must be no theme of religion or current politics, no couple on stage without a chaperone and any reference to the military had to be positive. *Leonore*'s story involved a political activist held captive in secret by a prison governor intent upon murdering him. There is a compassionate chorus for the prisoners in the first act, a rapturous love duet as the couple are reunited, alone, and a triumphant celebration of freedom at the end. What did Sonnleithner do about it? He simply moved the setting from France to Spain.

Luigi told me the censors had banned *Leonore* when I went to his latest lodging, on the pretext of retrieving a book I had lent him. He had moved yet again; now he was installed in a large apartment on the top floor of a massive building by the city wall, owned by his friend Baron Pasqualati. It reared up on a hillock next to the Mölkerbastei, looking over the ramparts towards the open field of the Glacis, the Prater's amusement park and, beyond that, the Vienna Woods. It took me several minutes to get my breath back after climbing four long flights of stairs.

'Spain? You thought that would help?' I asked.

'He thought it worth a try.' Luigi looked more angry than anxious; his movements had the pent-up energy of a furious creature that if released could cause mayhem of house-demolishing power.

'Ask them nicely.'

'I'm too ill to be nice to anybody. My stomach is tied in knots worthy of an expert sailor.'

'Get Sonnleithner to ask them, then.'

'Tesi, he is *trying*.'

Beethoven himself would crawl to nobody, but if his work were at stake, he did not mind his colleague doing so. What was the alternative? Coffee-house gossip throwing mud at him, the press sniping, Pepi disappointed, and cancellation of the work whose full title was *Leonore, or The Triumph of Marital Love*. The censors progressed like slugs; the copying was paused, the production postponed by five weeks. At last, with a few final tweaks, the ban was lifted. I wrote at once to Aunt Susanna asking if we could use the Guicciardis' box for the world premiere.

The next day I received a letter. It was from Toni – the first communication he had sent me in many months. I had tried to put him out of my mind, with appalling effort, some regret and a measure of success. At the sight of his handwriting, hope surged into me as if a sluice gate had opened. Might I have to revise my vow after all?

His letter had a wholly different purpose.

*'Please forgive me,'* he wrote, *'for my long silence. Times have not been easy and my regiment is now near Salzburg. I hope to see you again when things calm down, my dear Tesi, but for now please read this carefully and take action at once.*

*Napoleon's army is on its way to Vienna. It has already reached Ulm. I hold out little hope for its defeat, and soon we must encounter it at Salzburg if our surmise of his route is correct. If we cannot stop him, you will be in danger. Please go to safety – go home to Hungary – and make sure your dear sister and her children are likewise removed from the city. I cannot stress strongly enough the urgency of this. It may take a week from your receipt of this letter, perhaps a little longer if we are able to engage and damage them, but the French army will be arriving.*

*Ever yours,*

*Anton.'*

Strange to think that I was almost more interested in 'my dear Tesi' than in 'Napoleon's army', and more perturbed that he should sign himself 'Anton' instead of 'Toni', than by what he was telling me. I, a woman of thirty, must have had the addled, infatuated head of a little girl. Napoleon invading Vienna? French forces overrunning our unassailable bastion? Impossible! Laughable! Anyway, no army on earth could force me to miss Beethoven's opera.

A few hours later, a churning sensation in my stomach warned me that my confidence was premature. I should not keep this information to myself. I might have the fortitude to stay in Vienna; but others would not.

I sent word to Beethoven and received a reply to the effect that if the French forces were coming into Vienna, then they could go and see his opera. It was originally a French story, wasn't it?

I sent word to my family. Then I took the coach to Hietzing and told Pepi.

She jumped up from her sofa and called the servants. 'Start packing,' she directed them. 'We are going to Ofen.'

'When do you wish to leave, Madame?' asked Magda.

'As soon as we can. Tesi, do you think Franz would send the carriage to bring us home?' To her, 'home' was Hungary, despite all.

'I will write and tell him to.'

'And you must come with us.'

'I want to hear *Leonore*.'

Pepi stared. 'You would stay in Vienna with an invading army present just to hear an opera?'

My heart ached for Luigi, who would never know that while I could not be dragged away from his magnum opus, Pepi would not tarry a moment for it. Nevertheless – I glanced at the nut-brown hair of little Viky, who was sitting on the floor, playing with her doll's house. Pepi had to consider the children. Of course she would leave.

'I will come to Ofen the day after the premiere,' I said, 'but not before.'

'Very well.' Pepi shrugged. 'You have only yourself to think of.'

Five days later Franz's carriage arrived. Takács scarcely stopped for food, but tore into the house, swept up the luggage and then the children in armload after armload, and was almost ready to lift Pepi herself up and out when she hesitated, saying she had mislaid a favourite hat. I offered to help, but she ran past me on the stairs so precipitously that I nearly fell. 'I'm sure I have packed it, Madame,' said Magda, waiting by the door.

She came back without the hat, but stowing some papers down the front of her dress. I surmised she had rescued a love letter, perhaps received that day, perhaps abandoned somewhere it risked being found – by me.

'You're certain you won't come with us?' Her eyes were too bright; I reached out to see if her forehead was hot with fever. She shrank back at my touch. For a moment I doubted both my sanity and hers.

'I shall never forgive myself if I leave,' I said.

'And I will never forgive myself if I don't. Come to us as soon as it is done. And Tesi – tell me about the opera…'

I had promised to close up the house for her. I would stay in my room at the Palais and try to barricade the museum against any damage from the French – though as far as I was concerned they were welcome to do as they pleased with King Ferdinand.

With a whip-crack and a pounding of hooves, they were off. I watched the mud springing out from beneath the wheels and felt emptiness descending like fresh snow upon the barren house.

# 11

My dear niece,

November in Vienna, raw and slate-grey, presented Napoleon's army of fifteen thousand tramping men with little more than a strudel of wet leaves underfoot. Pepi and her children were not the only ones who had fled. The court and most noble families had packed everything they possessed and headed for the easiest or safest of their country palaces. A giant fleet of imperial horses pulled their carriages.

Letter after letter arrived, urging me to leave at once and go to Ofen (Mother), Siebenbürgen (Lotti), Martonvásár (Franz) or Venice (Julie). I disliked the notion of Venice. I would rather stay in occupied Vienna than visit those stinking canals, let alone in company with Countess Vanity.

I refused to be afraid, or at least to show it. During the one scant week between the French army's arrival and Beethoven's premiere, I would often wake in the small hours, darkness all around, hearing my heart battering like timpani in my ears. Napoleon's troops in Vienna? What a plight for a lone woman – for the sake of an opera? On brighter days, when more of the city's remaining inhabitants ventured out and I would not be alone in the streets, I would force myself to take a walk for the sake of my health. Once I came to the Danube and saw a convoy of barges, like a flock of birds sailing in formation, which I surmised must be carrying more stuff upriver towards Bohemia.

Watching the waterbirds drifting in their wakes, an idea took root in my mind. Material goods exist long after we ourselves are no more – but only people matter. Why, then, are we so preoccupied with inanimate possessions? Such 'stuff' should serve only our needs and nothing beyond. Someday, I decided, I would reduce my quotient of 'stuff' to essentials alone. Living in seclusion, while the city was dead to itself and its invaders, without power to divert oneself with new pastimes or make frivolous purchases, one might realise how little we need to be content, or indeed happy.

Napoleon himself was soon not one mile from where Pepi had lived. Hietzing was home to Schönbrunn Palace; there the 'Emperor' installed himself, amid the manicured gardens and the sprawling rooms where the child Mozart had once played with the little princess Maria Antonia. Its grandeur now went no further than the palace walls; the French, billeted everywhere, were hungry, thirsty and exhausted, but the city had frozen them out. Far from the mayhem I had feared, a peculiar stillness descended. The market places gaped without their stalls; huge brass padlocks hung on the bank doors; and the only activity to be found was the rehearsing of *Leonore* at the Theater an der Wien, where Luigi was in a storm of fury because his second bassoonist had not shown up.

Being alone, I was free to attend rehearsals to offer support for him. Most of his friends had left town, with a few exceptions – including, remarkably, Prince Lobkowitz: I spotted his familiar lithe figure and bright dark eyes across the theatre, with some amazement.

He had a rather too ready sense of humour that tended to antagonise Beethoven, if less so than Prince Lichnowsky's did. 'Your bassoonist is probably cooking rat-stew for the frogs,' Lobkowitz tried to joke to the composer during the break. 'You're lucky there's any orchestra at all.' He had a point.

Beethoven shot him a hellfire glare and ploughed on with the rehearsal. Soon he was shouting at the soprano, Anna Milder, who was singing Leonore; the unfortunate girl burst into tears. She had a bright, strong, silvery voice and held everyone's attention as soon as she stepped on stage, but aged only twenty she was under-experienced for what Beethoven expected of her. In the orchestra pit the musicians were sullen and unresponsive; they resented his yells, many not realising that half the extra volume was down to his hampered hearing. Besides, it was already obvious that no one would come to the performances, since almost nobody was left in Vienna.

If Beethoven looked to me for reassurance, I was not sure I could provide any. 'It will be fine, you'll see,' I said afterwards, hating myself for delivering falsity.

'Thank you, worthy Therese. I hope you are right. Now it's in God's hands.'

*Leonore* did not happen. *Fidelio* did. It turned out that the composer Ferdinando Paer had already written an opera on the same story; the theatre changed the title to avoid confusion, to Luigi's fury. Under the circumstances, I considered this a mild problem. It seemed astonishing they would proceed at all.

On opening night I made my way to the theatre through dank, almost deserted streets, fortunate to have found a cab.

A suffocating pall of humiliation hung over the city. Food was scarce and inflation – or opportunism – rampant; shops and banks remained locked and dark, while the French troops had seized all the supplies they could find. I had been slicing one salami and a tranche of Bergkäse for each meal for days; my head was light and spinning.

From my lonely seat in the Guicciardis' box, I stared down upon the gathering orchestra. In the parterre, the expanse of red plush was dotted with scant groups of curious listeners. Glints of blue and white, with golden buttons catching the candlelight, betrayed the presence of some French military; the air between them and the few local observers seemed as taut as a violin's E string. I glimpsed both Lobkowitz and Lichnowsky in their boxes. A great hole in the audience seemed to exist where Pepi should have been.

While Luigi and his performers went through the motions, I watched in a fug of sorrow. Some of the music was a glory: a rapt quartet in the first act and the chorus for the prisoners briefly released into the light were Luigi at his best. Could they save the opera? Yet the emotions were predictable, the recitatives were too long and the whole performance lumped onward; the necessary energy had leaked away. Worse, in the parterre, raucous squawks of laughter flared out from time to time. I fought the red fury behind my eyes, too far away in my box to tell those French soldiers to *taisez-vous*. What next? Luigi was bound to burn the piece, and I would never hear its considerable beauties ever again.

Backstage afterwards, I spotted him splashing cold water over his face from a bowl, while the chorus, stagehands and orchestra, wrapping themselves in their winter cloaks and hats, made for the stage door without saying a word to him.

Anna Milder, leaving with her mother, shot at me: 'Don't bother'.

I plucked up the courage to slip, well veiled, though the side streets to visit him the next day. 'It's a disaster and you know it,' he fumed. 'Don't tell me you're with those scoundrels who want me to rework the damn thing.'

That was news to me.

'Napoleon marches in, the audience marches out, the musicians are hungry, the singers can't cope, the theatre is empty, the bloody French flex their muscles by mocking my piece out of sheer swinishness – but no, they say it's *my fault* for delivering a bad opera and I must rewrite the entire score.'

'It's not a bad opera. It's just terrible timing…' I floundered.

'Any fool can see that. They are summoning me to a meeting at Lichnowsky's. Lobkowitz has *ordered* me to turn up and be willing to listen. Lichnowsky is even demanding his own princessly mother attends.'

As if Beethoven would ever listen to anybody. Sometimes, I reflected, his deafness was almost as metaphorical as it was physical.

'Shall I come with you? I will if it'll help.'

'Tesi, thank you – but no.' Luigi was visibly touched. 'Go to Ofen. Be safe. And please don't tell Pepi about this. I wanted so much to be worthy of her…'

'Read these.' Pepi opened a drawer at the bottom of her bedside cabinet and pulled out a pile of letters, which she deposited in my lap. I would know that handwriting anywhere.

It was a week after the premiere and I had reached Ofen in the stagecoach. I was reasonably sure that Pepi had spoken of Beethoven to nobody but me, not only for fear of what Mother might say, but also Father's younger brother, Uncle Joseph. He was the most prominent Brunsvik in public life, being a member of Parliament, and when he came to dinner and held forth at the table – that proud, confident Hungarian nobleman with magnificent moustaches and a hard-hitting way with the truth – Pepi sat mute with fear. I looked on and, over the roast duck, attempted to plan a strategy. I did not know which would horrify him more: the idea that Pepi was embroiled in a 'compromising' relationship with a musician, or the possibility that she might wish to marry him.

Now, during an afternoon when Mother had taken the children across the Danube to the Pest Christmas market and Franz was working in the office, Pepi and I could snatch a few private hours in which to talk. Some of the letters had been crumpled, then smoothed – perhaps those she had retrieved before leaving Vienna. By flickering candlelight, I looked at what Beethoven had been writing in secret to my sister.

The letters had begun months ago, in the spring – with *An die Hoffnung*. A long missive protested that the Prince Lichnowsky incident was not as bad as Pepi supposed; the prince had thought it a positive development if affection had grown between them, and as for who knew what about which, when and how, Aunt Susanna had known all along, because Luigi knew that Zmeskall and Lichnowsky had plotted to ask her to ask Pepi to ask Luigi to finish his opera...

'Aunt Susanna knew about this all along? What about Julie?' I demanded. My temples were aching.

'No idea.' Pepi looked defeated.

*'I here make you a solemn promise,'* wrote Luigi, *'that soon I shall stand before you more worthy of myself and of you… Oh, beloved Josephine, it is not desire for the other sex that draws me to you, no, it is just you, your whole self with all your personal qualities…'*

The letter rambled on and on, referring to 'our love': *'so noble, so firmly founded upon mutual regard and friendship – even a great similarity in our thoughts and feelings… Oh you, you make me hope that your heart will yearn – beat for me – Mine can only – cease – to beat for you – when – it no longer beats – Beloved Josephine…'*

'But this is impossible,' I said.

'Just try the next one.'

I read it. Slashed with dashes, disconnected phrases searching for words that were still never enough, longing for the expressive power of music and sensing even that as inadequate…

'He is barely coherent. Pips, what does Mother know? And Uncle Joseph? They have surely observed your state of mind. You must consider what they might do against him, to protect you and the children.'

'From Luigi?' Pepi gave a bitter laugh. 'As if he could harm us.'

'Don't you remember how Uncle Francesco laughed fit to burst when Luigi proposed to Julie?'

'Thank God for Uncle Francesco. I could not have borne it if Luigi had married Countess Vanity.'

'Be serious, Pips. Beethoven is not going to marry any woman of noble birth.' I thought of Luigi's continual fallouts: his own brothers; Ferdinand Ries; George Bridgetower, to such a degree that Luigi had stripped the dedication from the sonata intended for him and sent it to Rodolphe Kreutzer instead. His behaviour often did not match the noble inner self he had allowed me to glimpse. 'He is a commoner, his manners are lacking, he has a terrible temper, he is a musician and without property, land or reliable income, and he is going deaf. Find me any noble family that will accept such a person as son-in-law, let alone as stepfather to noble-born children. And what about the Deyms? Don't you see? They will stop at nothing to separate you.'

'We have not actually discussed marriage,' said Pepi, speaking slowly.

A man of Luigi's moral strength would not give vent to such passion if there were no encouragement. These were not letters of friendship. These were written in the knowledge that the recipient would not be unfamiliar with the ferocious emotions therein. He would write to her as 'beloved Josephine', then turn up to visit, surely expecting an appropriate welcome.

'Pepi, what exactly has passed between you?'

'I have granted him nothing... physical. At least, not much...'

'Pips! For heaven's sake! If you're not thinking of marriage, *they* will say you are compromising yourself and the entire family.'

'I have made him no promises. I have written, begging him to love me less sensually, because it's not that I don't feel for him—'

'You do love him, and obviously he knows.'

Pepi jumped up and swung away from me, hands pressed to her eyes. 'Dear *God*, I love him! But Tesi, what would you do if you received letters like these?' She pointed at the others in my lap, waiting to be read. 'There's more. Lots more.'

I had never received a love letter in my life. All I had was that scrawled note from Toni, urging me to leave Vienna.

'As Lotti says, you mustn't be alone with him – at least, not long and not often.'

I read on. Page after page of fragmented sentences, protestations of undying love. She is his angel, his only love, the person who has bound him to life in moments of the blackest despair. The brief gaps between meetings seemed interminable to him. She would have received the letters, and then she would see him, and be in that intimate contact of spirit, mind and body that music lessons so often can bring, and she had to respond, somehow –

It was more than six years since we first climbed the stairs to his mouse-ridden apartment in the Petersplatz. Had he loved her then too? And while she was married to Deym and having four children? Not that she had ever had a choice: scarcely had she got to know Beethoven than she met Deym and became engaged to him. She had been barely more than a child herself, in terms of feeling. In marrying Deym she thought herself noble, not self-destructive.

'I'm trapped,' she said. 'I can't marry him because my children would be taken from me. And I can't be his mistress…'

'It's all right, Pips. Take your time.'

The words spilled out. 'I count the hours, I calculate the minutes until I see him again, even though sometimes he's coming to the house every day. It's as if I am part of him, and he of me. It's not like being with another person. When he writes that we have such harmony of spirit, it sounds ridiculous, but it is true. But the physical side would ruin everything…'

'Then you must stop seeing him.'

Pepi let out another sob. 'I've lost one man I loved – must I lose another because of everybody else's demands?'

'Perhaps you must. Can you do it?'

Pepi sat down on her bed and hid her face on her knees. 'I want so much to be in control of my own life,' came her muffled voice. 'I can't think of one area, though, in which I am. Tesi, does every woman feel this way?'

'You must make the best of the situation. For instance, now you are removed from his world – out of sight and out of mind – and you can recover the strength to protect yourself when you return.'

Pepi pulled from inside her bodice a sealed envelope. 'I dare not open this one.'

There was a silence while we stared at her name on the front in his writing.

'Tesi, it's like a great flood and I'm drowning. And then I think "*I am drowning in Beethoven's love,*" and I start to think I am actually going mad…'

To me Luigi was Florestan from his opera – a freedom fighter imprisoned perhaps by his deafness, or else by his own indomitable spirit, longing for Leonore, who must be Pepi, to save him. If that was what he wanted from the woman of his dreams, perhaps he had chosen the wrong one.

'He thinks you are his soulmate,' I pointed out. 'But this is his imagination. Perhaps you are not.'

'We *are* soulmates,' Pepi stated, as if it were an accepted fact. 'But if I sleep with him, I will die.'

That did not make sense.

'If you'd experienced lovemaking, Tesi, you would understand. I will be burned up, destroyed, lost forever. And afterwards? Imagine the guilt, the shame, and I'd lose him because then I think you must either marry or part and we can do neither. I can't marry him, but I can't bear to lose him. I can't risk having a child out of wedlock, but I can't risk my children being sent away. There is nowhere to turn, nowhere to go, no way to move. I may die anyway, of grief.'

I took both my sister's hands, which were cold and sweaty. 'Listen, Pepi, if I do not say this, Mother will, or worse, Uncle Joseph. Stop seeing him. We will all help you through it. Here's my plan: we will stay here for the winter – there is no point trying to go back to Vienna while Napoleon's army is there. Then in spring, if all is well, let us go to Lotti in Siebenbürgen and help her have her baby.' Our sister was expecting her first child. 'That will revive your spirits, change the scenery and give us something to look forward to. What do you think?'

She stayed silent. I elected to take that as agreement.

'Good. I will write to Lotti today.'

'What about Luigi?'

'He will get over it. If you will not have him – and you will not – then he must learn to live without you. He will find a wife elsewhere. Men *do* recover from such passions. And so do women. It's harsh, darling, but it's the only way.'

'I need to sleep.' Pepi slid down, full-length on her bed.

She did not leave her room again for a week.


The nervous fever was back. This time I questioned my assumption that her illness was primarily physical, for my unfortunate sister began rambling about God, good, evil and music in such an incoherent way that Mother and I sent for a doctor. He arrived, with leeches. She was bled; she screamed; he left. In the middle of all this, yet another letter arrived in Beethoven's writing.

I looked at it. Then I opened it.

I read it. I thought long and hard. What effect would these words have upon Pepi in her current state? I could show them to her only if I wanted to kill her with the sorrow and longing they would induce. Biting back my heartbreak on my friend Luigi's account, I took it downstairs to the tile stove and fed it to the flames.

'He has stopped writing to me,' Pepi divined in the early weeks of 1806.

'Good.' I did not explain that he had not. The effect had been as intended: Pepi was regaining a measure of sanity and strength. 'Let's plan our trip to Siebenbürgen.'

Beethoven spent much of that year self-destructing, as Marianna told me, even while the city was attempting to reclaim its life around him.

First, the opera. He had agreed to rewrite it after Lichnowsky's meeting, when the prince's mother went down on her knees to beg him to comply, invoking the memory of his own beloved mother. Yet the revival, called *Leonore* to distinguish it from the old version, ceased abruptly when he became convinced the theatre was trying to con him out of his rightful income. He snatched the score from the baffled intendant's hands, took it home and sank it in the swamp of his chaotic apartment.

Next, another fallout: Lichnowsky himself. The prince took Beethoven with him for an extended stay at his country palace at Grätz in Silesia, and there held a soirée intended for the composer's benefit. But Luigi, spotting some French military types in the gathering, refused to perform in front of them. Lichnowsky then made the mistake of his life. He tried to force Beethoven to the piano. Luigi, who was the stronger of the two and, unlike the prince, not drunk, rebuffed him. He plunged straight out of the room and up to his quarters, where he scrawled a furious note.

'*You are just a prince,*' he raged in it at his importunate patron. '*You are what you are through accident of birth; what I am, I have made of myself. There are and will be thousands of princes. There is only one Beethoven.*'

He swept his few belongings into his holdall and strode out of the palace in the pouring rain, in the middle of the night. He walked for hours before looking for shelter or transport towards Vienna, even though the damp would damage the manuscripts he had brought with him. At home he had a bust of Lichnowsky. Though it was a journey of several days to reach the city, his anger must have been undimmed upon arrival, for in his apartment he smashed the prince's image into smithereens. After that, of course, Lichnowsky withdrew his annual stipend and Luigi found himself short of 600 florins a year. I am still trying to imagine the force of a fury that can destroy a statue.

Cometh the moment, turneth up the new patron. Once the court had slunk back to town, the Russian tsar's diplomatic representative in Vienna, Count Andrei Kirillovich Razumovsky, approached Luigi for music lessons, then commissioned a set of string quartets, asking that a Russian theme be included in each. The count, then in his mid-fifties, was a much-desired presence in the city's musical circles: partly for his charm, complete with accent full of dark Ls and missing its definite articles, partly for his supply of excellent vodka, and partly because he was the richest person anybody had ever met. At the Palladian palace he built for himself out in the Landstrasse region, beyond the city walls, he took Schuppanzigh's quartet into his employ, much to their delight; the three new Beethoven works would be theirs to premiere amid the splendour of those Grecian marble halls.

'I hear you have some Canova sculptures?' Pepi had asked him once at a ball, when we were both there.

The count's laugh boomed out as he bent to kiss her hand. 'Dear Countess,' he crooned in deep bass tones, 'I have entire hall of them! My walls are crammed with art. I love Dutch masters – Rembrandt, Van Eyck, Vermeer. And I have whole orchestra of finest Italian stringed instruments. You must visit – I will show you. But will take some time!'

When the new quartets were published as Luigi's Op. 59, Franz snapped them up and gathered his friends to play and listen. The first opens with an unforgettable cello melody; watching my brother perform it, I felt it held not only the joyous gratitude that Luigi owed his new supporter, but also Franz's whole bubbling, laconic and expansive personality. From beginning to end, the three quartets dedicated to Razumovsky held us all enraptured.

We had unfortunate lessons to learn, beyond the power of art.

The road to Siebenbürgen carried us over plains and through wide wooded hills, punctuated with plunging ravines. Viky stared from the carriage into the forests with wide eyes, and Carl and Fritz wanted to go fast down the slopes, for which Takács gave them a scolding from the driver's box. The roads were bumpy and moved in curves, not lines. Sephine vomited at intervals.

Pepi, exhausted, sat back with a vacant look in her eyes. 'Pull yourself together, Josephine,' Mother snapped. I wondered what the Telekis would make of us when we arrived – and vice versa. Uncle Joseph, our chief assessor of likely marriages, had visited them before the wedding and reported back, with his customary forthrightness, that he found them unsympathetic. Lotti, with uncharacteristic determination, refused to listen. 'Never give up,' she said, quoting my own motto.

We crossed three rivers amid a landscape ancient and fertile where wild horses grazed on an abundance of windflowers. The Teleki castle, overlooking all this from its hillside, was a well-proportioned baroque mansion, its façade of regular windows and three arched doorways appearing more welcoming than turned out to be the case.

When our carriage rolled up the drive, a small, dark-haired figure came dashing out towards us: Lotti, massively pregnant, ready to fling herself into our arms. Emerich strolled behind her: 'She has spoken of nothing but your arrival for weeks,' he acknowledged, with a heel click. Several dogs bounded up, barking, but soon made friends with the children, and Emerich calmed the creatures before taking our motley party inside to meet his mother. Behind us, Takács uttered a tactful cough.

'What about Takács?' I said. 'He is like one of the family, and he's not young.'

'The servants' quarters are above the stables. He can go up.' Emerich waved a lordly hand and turned his back.


Once we had settled into our rooms, with the children in one big 'nursery', we dressed for dinner, shivering with cold. The meal was a strained affair, served by two harried-looking servants in a cavernous dining hall in which it could still have been winter. After nightfall, we could hear wolves howling nearby.

Countess Teleki and Mother were not about to become

best friends. They were too alike in quite the wrong ways: both had replaced their capacity for affection with a determination to control others. The countess, long widowed, had a stare that reminded me of Deym's glass-eyed statues. The first disagreement was about church the next morning: the countess refused to touch a Catholic service. 'You may go, of course,' she granted us. Lotti made as if to speak. 'Not *you*,' barked the countess – and our sister shrank back as if expecting to be slapped. The marriage contract stipulated that the children must be brought up as Protestants.

'You should rest, dear Lotti,' Pepi encouraged her.

'Rest? She's idle as mud,' said Lotti's mother-in-law. 'Never lifts a finger to help me or her husband.'

'She is nine months pregnant,' I shot back, since my sisters were both too upset to speak.

'What would you know about that? I understand you are some kind of nun.'

'Either someone is a nun or she is not,' said Emerich, 'and Therese most definitely is – though no order dared take her on!'

At first I thought he was trying to make a joke.

'I intend to become a teacher,' I declared.

'Well, well,' said the countess. 'It's good to use your time productively. No man would want a misshapen cripple for a wife.'

Even Mother was dumbstruck. I rose and walked out, leaving my dinner uneaten. Oh, for the daring to take the plate and fling it at our hostess! At least a speedy exit would prove I was no cripple. Behind me I heard Lotti's gentle remonstrations and Emerich telling her not to interfere: troubled tones echoing from the bleak walls. If I were Luigi, I would simply have left, on foot, for home.

Having found a candle on a holder in the scullery, I made

my way up the back stairs to the nursery; Lotti's maid had brought the children their food and put them to bed. I stood in a pool of candlelight, trying to clear my head and pray for advice. Carl and Fritz were fast asleep, dark humps in their cots; Sephine was slumbering, thumb in her mouth. From Viky's bed, though, two bright eyes gazed at me. 'Auntie Tesi?'

I put the candle on the windowsill and went over to hug her.

'I'm scared,' she whispered. 'I don't like it here. There are weird animals outside.'

'Don't worry, darling. They can't get in and they're more scared of us than we are of them. And guess what? I don't like it here either.'

'How long are we staying?'

'We will stay to help Auntie Lotti when she has her baby. Then we can go home.'

'When will she have the baby?'

'I don't know, but it should be soon.'

'Supposing it's not for ages?'

'Then we'll think of something else – I promise.'

'Tell me a story?'

'Once upon a time, there was a young man who travelled from the north to a strange city. He had nothing except one extraordinary gift: for music...'

My tale put her to sleep before its hero had managed to win the beautiful princess. I kissed her forehead, then slipped away to my room, where I walked up and down for a while. Tomorrow I would start exploring ways to get us out of this terrible place.

Morning was no pleasanter. I could feel the countess's disapproving eyes on my substantial breakfast (I'd had no dinner, after all). Mother requested her youngest daughter's company at church and at once there was another row.

'Lotti, what do *you* want to do?' I cut in.

Lotti opened her mouth, but her husband interrupted: 'Lotti will attend our service at home.'

'Lotti can answer for herself.'

'Tesi,' my sister said, 'I will stay at home.'

I followed her upstairs. 'Darling, I'm worried. It's as if you have given up. You let him treat you like one of those Siebenbürgen Hounds.'

'The dogs are happy,' Lotti sighed. 'It's easier this way.'

'But – is he always like this?'

Lotti hesitated. 'Have you seen the library? It's enormous, even bigger than Father's. He spends most of his time in there.'

The library had not been part of our arrival tour; I went to investigate. It occupied one of the biggest rooms, looking out towards the distant forests, and smelled of old paper and damp stone. I picked a leather-bound volume off a shelf at random: *A History of the Bubonic Plague in Vienna*. Pulling down book after book, I divined that this devastating illness and its effect on Europe was Emerich's special area of interest.

Church gave us a chance to see the village. The chapel itself was wooden, its peaked roof thatched with dark straw. Simple chalets stood nearby, a tiny shop, and fields in which sheep and some donkeys were grazing; ox-carts trundled down the dirt tracks and atop the hillside perched an old stone inn. I took the opportunity to walk up there and ask whether they might have room for a large family of three women, four children and a coachman. It was clear they would be glad of our custom, should matters turn out this way.

Matters did. An argument at the luncheon table about popery, indulgences, corruption, puritan cruelty and the destruction of art propelled Mother straight back to her room to start packing. I intervened: if anything deserved fighting over, it was the appalling treatment of Lotti in her delicate condition. Countess Teleki was not used to being contradicted. Pepi, delicate herself, fled the table towards the small sitting room where Lotti was permitted a piano; soon we heard the distant strains of the *Andante favori* reaching out to calm us. The countess gave a mutter about the evils of modern composition.

At the piano, I found Pepi helpless with weeping, gazing at her would-be lover's name on a closed volume of his sonatas. She had been playing the *Andante* from memory. 'I can't bear it,' she said. 'Poor Lotti!'

'We'll go to the inn. I will organise it.'

Moments later a commotion revealed that we could not go yet: Lotti's waters had broken. I took cruel satisfaction in the fact that this had happened at the dining table in the middle of Sunday lunch.


For nearly twenty-four hours Pepi, having switched in a trice from fragile widow to sensible midwife, guided our sister through a labour that intensified through deceptive lulls to great tidal surges of pain. As the night deepened, Lotti clutched my hands until her nails drew blood. Sometimes she stopped her cries for long enough to thank us for staying with her. The nearest doctor was thirty miles away and the countess did not seem minded to assist at anything as unpleasant as childbirth.

At three in the morning Pepi, her eyes red and shadowed, beckoned me out of the room. 'The baby isn't coming – something must be wrong. I'm scared, Tesi. After all this, we might lose them both.'

I fetched Mother to ask her advice. We stared down at poor Lotti, writhing on the bed, her legs drawn up to her distended form.

'Lie flat,' Mother instructed.

'I can't,' Lotti moaned. 'I want to move.'

'Take my hand,' Pepi whispered to her. 'Stand if you want to. Do whatever feels right.'

'She must lie still and save her energy!' Mother snapped.

'I never did, not after the first one.' Pepi held out her hands and helped Lotti to roll to the side and up. Walking back and forth, leaning on Pepi, seemed to ease her agony. Mother, overridden, strode out in a huff.

'Thank goodness for that,' growled Pepi – and at last Lotti managed a smile.

The process took its terrifying course, but after almost a whole day and night, the first cries of Lotti and Emerich's daughter set us laughing for joy. The baby settled on her exhausted mother's breast and soon we could take turns holding her. My beloved niece Blanka's tiny fingers curled around my thumb and held tight. She already had dark eyes, just like Viky's.

'She's enormous,' Pepi remarked. 'No wonder that was difficult, darling.'

'It's over now,' Lotti said, smiling.

Emerich, to his credit, became tearful upon seeing the baby and finding his wife alive and recovering. The countess looked in and nodded – 'A girl? What a pity.' The children were enchanted. 'How big and strong she is,' said Viky. I imagined them together in twenty years' time: intelligent, passionate women of great character who would set out to change the world, with my ageing self as guide...

As it turned out, I was partly right.

Once it was clear Lotti and Blanka were as healthy and happy as could be expected, we moved with relief to the inn.

Pepi, the children and I walked thigh-deep through a sprawling meadow of flowers. On such a day, Siebenbürgen could seem a paradise; and from the village Biergarten we could hear the distant whirls and plucks of a Gypsy band. Only the Teleki castle and its mistress remained cold and hostile.

'I can't bear to abandon Lotti in that godforsaken house,' said Pepi.

'Do you think she would leave and come home with us?'

'Never. She's devoted to Emy.'

'Why do women stay with men for "love" when they make existence a living hell?'

'Believe me, it is not easy to be a wife and contemplate leaving your home and husband.'

'We're inculcated from earliest childhood with how we must behave, and it's almost impossible to change someone's mind after that has happened. I'm sure it's in the earliest years that we learn patterns that bind us for the rest of our lives.'

Pepi agreed: 'As the Jesuits say, give them a child until he is seven and they will form the man.'

I confided in her my own vision: our house in Ofen had space enough for a school – perhaps twenty to forty little girls, a garden of angels...

'But *how* would you teach them?' Pepi wanted to know. '*What* would you teach them? How will you persuade the good people of Ofen that their tiny daughters should be schooled – and by you?'

'Well, don't you want to school Viky and Sephine?'

'Not particularly,' said Pepi, to my horror. 'Carl and Fritz, yes, but I wouldn't send the girls away from home. It would be unbearable – how would I ever know they were safe?'

'Then we will set up a school to which mothers such as you *are* content to send their daughters – because the girls will be happy, protected and learning well.'

'Let's research it,' Pepi suggested. 'We'll investigate the best educational methods – I for my boys, you for the girls.'

That was why we were ensconced in Ofen, reading about another man who was about to change our lives, Johann Heinrich Pestalozzi, when Marianna wrote to us from Vienna with the latest news: Beethoven was in trouble for importuning a married woman.

## 12

My dear,

Maybe you met the beautiful Marie Bigot. She was as fine a pianist as you are. She could sight-read even the most complex of Beethoven's sonatas.

'Don't be jealous,' I told Pepi. '*You* won't have him. You can't blame him if he looks elsewhere.'

'She's married,' Pepi fumed. 'To Razumovsky's librarian! Luigi would never pursue another man's wife. He's said so a hundred times.'

He had even left Pepi alone while she was married to Deym. No wonder she was annoyed.

Franz made discreet enquiries. It was, of course, a tremendous misunderstanding. Beethoven, seeing a beautiful sunny day as an opportunity for a drive into the countryside, sent Marie a note asking if she and her little daughter, who was three, would like to go too. Her husband was at work, so he could not join them. The startled wife showed him the letter.

'Beethoven is not one to write between the lines,' Franz insisted. 'If he says something, he means it, no more, no less, *finito*. And if he doesn't mean something, he doesn't say it.

You always know where you stand, and you can trust his word. Besides, it means that praise, should he utter any, is genuine.'

'Is that a Rhinelander characteristic?' I asked. It was certainly not the Viennese way.

'I don't know,' said Franz, 'but it is a Beethoven one. He simply saw nothing wrong with inviting a pupil and her child to join him in the sunshine.'

We had been away from Vienna for almost a year: it left a great emptiness in our hearts, but we were afraid to return, to find the city demoralised and drained of its status. By now, Napoleon had succeeded in obliterating the world order of a thousand years.

Our army was all but destroyed at Ulm, as Toni had warned. A few months later the forces of the Third Coalition – England, Russia, Prussia, Austria and Sweden – were crushed with devastating losses at Austerlitz. Emperor Francis was forced to surrender. The German states gathered together and declared they would form a Confederation of the Rhine, controlled by a 'prince-primate', but with Napoleon as – oh dear – 'protector'. The so-called rulers of this new group had to pay Paris handsomely for the privilege. Nobody was fooled. Then on 1 August the Germans declared they would secede from the Holy Roman Empire, and before the week was out, Emperor Francis gave up, declaring he would lay down the imperial crown. The Holy Roman Empire had seen its last sunset. Francis II now became Francis I: the first emperor of Austria and Hungary, shorn of his former territory, humiliated before the world.

He had still not sent Pepi the help she thought he had promised. No doubt he had other things on his mind.

'We should go back when the season begins,' Pepi

decided. 'The soldiers have left, and it is not going to be easier if we leave it too long.'

'You should take a cure,' I said. 'Spend a little time in Baden and rest properly. Then you will be all the stronger for when we return.'

'Exactly. And then it will be time to start rebuilding. Tesi – you will come back with me, won't you?'

I felt somewhat gratified: my sister had recognised that she could not do without me.

Count von Sauer was not best pleased to see Pepi when she swept back into the Palais and the museum. He was still less pleased to see me; mine was the watchful eye that would be cast over twelve months' worth of his documentation. I mollified the effects with a quiet behind-the-scenes financial deal in his favour.

My plan now aimed to build Pepi's strength and look to the children's future. To that end I timetabled all our hours, with allocations after my office duties for a constitutional walk, piano practice, painting, playing with the children, visiting or receiving friends, and attending what concerts, theatre, opera and salons could be found. One hour was reserved for reading about educational theory; this soon extended, for me, to two and beyond. At my easel, I was copying a portrait of myself by Johann Baptist Lampi the Elder, in which I am shown as a Grecian priestess, my hair wound with long ribbons. This task was neglected when I lighted upon words I felt I had been seeking all my life.

Pestalozzi echoed my deepest instincts. In *My Inquiries into the Course of Nature in the Development of Mankind* the philosopher suggested we must each be responsible for our own moral and intellectual state; education should therefore teach us to think for ourselves. In an era when all we had deemed firm and immovable was being dismantled, to be replaced with thought and ambition on a terrifying scale, developing sound judgment was vital – for us and for the children too.

I began letter after letter to the great man at his institute in Yverdon, on Lake Neuchâtel, but tore them up. Nothing I wrote seemed eloquent enough to convince him to accept me as his disciple.

I was so absorbed in my research that I did not check whether Pepi was sticking to our routine, or to whom she was writing letters. Therefore when a servant from the museum tapped on my office door one fine September day to say we had a personal visitor, but Countess Deym was nowhere to be seen, I bustled down the stairs to be faced with a sight that stopped me in my tracks.

In the hallway, hat in hand, stood a familiar stocky figure in a blue coat.

The house was too quiet; there was no sign of Pepi or the children. I made sounds of greeting, of surprise and delight. 'My dear Beethoven! I'm afraid Josephine is not here at the moment, but please, come upstairs and have some coffee and cake…'

He grunted his thanks, evidently disappointed. I was shocked by the change in him. His dark hair was threaded with grey and he had gained weight. His breeches and shoes were muddy; the latter were, I was certain, the same ones in which he often used to walk to Hietzing, with wear and tear to match.

'I thought she wanted to see me,' he said. I called the maid to bring coffee, good and strong; she looked askance at the unkempt visitor, who was seated, but could not keep still. 'Of course,' he added quickly, 'I am overjoyed to see you, dear Tesi.'

'Luigi, it is *wonderful* to see you – I have missed you – but did something happen?'

'She wrote to me. She said she wanted to be friends…'

If Beethoven could be self-destructive, and my sister was his soulmate, that meant she could be too.

'Look.' He handed me a letter in Pepi's writing.

*'For a long time I had wished for news of your health, and I would have inquired long ago had modesty not held me back,'* wrote Pepi. *'Now tell me how you are, what you are doing… The deep interest that I take in everything concerning you, and shall take as long as I live, makes me long for news of this. Or does my friend Beethoven – surely I may call you this – believe I have changed?'*

Why, oh why? And why now? Did she not know his volatility? Was she cruel enough to rekindle his feelings? Or could she not control her own?

'Well then,' I said brightly. 'How *are* you? How is everything going?'

Beethoven gave a resigned sigh. His voice was louder than before; I surmised he could not hear well enough to judge his own volume. He had been back a short time in Vienna after a long sojourn in Eisenstadt and was planning to visit for a while one of his patrons, a Hungarian countess named Marie Erdödy, at her estate north of Vienna at Jedlesee. She was about Pepi's age, had three small children and, most unusually, had separated from her husband.

'It's not what you think,' Luigi barked. 'She is disabled – walking is almost impossible for her – and I think she takes too much laudanum to control her pain. Often she does not come out of her room for days. It will reassure her to have a man in the house besides the servants, even if only me. The peace is good for my work. It will suit us both.'

'And music, Luigi? What are you writing?'

He leaned towards me. I repeated the question at greater volume.

The smile turned to gloom. 'A symphony, in C minor. You will like it, I think. It is rather different – it includes trombones. But I had a useless summer. Headaches – all the time headaches. And stomach pain. My innards are disasters by the dozen. I went to Baden, I saw doctors, I had those fearful leeches, nothing helped.' Of his hearing, he said nothing, and I dared not ask.

'Pepi went to Baden too,' I remarked, then wished I hadn't.

'I saw her name in the hotel register.' His voice cracked a little. 'Our paths did not cross. Anyway, I found it difficult to work. I wrote a Mass for Prince Esterházy, and he didn't like it. Nobody liked it, except me. Tell me, Tesi – how is she?'

'She is well.' I tried to keep my expression neutral. 'Life has been difficult; she was quite ill and sometimes relapses. But she is rebuilding her life. I beg you, Luigi, do not disrupt her peace of mind. It is hard won.'

He gave a snort. '*She* wrote to *me*.' With a sudden motion that pushed two cushions to the floor, he jumped up. 'Thank you for the coffee, Tesi. Please tell her I was here. I'll try another day. For now, I will leave you in peace.'

I bided my time when Pepi and the children returned – they must have slunk out the back way and had driven to the Prater. After the children were in bed, I confronted her.

'Pepi, you wrote to him. Are you quite mad?'

Pepi turned first pale, then pink. 'It's been over a year. His name is always being linked with other women. Surely he's forgotten me?'

That was as disingenuous as 'It's only piano lessons.' Of course she had been listening for news of him and his attachments; those were news to me, unless she meant Countess Erdödy – which was news even to him.

'Pepi, he is in a *ferment*. He said he'd come back.'

'Oh God. What have I done?' mused Pepi. She must have known, full well, exactly what she had done.

He returned the next day. This time, everybody was out. A letter came soon.

*'Dear, beloved and only J! … How often have I wrestled with myself, beloved J … but it is all in vain. A thousand voices are always whispering to me that you are my only girlfriend, my only beloved. Oh, dear J, let us walk without constraint along that path where we have often been so happy … I called on you twice – but I was not so fortunate – as to see you – That hurt me deeply … But I still hope…'*

Hope. The curse of eternal optimism. The blaze of sunset on the cloud's bright hem. Even if Pepi did miss him – so much that she could not stop herself from writing to him – her situation could not and would not change. Reawakening this love affair meant encountering yet again everything that made it impossible.

'If he comes back,' I said, 'you must not see him.'

'If he comes back, tell him I am not here,' she instructed the servants.

He came back. Again and again. He would not give up.

'Idiot,' I accused Pepi.

'Heartless spinster!'

'I want no further anguish for either of you.'

Pepi covered her face with her hands, like one of the children pretending it made her invisible. 'I don't want to talk about how rare it is for our class of women to be permitted to choose our husbands for love. You can have no idea what a tragedy it is until it happens to you.'

He wrote again: suffering, offended by the servants' refusal to admit him, assuming she did not wish to see him, still unable to believe it. The least he deserved, he wrote, was her honesty. I had, silently, to agree.

Pepi locked herself in her bedroom. 'She needs time,' I told the anxious Magda. 'Time must heal all.'

'If she is having to freeze him out,' Magda mused, 'he must mean a terrible lot to her.'


While Pepi was recovering from her latest bout of nervous fever, I rushed around Vienna, charged with looking after the family. Viky needed new shoes, the boys must have exercise books, and perhaps I would buy a doll for Sephine...

Emerging from a toyshop close to the Stephansdom, laden with parcels, I nearly walked headlong into Luigi himself. He was marching in the direction of the Rotenturmstrasse, carrying a flat brown package. We both stopped short as if we were Monostatos and Papageno in *Die Zauberflöte*, each more alarmed than the other.

'I was bringing something for Josephine to give to your brother at her earliest convenience,' he said. 'It's dedicated to him.'

He did not wait for my response, but pressed the package into my arms, then vanished amid the throng.

A note was attached. *'Please deliver this sonata to your brother, my dear Josephine ... You want me to tell you how I am. A more difficult question could not be addressed to me – and I would rather leave it unanswered than – answer too truthfully.'*

He could have posted the sonata to Franz. Instead, he sent it to Pepi, knowing she would be the first to read it. She was up and about when I returned – and she could no more resist trying to play it than I could.

I can still feel the shock of it.

Imagine the hottest summer day you have ever experienced, and the storm it triggers. That is nothing compared to this music. I wondered if Luigi perhaps had a new piano and was running it to its extremes, like a warhorse that refused to be broken. I'd had no idea that music could contain such violence.

Pepi turned a page and faced a deluge of notes. She pulled her hands from the keyboard as if out of a naked flame.

'Tesi, what *is* this?'

The first movement progressed in volcanic eruptions and sonic blazes, culminating in a cadenza that felt like a complete conflagration of the keyboard. The second seemed to bring us back to good sense: a clear, simple theme with several variations – but then...

With one shattering chord – hammered out, jagged, in anguish fourteen times – peace was banished and there ensued the finale.

'This is impossible,' said Pepi. I took her place and began to read the last movement's seething perpetual motion.

Today this sonata is termed the 'Appassionata'; again, a publisher trying to be clever, to Luigi's annoyance. Passion? No, this is elemental fury – oddly punctuated from time to time by what sounds like the syncopated rhythm of a Hungarian dance. Yet just when you thought he has gone as far as anybody could, he goes further still. The coda accelerates and Beethoven ratchets up the tension to its summit before the last plunge from the top of the keyboard plummets us down to what feels like the deepest pit of hell.

One could not imagine a work more at odds with our peaceable, irony-prone brother, never mind his modest piano technique. At the end we sat together at the keyboard, staring at the music in silence.

Why dedicate this to Franz, of all people? Franz was not much of a pianist, but his sister was. Franz was not a target for anger, frustration, desperation – but his sister was. Franz, whom Luigi termed his 'brother and friend' – I could not help but wonder what the two of them talked about together. Whether they discussed Pepi. How Franz, however close the two men were, could have stood in the way of any potential marriage. Was I doubting my own brother's integrity? He could love a commoner as a friend, even as a brother, yet not if that friend wished to marry his noble sister. He would, of course, have been seeking to protect Pepi and her children from the Deyms' potential retribution, but Luigi would not have seen it that way.

Neither Pepi nor I wished to admit that we were frightened, viscerally so, by a piece of music.

For three days my head pounded with the agony that Beethoven's sonata had unleashed into it. If Pepi felt as shaken, she did not show it. Instead, she was learning to play the accursed thing.

'Tesi, be reasonable,' she said, when I found her taking the finale to pieces in slow practice. 'You know Luigi doesn't just sit down and write a piece because he feels something. It's a ridiculous idea. He goes very slowly and he always writes several different things at the same time. You'll see, he will have been working on this one for *years*.'

'That's what worries me.' This despair, this overt confrontation with fate, was nothing new. Later I learned that Pepi was quite right: he had begun the sonata in 1805. This was the manuscript that had been half drenched in the torrential Silesian rain the night he broke with Prince Lichnowsky.

After a week I could bear it no longer. Early in the morning, I located a coach that was travelling north and set out to try to find him.


Jedlesee is up the Danube, east of Heiligenstadt: an easy trip to a peaceful place transforming from village to suburb. From the coach, I walked up the road to a long, low building, fronted in yellow ochre: the gateway to the sizeable estate and its grounds. There, however, I found soft, suppressed mayhem.

Countess Marie welcomed me – we had met at several soirées, when she was well enough to go out – but now her delicate features were wracked with not only pain, but anxiety. She moved with difficulty, supported by a walking stick, and was attired in a gown better designed for the bedroom than for the living room.

'Please forgive me, Countess Therese.' She rang for a servant to bring coffee. 'My medicine slows me down.'

'Do you mind me asking what happened?' I ventured.

'We are women together, so I will explain.' Countess Marie smiled, resigned. 'When I had my first daughter, some damage was done. I was not sixteen. The next two babies made it worse. Something in my skeleton has never been right since.' She indicated her hips, pelvis and spine. 'I spend more time confined to bed than I would like. The poor children, they just want me to get up and be well, like a normal mother.'

'Beethoven's music must be a great comfort to you.' I had noticed – and Marianna had confirmed – that Beethoven could only be persuaded easily to improvise for someone if they were ill or depressed. He could tap into the atmosphere around them, translate it into music, and turn it inside out to uplift them. It always worked.

'It would,' said Countess Marie, 'if I knew where he was. He's disappeared. I thought he must have gone back to town, but I didn't understand why he wouldn't have told me first. I panicked a little and the servants checked his rooms. All his luggage is still there. They have been hunting for him the whole of yesterday and today.'

The last time Beethoven disappeared was Heiligenstadt. 'When did you last see him?'

'Three days ago.'

I could not conceal my disquiet. Had he returned to Vienna? Or to Hietzing where he and Pepi had spent so many happy times? The Danube was close by; had he perhaps thrown himself into its waters?

Countess Marie's manservant had alerted the police, the neighbours, messengers, coach drivers, shopkeepers – but nobody had seen anyone answering to Beethoven's description. A man so distinctive would find it difficult to vanish.

'He'd want to be entirely alone,' I said, 'somewhere secluded, unobserved. What worries me most is that if people are calling his name, he will not be able to hear them.'

'So he might never have left the estate...'

'Let me go with the servants to look for him.'

We walked through the grounds for almost an hour. It began to rain. The manservant held an umbrella over me, but I was keen not to slow our progress.

'We have looked almost everywhere, Madame, and there is only one more place left to try.'

'Then let's try it.'

'Near the stream by the perimeter wall there is a type of natural grotto.'

'Somewhere he might shelter?'

We marched on, the drizzle soaking through our clothes, the ground waterlogged under our feet and the autumn wind picking up around our ears. After some twenty minutes, we spotted the brook and, close by, a patch of darkness beneath a grassy bank that sloped up towards the estate's outermost edge. An acrid human smell reached my nostrils. My skin prickled. What if he were dead?

'Wait here,' I instructed the servants. I went forward alone towards the darkness.

It was more than a hollow, but less than a cave. Through the fading afternoon light and the pelting rain, I glimpsed a figure on the ground, huddling against the earthen surrounds, wearing a mud-splattered blue coat. Thank God…

'Luigi! It's me, Therese. I've come to take you home.'

'Tesi?' An incredulous croak. My throat tightened with tears.

'Please, Luigi – come with us.'

Uncurling, he rose and dragged himself towards me with faltering step.

'When did you last eat?'

He shrugged.

'When did you last sleep? And where?'

'No idea. Maybe three days.'

It takes a lot to make me utter expletives, but one may have escaped me then. Beethoven, weak with cold, exhaustion and hunger?

'Were you lost?'

'For heaven's sake,' shouted Luigi. 'I wanted to be alone!'

'For three days?'

He stared me straight in the eye. 'I wanted to die.'

My only comfort was that he used the past tense. We would take him back to the house, give him a bath and a good hot meal – and with a long sleep he should be over the worst. My fury at my thoughtless, selfish sister tightened my throat. Did she not know her effect on him? How could she think herself free? Above all, how could this possibly be the end of it?

## 13

My dear niece,

By now you know Luigi well enough to guess that he would pick himself up. Indeed, he did, with Countess Marie Erdödy's help. He moved into her city apartment on the Krügerstrasse. He lived at the front, which was dark and dreary; she and her children lived at the back, which was warm and bright. Prince Lichnowsky, of all people, lived upstairs, but they rarely spoke.

Somewhat fascinated by Beethoven and the countess's relationship, not to say nervous about it, I broached the subject carefully with Pepi. 'I think they can be close,' I suggested, 'because they are no threat to one another. She is not well; he is going deaf; neither can attract the other. He even calls her his "father confessor".'

'*Father?*' she echoed, before fleeing the room.

In an attempt to help Pepi regain her spirits – which was altogether less straightforward than it was for Luigi, who could focus on his art – I insisted we retreat to Hungary, leaving Sauer in charge at the Palais. From Martonvásár and Ofen, though, I spent most of my time writing letters home to Vienna.

Countess Marie certainly had Luigi's interests at heart. That autumn he was offered the post of Kapellmeister in Kassel for the King of Westphalia – and intended to take it, despite being unsuited to such a job in temperament, attitude and health. The king was Napoleon's younger brother, Jérôme Bonaparte, installed by his sibling and trying to dress up his court as more than a marionette theatre. Countess Marie set about rescuing Luigi from this dubious move.

She had a quiet word with the idealistic young Archduke Rudolph, the emperor's youngest son, who was only twenty and revered Beethoven like the god the composer possibly aspired to be. The archduke gathered a group of aristocratic supporters who together could provide Beethoven with an annual stipend – on condition that he remained in Vienna. Prince Kinsky, Prince Lobkowitz and the archduke each contributed a tranche to this most unusual scheme, giving the composer a total of 4,000 florins a year.

What a contrast from Haydn, who was now elderly and frail, living in his Gumpendorfer Strasse home with a devoted housekeeper and a noisy grey parrot; he had spent most of his life as a liveried Kapellmeister. When Johann Peter Salomon took him to London in the 1790s, he arrived to find himself an international celebrity, to his own amazement. Such an artist should not have had to wait until old age for due recognition simply because he was of humble birth and impecunious background. Luigi would have an advantage far beyond any his professor had known.

Bolstered and regaining his confidence, Beethoven planned a return to the scene of the *Leonore* fiasco, the Theater an der Wien. Given his persistence, and many appearances at charity events there through the year, the intendant, Hartl, agreed to let him stage an Akademie concert on 22 December 1808, including the public premieres of his fifth and sixth symphonies, his Piano Concerto No. 4 and an extravaganza of a piece that would begin with a fantasia on solo piano and end with full orchestra and chorus. There would be sections from his Mass in C – the work that had flopped at the Esterházy palace – and a concert aria for soprano entitled, somewhat to my distress, '*Ah! perfido*'. In between, Luigi would improvise; for this alone nobles and bourgeoisie alike would flock in, from far beyond Vienna too. Were it successful, this concert would spread his repute further through a Europe agog for new music for our new century.

Because of that concert, Pepi and I faced a decision. Fritz and Carl were nearly of school age; if we were going to Yverdon to see Pestalozzi, we could put it off no longer. We conferred in my room; we did not want to be overheard by Mother, who would happily have sliced off Beethoven's ears to keep him away from Pepi, or by Franz, who was flattered if nonplussed by the 'Appassionata' dedication – despite a sun-filled cello sonata, Luigi's Op. 69, having reached his music stand since then.

Pepi wanted to be back for 22 December. 'It's just a concert,' she said in that innocuous tone I knew too well. 'I don't have to *speak* to him.'

I am sure she would have written to Luigi again, if left to her own devices. All the more reason for us to travel and expand our horizons. As a compromise, I agreed in principle that we could aim to return in time for the concert. Apart from anything else, I longed to be there myself.

The trip would nevertheless be lengthy. 'We can't take all four children,' Pepi decided. 'It's too unpredictable. As it is the boys' education at stake, they should come with us. The girls must stay behind.' I made my usual insistence that the girls too should be schooled, which Pepi, to my annoyance, dismissed as unhelpful.

First, we'd go with Mother to Karlsbad for curative hot springs; then we would be in the best possible shape for our great journey.

We went briefly to Vienna to lodge Viky and Sephine with the Bigots – Count Razumovsky's librarian and his wife Marie, over whom there had been such a ludicrous scandal with Beethoven. She and Pepi had since become the best of friends.

'I am slightly concerned about your timing,' Marie remarked, furnishing the little girls with cold drinks. 'It's a long way and by the time you come back it will be winter.'

We agreed, tacitly, that we should probably have left sooner; but now, in golden September, it was hard to believe the beckoning countryside could ever be less than hospitable. 'Please don't worry,' I assured Marie. 'We'll be home well before Christmas.'


Karlsbad, that snug spa in the Bohemian hills, full of sugar-hued hotels and sprawling parkland, lulled us into a false sense of security. The boys played in the gardens, observed by their censorious grandmother. Pepi and I walked along the forest trails, relaxed in the new steam baths, drank healing waters – which tasted horrible – and treated ourselves to the latest hairstyles.

'You are spoilt, dreadful, wanton creatures,' Mother scolded, finding us lounging over a glass of something that was not sulphurous water. The town had invented a noxious digestif named Becherovka. 'Dolled up as if you think yourself empresses, drinking alcohol! Take care, Josephine, that you do not sin against God.'

'Oh, Mother,' Pepi groaned. 'We're on holiday... But Tesi will keep an eye on me. She always does.'

By the time we set out, we felt ten years younger, ready for every excitement life could deliver. We were travelling in Pepi's own barouche, which was semi-open, though sheltered enough from rain – 'perfect for summer,' Pepi insisted, though I had my doubts. We could sit in comfort in the hooded seat, or open it to the elements; the boys loved to ride up on the box behind the coachman, but could take to our laps if the weather turned. The front wheels were small, the back ones taller than Carl. Pulled by two horses, and driven by an expert coachman whom we had hired, since Takács was driving Mother to visit relations in France, this contraption would carry us further west than we had ever gone before.

'How far *is* it?' Pepi stared at the map.

'I don't know,' I admitted. 'It can't be so bad – people do it all the time.'

As we headed out of town the horses began to trot and the forest-clad hills loomed blue and purple ahead of us. We laughed and joked, intoxicated with our sense of liberation.

We reached Yverdon later than planned; in Frankfurt Fritz had caught a cold and had to stay in bed for several days. From there, the route had brought us to the great river beside which Luigi had grown up. Awestruck, we watched the Rhine's magnificence glinting silver under the clouds. Beside it we travelled around five hundred kilometres, to arrive exhilarated, but exhausted.

In our hotel, Pepi threw herself onto her bed; the boys

were tired and quarrelsome; everyone needed rest. My jaw was painful from the gritting of my teeth. 'Supposing I take our letter of introduction round to the Pestalozzi institute,' I volunteered. 'A walk will do me good.' I did not add that solitude would be equally welcome. Moments later I was marching downhill towards the lakeside; here Pestalozzi's establishment had opened a few years earlier in an ancient chateau with high white walls and four round towers.

The town cradled the southern curve of Lake Neuchâtel; across the turquoise water, gentle wooded hills rose into a soft sky. The castle was easy to find, being the largest building in the place; I rejoiced that such a special setting should be given to experimental education. Walking up to the huge wooden door, I was wondering what it would be like inside, when a remarkable sight caught my eye.

Snaking up the road towards me, dressed in dark uniform and walking tidily in pairs, was a stream of small children. Specifically, small girls, shepherded by several women in cloaks, presumably their teachers. As I waited, they trooped past, filing through a gateway into a long, low building next to the castle. Pestalozzi did not only have a school. He had two. The second was for girls. Just like the one I dreamed of creating.

Unexpectedly rejuvenated, I floated up to the entrance to present our letter.

Starting with Pestalozzi's prayers at 6 a.m., the next day we witnessed some of the lessons given to the 190 boys by the great man and his assistants, who were mostly his former students. Some had travelled from much further afield than Vienna. Over lunch, which everybody took together in the great hall, we chatted to a young man who spoke dubious

French with an accent that gurgled like running water; he was American and had undertaken a perilous ocean voyage for the sake of Pestalozzi's system. We heard someone speaking Russian, a tone we recognised well from Count Razumovsky. Others came from Italy, England, Croatia. We could have talked all afternoon and heard stories of faraway lands and peoples long into the night.

Therefore we arrived, somewhat out of breath, a few minutes late at a lesson in philosophy. The teacher turned and gave us a hard glare. He was about our age, a gangly figure topped with fair curls and blessed with vivid blue eyes set a little too close to his nose.

'Friends, if you are coming in, please do so quickly,' he said, drawing unnecessary attention to our tardy arrival. The gazes of all the boys swung towards us. The teacher caught Pepi's and held it for a moment. I could sense his struggle not to stare at her beautiful figure while delivering his lecture. Settling at the back, we listened to his well-modulated arguments about Jean-Jacques Rousseau's *Discourse on Inequality*. His French had an unmistakably Russian twist.

At the end we went up to introduce ourselves and apologise for our lateness. To our surprise, no admonishment issued from his narrow lips, but instead mellifluous words accompanied by a bow and a heel click: 'Baron Christoph von Stackelberg, at your service.'

'You must be Russian.' Pepi smiled. She had always been a little bit too susceptible to superficial charm.

'I am from Reval in Estonia, which some consider Russian and others do not. Do you know it? It's a Hanseatic port, extremely beautiful. Our estate is not far from the town, and within easy reach of the Baltic coast. I recommend it if you are on your travels.'

'These are my sons, Friedrich and Carl.' Pepi motioned

the children forward. 'Since my husband died, my sister and I have been preoccupied with finding them the best possible education…'

Baron von Stackelberg was much more interested in Pepi than in Fritz and Carl, but when Pestalozzi and his wife came to visit us at the hotel in the evening, the philosopher – a wiry, ascetic man in his sixties – seemed delighted that we had made such a warm acquaintance. 'Sometimes I think Stackelberg is more theoretician than animateur,' he said, 'but his understanding and communication cannot be faulted. He is quite an asset.'

I was eager to ask them more about the girls' school and to seek their advice regarding my hopes for setting up one of my own. Madame Pestalozzi laughed when I told her what I had in mind.

'I can tell you how *not* to do it,' she said. 'You saw all those people at lunch? You know why they are there? They come for free food. We pay for everything.'

This shocked me. 'They do not all seem needy.'

'They are not. But I cannot persuade my husband that we should cease this practice, because he argues – correctly, of course – that it would harm those who genuinely need our charity.'

'How is this sustainable?'

'He always says that for the good of the people and the country, we must give our best efforts and make sacrifices. God will reward us in the next world, and the gratitude of those few appreciative children will be our sustenance in this one.'

I was beginning to understand how I would have to change my own life.

\*\*\*

Our week in Yverdon became a fortnight: having travelled all this way, we should reap the benefits. The boys started to make friends; the young teachers, headed by Baron von Stackelberg, flocked to Pepi to regale her with information and encouragement, and Madame Pestalozzi showed me around the establishment for girls. During my own year in a school, I had encountered nothing of this quality of teaching, nor the girls' excitement over activities from which later in life they might be discouraged: studying sciences, writing stories and creating music. Yet boys were handed the keys to enlightenment just because they happened to be male? Why the ability to bear children should override the development of the mind is one thing I have never managed to learn.

It was October and the trees gleamed bronze through the lakeside mists. There was still time; no need, yet, to rush away. Pepi agreed; it put off the moment when we must make a decision about the boys. The Pestalozzis had already offered to board them in their own home should Pepi resolve that they would stay.

November arrived, and the cold and the rain; now we had no wish to set out in the barouche. By the time Pestalozzi invited us to his office and motioned to us to sit down for a serious chat, winter was setting in.

'We would love to have your boys here in the school,' he said, 'and as you know, I would guarantee them excellent care.'

Pepi cleared her throat. She was not happy. It was such a long way from Vienna…

'I find it extremely difficult to contemplate being separated from my children,' she admitted. 'I have another idea.

Is there any way we can teach them in your system at home?'

Pestalozzi, visibly crestfallen, thought about this. 'You could perhaps employ a trainee teacher from this institute. It would be a fine prospect for one of them. Still, as you know, they come from far-flung locations, and we may have to be persuasive.'

After my initial disappointment, I spotted the advantages: if we had a Pestalozzi teacher with us, I could learn the system from him and build my knowledge for my own school.

The first young man Pepi and I interviewed blanched at the idea of travelling so far. He was only sixteen. A second youth, too, balked at the word 'Vienna'.

'Whatever are we to do?' Pepi said, glum in our hotel sitting room.

'They're too young. We need someone older and more experienced.'

Just then there was a knock on the door: the concierge. 'Mesdames, there is a gentleman downstairs asking to see you. He says he is from Pestalozzi and that you know him.'

We exchanged glances. 'Please send him up,' Pepi said.

A minute later the door swung open; there was a swift motion of a tall, fair figure with a long stride. Baron Christoph von Stackelberg stood before us.

'I understand you are looking for a private tutor,' he said.

If we were to reach Vienna for 22 December, we would have to leave soon. As I'd feared, our time and money were running short. After some calculations, I surmised that we could reach Munich, whereupon we wrote to our banks requesting that money be sent there for us to collect, to cover the last stage of the journey. Pestalozzi offered to come with us as far as Solothurn, together with Stackelberg – who as our tutor designate would join us in Vienna in the spring.

We bade farewell to our new friends at the institute – and, for me, at the girls' school – and took to the road. Marianna had written to me that Vienna was aflutter with anticipation: two new symphonies by Beethoven, whose repute was growing by the second, would be heard for the first time. The cognoscenti were already ecstatic over his Piano Concerto No. 4, which he had performed in private at Prince Lobkowitz's. We could still make it, assuming all went according to plan.

On the dinner table at the Solothurn inn, we spread out our map and showed our companions our intended route. Zurich, Friedrichshafen, Munich, Salzburg, Linz, Vienna; and after Beethoven's concert I would continue to Ofen, while Pepi and the children went home. Pestalozzi nodded, and Stackelberg looked on, inscrutable.

I dislike inscrutability. People sometimes say Beethoven was inscrutable, but I disagree: he had little to hide, at least from us. I could read him like the proverbial book, and Pepi understood him so well that she knew the writing by heart. Stackelberg, in contrast, I could not work out at all; this had struck me upon our first meeting. Yet I was growing to admire the way he weighed up his words; his speech and his attitudes conveyed a gravitas that was not always reflected in his face. The boys liked him, not least because he offered to teach them how to play chess.

When the two men finally waved us off on the road to Zurich, Pepi gazed back at them over her shoulder, one arm raised high.

Napoleon, as far as I knew from the newspapers, was in

Spain, dealing with a widespread uprising and trying to retake Madrid. So it was with some surprise that I read a letter from Stackelberg that reached our hotel in Zurich soon after we did. It was addressed to Pepi, not to me.

'*Do not go via the northern route,*' he advised. '*May I suggest that you bypass Austria and aim straight away for your Hungarian homeland. My military contacts tell me that there may soon be a renewed state of war against Napoleon. There is talk of an uprising against him in Vienna.*'

Pepi's girls were still there, with Marie Bigot, who had written to us that all was well and they were looking forward to seeing us soon.

'Read me the rest? I can't bear to look,' Pepi pleaded.

Count von Stadion, in charge of Austrian preparations for war, considered rightly enough that Napoleon represented an existential threat to monarchial Europe; therefore any attempt to reach a compromise or agreement with him would be flawed, if not impossible. War would be an inevitable result of this attitude – and the fault of Napoleon alone. Austria, its teeth pulled, could no longer afford such extensive armies; instead, the count was planning to expand the forces through reservists and militia men tempted by the drumrolls of patriotism. If you love our great Emperor, fight for the Fatherland! If you are a true patriot, join up!

Why do people fall for this guff? The only way to be a true patriot – as I am – is to give your all for your country's future by building its repute, spreading its learning and culture, and above all, educating its young people. Do not send them to the battlefield to be mown down like grass by Napoleon's army!

'Yes, Tesi,' said Pepi, 'but what are we going to do?'

'Napoleon is still in Spain. This is something the baron

suggests *may* lie ahead. That does not mean it *is* going to happen.'

'Do we take the risk? Or…'

Stackelberg's letter continued. Instead of waiting for spring, he would come to us in Zurich, escort us via a different route to Hungary, and remain the boys' tutor thereafter.

'Oh, that's wonderful!' Pepi's eyes lit up. 'What a fine man – how noble and kind.'

I was dismayed. No Vienna? What of the concert? I could see nothing in the newspapers of the situation he described, and I always read them from first word to last over breakfast. Pepi thought it was not 'ladylike', or befitting to our class, to take such a keen interest in politics, but I was past thirty and past caring.

'It's not that I don't believe him,' I said, 'it's just that I am not sure he is not… over-anxious.'

'Baron von Stackelberg? Over-anxious? That seems a contradiction in terms.'

'Then… looking for an excuse to join us.'

'We would be fortunate to have him. I'll go and tell the front desk we will stay a few more days.'

'Are you sure, Pips? Aren't you worried about Viky and Sephine?' I could not have missed Viky more if she were my own daughter.

'They'll be fine. The Bigots are the most responsible of families. Everything has been perfect until now. Why should it not be?'


Baron von Stackelberg arrived two days later in a great tide of carriage, luggage and rosemary-scented eau de Cologne. He had worked everything out – and planned a longer trip than we had anticipated. Since the boys would receive their education from him en route, why should we not travel south? We had never seen the Italian lands. It was high time we did. We could therefore go via Trieste to Milan.

'There is one problem,' I said. 'We will soon run low on funds and we have requested that money is sent for us to collect in Munich. This route goes nowhere near Munich.'

'Please don't worry, Countess Therese,' Stackelberg said. 'I'm expecting some money from my estate soon, so I can cover everything until your funds have been secured. Just think: travel is the greatest education there is, and this would be an education for us all.'

Thus it was that a few days later, instead of heading towards the Rhine, we found ourselves going in the opposite direction, back towards Yverdon and beyond, towards Geneva and Mont Blanc. It was early December and the cold was ferocious, but under several layers of blankets we huddled in the carriage, with Carl on Pepi's lap and Stackelberg with Fritz in fur wraps up on the box, gazing at a great mass of white mountain rising from the black forests below. 'Just think, we might have missed this!' said the awestruck Pepi.

Descending towards Geneva, we began to feel the sting of a sharp wind, full of ice. The coachman whipped the poor horses to travel faster, but the clouds were turning a strange, evil bronze. Soon snow began to tumble as if emptied from a celestial gunpowder barrel. We were all shivering. The boys found it desperately exciting.

In Geneva, numb and shuddering with cold, we hurried to find a hotel; Stackelberg took a room a modest distance down the corridor from ours. We bundled the children into dry clothes and piled wood into the iron stove in the hope of thawing out. I hurried downstairs to order a hearty stew to be sent up to us for dinner, using extra cash to persuade the kitchen staff to work fast.

When I returned, Fritz was waiting for me in the doorway. 'Aunt Tesi, look at Mama.'

Pepi was lying half undressed on her bed, shaking and coughing. I felt her brow, which seemed hot as flame.

'I just need to rest,' she said. A spasm shook her. A damp scarlet spot appeared on the pillow case.

When Stackelberg tapped on our door, I was on the point of panic, donning the warmest cloak I possessed to go out and look for a doctor. One could see barely a metre beyond the window into the blizzard. Stackelberg saw Pepi and gasped with fright.

'Leave it to me,' he insisted. 'I know where to find a good physician. You stay here and take care of her.'

It was the onset of a terrifying illness. Stackelberg brought a doctor, who diagnosed colic. What rubbish. Delirious and weakened by a cough that was stronger than she was, my beloved sister walked in the shadow of the valley of death. Several nights we feared she would not live to see the dawn. Many times I thanked God for Stackelberg's good sense and solid presence; supposing this had happened when we were alone in a strange, frozen city?

After Pepi was asleep, and the boys too, Stackelberg and I would sit close to the stove and talk long and late into the night. There seemed nothing we could not explore: the will of God and our duty as His servants; the role of good education in producing responsible citizens; and how primitive our medical resources could one day seem as science developed. That might be too late for Pepi.

'I feel this is all my fault, Therese,' he mused one evening.

Thrown by circumstance into unexpected intimacy, we had begun to call one another by our first names. 'If I had not suggested this detour, you would have been safely back in Hungary, and Josephine reunited with her daughters.' The French, contrary to his expectation, were nowhere near Vienna.

'Please do not blame yourself, Christoph,' I said. 'Nobody could have foreseen this.'

Nevertheless, staring into the stove's glowing embers, I could not help thinking that perhaps I should have. I had seen our father suffering with consumption; and I knew Pepi had a chronic illness, one that could be with her for years at a low grade before overcoming her. It was no surprise if it flared up when she caught a chill or was under strain.

'Let us pray beside her,' he suggested. I agreed; it would help us feel better, if nothing else.

In her bedroom, Pepi was slumbering, her breath laboured. We placed our candles a safe distance from her. Damp with sweat, her hair clung to her cheek and neck. One bare arm trailed across the top of her bedclothes. Stackelberg averted his eyes for modesty's sake; nevertheless, I'd had time to notice him drinking in the sight of her slender form lying there, illness and all, with an expression that reminded me oddly of an owl assessing a distant mouse.

By the foot of the bed we knelt and uttered prayers, official and unofficial, Catholic and Protestant (he was a Lutheran), Latin and French. We put aside all differences of faith. It crossed my mind that if Stackelberg were in love with Pepi, if he could help her recover and give her a new life, then so be it. She could do much worse. When we had run out of prayers, we stayed for many minutes, deep in contemplation.

Then came a weak call. 'Tesi?'

I scrambled to my feet. Pepi was trying in vain to sit up against the pillow. 'Where am I?' she said. 'What happened? I remember being cold...'

'Countess Josephine!' Stackelberg's face lit up. 'You have come back to us.'

'What day is it?'

'You are our early Christmas present – it is 22 December.' He took her hand gently. 'You have been ill for weeks.'

Pepi gazed at me, her eyes filling with tears. 'That day?' Vienna was far away and Beethoven even now would be celebrating his success with his friends, and without us, in a favourite tavern...

We did not know until much later that, at this precise moment, the concert was still limping forward. It had started at half past six, was under-rehearsed, poorly delivered and unheated, and did not finish until ten-thirty. By the time the last notes of what became known as the 'Choral Fantasy' had faded into the winter night, most people in the chilly theatre had given up and gone home.

## 14

My dear niece,

Today you find us trapped in Geneva. We could not leave until Pepi was well enough, and so, as a strange family of mother, sons, aunt and tutor, we stayed for Christmas and New Year. Each day we encouraged Pepi to walk a little further with either me or Stackelberg. Two weeks into January she was strong enough for us to contemplate our departure. Nevertheless, the journey home was a frightening prospect, given the snowy mountains we must cross.

'It's unfortunate timing,' said Stackelberg. 'Really it would be better for you to be somewhere warm.'

'Ahh, I would love that.' Pepi gazed out at the snow. 'It's beautiful here, but I would love to feel sunshine.'

'Nowhere is warm now,' I said.

'Further south,' said Stackelberg, 'is… less cold. Have you ever been to the region of Tuscany?'

Pepi's eyes filled with longing. 'Oh, Tesi – couldn't we go? We'd see the palaces and galleries of Florence and the Leaning Tower of Pisa and—'

'We could!' Stackelberg encouraged her. 'We can find a spa for you to rest, then go and soak up everything Florence has to offer. Surely this is too good a chance to miss? When would you have another?'

'That's true. We should… We must…'

'How will we pay for it?' I reminded her. Of our small trunk of paper ducats, a scant few notes remained. We had not yet solved the Munich problem.

'Franz will help us if we ask him to send money to Florence. And Sauer must send me my income from the Palais.'

'My funds are on the way from Reval.' Stackelberg had already grabbed the map from his travelling case and was scanning it for routes. 'There are hot springs in Pisa, and from there it is an easy trip to Florence. I shall be your guide.'

To reach Florence, though, we would have to take not the easy road to Trieste, but a mountain pass.

'Mont Cenis.' Stackelberg pointed at a dramatic-looking conglomeration of lines on his map. 'This is the fastest and nearest. It will bring us over the Alps and down to Genoa and it's a good new road, built by Napoleon. But it is steep and high. Are you sure about this? Are you strong enough?'

Pepi rose to his bait. 'We are proud Magyár women and there is nothing we can't do. If I can survive such an illness, I can survive anything.'

'Therese?' Stackelberg glanced at me, as if in an afterthought.

'Thanks for asking,' I snapped. 'Very well, if we must.' Stackelberg and my sister had the bright, set look of fanatics who had made up their minds and would be swayed by nothing, however crazed the plan.

Saying 'Leave it to me,' Stackelberg went out to make arrangements; a few days later we were ready to go. He recruited a coachman with a closed carriage in which Pepi, the children and I would travel; he would follow, driving our barouche himself. A group of Savoyards would be our guides, for a healthy fee.

We set out into the first rays of dawn; our carriages were taken off their wheels and mounted onto sleds. Workers were busy shovelling a way through the drifts; to either side of the road, mounds of snow reared up above us. In the rising sun the ice glittered pink and gold; if it were to collapse, we would be in trouble. The boys shouted. Pepi gazed with bright eyes at the beauty all around. I folded my hands and prayed.

Soon I had to say Hail Marys in earnest. Coming up the pass the other way was a mule caravan carrying a cargo of massive wooden boxes. Our coachman, cursing, pulled us close to the snowy roadside, but with the swaying loads, the tramping animals and the trundling sleds, we stood not a chance. I leaned out and shouted, 'What in heaven's name do you think you are doing?'

'Madama,' came a yelled reply, 'you speak-a Frenchais? So leesten: *shiftez-vous.*'

Shivering, terrified and squashed, we clambered down. 'Italian drivers,' Stackelberg muttered.

Amid the mule droppings, the Italians clustered around our carriage-on-sled and between them and our guides hoisted it onto the mountain slope and a jutting ledge of rock above the road. We had to stand, backs pressed to a wall of snow, the river roaring in the ravine, while dozens of sleds passed by, the slush flying into our faces. Whatever would this do to Pepi?

After what seemed a decade, the end of the caravan became visible. Stackelberg and our guides importuned the last few men and persuaded them to move the carriage back down to the road – otherwise they would have left it, and us, sitting there.

Amazed to be alive, we went on our way. Now the full magnificence of the pass came into view. White upon blue, the mountains sang their beauty; sunbeams caught in the ice and scattered rainbows over us. Pepi, the cold forgotten, leaned out and cried out for joy at the glory. The boys followed suit. Until –

'Mama, look! Soldiers!'

'Soldiers? What soldiers?'

A sizeable battalion was riding towards us. Our sled came to an abrupt stop.

'They're Napoleon's. We have to let them pass,' the coachman informed us.

This was intolerable. Pepi's shaky health had been put in peril through the incident with the mule caravan; now this lot could take hours to pass while we waited, yet again, in the snow. Even though instinctive terror of a mass of men chilled me still further, I don't believe I remembered to wonder what Napoleon's soldiers were doing, marching towards Savoy.

Stackelberg leapt down from the barouche and ran forward to us: 'Don't worry, they will soon be gone. They will be conscripts and no more eager to attack us than they are to serve His Nibs.'

'There must be hundreds of them.' I glared at the incongruous ranks of men with the crests of their uniforms glaring in the sunlight. 'We need to get Pepi out of the cold.'

'I don't think there's much we can do against the French army...'

Pathetic! I threw open the carriage door and jumped into the slush. I heard Stackelberg's voice behind me, protesting, but if a grown man would not do his job and protect us, I would do it myself.

The French commander, no doubt startled by the daring of this strange, small woman, brought his men to an abrupt halt. I half walked, half slid towards him, then stood in front of them all, my ankles shaking with fright beneath my skirts.

'I beg of you, good sirs – in the name of my sick sister in our carriage, might you, on this occasion, be kind enough to let us go by first? She has been in mortal danger. I would give my life to save hers.'

I have to hand it to the French: at their best they can be gallant. The officer at once raised one arm and gave a shout; and the conscripts ranked themselves to the side of the road. To our astonishment, Napoleon's troops waited while our carriages slithered past them towards the mountain slope.

Once we were through, safe from any misdirected or malicious guns, our laughter was intense – and the downward road was much faster than the upward. Pepi's face was suffused with happiness: 'Tesi, you're incredible! You have saved all our lives.'


Genoa! Sparkling before us was the sun's path on the water, the same conduit to heaven that opened to me on the Martonvásár lake and at Yverdon – but now it was infinite, its golden light pulsating towards the wide horizon. Pepi and I joined hands to share the thrill of this, our first sight of the sea.

'In my country, you can sit on the beach and watch the sun setting into the waves,' Stackelberg told us while we strolled under the palm trees by the harbour, breathing deep on the salty air. 'Every summer thousands of people come from far and wide to sing together on the shore. You would love it, Josephine.'

Sometimes the smallest signals betray the greatest perils, if only we could notice. That day, I was merely a little annoyed that Stackelberg would address Pepi with such a phrase, but not me.

Those signals, individually, might have seemed insignificant, but together they built. Day after day, they took us further down the road, further from Vienna, further from safety, into a danger of which we still knew nothing. Lulled by warmth and luxury, I tried to forget my doubts.

From Genoa, we travelled to Pisa; Pepi relished the hot springs, Stackelberg brought her glasses of healing waters and I took the boys to see the Leaning Tower. We went up its slippery marble steps together, until I disgraced myself by glancing over the precipice that was its interior void, becoming convinced that the building was about to collapse and insisting we must get out at once.

'It's terrifying,' I told Pepi and Stackelberg later. 'I wasn't prepared for that.'

Stackelberg looked amazed.

'You haven't been up there?' I asked. 'I thought you knew this country like the back of your hand.'

'Not all of it.' A graceful acknowledgement, delivered with his warmest smile.

The Leaning Tower, my dear, is still standing to this day. It was in Florence that another edifice began to crumble beneath me.


At first, even I was overexcited. Walking by the Arno; crossing the Ponte Vecchio, where shop windows glittered with golden trinkets; navigating the narrow lanes of terracotta and ochre houses until we rounded a corner to see the black, white and green marble of the Duomo, the Campanella and the Baptistry ahead of us against the aquamarine sky. Eating dinners trimmed with fragrant basil and tomatoes bursting with juice. Walking past the Palazzo Vecchio on the Piazza della Signoria, where Fritz and Carl stared, astonished, at the naked form of Michelangelo's David.

Then... queuing at the bank for our money from Vienna and Ofen. Franz had sent some, but not much. He had also written us a scolding note, wanting to know what we were doing in Florence in any case and reminding us to write to Marie Bigot to explain the delay.

Sauer had sent Pepi some of the money due to her. 'Are you sure that is all?' she asked the bank clerk. 'It should be at least double.'

But the figures on the paper matched the banknotes in the envelopes that the clerk presented to us. We counted them three times.

'Has my money come from Reval?' our companion enquired. 'I am Baron Christoph von Stackelberg.'

Our clerk, with a little bow, went to a back room to check. He returned, shaking his head: 'I'm afraid, my lord, we have nothing in this name.'

Stackelberg's eyes narrowed and when the clerk shrank back, he let fly. Pepi and I winced with embarrassment: this was not the behaviour one should expect of a nobleman.

'Come, dear tutor,' I intervened at last. 'It is not this gentleman's fault if someone in Reval has failed to do his job.' Were we going to have to support Stackelberg after all? I was beginning to fear so.

'What's the matter with them?' Stackelberg fumed while we walked back to our hotel. 'Who *do* we blame – those who are sending the money, the Florentine postal service or the bank staff filching it for themselves?'

Pepi tried to soothe him. 'These are good, hardworking people. We should not judge them so cruelly.'

'You always see the best in everyone, Pepi,' I encouraged her.

'You are quite right, Josephine.' Stackelberg, apparently contrite, paused in his tracks. 'Wait here. I wish to make amends.' He dashed away down a side street where we had spotted a florist's shop.

A minute later, he was filling Pepi's arms with branches of spring blossom. Above the florets, her eyes were luminous, and the sun lifted the golden lights in her dark hair. In a pink and white spring dress, she looked angelic even to me. It was, as Luigi had written, her whole being that drew him to her; and here was that entire, enchanting self, shining out at us. A lost expression filled Stackelberg's face. 'Please forgive me, Countess Josephine.' He bowed low to her. 'I, your tutor, have learned a lesson from you today.'

'Dear tutor,' Pepi said, 'I think I would forgive you anything.'


The hotel in which we had taken rooms was within a small Renaissance palazzo; in the central courtyard, blossoming orange trees surrounded a delicate fountain. Waking the next morning, I could hear nothing but the soothing trickle and the breeze in the leaves. I seemed to be alone. Pepi had left a note: 'We are taking the boys for a walk.' I waited, but they did not return.

After several hours, I put on my hat and wandered off to tour some churches by myself. I sat for a while in the cool marble of Santa Maria Novella, then lit a candle for my father.

'Look at Auntie Tesi – she's *so* disapproving,' Pepi joked to the boys over dinner later on. 'Dear, dear. We went out without her!'

'I'm glad someone thinks it's funny.' I was still smarting from the upset.

'Don't worry, Therese,' said Stackelberg. 'We will make it up to you. Leave it to me.'

Pepi's name day fell on 19 March. At daybreak I heard Stackelberg's step outside my door. I slipped out to see what he was up to.

'Shh.' He smiled. 'I have placed a little order at the flower shop. Leave it to me, and don't wake her up – I'll be back in ten minutes…'

When he returned, he was carrying a mound of garlands of golden and white blooms: 'If we put them around her very quietly, she'll find them when she opens her eyes.' The flowers smelled so sweet, the idea was so touching and the carefree atmosphere so irresistible that I assented.

Pepi did not lock her door lest the children should need her in the night, so we slunk in. The curtains admitted just enough sunlight for us to see what we were doing – and Stackelberg reached up to loop the garlands around the crest of the bed and its baldachin canopy, while I balanced the remainder over the marble bedside table and the hump of my sister's feet under the coverlet.

She did not stir; we left her to sleep while we fetched coffee and custard-filled cakes for breakfast. Waiting outside the door with the two excited children, we finally heard her cry of delight, which we took as a cue to carry the lot in to her, singing.

How could I have let Stackelberg go into that bedroom? But by then he was part of the family. He had made himself indispensable, guiding us through the treasures of this Florentine paradise, finding lodgings that befitted us, giving the boys lessons every day and making sure we all prayed together in the morning and evening, though I could have seen to that myself. Even so…

After breakfast we walked to Fiesole, together this time – for more than a week now, I had been left behind, always with a different excuse. This excursion led us uphill beneath dark cypress trees and past grand villas that enjoyed views across the russet-tiled rooftops and the hills beyond the city, everything topped like a cherry by the red geometric dome of the cathedral. When Pepi stopped to get her breath, Stackelberg offered her his arm. The boys bounded ahead; I brought up the rear. I felt like an extra in this little party. What nonsense: Stackelberg was the stranger. Why were they excluding me? I banished such thoughts; I did not want to spoil Pepi's special day.

Later the spring sunset blazed amber and lilac, and after putting the boys to bed, then dressing in our favourite splendours for dinner – I in white with a yellow shawl and my pearls, Pepi in blossom pink with her ruby necklace – we went out to an esteemed restaurant across the street to continue celebrating, flushed with our day of exercise and fresh air. Stackelberg ordered Italian red wine, an eighteenth-century vintage. 'This is exceptional – one of the best Nebbiolos I've tasted.' He swirled it in its glass under his long nose. 'Therese, some more? Josephine? It suits you so well. It matches your ruby.' He lifted his glass, then reached across to hold it close to her, so that the candlelight cast the liquid's purple glow onto her skin.

The bottle was nearly empty when Pepi asked about Stackelberg's trips to the Italian lands. When had he been here? Where did he travel?

'This is my first time,' he declared.

We were speechless for a moment.

'But Christoph,' I said eventually, 'you are our guide, you organise everything, you know your way around...'

'True.' He laughed. 'Yet I am as new to Florence as you are!'

There was a startled, almost anguished pause. Then Pepi began to giggle, and couldn't stop. Stackelberg and I joined in despite ourselves; the other guests tried not to smile at our peculiar trio's hilarity. I had a sip of wine to calm myself down, then another, and by the time we crossed the hotel courtyard and climbed the stairs to our rooms, I was so tired and tipsy, to my shame, that Stackelberg had to take my arm as well as Pepi's. At our doors, we stopped. Stackelberg opened mine first. 'There you are, dear Therese. Goodnight! Sleep well.'

'Goodnight, Christoph, goodnight Pips.' I felt as if I were in a fairground, playing a game of catching the furniture as it spun. Somehow I managed to disrobe, wash and tumble into bed. My head was too furry to make sense of Stackelberg's revelation. He had given us the impression that he knew this country well... hadn't he? But I must have fallen asleep within seconds.

In the dead of night a sound woke me. What was it? Muffled voices? A woman's high tone; a man's low one, soothing, trying to hush her. Was it from the street? Locals having a domestic tiff? Was I dreaming? There came a soft cry; then silence.

My curtains bled moonlight; the scent of orange blossom drifted in on the night air. I was settling back into slumber when another cry jolted me, then a soft, regular beat, as if an item of furniture were being shunted back and forth. The tempo picked up; the volume too. There came the woman's cry, louder – and now I shot to consciousness, for it was Pepi – and then a low, loud grunt from the man. Silence. And... tension released; a voice, strange, relaxed...

By the time I understood, it was much too late.

Oh, my sweet sister. My dear, profound, delicate, ruby-red, damaged sister. I should have seen it sooner. I was deceived; I failed to guard you.


The boys and I went down to breakfast early. Pepi trailed in later, pallid and rather dishevelled.

'I am not well,' she said. She scarcely looked at the children, took some coffee, then excused herself. After a few minutes, Stackelberg sauntered in with a brusque greeting, swallowed a pastry in a few gulps – and disappeared too.

I knocked on Pepi's door. She was back in bed, fortunately alone.

'Please, Tesi, let me rest,' she begged. I did not see her again until dinner time.

The next day the two of them announced they were taking the boys to see the Botticelli paintings in the Uffizi Gallery – and left me behind.

Now it was too late to stop anything at all.

## *15*

My dearest niece,

You have not known the power of silence until you have experienced my mother's. The silence, for instance, with which she and Franz greeted our bedraggled party when we walked into Martonvásár out of a summer rainstorm, home at last – though still without Pepi's girls – after nearly ten months.

Their gaze fell not onto the boys, who were unusually quiet; nor upon me – perhaps they mistook me for the maid, since due to general anxiety and much reduced intake of food when we ran out of money, I had lost a great deal of weight. No: they stared at the shape of Pepi's body. Her waist had expanded; her swollen breasts strained against her bodice. Pepi had had four children. We all knew exactly how she looked when she was pregnant.

'I'll, er, help bring our stuff in,' I faltered.

Pepi's eyes glistened with tears of shame.

We passed a terrible evening. I tried to play the piano; my fingers were stiff and awkward after months removed from their accustomed exercise. Mother locked herself in the office. Franz saddled his horse and went for a long ride. Pepi stayed in bed and wept. She was bereft on another front besides: Vienna was occupied by French soldiers and she had no idea how her girls were.

I offer you no reward, my dear, for your guess as to who had to present an explanation for her condition. Suffice it to say it was not Pepi.

'Where is he? I shall challenge him.' In Franz's eyes shone a genuine desire to murder Stackelberg.

'In Pest, awaiting word.'

'Why isn't he running for his life?'

'He wants to marry her.'

'Why hasn't he, then? I shall kill him!'

We had no idea how good a shot Stackelberg might be. I would hazard a guess that Franz could fell him with one stroke, if sober. But a duel might kill one of them, either leaving us without our beloved brother, or Pepi without the father of her unborn infant. Moreover, there'd be extra public scandal to add to the disgrace of an illegitimate child. There was only one solution.

Mother and I ventured together to Pepi's room and found her in bed, nauseous and crying.

'You must marry him at once,' Mother said.

Pepi sat up, her face distorted with fury. 'I will not!'

'Don't be silly.'

Pepi fixed Mother with a glare almost as terrifying as her own. 'You wanted me to leave Deym when I already had Viky, because he hadn't any money. Do you believe Christoph von Stackelberg is any better?'

'It's a bit late for scruples. Pepi, dearest.' The word

clunked. 'You must have feelings for him if you have got yourself into this state.'

'"Got myself into this state"?' Pepi echoed. 'Mother, have you *any idea* how wrong you are?'

'Are you saying he forced you?' I asked.

'You were there. You were next door. You could have stopped him. You believed all his rubbish. You thought he was an honourable man.'

I reeled. 'Oh, it's *my* fault?'

'Couldn't you see what he was doing? Couldn't you have intervened?'

I was so hurt – since *she* could not see what he was doing in excluding me from their excursions – that words failed me.

'Tesi,' said Mother, 'please explain.'

'At first Baron von Stackelberg painted himself as the ideal tutor for the boys. He was our rock, our organiser, our spiritual leader and a man of principle. We trusted him. And then he began to separate Pepi and the boys from me. Pepi, I thought it was simply that he wanted you to himself, and you concurred. I would wander alone, while you went off together, taking Carl and Fritz. Quite the little family. And then it was your name day…'

'I have never seen you as affected by wine as you were that night,' Pepi said.

'Tesi, you were drunk?' I thought Mother would strike me.

'So were they.'

'I had been so ill.' Pepi was seized by a fresh flood of tears. 'I nearly died. I was weak and could not fight back.'

'Pepi, *did* he force you?' Mother demanded. 'Then Franz must kill him.'

What I'd heard that night had not sounded like a rape. Pepi's cries had been not pained or frightened, but rather joyful… hadn't they? Had I been too dim-witted through wine to know the difference? Still, I had seen no evidence that he had spent a night with her since. I'd heard him once, knocking at her door, whispering her name, to no avail.

'I don't love him,' said Pepi. 'I don't want to sleep with him, I don't want to live with him, I don't want to marry him. I don't see why I must be trapped forever with a man I do not even *like*.'

'You're saying not that he violated you, but that he took advantage of you,' I suggested. 'He seduced you. He used every trick in the book.'

'Where does one stop and the other begin? He made me feel sorry for him… he made me feel compassion for his suffering in his longing… but it *was* against my will. I was not physically strong enough to stop him. Oh, dear God…' Pepi doubled up again. Mother and I looked down at the wooden floorboards while she vomited into the bowl beside her bed.

I could find no sleep that night. In the end I slunk out into the grounds, avoiding the dogs, and made my way by moonlight to Father's memorial. There, on the cool grass, I turned over and over in my mind the errors and deceits that had landed us in this desperate position. What should we do? The girls were still with the patient Marie Bigot. Someone would have to fetch them from French-occupied Vienna and explain – at least to Viky, who was old enough to understand – the minimum of what was going on.

Our family honour was at stake; if Pepi's disgrace became known, it would besmirch us all. I had not dared write even to Lotti of these events. Obviously Pepi must marry Stackelberg, and retire out of sight until the baby arrived; then they must somehow convince everyone that the birth took place nine months after their marriage. This was a social issue, not a religious one; my faith is strong, but I do not see it as a stick with which to beat my sister. At least the Deym children would probably not be taken away if she married Stackelberg, who was a nobleman, whatever 'noble' meant. I ran one hand over my father's engraved name. For once I felt grateful that he was not here to witness this mess.

My heart bled for Luigi. I made up my mind: I must go to Vienna myself to collect Viky and Sephine, and I must see him.

I had no idea what I might find there. The French forces had beaten our troops to pulp at the battles of Wagram and Znaim. Around 72,000 men on both sides had lost their lives. Vienna had been under siege in May; this invasion, unlike the last one, had been ferocious and destructive from the start. Now Napoleon was installed once more at Schönbrunn. I imagined him strutting through the grounds, putting his chubby little hand through the menagerie wires to pat the wallabies.


Mother went silent again when I told her my plan. My stomach contracted at the thought of my friends – Marianna and her sister, Countess Erdödy, Beethoven himself. We had been too wound up in our own problems to worry much about anyone else.

I wrote frantic letters. Marie Bigot wrote back: all was calm, if damaged, and inflation was desperate, but Vienna was still Vienna; they were at home, the girls were well and I must come and stay. Marianna wrote too: life had been difficult and the currency was being destroyed. Worst, though,

Haydn had died in May – not in war, but of old age. While he lay on his deathbed, the cannons were roaring at the city walls. Marianna was still weeping for him.

No word of Beethoven. Nor any of Toni. If he had not been slaughtered earlier by Napoleon's troops, the numbers involved in the latest battle were so vast that one could scarcely hope he had survived.

I wandered alone through the streets of broken Vienna, observing, keeping clear of military patrols. The shelling had blown gouges from the city walls, which looked as if a Titan had taken giant bitefuls, crunched and spat them out. Workers were busy, three months after Napoleon's second triumph over us, clearing rubble and rebuilding, their necks and faces carmine with effort in the summer heat. The palaces on the nearby streets were peppered with the marks of bullets and shrapnel. At the Palais Deym, seeing a group of soldiers bounding out of the main entrance, I concealed myself round a corner, deciding against venturing in. Incredibly, it was still intact. Other buildings close to the walls were ruined, their entrails exposed, those once grand interiors coated in grime. Clambering weeds had sent exploratory tendrils through the glassless window frames. Urchins were scavenging for objects of value amid the wreckage.

Out of curiosity I drifted towards the palace where we had attended our first party and met Marianna and Schuppanzigh. The roof was shattered; broken slate and glass littered the courtyard through which we had pranced for joy ten years ago. I forced back a lump in my throat, and pressed on.

Anyone who could leave had gone. The Guicciardis'

home was shuttered and boarded: our aunt and uncle were in Naples with Julie and her family. The Graben, usually teeming with shoppers, diners and pleasure-seekers, was empty and stinking of refuse. Rats scuttled past the abandoned plague memorial. The void felt more alarming than angry crowds, the heat more threatening than the snow-drifts on Mont Cenis.

Groups of Austrian soldiers nevertheless stood carousing outside the taverns; Napoleon had decided to let ten thousand members of the Vienna national guard remain armed and nominally in charge. Two young maidservants, concealed in shawls despite the summer heat, hurried by, heads lowered. The men's lewd shouts and whistles followed them like dogs. I hung back – would they chase and attack those poor girls, and if so, would I dare intervene? Thank goodness, they were more interested in their drink, and as I slipped past, they left me alone; in my old-fashioned black dress I was unobtrusive, almost invisible. This was useful. Perhaps it was then that black became my habitual garb. Why would I need any other?

I fell into Marianna and Antonia's welcoming embrace. We settled in their music room with herbal infusions to drink: coffee could not be obtained. They hoped to restart their salon concerts in the autumn, should anyone be able to manage what used to be called a 'season'.

'Everything costs double what it used to,' Marianna said. 'Oh, Tesi, how I wish I had seen Haydn again – the streets were too dangerous for two old ladies…'

'You mustn't chastise yourself,' I said. 'He can see you now, from a better world.'

'God willing,' said Antonia. 'How is your lovely sister?'

I had rehearsed some lines. 'She was very ill during our

travels. She is better, but fragile, which is why I have come to fetch her daughters.'

'You must have loved Italy,' said Marianna.

'I was pleased to experience it.' Not to be open with someone I trusted brought home the misery that Pepi and Stackelberg had unleashed upon us all. 'Marianna, please tell me, what news of Beethoven?'

'He is in Baden at the Sauerhof Hotel,' she said. 'He's not dared to go back to the Pasqualati House, though by some miracle it is still standing. You should see him if you can face a trip out of town.'

'What has he been doing? And writing? And how surviving?'

'He has written a wonderful piano trio, but I could not say what else. Things are not easy, as you can see. Napoleon turned twenty howitzers upon us and the noise – it was unbearable, you had to stop up your ears... You know Beethoven's brother Kasper Karl – or rather, his wife, Johanna – has a house in Alservorstadt with a good, deep cellar? He went there for shelter, and had to press pillows around his head to protect what remains of his hearing.'

I closed my eyes; I could see him. Our Master, cowering in the dark, crouching as he had by the brook at Jedlesee. All because of the man he had once revered.


It was a coach ride of several hours through the countryside to the resort that Luigi loved. Here there was no damage: no bullet-holes, no atmosphere of imminent doom. Arriving at the sprawling Sauerhof Hotel and asking for Beethoven, one might imagine oneself still as safe and secure as if the Holy Roman Empire had never fallen.

In his room, Luigi's back was curved over a desk in the

window; I heard the thread of a hum and the scratch of his pen before he turned. The sight of me sent a shock wave through him.

'Tesi? You, here?'

A second later his palms were wrapping around mine. We clasped hands for a long time, as never before. Had he been my brother, I could have embraced him, so powerful was the relief and joy at being together again. 'How splendid it is to see you,' he said. 'At times I've wondered if you would ever return.'

'Luigi, how could I not?' I turned my head so he would not see the tears in my eyes.

His face had acquired shadows like rainclouds. His stock was fastened close around his neck, despite the warm weather, and his waistcoat and jacket hung loose upon his torso. Being an elegant spa hotel, this room had had no chance to acquire the usual Beethovenian chaos, but he had brought a piano, on which perched a hefty supply of books, on the top a volume of Christoph Christian Sturm, whose writings he had always loved. A copy of Goethe's *The Sorrows of Young Werther* sat splayed beside an armchair and a box of brand-new, printed music lurked in one corner.

'You must have the new trio,' he mumbled, rummaging in it. 'Here.' He straightened up, volume in hand. 'Franz will do the cello part well and I'm sure our Lord Falstaff, dear old Schuppanzigh, will play with you. You know he got married? To a woman as fat as he is! They make a fine pair.'

'Luigi, you look too thin.'

'What's that? Speak louder.'

I flushed, then obeyed.

'Curse these ears. Curse this war.' He stared beyond me to the window, the view affording only greenery and calm. 'It is madness how much everything costs now, while my income only decreases. I am trying to induce my publishers to pay me a little bit faster, or in other currencies.'

'Do you think we will have peace again soon?' He was one of few men I knew who did not object to women interesting themselves in world affairs.

'What worries me is that Napoleon did not come legitimately to power.' He paced away to fetch me a glass of water. 'Spa water. Sulphury, but good for you... He will want to hold on to it – power, that is, not sulphur – and for that purpose there has never been anything as useful as war. It makes him look stronger than he is. One day he will overreach his ambitions and be destroyed by his own errors of judgment. That is the only way we will ever have peace.'

'So many lives are lost. So many people destroyed. And more, if he continues.'

'Don't imagine that he cares. He does not. And I speak as one who admired him – to be truthful, I still do, in a peculiar way. Enough... Tesi, tell me – how is...?'

I did not want to have to shout this, so I moved closer to him. 'Luigi, it is not good news.'

'She is – alive? Or not alive? Tell me, quickly. I can't bear it.'

'She is alive. She was ill at the start of the year, but we travelled to Florence and the hot sun has healed her.'

'God be praised. May I... see her?'

'Luigi, she will remarry. He is a baron, from Reval on the Baltic Sea, a disciple of Pestalozzi. He became tutor to her boys after we visited Pestalozzi's institute.'

'And they are in love.'

'He is in love with her. I would not say she is in love with him. But I think they will marry.'

'If she is not in love, she should not,' he said at once.

'She is...' I lost my courage. 'Alone.'

'And it must be a nobleman. The same old story. Dear God, what will it *take*?' He stamped a foot. I hoped the hotel floorboards were strong. 'Such misery, Tesi. Such loneliness, facing the world without a true companion – and it is so unnecessary.'

He had not even begun to forget her.

'Supposing it were to turn out,' I ventured, 'that she was in some way unworthy of you?'

'Impossible. Nothing could make her less than perfect. Nothing can wrench her from her place in my heart. Tesi, if she is lonely, may I not hope? Might she take the risk of defiance?'

Was he insane? Could he *still* be hoping for her, an Enlightenment optimist after all? 'The external forces are so immovable now that there is no point maintaining any hope. It must be over, and forever.'

'So that she can marry a man she doesn't love... Tesi, thank you for being patient with me. My sphere of mortal longing is far from your ideal life of learning and wisdom. Whatever happens, please will you look after her for me?'

The gentleness, directness and openness of his words was so far removed from anything I had heard Stackelberg utter that I could have cried.

Later, he walked with me to the stagecoach. Our pace slowed as the moment of parting approached.

'Please, write to me in Hungary,' I said. 'Do not vanish from our lives, however painful it may seem, because we Brunsviks cannot live without you.'

'Nor I,' he said, 'without the Brunsviks. Will you send me your portraits – all of you?'

'We will. You shall have my painting as a Greek priestess, and miniatures of Pepi and Lotti...' If I spoke further I feared losing control over my emotions. Sending portraits was a way of parting on affectionate terms, but parting nonetheless.

The coachman sounded the horn call: it was time to go. Luigi handed me up into the carriage. 'Farewell, worthy Therese,' he said. 'Thank you.'

When Viky, Sephine and I reached Martonvásár, Pepi and the boys had gone.

'Neither I nor Franz want her here,' Mother said.

I forgot my sex, my station, my nobility, and yelled at her. 'You can't throw out your own daughter when she's pregnant!'

'Try me.' Mother was as icy as Geneva. 'She has shamed us. We told her, your brother and I, that we will accept her back once she has married *him*, and not a moment before. I researched it, Tesi: I wrote to a nobleman of my acquaintance in Vác and arranged for her to take a house he owns. I packed her trunk for her. I gave her everything she will need and Takács drove her there, to escort her and help her unpack.'

'But how she must have suffered from such rejection!'

'Mind that shrewish tone with me, Tesi. Your sister has sinned against God. I always knew she would. She has in her the marks of lascivious living, the taste for sin, and for such a woman to be widowed while in her prime…'

'You are talking about your daughter. The mother of your grandchildren.' I turned away in disgust. 'Speaking of whom, does this mean I must "return" our two little angels to Vác? And what of him? Are they married?'

'*He* is living nearby and visiting – as tutor. She is consulting those high-and-mighty Deyms, ascertaining the status

of the children in the event of this marriage, but she says she
*has not decided.*'

'And Franz...?'

'Refused to challenge him. In short, your brother is a coward. Men are not what they used to be in my young day...'

Vác sits among fertile hills at the crest of a bend in the Danube, about fifty kilometres due north of Ofen and Pest. Takács could drive us there in half a day. I had coaxed Magda back to Pepi with a pay rise; she was with her now, thank goodness. Pepi knew nobody there – a good reason to choose the place – but she would have nothing to do except wait.

The baby, a little girl, was born in December. In February 1810, Pepi quietly married Stackelberg. This outcome was inevitable, even if it had taken a long time under the circumstances.

'What did you tell the neighbours?' I asked Pepi when I was allowed to visit them for a few days. We were alone, the baby nursing in her arms.

'That I am a widow – which I am – and that Stackelberg is our saviour in our misfortune.' Her tone was flat. 'We are looking forward to a bright future together.'

'Don't they suspect?'

'I expect so. But there are many widows today, Tesi, all over the Empire. Come, look at Laura – isn't she a darling?'

Maria Laura: a name for an angel. Pepi handed her to me. I cuddled her, a tumult of mixed emotions sweeping over me. A newborn girl, curling her fingers around one of mine just as all her siblings and eldest cousin had in their turn. How could such perfection be the result of coercion and deceit?

'Why "Laura"?'

'Because of Petrarch,' said Pepi. 'She was... conceived in Petrarch's land.'

Laura was the great Italian poet's eternal beloved and muse – one who married someone else and could never be his. I doubted Stackelberg appreciated the irony. As far as he knew, Beethoven was no more to Pepi than a favourite composer.

'I shall put her out with a wet-nurse,' said Pepi, 'and she will stay there for a few years.'

'Years?' I echoed. The baby's hand was still clutching my finger.

'Well, we can't stay here forever. We'll have to go back to Vienna sooner or later. I can't just... appear with a baby.'

'But later you can't just appear with a three-year-old.'

'It will be easier by then to conceal her age. Don't worry, Tesi – I will have her back, I just need to be careful about how I manage it.'

'What of the Deyms? Are they content to let you keep the children?'

'Thank almighty God, I have persuaded them that Christoph is an honourable man from a fine, noble family.'

Who knows, I thought, kissing Laura's forehead. Perhaps everything will turn out well. Storms can sometimes give way, as in Beethoven's *Pastoral Symphony*, to beautiful sunsets and a song of thanksgiving. Perhaps you, my new little niece, will be the one to heal us all.

Wrapped in our winter coats and cloaks, we walked down to the Danube, leaving Magda in charge of Laura at the house. The river, swollen with snow and rain, powered by in a magnificent curve. We shivered, watching it from beside a low railing on the embankment. Sephine began to whimper; Pepi bent at once to comfort her. Viky and I gazed down into the surging water that slapped at the stone beneath us.

'What's that?' Viky pointed.

A shape was drifting towards us; long, sallow under the waves, like a bizarre sea monster with a disarray of protruding sections. I grabbed Viky and turned her away. Nausea was sweeping across me. The object was a naked corpse, its features indiscernible in the grey-green mess of its visage, the thigh bone and hip socket exposed where the flesh had washed or rotted away.

Pepi did not divert her eyes from her children. 'I've seen these before. They are carried downstream from the battlefields.'

'The battles were months ago!'

'But there seems no end to it. Dozens of thousands of young men, slaughtered like animals – for what? That maniac's ambition to rule all of Europe? Even their clothes were looted from them on the field.'

'What does Stackelberg say about it?'

'He says we must look the other way and pray to God.'

'He's never been a soldier, then.'

'Him? He wouldn't last two seconds in the military.'

'I don't suppose he would.'

'I thought you would agree with him,' Pepi needled, 'you being so avid about prayer.'

I hoped Pepi's words did not bode ill; this was no time to alienate her family. 'There's no point praying if you are not willing to do something practical in which God can support you.' I am a great believer in the maxim that God helps those who help themselves.

I had sent Beethoven the gift of our portraits. Now at

Martonvásár a return present awaited me that eclipsed any I had ever received. A manuscript. A fair copy, in his hand and with his signature, of a work about to go to print: a new piano sonata. Unusually, it was in F sharp major. Where the 'Appassionata' was furious, this one was soft and wise. The melodies were carefree, as if this remote and spiritual key lifted them above all worldly troubles. Clarity, good sense and balance were required throughout its two movements: a voice of reason in a dark world, the sonic image of the way that I personally function. It was fiddly to play, with tricky repeated notes and an unforgiving passage of octaves in contrapuntal voices between the hands – but the Master knew I liked a challenge.

At the top, the words: '*À Comtesse Therese von Brunsvik*'. Beethoven had written a sonata that was not only dedicated to me, but written *for* me – in a way that nobody but I and those closest to me would ever understand.

# 16

My dear,

Jean-Jacques Rousseau might disagree, but people do not change just because they sign a piece of paper declaring them married. Pepi did not lose her sensibility, her tenacity and her tenderness – though she was thirty-one and her bloom was diminishing through illness and exhaustion. Stackelberg, for his part, did not stop being a deceitful, manipulative, pretentious liar. At first, he seemed to try – but with him, the important word would always be 'seem'.

I steeled myself for another sojourn with them. 'I love her so much,' he said to me, after dinner one evening. 'I can never love any woman but her. She is my ideal, my muse, my Julie of whom I have always dreamed.' Rousseau's *Julie, or The New Heloïse* was Stackelberg's favourite book, with a heroine whose inner conflicts were resolved by the triumph of head over heart, transformed by her voluntary renunciation of extraneous passion upon her marriage. (I suspect Aunt Susanna, who loved reading as much as Father did, had named her daughter in tribute. There any resemblance ended.)

By rejecting true love for the sake of her children, Pepi

had perhaps forced her will to conquer her emotions. To me, she was more like the Greek princess Iphigenia, sacrificed upon the altar at which she had expected to be married.

'I would rather be *Goethe*'s Iphigenia, and I'm sure you would too,' said Pepi, well out of Stackelberg's earshot. In Goethe's version, Iphigenia has escaped murder and become a priestess. At one point she explains that a woman's words can be as powerful as a man's sword.

'Tesi, listen.' She was twisting her hands together. 'We will be moving back to Vienna soon. Christoph will manage the museum and will not after all be tutor to the boys. So, I was wondering: would you consider coming with us, and teaching the children? Viky is keen to be schooled and she will prove your most willing student. And we won't only be in Vienna, of course. We're buying a country place for the summer months.'

I wondered if the truth was that she could not face life without some company. Being with Stackelberg must be far worse than being alone. My spirits lifted a little, nonetheless, at the idea of educating Viky and Sephine.

'Where in the country?' I asked.

'We are looking for something that befits our station.' Pepi's nose lifted a little. She was now a baroness, a diminished status from that of countess, but this did not seem to sway her towards modesty. 'Christoph found a house near Prague, but it was far too small.'

'So where will you look?'

'There is a truly wonderful estate for sale at Witschapp.'

'Where's that?'

Pepi beckoned me into the room she was using as her study – a piano, a desk, piles of books – it almost reminded me of Beethoven's propensity for mess. Spread out on the piano was a map. She pointed. This estate, about which she had been enjoying a lengthy correspondence with the current owner, was near Znaim in Moravia, not too distant from Vienna. As she described it, I wondered how much of it was real.

The castle belonged to one Countess Trauttmansdorff, a widowed representative of a royal family with branches in many corners of Europe and even in England. The building's oldest parts dated back to the twelfth century. It had an English-style park full of oak trees. Its estate included a sprawl of good farming land, well populated with sheep, cattle and, not least, vineyards. 'Christoph is very experienced in farming, from the estate in Reval,' she said.

Farming? Stackelberg? He had spent most of the past decade travelling through Europe with his archaeologist brother, dreaming of finding a Rousseauesque Julie, talking to God and studying, supposedly, with Pestalozzi. Still, perhaps he would enjoy developing expertise in winemaking; this place was in the best Moravian region for viticulture.

I browsed through the letters, with her permission. Then I sought Stackelberg out in his own study.

'Christoph, this estate – it's enormous and it costs a fortune. Please forgive me, but is this wise?'

Stackelberg sat back, folding his arms behind his head and looking past rather than at me. 'It will pay off. You'll see.'

'Did you consider anywhere else?'

'I purchased a smaller estate in Bohemia, which seemed perfect, a secluded and modest little paradise for our child. But I had not realised Josephine harboured such ambitions. She has an imagination on a grand scale. I resold it and we are now gathering funds for Witschapp.'

'Please can I see the paperwork?'

'Oh, Therese, don't *worry*. It's not your problem. Leave it to me.'

I had come to associate that phrase from Stackelberg with a sinking sensation.

In the morning I was passing Pepi's room on my way downstairs when I heard the telltale sound of retching. She was pregnant yet again. At least she and Stackelberg must be getting along well.

At Schönbrunn, Napoleon too was on his second marriage. He had divorced his Josephine when she was unable to bear him a child and heir, even though he still loved her. Instead he married our own Archduchess Marie Louise of Austria. This would stabilise relations between his country and the Habsburgs, but presented our unfortunate emperor, the archduchess's father, with the most painful of all his many humiliations. Beethoven had revered Napoleon as a self-made hero; then Bonaparte became the worst enemy known to mankind; and now we were virtually related to him.

Still, with the troops gone at last, it was time for us to return. I was happy to be back. Here was the simple if shrapnel-pocked stone façade of the Palais Deym. Inside, the museum was dingy and coated in a dense layer of dust, and the bust of Ferdinand IV –

Had gone.

In my bedroom, too, a shock awaited. The place had been stripped of its contents except the heavy armoire and the bed frame. On the parquet I spotted the marks of military boots. I flew downstairs to accost Sauer.

'Napoleon's soldiers were billeted here.' He gave a shrug. 'We have a bill of 16,000 florins for it. I shall pass this on to the countess.'

'There are valuable waxworks missing, the handiwork of Count Deym himself!'

'The former Naples royalty have, shall we say, lost their jobs. We are no longer permitted to display them. Don't worry, Countess Therese, the statues are in storage.'

I had never thought I would be upset by the absence of Ferdinand IV.

Pepi bustled in with a bright smile – 'It's so good to see you, so wonderful to be back!' Sauer responded with mono-syllabic surprise; Pepi was not often so enthusiastic. Compared to where she had been, this place at least represented home.

Then Stackelberg sauntered in. Pepi, flustered, introduced them.

'My dear fellow, I shall be dealing with the business affairs from now on,' Stackelberg announced to Sauer. 'My wife is much too delicate for such matters.'

'My lord?' His valet appeared in the doorway. 'There is a delivery.'

'My books!' Stackelberg hurried downstairs to the entrance hall – where a delivery boy was unloading a veri-table haystack of brown paper packages. It looked as if my new brother-in-law had bought half the stock of Vienna's finest bookshop.

All this upheaval was unsettling at best, distressing at worst. I tried to calm myself by taking the children to Mass at the Stephansdom; Sephine was enchanted, though I did not know then that there was more to her fascination with the service and with God than the pretty colours on the cathe-dral roof. The next day I went to see Marianna and Anto-nia; the sisters were both unwell, coughing and housebound, yet looking for the good in the world, as always. And then, without telling Pepi, I called upon an old friend at the top of the Pasqualati House. As I climbed the stairs the sound reached me of a pounding piano and someone roaring in there as he wrote.

He was as pleased to see me as I was distressed to see the state of his apartment, although his clothes were pristine. A smell of decay caught in my throat: an earthenware plate beneath the piano was encrusted with what looked like left-over potato furred with silver mould.

'You have been away a long time, Tesi.' He swept some papers off a chair for me.

'Luigi, you look very… dapper.' I made an effort to keep my voice loud and clear, and to hold his gaze while speaking. It seemed, for the moment, to work.

He allowed himself a wry smile. 'I tried to get married.'

I was struck dumb.

'I bought some new clothes, I went a-courting, I even persuaded a friend to dig up my baptismal certificate. Now I know how old I am!' He trumpeted a laugh. 'I am thirty-nine. I will be forty in December. I'd had no idea. At this age a man should have some settledness…'

'You got the certificate, then looked for a wife?'

'No, I found the girl first. The only problem is, she would not marry me!' He laughed still louder.

'Oh, Luigi.' I tried to look sympathetic. 'Who was she?'

'She was called Therese. It's a name I associate with goodness and honour, for some reason…'

This was genuinely touching.

'She was not a complicated aristocrat, forbidden to marry beneath her. She's the daughter of a merchant, Malfatti. A sweet girl – pretty, healthy, rather young.'

'How young?'

'Eighteen. I wrote her a piano piece, but I did not send it to you because it is not on your level. It's a little bagatelle, very easy. She plays well, but she wouldn't play in front of me, even though I told her I could scarcely hear her anyway.'

This did not sound to me like a match made in heaven. 'It's a big age gap.'

'I imagined it could work. I could see us living together, finding a way of being, raising a child, maybe several. Many marriages are built upon good companionship, rather than overwhelming spiritual passion. Others have this; why not I? But I suppose she thought she could do better.'

'A silly girl.'

'Most women – and their families – simply want status and a stable income. I can guarantee neither.'

The issue of his hearing hung unelaborated. What family would happily marry their precious, protected daughter to a man with whom conversation would someday become physically impossible?

My dear, it is straightforward for you to read as I write it here – but in reality this discussion was slow, painful and full of repetitions. I had to shout to make myself heard, and Luigi could not judge his own volume, so he shouted back. Dear God, what a situation for a musician. What a difference a kind, understanding, loving wife could make – and how unlikely that he would ever find one.

'You haven't seen my new sonata, I imagine,' he said. 'It's a new concept. It has a narrative.'

'Luigi, would you play it to me? Please?'

Although he spat brimstone over the publisher who had seen fit to call the piece 'Les Adieux' – 'the farewells', plural – instead of 'Das Lebewohl' – 'the farewell', singular – the music cast an irresistible spell. The first movement was the leave-taking; the second, hovering between smiles and sorrow, was the absence; then in the finale the return takes place with a flurry of jubilation and ecstatic trills. 'Nameless joy.' Beethoven's storm-prone face was transfigured.

'Why "Das Lebewohl"?' I asked, patting away my tears after the last notes had faded.

'Patrons.' This sonata was for the one he liked the most: the archduke, whom he considered a devoted, principled and spiritual intellect. Along with most other aristocrats, the archduke had fled before Napoleon shelled the city; now he was back. Farewell, absence, return. His Imperial Highness adored it. I surmised, unspoken, that it was more crucial than ever, given the financial chaos around us, for Beethoven to maintain good relations with any prince who still supported him.

'And you?' I asked. 'Do you adore it too?'

'Of course. But you, Tesi, are the most perceptive and the wisest of my friends. You can see, can't you?'

'You are thinking of another absence...?'

'What if I am?' He gave a shrug. 'It is of no importance. The music is sufficient to itself. Would you like to try it?' He motioned me towards the piano.

I sat at the keyboard and began to read the last movement, the theme of which – with rising and falling arpeggios and some repeated notes – reminded me of something I had heard long before: the reunion duet from *Leonore*, 'O namenlose Freude'. That was it. 'That's why you said "Nameless joy"...'. It was getting dark now, but Luigi and I were in our old space, the teacher–pupil session in which we existed together in music alone. For a good hour we talked the sonata through, exploring its difficulties and its aims. Every precious moment I held close; things being as they were, I had no idea when I might return.

A chunky, well-thumbed manuscript was sitting atop his desk. 'What's that?' I asked, before reading the title upside-down. *Leonore*, no less.

'I'm thinking of revising it,' he said. 'Only thinking, mind. Tell me, Tesi...' Here came the question he had been wanting to ask all afternoon. 'How is *she?*'

As I spoke, in the golden lamplight I watched the joy drain away from his eyes.

'I wonder if I will ever see her again.'

'Luigi, you found someone you thought you could be happy with. There will be others. Please, don't stop looking. Marriage would be a wonderful thing for you.'

'And for you?' His gaze burned through the bridge of my nose. 'You encourage me towards something that you will not countenance for yourself, and that your brother has not considered either. Marriage, this wonderful institution – tell me, how is that working out for your sisters?'

My flush of pain told him all he needed to know.

'I can thank Pepi and Lotti for my two nephews and five nieces, all of whom I could not love more were they my own,' I declared. Lotti and Emerich had had a second daughter, named Emma. 'It is a different issue for a man, an artist. You need someone to take care of you.'

'I can take care of myself, Tesi. What of your school? When will you begin?'

'I *will* begin. But my first duty is to my family, as I promised my father on his deathbed. I must make sure they can manage without me. At the moment I'm not sure they can. Soon I must go to Mother in Ofen, and in summer to Moravia and Pepi's fancy new estate, with a fancy new carriage and four Polish grey horses on which she has set her heart.'

'Is that what she wants?' Beethoven glared. '*Horses?*'

'I don't want you to go,' Mother declared at the dinner table in Ofen. 'No good will come of this marriage, mark my words.' Her blotchy rash was threatening her features once more.

'That's what I said last time, and you wouldn't listen.'

'This is worse. He is a Protestant. She is following her younger sister's unfortunate fate.'

'Lotti is fine. Anyway, *you* insisted they must marry. Pepi would not have agreed, given the choice.'

'Oh, my children! Two daughters who have taken up with Protestant cranks, one who refuses to marry at all, a son who fritters away his estate's income on drinking, cards and whoring...'

'Mother, don't fret. Franz will settle down someday. I am here to make life easier for my family as long as necessary. When none of you need me any longer, I shall found my school.'

'If you wish to make life easier, stay and live with me. We could found the school together,' Mother said, to my surprise. 'I could help you.'

'Mother – that is kind of you. What's the matter? Are you lonely?'

'Of course I'm lonely. What do you expect? None of my children seem to care. But I do believe I could be useful to you, for this school of yours.'

'You don't disapprove?'

'It is your dream, and I believe it is a good development.'

'I appreciate that, Mother. But Pepi needs me too much. For now, I will be governess to her children, happily so. Why don't you come too?'

'I would prefer to live here with you than there with her and *him*.'

'But you don't have that choice. I am going, and I suggest therefore that either you come with me, or you take up a profession. You are more than capable. You would feel better if you had a worthwhile occupation.'

I left her sitting there, silenced with astonishment, while I went upstairs to begin packing my few things for my journey to our new life.

## 17

My dear,

On my third night at Witschapp, from my small bed in a huge bedroom, I heard a strange noise. At first I thought it was in one of the children's rooms, close to mine – but when I lit a candle and slunk out to investigate, the distant raised voices were coming from Pepi and Stackelberg's bedroom downstairs, with the plaintive thread of a sob. What had woken me was a thud, perhaps someone bumping into furniture in the dark. Not that they had much furniture. I hesitated on the stairs: should I go in and make sure all was well? Once before, I had not intervened when I should have. Yet I decided against it; despite all, it was not seemly to invade a marital chamber.

Pepi did not come down to breakfast. I found her in bed. A purple bruise was spreading across her left cheekbone.

'It will get better.' She would not meet my horrified gaze. 'Tesi, what are you planning for the children today? Something... outdoors?'

Evidently I had to keep them away from her.

'The little ones won't understand, but Viky will. Try and make sure she's occupied until I can... fix how this looks.'

Stackelberg was nowhere to be seen. I found Magda in the kitchen, which had a fireplace large enough to roast a whole baron on a spit. She was scraping ice from a block to make a cold compress, a bowl of mixed cream and soothing herbs beside her.

'Oh, Madame,' she sobbed. 'Poor Countess Josephine. And expecting, too.'

'Where is *he*?'

She shrugged. 'Out riding.'

'And the children?'

There a fresh horror awaited. In the schoolroom I had set up, I found Viky, Sephine and Fritz, pasty-faced and silent. 'Where's Carl?'

'Go and see,' said Viky.

I ran upstairs and flung open Carl's door. The room was dark; I pushed back the shutters to admit the morning sun. There, staring at me from his bed, lay my youngest nephew. He had not spoken because tears were streaming down his little freckly face. A length of rope had been wound round and round him, crossing over his body and under the mattress. A damp stain on his clothing indicated he had wet himself.

I shrieked aloud before diving over to battle with the ferocious knots that had been used to tie down a seven-year-old child. 'What happened?'

'Papa said I was naughty.'

'Were you?'

'I didn't do anything! I was on the floor – me and Fritz had a game – and – and – Papa said it was naughty to roll on the floor.'

'Let's get you out of here.' I rushed downstairs for a knife to cut the rope.

If only Franz had challenged Stackelberg and killed him

before he could wreak such havoc on our family. Blade in hand, I wished I could do so instead.

Those close-set eyes; that nonchalant stance, belittling others' concerns; how could I ever have been fooled? I had seen only what I wanted to see: a gallant, well-spoken, well-read saviour for my sister. While I shouted, he stood with a smirk on his face, leaning on the banister, one leg crossed over the other.

'Pestalozzi!' I cried. 'What would Pestalozzi say? You, his disciple, believe such cruelty a fit punishment for a tiny transgression by a tiny boy?'

'You've made your point, Tesi. There's no need to go even crazier than usual. The great man is not here to witness your fervent support. Come, let me show you something.' With a click of his fingers, as if summoning a dog, he motioned me towards his study. I was still shaking with fury.

Calm as a disused drainpipe, he handed me a sheet of paper from his desk. 'These are my house rules.'

I read his 'statutes' twice through, to make sure I was not imagining it. He decreed that if the children touched something that did not belong to them, their hands should be tied together. That if they rolled on the floor, they would be tied to the bed. And so it continued.

'Since you are the schoolmistress, you will ensure that my rules are followed to the letter.' He took the paper, smoothed the creases out of it, then slammed it down on the desk.

A man only has authority if you grant it to him. 'If *Pepi* wishes me to obey "rules",' I said, 'then I shall.'

I knew she would not, because I had been reading her notebooks, containing her own ideas about how she wished to raise her children. She liked to start each day with something positive. She discouraged rivalry. She wanted them to learn to do good for its own sake. As for punishments, she scarcely believed in them at all.

Dear, gentle, great-hearted Pepi – harnessed to this brute, who hid his true self beneath a veneer of false civility? This palatial house, the elegant new carriage, the beautiful horses (the girls and I went to the stable to feed them apples every day) – was this bribery enough to secure her loyalty?

Stackelberg found some excuse to go back to Vienna. Without him, this unfamiliar mansion, full of locked doors and superfluous, disused rooms, felt warmer at once. I watched the children playing on the lawn, while the gardeners were clearing up the first falling leaves of a golden September. How much did the place cost to run, with its army of staff? Magda, the footman, the coachman, the cook, several other maids, Stackelberg's valet, the gardeners, the stable boy... The estate included offices for justice, management, land registry and forestry. It extended over eleven villages, fourteen dairy farms, vineyards, innumerable sheep. It should have been a handsome earner for its proprietors – but how would my dreaming sister and her clueless, lying husband ever manage to make it pay?

Stackelberg's absence was the perfect opportunity for me to invade his office, which with astonishing lack of foresight he had left unlocked.

I spent several hours in there, after everyone else was asleep. By one o'clock in the morning I was angry, miserable and anxious. While the moon poured silver light through the tall windows, I mused upon how much Pepi knew of what I had discovered; and, if she did not, how I was to tell her.

We were walking together in the parkland the next day, after the children's lessons were finished, when I broached the topic. Pepi, seven months pregnant, was calmer with her husband away. The bruise was fading and the bloom of her fertility seemed to hold back the recurring fever and cough that we dreaded.

'This is a wonderful place,' I began. 'I can see why you wanted it.'

'We could create a heaven here, as Father would have called it. A place where we can be protected from the world.'

'It is difficult, darling, to be wholly protected. Tell me, what do you know about the purchase of this estate?'

'It's taken everything we have.' Her tone suggested that that was entirely natural. Then, with a sideways glance, 'You were up late. Were you in Christoph's office? What did you find?'

'I was more interested in what I did *not* find: any evidence that your husband is receiving funds from Reval.'

'He says he's expecting some.'

'He was saying that in Yverdon.'

She shook her head, inexplicably smiling.

'So you've made the entire down payment on this place yourself – from your inheritances from Father and Deym?'

Pepi burst out laughing. 'Darling, I organised the whole thing! I wouldn't leave something that important to *him*.'

'But which lawyer did you employ? I couldn't find any official papers, just some personal documents with Christoph's signature...'

'We don't *need* a lawyer – it's a private arrangement among aristocracy.'

No lawyer? With paperwork that had agitated for an overdue down payment of 200,000 florins? And a notification that their purchase was still short of the very sum that they had forked out for the carriage and those four lovable horses?

'So… you've signed the documents, you've moved in, but you have not finished paying and there is a bit of a way to go. And I found the most extraordinary statement: that because your husband is new to the area and does not know the system, he must have a probationary year before this is definite, and that to complete this takeover, he has to be inaugurated into the Knights of Bohemia, because otherwise he is just a foreign baron. Yes?'

'Sort of…'

'And you do know, don't you, that your beneficent Countess Trauttmansdorff can take this away from you any time she likes?'

'That is in accord with the law.' Pepi seemed untroubled. 'But she has given her word.'

It was worse than I thought. Pepi did know – but she did not care.

'Where is she now?'

'We have taken a house for her in Lessonitz until the purchase is finished.'

'*You* took a house for her?' More expense? No wonder they wanted an unpaid sister as governess, rather than sending the boys to a pricey school… 'But supposing she changes her mind? You could lose everything.'

Pepi thought for a minute, one hand resting on her bump. 'Supposing she *doesn't*?'

'Pips!' I groaned.

She tucked her arm through mine. 'The countess is a charming woman, intelligent and sociable and only too happy to see her beautiful house given over to a young, growing family. I would trust her with my life. Besides, I've enough to worry about already, without adding things that are never going to happen.'

Having failed to clean up the financial mess around my sister's country house, when autumn set in I turned my attention to Vienna instead. It was little better. Despite demanding that the museum's administration was left to him, Stackelberg had not a clue how to go about it. I spent long evenings in the office, putting the papers in order and paying invoices because he had forgotten again. Often I was obliged to slink off to the bank to deposit the museum's takings because they had been left in an open box on the desktop, where any passing servant could help himself.

Stackelberg, meanwhile, would be meeting his friends in Ludwig Dehner's café opposite the Burgtheater; most of them were booksellers with whom he could discuss philosophy, educational theory and the writings of Goethe, Rousseau or Schiller over tankards of beer. He must have been these individuals' best customer: they usually treated him to the drinks. New parcels of books would arrive every week, faster than he could read them, and Pepi had to struggle to gain his attention.

She rarely practised her piano; Stackelberg disliked music and did not see why his wife should waste her time on it. I ignored him, and started giving the little Deyms piano lessons, but it is off-putting to any child's musical progress if their stepfather marches past uttering insults. He preferred in any case to vanish amid his books – easier to deal with than living, breathing, demanding children. Soon there was another: a baby girl, to whom they gave the poetic name Theophile.

\*\*\*

I saw Beethoven at Prince Kinsky's salon in the first gathering of the autumn season, at which his latest piano trio was being played. Marie Bigot was the pianist and Schuppanzigh the violinist; on the cello, his quartet colleague Joseph Linke. Beethoven had demurred from playing. I arrived late – I had been working in the office – and tiptoed up the opulent staircase, offered pastries en route by a kind servant. Schuppanzigh's little eyes gave me a gleam of welcome over his violin. There was no sign of Marianna; she was too ill to attend. By the tall mirrors the composer was standing with his back to the room. Then he turned and I caught a clear glimpse of the face I knew so well: anguish in the eyes, anger in the jaw.

When everyone rose at the end, he made his way to me through the throng. In his hand was an odd brass contraption, somewhere between a long pipe for smoking, a musical instrument for playing and a miniature bed-pan.

'Therese,' he greeted me, 'say something. Speak into the bell.' He held the thin tubular end of the object to his ear.

'Hello, Luigi,' I experimented.

'I can almost hear you. An inventor called Mälzel made it for me. It's no cure, but it amplifies sounds in a helpful way.'

'Luigi, you look terrible. What is going on?'

'Let's go to Kinsky's study and talk.' He took my elbow and steered me towards the door. People stood aside to let us through; some eyes were raised, glowing, towards him while others were lowered as if the great man's presence might be too much to cope with. My friend was no longer merely respected or admired, but venerated.

A safe distance away, in a room panelled with glowing

wood, we sat together on a sofa, the ear trumpet poised between us.

'Have you heard of a critic named Hoffmann?' he asked me.

I knew of a *writer* called Hoffmann. Ernst Theodor Amadeus Hoffmann. Though I was not sure if Amadeus were his real name.

'Assumed, after Mozart,' said Luigi, 'to show how devoted he is to music. He has published an article about my Symphony No. 5, and for once people read it and are actually listening to a critic's opinion.'

'I hope it's good?'

'It is extraordinary, far more than I deserve. I will show it to you. But it's part of a strange process. Tesi, the only other thing I've finished this year is the incidental music for *Egmont*, the Goethe play, and it was not difficult because it was commissioned, the format was clear and my task was merely to provide the right kind of music at the right moment. I'm not writing with the ease I used to, or the speed – partly I can't hear, but partly I can't feel. My heart is rather numb. I'm sure you understand.'

'But I heard *Egmont* went well?'

'Goethe was happy and has written to me about it – imagine, I have an actual letter from Goethe! Yet every day I receive a heap of letters, mostly from people I've just met, all manner of them, seeking me out, wanting something. The more correspondence and callers and requests, the less equal to it I feel. I keep getting sick – this ridiculous colic will not leave me alone, I have headaches all the time, my foot is sore, it's problem after problem.'

'My father used to call that an organ recital,' I told him. He had the grace to laugh. 'What are you writing now?'

'A string quartet. I was pleased with the set for Razumovsky, and the piece after, which those bloody publishers call the "Harp" just because it involves a little bit of pizzicato. I'm not sure I will publish this new one.'

'But you can't not publish a new quartet.'

'I don't want it performed, either – except in private, for people who will understand it.'

'*I* will understand it.'

'You will.' I wondered what he meant, given his reference moments earlier to my comprehension of his numbed heart.

'May I see it, at least?'

A nearby footstep sounded and the prince himself bounded in. 'My dears, we miss you! Everyone wants you, Beethoven. Can I spirit you back with me?'

We stood. 'May I visit you tomorrow?' I said. 'May I come to yours?'


The next morning I sat at Beethoven's big walnut desk, trying to read his handiwork. The new quartet was in F minor, the same furious, lovelorn key as the 'Appassionata' Sonata. Terse motifs, rapid development, supremely condensed. He looked on, over my shoulder. 'There's no Spanish Riding School dressage, no imperial ceremony,' he said. 'Nothing extra. You have to grasp it at once, or not at all.'

A little way into the scherzo something made me turn back a page. That motif. *Jo*-se-*phiiin*-e. *Jo*-se-*phiiin*-e. The whole movement sprang from it, her name over and over again: anger, resentment, restlessness. 'Is this what I think it is?'

'I don't *know* what you think it is.' Was he being disingenuous? His face wore his habitual work aspect: severe, calm, with downturned mouth. These days it gave little away.

Our first lessons with him were more than a decade ago. That song, *Ich denke dein*, which Pepi and I had played and sung so often together, had in it something resembling that motif. Then he had let it flower in 'her' Andante, and in the minuet of the Sonata Op. 31, No. 3. Now here it was again, in a new, fearsome disguise. It was never exactly the same; yet beyond the surface it was no different.

'You are thinking perhaps of your Goethe song?'

'Indeed. And other pieces.'

A silence loomed between us. Was Luigi really confessing, without words, that he was peppering his music with Pepi's name? If I asked outright, whatever would he say?

He changed the subject. 'I'll find you that Hoffmann article, or some of it. I don't believe I have ever seen such a lengthy essay about a single symphony...'

He swooped onto the piles of papers on the floor, pulling volumes and notebooks down around him while he hunted. The dust made him sneeze. At last he found a folded cutting, its edge jagged from being ripped from its journal.

*'Instrumental music', I read, 'is the most Romantic of all the arts – almost the only one that is purely Romantic... Music reveals to mankind an unknown kingdom: a world that shares nothing with the outward, material world around him, and in which he leaves behind all feelings that can be conceptualised to surrender to the ineffable...'*

It perfectly encapsulated the enveloping comfort Luigi's music brought me.

*'Thus Beethoven's instrumental music also unlocks for us the realms of the vast and the immeasurable ... awakening that infinite longing that is the essence of Romanticism.'*

'"*Sehnsucht*" – infinite longing? That is nothing new,' I

said. 'It is in Mozart, Haydn, even sometimes Handel. Why should Romanticism claim this for its own?'

'Perhaps it is a matter of making it central to life,' said Luigi.

'But when it is fulfilled, it ceases to exist, and this aesthetic idea with it.'

'If you assume it will be fulfilled, then yes. But that is a large assumption – and unlikely for some.'

On his desk beside the quartet manuscript lay a letter in lavish, bold script, many pages long, the final sheet signed with a huge 'B'.

'Who's "B"? Another person of infinite longing?'

'Her name,' said Luigi, 'is Bettina Brentano.'

Bettina. Black eyes, open heart, sparkling soul and too much imagination. 'She thinks herself for me. She is wrong. Still, she writes well and I like her very much,' was Luigi's explanation.

He had met her through a new and special friend. When he mentioned those people he had recently got to know, he really meant Franz Brentano and his wife Antonie, née Birkenstock. Unlike most others, the Brentanos sought his company not for what he could do for them, but for what they could do for him.

They lived in Frankfurt, where Franz's business interests were based and where their five children were born; but they had come back to Antonie's native Vienna, first to care for her dying father and then, after his demise, to organise his estate, which centred on a substantial art collection. Franz's half-sister Bettina, who was twenty-five, leapt into Romanticism as if diving naked into a mountain lake, eager to follow the example of her other half-brother Clemens, a distinguished author in the Heidelberg group of Romantics. She had been working with him and the poet Achim von

Arnim on a collection of folk songs, *Des Knaben Wunderhorn* (The Boy's Magic Horn) – which I had not read, being more concerned just then with tackling the language of Euripides and Aristotle. 'She corresponds with Goethe and says she will introduce me to him,' Luigi said. 'She insists he is in love with her... She loves the fantastical so much that I fear she sometimes neglects reality for it.'

She was nevertheless determined to bring together the two men she most admired: the author of *Faust* with the immortal *Tondichter* (he preferred 'tone poet' to mere 'composer'). This was perfectly realistic.

'How will you meet Goethe? Will you go to Weimar?'

'I'm wary of meeting someone I revere. Writing to him is fine, but in person, whatever will he think of me? I'm a bit of a boorish fellow, I have no airs and graces, I care for little but my art, and I will not be able to hear him when he speaks. Perhaps it is better to stay away.'

'But Luigi, none of that would matter, even if it were true. He reveres you in return, I'm sure.'

'Worthy Therese.' Beethoven's face might hold a defiant scowl, but his hand – gentle, warm and certain – rested for a split second on my shoulder, with gratitude.


In the Palais, holding a candle high, I searched Pepi's bookshelves for an old copy of Goethe's *The Sorrows of Young Werther*, its pages loosened by dedicated perusal. I sought the passage in which Werther reads Ossian to Charlotte. The poetry moves her to admit her love for him. The evocation of long-departed friends: Fingal, Ullin, Alpin, Minona, Selma. '*Minona came forth in her beauty, with downcast look and tearful eye...*' Oh, how are ye changed, 'Ossian' laments – and we, too, so changed since the glory days of our youth –

'Tesi?'

I looked up through my tears. Pepi stood in the shadowed doorway in her nightgown, staring at the book. 'You saw *him* today, didn't you?'

I put down book and candle and held out my arms. She plunged across the room to my embrace. I could feel how weak her body was becoming – and how much emotion still boiled within it.

'Don't cry, darling. It does not befit an artist like Luigi to be too content. He needs conflict to feed his art, like a grain of sand in an oyster. Struggle and the overcoming of spiritual pain is at the heart of all he writes. To be frank, he is too celebrated for his own good.'

'I miss him so… And you are talking nonsense.'

'Oh yes?'

She sat back on her heels on the floor, her face transformed by the mere thought of him. 'Imagine if I *had* married him. Instead of the chaos he lives in, he would have had a good home, security and love. Nothing could prevent him from working all day, every day. He could have written three times as much music! What artist could wish for more?'

I hesitated. Hoffmann's word came to mind: *Sehnsucht*. Infinite longing. The essence of a dawning age.

'I don't know,' I said. 'I don't know what to think any more, about anything.'

'You are worn out.' Pepi stood and held out her hands. 'Look at the two of us, both in tears – sisters ever. It's time to sleep.'

I assented. Pondering Romanticism was a welcome pastime, but in the morning, we must contend with practical problems. Not least, Austria – in all but name reduced virtu-

ally to a vassal state of Napoleonic France – was going bankrupt.

## 18

My dearest niece,

Picture now the post-chaise, its giant wheels slithering to a halt on the snowy road outside the gate to Witschapp, where we had uncharacteristically retreated for the winter of 1810–11, soon after my encounter with Beethoven and his quartet manuscript. I was with the children, clustering beside the schoolroom's iron stove playing a Greek vocabulary game, when the servant came in with a letter for me. At the sight of the handwriting my heart jolted.

'Viky, carry on without me for five minutes?' I instructed my youthful second-in-command, before dashing downstairs to open the missive. It was by now several months since I had heard from Luigi.

'*I beg you, please send me again a little drawing which I have been sorry to lose,*' he wrote. '*It shows an eagle, staring at the sun. I can never forget it.*' He signed off: '*Farewell, worthy Therese, and remember sometimes your friend who truly reveres you.*'

Pepi had drawn that eagle for him years ago; we had spotted the creature in the distance during one of our walks in the hills. Often I had seen on his piano pictures, poems, perhaps an extract of Christoph Christian Sturm describing the heavenly spheres – as if for his inspiration, not that he needed it – and the eagle had sometimes been among them. Now I was not sure which troubled me more: that he had lost the sketch, or that he had kept it so long and still wished for it.

My sister was in bed with a fever, nervous or otherwise. I looked in to see if she was asleep. 'Pips, Luigi has written. He asks if you could redraw his eagle. He has lost it.'

'Leave me alone.' Pepi closed her eyes.

'I tell you this only because he is pleading for it.'

Pepi pulled the coverlet over her head.

'Careless oaf,' said Stackelberg, later. 'He lost the picture – why send him another? He'll lose that too.'

'Nevertheless, I will make sure she draws it.'

'Don't nag her!'

Nagging has a positive side if it persuades someone to exit her bed and do something productive. Pepi had no choice: I would not leave her in peace until she accepted the sketchbook and pencil, then rose in search of better light.

By the time the eagle was on its way to Vienna, Pepi was up, dressed and feeling better. I stood at the gate gazing after the coach, wishing I could go as well. The city was now much too dangerous. Full of soldiers and the destitute in troubled symbiosis, the rule of law limping along in ruined boots, and looting of damaged shops and homes breaking out only to be crushed with live ammunition – this was no place for the lotus-blooms of my sister and her children, or indeed for their maiden aunt.

War is an expensive business. So is a monarchy accustomed to its luxuries. Decades ago, the Seven Years' War cost the

state nearly 300 million florins. Once the situation had sta-
bilised, there were uprisings to be dealt with, then the Austro-Turkish War; no sooner was that over than the French
executed their aristocrats and soon Napoleon came onto the
scene. Now our depleted government, imagining itself still a
great imperial power, was trying to secure loans, but neither
England nor Holland would lend to us. The state resorted,
instead, to printing money.

During 1810 a rising flood began to threaten Vienna:
one made of paper Bancozettel – the notes in which Pepi
and Stackelberg had paid their deposit for Witschapp. Supply soon far exceeded demand. The oh-so-surprising result:
worthlessness. On 20 February 1811 came the Financial
Charter, a pathetic euphemism for the formal bankruptcy of
the state, which reduced the value of this cash to one-fifth
of what it had been: 'Redemption Bills' for the new Vienna
currency replaced the withdrawn Bancozettel, one new bill
to five of the old. This meant not only vast upheaval for all
affected – which was everybody – but years of turbulence
ahead, striking hardest at the people who could least afford
it and who moreover bore least responsibility for bringing
about this sorry situation.

I escaped into ancient Greek, trying to memorise forty
new words per day. The rest of the time, I could observe the
knock-on impact of world events on individual suffering.
Among financial instability's immediate effects is extreme
anxiety. This heats tempers that are short and plunges
depression-prone souls into the blackest depths. Those close
to them, also anxious, grow less able to offer comfort. You
try to edify yourself with books or music, but the worry is
waiting to pounce: how will we eat if this carries on? How
are we to feed the children? All things are bound invisibly

yet intimately together; sometimes, under strain, you can hear the ropes snap.

The first casualty was what little remained of the relationship between Pepi and Stackelberg. He, thinking only of himself, carped and sniped at the family; she despaired while he sought refuge in reading, from which he often refused to emerge.

'Christoph,' Pepi said, 'I need to talk to you.'

He sighed, crossed his legs and continued to read.

'Christoph, it's about Countess Trauttmansdorff. This is serious.'

Stackelberg turned a page and ran one finger across his moustache.

'I've had a letter. She says...'

'Shut up, Josephine. I'm trying to read.'

Pepi strode to him and tugged the book from his hands.

'I heard you the first time, dear,' he grunted, without a hint of perturbation at her fury. 'We'll talk tomorrow.'

'Christoph, I need you to listen, now, this minute.'

'Give me that.' He snatched the book back from her. 'You've lost my place for me.'

'For God's sake!'

I jumped up, horrified: Pepi never resorted to taking the Lord's name in vain. She shot past me out of the sitting room, overcome with sobs of frustration. I followed her.

'I can't go on,' she howled onto my shoulder. 'I can't stand it. I'm beside him, crying, and instead of saying one word to help me, he carries on reading! He ignores me, but demands I let him make all the decisions... How can we still be married if he cares so little about me?'

I guided her away, up the stairs and through to my schoolroom. She sat on Viky's chair, fighting to catch her breath, her fists clenched. Anger brings energy; it is far more useful than despair.

'It isn't right to suffer like this,' she said. 'One has to change things, or find a way to be content with them. Otherwise, one must revolt against those who cause the suffering.'

'Leave him, Pips.'

'I can't give up. I can't throw everything away – if I do, all my sacrifices will have been worthless. Tesi, do *you* want to know what's happened? I had a letter today. We're going to lose the house. The estate. The money. Everything. Countess Trauttmansdorff has changed her mind and is calling in her right to demand repurchase. And Christoph won't listen.'


You can blame Countess Trauttmansdorff for going back on her noblewoman's sacred word. You can blame Pepi for naivety, or worse; you can blame Stackelberg for – well, for being Stackelberg, but mostly for inducing his wife to seek emotional comfort in material things. You could blame me, too, because my words made no impact upon my wilful sister – which means I had not protested or advised hard enough, even if I thought I had. In the end, though, the blame is upon Napoleon Bonaparte: his overweening greed, ambition and aggression was the root cause of all. Knowing this did not help.

'She offers us the chance to repurchase the estate,' Pepi said, 'not for 50,000, which we owed, but 100,000. Otherwise, we lose everything.'

What kind of law was this, that assumed that anyone of the aristocratic elite was automatically honourable, yet licensed them to ruin a family in one stroke?

'We should leave. Cut the losses, as Franz's gambling friends would say.'

'No! We can't just give up.' Pepi sprang to her feet and began to pace up and down beside my blackboard. 'I want this place for my children, to be their paradise as we planned. She can't go back on her word. I can't believe it is legal. We'll try everything. We'll find the best lawyers in Brünn, in Prague, in Vienna. The courts must be able to sort this out.'

'I admire your determination.' Into this estate Pepi had sunk her entire inheritance; everything she had was at stake. My inward Cassandra twisted in my guts, lest whatever money Pepi and Stackelberg threw at a lawyer should turn as bad as the funds they had poured into a place they could not afford. Witschapp was pure fantasy. It could never be real because from the outset the notion was fundamentally flawed.

My dear, where legal matters and personal letters collide, it is better either to devote the entirety of the latter to the former, or include them not at all. You know, in any case, how this was going to turn out. I will spare you the anguish of the court cases; the weasel words of the lawyer Pepi found in Brünn, who naturally assured her that should she engage his services the court would find in her favour; and the lazy indifference of her husband.

Twice a day, Stackelberg led family prayers: for ten minutes we knelt together while he intoned grave words about mortal terror, pathetic mankind and judgmental God. In between I tried to keep the children away from the fights. All the time I had to conceal my fears. Pepi's gaze burned with inner fire, but her body was racked by coughs and her soul by an inexpressible anguish.

When the snow had thawed, Franz came to us, having ridden all the way from Martonvásár. His bright eyes gazed around at the chilly grandeur while he escorted his tired horse to the stable boy for a wipe-down and nose-bag. 'Nice place,' he said. 'Shame about Countess Old Trout.'

Everyone pulled at Franz from all sides: the children were excited by the arrival of a rare uncle, Pepi and I wanted news from home, and Stackelberg offered to show him around the estate, as if it were still his.

Once we had rid ourselves of Stackelberg – who stayed in the chapel for solitary contemplation beneath the frescoes after evening prayer – we packed the children off to play and took our brother to a sheltered terrace outside, where our shadows lengthened beneath the sinking sun.

'I've been hunting for more lawyers for you,' Franz told Pepi, 'and I have two pieces of advice. First, your best bet is a man in Prague, named Liebert. He is expensive, but the only one I've found about whom there is no adverse gossip. The second is that when Mother writes to you, try not to take anything she says personally.'

'What *does* she say?'

'She will say all this is because you sinned against God. As I said: don't take it personally.'

'My sin was not against God. It was against myself, against my better instincts. Thank you, though, for the lawyer.'

'Franz, how is Beethoven?' I asked.

'I saw him a few times when I went to Vienna last month. I think he is depressed, but so is the whole city. I asked him to come with me to Berlin, but his doctor says he must stay two months in Teplitz for a cure. If war breaks out again, he says he will come to Hungary – and he asks if he can address me as "brother" because he has nobody else he can call this. Except that as I remember it, he has two of his own and doesn't much like them.'

Pepi and I exchanged glances.

'Otherwise,' Franz went on, 'he is not too bad. He's being distracted.'

Pepi sat up. 'By whom?'

'He spends almost every evening with those Brentanos. Franz Brentano has opened his doors and his bank account to support him – you know Luigi's consortium is falling through? None of them are paying properly. Kinsky gave him less than half. The archduke tries to help, but demands endless piano lessons – when he's in town it's several times a week and they go on for hours. Poor Luigi is always looking for excuses to cancel them. As for Lobkowitz, his investments are prey to the inflation. There isn't much Luigi can rely on. So he goes to the Brentanos, and there the half-sister, Bettina, is a kind of elf, an adult child, bouncing around him, bringing him pastries and wine and chocolates and rabbiting on about Goethe and her almost-love affair with him, which is unseemly since the man is almost forty years older than her and very married. If you ask me, she's making it all up. Franz's wife, Antonie, is quite the opposite: a sad, willowy woman who droops about like a lily of the valley – she has long been mourning her father, but cannot pull herself out of her grief. Luigi sits her down on a chaise-longue by the piano and improvises for her.'

I remembered his fondness for aiding others in this way.

'He will never play to order, as we know from Lichnowsky. But when he wants to, just you try and stop him.' Franz grinned. 'Did you see the last thing he dedicated to

me? That crazy piano Fantasia? That's rather like his improvisations – only his actual improvisations are better.'

'I don't know this piece,' said Pepi. 'You are very mean
about it.'

'Don't worry. You haven't missed much.'

'Send it to me? *Please*?'

'Oh, Pips.' Franz glanced at her, mocking. 'Anyone would
think you simply couldn't bear to miss one note from the
great man.'

'Well, neither can I,' I declared.

'All right, all right... The ladies shall have their
Beethoven. And Beethoven, no doubt, shall have his ladies.'

'What of the Brentano ones?' I demanded. 'Is he – *caught*
there?'

'Beethoven is not a man easily caught, any more than I
am. Pips, is there more of that wine? I had no idea Moravian
wine was so good.'

Pepi gestured to the servant. Franz stood and paced about
the terrace; after riding for many days, he was pleased to sit
no longer.

'Bettina would love to catch him, but if you ask me, she
is soon to be caught herself, by Arnim, who is madly in
love with her. Luigi gravitates more towards the sad young
Antonie, whom they call Toni. She and he can help one
another. His music can soothe her soul; and playing to her
gets his juices flowing, so to speak.'

'So this musical connection...' Pepi faltered. I was silent,
nursing a bee-sting from the name 'Toni'.

'If it's any comfort...' Franz needled Pepi where it hurt.
'He does the same for Baronin Dorothea Ertmann, whose
only child died – she was inconsolable. A man like
Beethoven cannot pay court to an aristocrat, as you well
know, and even if Vienna is bursting with people getting

up to all sorts behind the scenes, our Beethoven is too principled, high-minded and downright stubborn to approach a
married woman, even an unhappy one. So he can speak to
them of love in music alone, then say that it means nothing
because it is only music.'

'He would never say that,' I protested. 'It is never "only"
music, least of all to him.'

The servant brought Franz his wine; he drained the glass
in a gulp, facing out across the wooded parkland. 'My goodness, this view is stunning. Shame you'll have to leave it so
soon.'

'Franz, you are wrong about Luigi,' I said gently; I could
sense Pepi shrivelling up with misery. 'I know what he's
doing. He has found a magic power in music and he is using
it to heal these women.'

Franz gave a bellow of laughter. 'You are worse than little
Bettina! *Magic?*'

'You call yourself his friend, and he calls you his brother?
Have you not seen how people weep when they hear him
play? He senses their emotional condition, translates it into
sound and reflects it back to them; it loosens their restraint
and they find release in tears. Afterwards, they feel better. Is
that not magic?'

'Medicine, perhaps, more than magic.' Franz now looked
thoughtful. 'I suppose it's logical.'

'Franz,' said Pepi, 'can he *hear?*'

'I don't know if he can hear his music,' said Franz. 'But he
can feel it.'

There now ensued some extreme legal – and possibly illegal
– events. Pepi's appeal against the countess's decision was
successful, finding in the Stackelbergs' favour. Franz's taunts

were misplaced; Pepi and Stackelberg were briefly united in a mutual gloat.

Then it was the countess's turn to appeal to the Landrecht. She, too, was successful.

Pepi still would not admit defeat. The next stop was the Supreme Court. It decided against her.

'*Why won't you come back to Ofen?*' Mother wrote.

'*Come back to Vienna,*' wrote Sauer.

'Never give up! We must have a retrial,' Pepi decreed.

To go through the entire process again would not be easy. We turned for help to Uncle Joseph, who was now head of the Hungarian Treasury. His intervention secured the retrial. The countess then, as I later learned, sent the wife of the councillor in charge some handsome jewellery. If she could spend that much on bribery, surely she could afford not to leave the Stackelbergs penniless? Then again, perhaps she loathed Christoph as much as I did.

Napoleon's fault? No – this was Stackelberg's alone. Going through the paperwork, as had become my reluctant wont, I discovered a crucial fact that I suspected had escaped Pepi's notice. The Stackelbergs had paid for all manner of improvements on the estate – irrigation, drainage and so forth; and they had put down, as we know, a substantial deposit. They should have had recognition of their expenditure and they should have had the deposit back. They did not – because Stackelberg, who had insisted upon being the sole signatory despite using Pepi's money, never requested it. Why was that? Because he was not there and could not be bothered.

While we packed up our household effects and departed in ignominy and despair, he washed his hands of our travails. Back at the Palais Deym we pulled the dust sheets from the furniture in the family apartments. 'At least they can't take *this* away from my children,' said Pepi, staring in gloom at what remained of the neglected waxworks. I set about cleaning my old room from ceiling to floorboard. Stackelberg, when he deigned to appear, troubled himself solely with his library. I should have anticipated the worst.

'Tesi,' said Franz – who would arrive for a few days, order us about, tease us, then vanish again – 'you are being treated like a servant here. I don't like it.'

I assured him that I was useful, hence content.

'You are a countess, not a governess. You deserve a decent life. You're – how old now?'

'Thirty-six.'

'You should be living like the elegant lady you are, not slaving for an ill sister and her wastrel husband. I have an idea.'

Oh no… I waited, tapping my fingertips.

'Are you acquainted with Baron Carl Podmaniczky?'

'Baron Thingy Whatsit von Wheresthat?'

'Tesi, be serious. He is a fine philosopher, a scientist, a gentle person. He is forty and wishes to settle down. He would make a fine husband for you. I shall arrange a meeting…'

I laughed in his face. 'If you don't know me by now, Franz, you never will. I have taken a vow never to marry.'

'But if that very tall officer had come back for you – what was his name? Toni von Thingamajig? You'd have gone off like a shotgun.'

'That is cruel, Franz.' I kept my head high and my dignity intact. 'Yes, were I ever to break my vow, it would be for love alone. I have seen the results when a marriage is *not* for love. Look at Pepi. Would you wish that misery upon me as well?'

'I would not wish *that* upon my worst enemy. But this baron is not like Stackelberg. He is a true Hungarian gentleman. You would be a perfect match, and it would gain you independence and a home of your own.'

'Dear brother, do excuse me.' I rose with a smile. 'I have to study my Greek.'

I was in the corner room that I was transforming into the children's school, setting up the blackboard on its easel and positioning the desks around it, when the door opened a fraction and Viky's lithe little form appeared.

'Auntie Tesi?' She tiptoed in. 'Has Uncle Count Ego left?'

Count Ego! I would never think of Franz, thereafter, as anything else.

Viky was nearly twelve, but despite her sharp sense of humour, she had the expression of one ten years older. I brought my candle closer. 'Darling, you've been crying. What is it?'

'Mama and Papa were fighting again,' she said. 'He was saying the most terrible things, accusing her so horribly, and I can't do anything to stop him. Is it my fault? I keep thinking about it – that she married him so fast because she did not want to leave us without a father in case we'd be alone if she were to die...'

'Viky, Viky, wait! What *is* all this?'

'She's so unhappy – all because she wanted us to have a father...'

'Oh, my poor angel – listen, this is not your fault in any way. I swear to you.' Hugging her close, I could not tell her that what she had surmised was true in part: Pepi did not want *Laura* to be without a father. How could Pepi possibly go on like this? As she had said, in a painful situation the choices are to accept it, to change it, or to revolt.

Finger by finger, nail by nail, Pepi began to prise Stackelberg away from her. First there was the Palais' management. Stackelberg sat in the office, supposedly working, but more likely poring over a recent literary acquisition, already bored by his last ones. When no new rental arrangements arrived and a complaint from a museum visitor went unaddressed, Pepi and I were obliged to step in; I dealt with publicising the rooms' availability, and she, with charm aglow, went down to meet the dissatisfied customer. Stackelberg did nothing. Pepi took the office keys out of his pocket.

She tried to suggest a musical evening in the salon, which was still under dust sheets. He would not hear of anything so vulgar. We considered going ahead in any case – until I realised we could not afford it. As prices erupted, our income decreased, and growing children have healthy appetites.

'You're a fine teacher. Can't you find professional employment?' I challenged my brother-in-law. 'It would make a big difference to your wife and children.'

'There's money coming soon from Reval.' He did not look up from his book.

'Christoph – there isn't.'

'What do you know, oh "worthy Therese"? It will be fine. Leave it to me…'

Of course it would not be fine. Of course there was no money from Reval. Later, when I learned more about the Stackelbergs – who in Estonia were considered world-famous – I was frankly astonished they did not send him anything. But in any noble family, there might be one bad egg; among ten siblings, that is almost assured; and that bad egg, I surmised, was Christoph. Pepi decided she must take more extreme action.

I awoke one morning in late spring to a clamour beyond the usual sounds of a fractious household. Hastening out of my bedroom, I found Fritz and Carl, still in their nightclothes, on the back stairwell, looking down through the banisters.

'Papa's got no clothes on!' sang Carl in delight. He had never forgiven Stackelberg for the rope incident, nor should he have.

Stackelberg, wearing only long underpants, was on the landing below, running up and down.

'He looks like a chicken,' Fritz snickered. I tried hard to stay solemn and tell them to speak of their stepfather with respect, but Stackelberg really did look like a chicken, his red-gold hair sticking up like a rooster's comb, his chest – puny without his clothes – pushed ridiculously forward and big feet sticking out at the end of his spindly legs.

'Josephine! What have you done?' he was roaring. 'Jose-*phin*-e!' His version of her name was not Beethoven's elegant motif, but sounded like the crowing of a cockerel. We fought to stifle our laughter.

'She hid his clothes,' Viky whispered, joining us. 'I helped her last night.'

'I won't unlock them until you change your attitude.' Pepi stood, with arms folded and her best haughty expression, outside her bedroom (they no longer shared a room, let alone a bed). 'And I shall give you no more from the house income for your personal spending. The children come first, the house comes next, and there is nothing to spare. Today

I shall hand you some garments on condition you use them to go out and find a job.'

'How dare you!' screamed the chicken. A loud guffaw from Carl made Stackelberg glance up and spot us. 'Humiliating me in front of my family!'

'You are no family of mine, Christoph von Stackelberg, unless my sister wishes you to be,' I informed him.

'Or mine!' Viky imitated her mother's dignity.

'Or mine. Or mine.' Carl and Fritz were not to be outdone.

Stymied in his underwear, Stackelberg made for his bedroom and slammed the door. 'Let me know when you're ready,' sang Pepi.

Viky ran down the stairs to her; together they danced away towards the music room and a moment later they were playing a piano duet. It was, of course, *Ich denke dein*. Strange to think that Viky was only eight years younger than Pepi was when she first met Luigi and Deym.

This was the perfect way to smoke Stackelberg out. The wretched man hated music. While he stamped in wearing a dressing gown and shouting with fury, Pepi drowned his yells with the 'Waldstein' Sonata. When he slammed the piano lid, just missing her fingers, she threw it open again and began the minuet that held her name, a blissful smile warming her face.

Stackelberg began jumping up and down. 'Give me my bloody clothes, you bloody stupid woman!'

'What will you do when you've got them?' Her fingers continued to dance over the keys.

'None of your business.'

'You can wear them to find a job. Until then, you are only my children's guest here.'

'Stop that damned racket!'

'You are talking about Beethoven,' said Pepi, with all the magnificence she had lacked while Stackelberg had the upper hand. Maybe she'd decided that she had nothing more to lose.

He capitulated at last. 'If you stop that infernal noise, I will go out and look.'

She stopped and stood. 'Viky, will you find the key, please?'

Ten minutes later Stackelberg was dressed – but for his shoes. He was trapped on the landing, glowering at us.

A long moment went by. 'Where are they?'

'Christoph – you *are* going to seek work?'

'Yes. Give me my shoes.'

Viky drew another key from her school-dress pocket and unlocked a small cabinet in which her stepfather's yellow leather shoes were concealed. She handed them to him. He bent and tied the laces while we all watched. Then, without another word, he was off – past the museum entrance and down the stairs, startling a group of would-be sightseers who were coming to pay their respects to the handiwork of the late great wax sculptor Joseph Deym.

'Won't there be a nightmare when he comes back?' I feared another black eye for my sister in retribution. She had only been safe in shaming him thus far because even Stackelberg was too proud to attack her in front of the children.

'I'll worry about that later.' Pepi gave a sigh of contentment. 'How wonderfully quiet it is. We need no money to enjoy such peace.'

When Stackelberg still had not returned by midnight, we wondered whether it was time to worry about him.

## 19

My dearest niece,

I am sure you have noticed that while we have stability, we think it dull. Yet it is more fragile than we ever suppose – and when it's gone, we long for our old, boring, carefree life, untroubled by the terror of what might happen in a few weeks or months. Would our city still be standing? Would we still be alive?

Napoleon had conscripted some 30,000 Austrians into the forces for his biggest endeavour yet: the invasion of Russia. His aim was to liberate Poland from Russian rule, or so he said. He called it the Second Polish War and he would send into it, as we later learned, a total of around 685,000 men, about two-thirds of them French, the rest from the lands he now occupied or that were allied to him.

This ferment of preparation was taking place at the same time as Pepi's rift with Stackelberg. Our first thought, when he disappeared, was that he might travel back to his family, ready to fight the Napoleonic forces from the Russian side – and Pepi's particular hope was that she could be rid of him forever when Napoleon won. So far, nothing and nobody had repulsed the French 'emperor'. Still, Russia would be an unprecedented challenge; and supposing the tsar were to counter-attack and sweep through Poland, Bohemia, Hungary and even Vienna? Nothing was impossible; and our worthless currency, to be drained by war yet again, would no doubt paralyse us. How would we seek safety?

A note came from Stackelberg. He was indeed planning to go away – he did not say to where – but he had not yet left. He had taken a room on the other side of Vienna and was praying for guidance day and night.

Pepi, copying my efforts, scoured his study for clues. I had found bank statements. She found his diary. We read it together, horrified.

When Pepi looked up from the scrawled page, she was smiling, but there were tears of pain in her eyes: she had seen how her husband wrote of her. His description of me as 'the madwoman' only made me laugh, but his words about his wife were less mild. If this diary reflected his soul, we had been harbouring the most poisonous of reptiles in human form. 'It should not be such a surprise,' I remarked.

'He's been using up my children's inheritance. He's spent all the money that Franz lent him and that Mother sent me – he owes Franz thousands. And he's writing all this portentous rubbish about religion, relinquishment and self-sacrifice?'

'Be steadfast, be determined: you have to divorce him.'

'At the very least, before he goes I will ensure we have legal papers regarding his rights or otherwise where this family is concerned.'


This process was rapid, as Stackelberg made no objection. Pepi would take sole responsibility for the children. He would send nothing.

She did not sleep all night. I found her at the breakfast table in the morning, downing what coffee there was, making lists. 'It is useful to make lists,' she said, without looking up. 'Tesi, I think I must go to Prague. I need to talk to people. I need advice. I can see our Uncle Seeberg.' Our mother's brother, Baron Philipp Seeberg, was court councillor there, responsible for coinage. 'And Victoria Golz and Casimir Deym, who are the best in-laws in the world, and Prince and Princess Kinsky. The whole court is going there, too, after the Fürstentage in Dresden. Perhaps I can remind the emperor of his pledge.'

Not the emperor again? How stubborn *was* my sister? 'What about the lawyer Franz recommended?'

'Yes, indeed. I want a cast-iron guarantee that nobody can take my children away from me.'

'Then you must go, darling. It will be easiest if you go alone. I shall look after the children while you are away.'

'You know me well.' My sister smiled.

'You know me well too. Why don't you take a little longer? If you're going to Prague, why not Franzensbad or Karlsbad as well? Take a few days, or a few weeks. You deserve a rest. I will find a quiet house in the country.' A carefree summer alone with the children would be my own reward, if I could find a place that would hold us all without costing too much.

'Christoph has wrecked my health,' Pepi acknowledged.

He had half wrecked mine as well, and I was not married to him.


By the time Pepi had made her arrangements and I had located a suitable retreat, it was mid-June 1812. Magda came with me and the children, for Pepi insisted we needed her more than she would. For once, my sister was taking up my maxim about travelling light and travelling alone. Aged thirty-three, she had never before made a journey by herself.

'Don't tell anyone about this, please,' she said to me while the coachman loaded her small trunk into the rack. 'The fewer people know I'm there, the better. I'll be at Victoria's house.' I waved her off, saying a quiet prayer for her safety.

I remembered Prague well from my last visit, when poor Deym died; to me the city was becoming an emblem for moments of change or transition. Pepi faced there the death of her first husband, and now perhaps a legal separation from the second. What a marvel, though, to see this impressive city in its June finery, with everything to look forward to, freedom and independence…

So dreaming, the children, Magda and I set off for Hacking, not far from Hietzing, where I had located a cosy villa to rent, with a small courtyard and sizeable garden. I intended we should spend in it the most idyllic summer we had ever known.

At the beginning of July it started to rain. Low clouds rolled in like smoke across the Vienna Woods, then unleashed their load. The children sat on window seats, staring at the deluge in dismay – one step out of the door and we would be soaked to the skin. 'We will practise playing chess, then have a tournament,' I suggested. 'When we finish, the rain will stop.'

My charges played until Carl grunted that he never wanted to see black and white squares ever again – but my prediction failed; raindrops pattered on against the window panes. 'I shall pray for sunshine,' said Sephine, who had decided she loved God more than human beings (and who could blame her?).

Even the sensible Viky was miserable. 'Do you think it's raining on Mama as well?'

I glanced out towards the northeast. The sky was pewter and an angry wind tore at the woods. 'Probably,' I said.

Unlike the storm in Beethoven's *Pastoral Symphony*, ours was not redeemed by a tranquil sunset. It continued all week. Roads turned to rivers, fields to marsh. The delivery boys, fighting through the mud in clogged-up boots or on reluctant horses, lamented that the harvest would be ruined. Time dragged. The toddler Theophile caught a cold.

I'd heard nothing from Pepi but one scribbled note, saying she had arrived safely. Victoria was away in Nemischl for the summer, as it turned out, so Pepi had the Prague house to herself. I wrote back, describing Hacking's tranquillity, the pretty surroundings, everybody's robust health. The last thing she needed was anxiety on our account. Looking after five children on my own, I began to award myself marks for self-control and sensible behaviour. I accepted an extra point for this letter.

After the little ones were asleep, I sat up late, reading Madame de Staël's *Delphine*. '*How many women without inner unity and attitude perish worthlessly, although they boast of having complied with the senseless letter of the law*,' I noted. Surely it was better to rise above the 'law' and keep faith instead with one's own higher nature? Imagine the joy of a free, equal companionship between like minds, given through volition, rather than compelled by a law artificially declaring people bound to one another...

Just then there came a noise from the courtyard: horses, wheels, voices. It was five minutes to midnight. I dropped the book. From the window I could see dim silhouettes in the black space below: a figure clambering down from a carriage, a coachman unloading something, horses stamping and shaking the rain from their manes. A fast-moving lantern within our windows indicated that Magda had woken and was running to investigate. I wished abruptly that there could have been a man among us – though this arrival did not look like a band of robbers. I pulled on my gown and dashed after her.

'Madame, come quick,' she called up the stairs. 'It's Countess Josephine!'

'It can't be! She was going to Franzensbad…'

Her eyes were wide and terrified. 'She is not well. She can hardly speak.'

I flung myself through the hallway and out into the rain. My sister stumbled across the cobbles into my arms. Her shawl, dress and hair drenched and dripping, she was holding onto me and shivering with – what, exactly? Fever? Fright? Madness? I had seen my sister in a state of nervous collapse and in danger from mortal illness – but nothing could provide me with a model for what to do with her now.

I did all I could. I helped her out of her wet clothes, took her to our sitting room and lit a fire in the stove, July or not July. Magda made her some warm spiced wine and brought a towel for her hair.

'Don't let the children come down,' Pepi managed to say.

'It's all right, Madame, they are fast asleep,' Magda promised.

I waited. When my sister's breathing had calmed a little, I took her hands.

'Darling, are you ill?'

'I don't think so.' She could scarcely look at me.

'What's happened? Why aren't you in Franzensbad?'

'I am... not sure... I can... explain.'

'You have to, because if I don't know, I can't help. And what do we tell the children?'

'Tell them nothing.' She was suddenly alert, blazing with – was it anger or fright? 'This has to stay secret.'

I calculated quickly how long the journeys would have taken. 'You cannot have been in Franzensbad at all. You came straight from Prague. Why?'

'Tesi, I need to sleep.'

'So do I, but I won't sleep unless you tell me, because I'll be too worried. You went to Prague. You wrote to me from Victoria's house. What then? Did Liebert not help? Could the Deyms not give you a loan or—'

'Tesi, the whole thing is off. I must write to Christoph. I must get him back, straight away.'

All I could say was, 'Are you mad?'

'It's not what you think.'

'I don't think anything! Why summon this frightful man back into your life?'

'Because he is my husband.' Pepi's tone was flat as I had only heard it once before: in Vác, when she told me the 'story' she had given the neighbours about her situation and her baby. Oh God – might she have encountered highwaymen and been robbed, or worse?

I lifted her hand to my lips and stroked her arm. 'Darling, you're safe now. Tell me – were you attacked? Have you been violated?'

Pepi actually smiled. 'If only it were that simple.'

Then she took a breath and uttered a name.

If I had thought myself shocked by her chaotic return, her sudden reversal towards Stackelberg, or anything else that

had ever befallen our crazy family, that was nothing compared to the lightning strike that now split my mind in two.


Pepi's story reminded me of Luigi's letters: fragments of
emotion wrung out onto the page between long dashes
when he could not find the words.

'I'm sorry,' she wept. 'I'm tired, I'm frightened, I don't
know what to do. I can't think straight.'

'Start at the beginning. You had no idea he would be
there, nor he you?'

'Of course not! How could we? But... the Kinskys... I
went to see Princess Caroline – you remember the pink
palace on the old square? And I heard something...'

'A voice? A piano?'

'His voice. Distant, but you know how he shouts, because
he can't hear. He was visiting the prince, trying to persuade
him to provide at least part of the money he is owed... He
was on the way to his spa cure and it was the perfect opportunity to see Kinsky and some other friends. I heard him
in the prince's morning room and I didn't mean to intrude,
but...'

She was deceiving herself. Of course she ran to him. Why
wouldn't she?

'I spoke. He could not hear me – it is so long since I last
saw him and I did not know how much more hearing he has
lost. And when I realised that, I could not help it, but I wept.
Kinsky must have known something of what this meant to
us, because he left the room and said he would come back in
a few minutes, and...' She stopped, mopping her eyes with
one sleeve.

'So you made a plan to meet?' I prompted.

'He was supposed to meet a friend for dinner, but he cancelled it.' Tears were gleaming against her nose. 'I need to sleep.'

'Sleep, then,' I soothed. 'Magda is making up a room for you. In the morning everything will seem clearer.'

Pepi picked herself up and, as if walking deep underwater, moved towards the stairs.

I close my eyes: there they are. Pepi, ravaged by sorrow and strain, is no longer the soft, pretty, ruby-red girl who captured his heart thirteen years earlier, but a mature woman, her intensity fashioned in the fire of experience. She, in turn, sees the would-be lover she adored but froze from her life: older, worn, celebrated, deaf and slightly lost.

Perhaps the rain has stopped for now, at least in Prague. They walk together, maybe for hours: through the charcoal-dark medieval squares and narrow lanes, across the Charles Bridge over the deluge-swollen Vltava, up the hill and into the park. Prague spreads its treasures beneath their feet; the two of them are moving in step again, just as they used to when they were younger, happier and filled with hope. Breathing the cold summer evening under the greenery, hidden deep in the shadows, perhaps they embrace at last. What could be more natural during troubled times than to hold close someone you love, someone you have loved for thirteen years? How could I ever have accepted Mother's view that Pepi must marry a nobleman, not a musician? How could I possibly have tried to dissuade her from loving Luigi?

Pepi has the run of Victoria's house. So, then, a quiet dinner for two; give the servants the night off. He would never enter into an affair with a married woman, but Pepi no longer considers herself married; she is seeking papers to separate her from Stackelberg forever. In the quiet of this darkened mansion, in a Prague which no longer signifies death but the essence of life, they are alone. The surroundings are silent and so, with the light of an oil lamp and the aid of a pencil and paper, they can talk. He could go back to his room at the Black Horse Inn, three minutes away. Perhaps he does. Perhaps he does not.

Many years have passed, yet to a constant heart that is only a blink. Who would dare say to me that were my Toni to appear, I would not run to his arms? We never touched. We never kissed. I do not even know if he loved me. But supposing he did? Supposing we had always loved each other, but had been forced apart by fate, as indeed we were – then met by chance when our guard was down, away from our home spheres, our time uncommitted, our situations likewise, knowing we might never again find such a moment of inadvertent freedom? Would we not have done the same?

Perhaps Pepi lights extra candles in her bedroom. The glow strokes their skin as they emerge from their discarded clothes. Perhaps the heat is soon too great and the sheets and blankets tumble to the floor. Perhaps, long after the flames have subsided to darkness, the fire in this bed burns as bright as ever. Perhaps they collapse into slumber in one another's arms. Perhaps they do not sleep at all.

I could not sleep either, for Pepi's confused words had set off a flood of waking visions. Around seven in the morning, I dressed and went down to the living room. Pepi, wrapped in her Paisley shawl for warmth, was at the writing table, quill in hand, looking as sane as I had ever seen her.

'I feel better now,' she said.

'What are you doing?'

'Writing to Christoph. Don't you see, Tesi? He has to come back, because otherwise – if I...'

Pepi – nervous illness, chronic lung condition or none – had never had difficulty conceiving her babies. I counted to five, allowing the dagger attack of fear to withdraw a little before I spoke.

'But darling, you won't know for weeks yet. If you write to him now and he returns, then you're trapped – but there might be no child – and then what have you done?'

Pepi's eye sockets were lilac with sorrow. 'I have to take the risk.'

'But why? What would Luigi say? You must have discussed this with him?'

'He said he would stand by me no matter what happens. But that's only about us being... us. Beyond, in society, everything looks different. It's not as if I haven't thought it through – honestly, Tesi, I've just had days on the coach thinking of nothing else.'

'Where is he? Isn't he coming back too? We should see him – talk to him properly...'

'He's gone to Teplitz. He has an arrangement there to meet Goethe.'

'Please, Pepi, don't ruin your life more than you have already.'

'Oh, it's *my* fault?' she snapped. 'All I'm trying to do is protect my children. It's all I've ever tried to do.'

'But... didn't you think? *Before?*'

What a silly question – obviously she had not. 'If you don't understand, Tesi, then I can't explain,' she said.

'What do you want to do?'

'What I want, and what is possible, are two different things. I had one day of pure happiness. That must be enough.'

'Pepi, for pity's sake leave bloody Stackelberg and be happy with Luigi in whatever way you can. People do have affairs, like it or not, and you've both suffered too much.'

Pepi deflated a little. 'An affair is not enough. He knows it won't be easy, but he wants us to live together completely – this in-between land is a purgatory.'

'But he thinks you can find a way?'

'I don't know how to make it happen. Imagine: even if Christoph does divorce me – but then I have a child – and then Luigi and I marry – what kind of scandal is that? Nobody knew Christoph in Vienna or Bohemia and *that* was difficult enough to keep quiet. But…'

Everyone knows Beethoven. Of course they do.

'Would he care?'

'He might not, but I do. I would certainly lose the children, and then what would all that suffering have been for? I will never give up my children, Tesi – and if you think I should, then you are as mad as I am.' She dipped the quill into the inkwell.

'Pepi, supposing Christoph won't come back?'

'At least I will have tried.'

She turned back to her letter and signed it with a flourish. I watched her fold the paper, ready for the post.

'What will you do now?'

'Go back to Vienna,' said Pepi. 'And wait.'

## 20

My dearest niece,

To come through spring, summer, autumn and winter, through all the suffering life brings, and still sing a beautiful song – that is what creates a Master. The words of Hans Sachs, poet, shoemaker and founder of all German literature since the sixteenth century, come to me as I sit transfixed under the university hall's vertigo-inducing murals, experiencing a sound that lifts my spirit clean out of my body. It is 8 December 1813; this concert, staged by Luigi, is raising money for the tens of thousands wounded in the Battle of Hanau against Napoleon.

One bleak chord, poised in the woodwind. Then, low in the strings, a motif, a rhythm with a simple progression of chords. When it has run its course, the violas take it up while the cellos play a countermelody. It's a fraction louder. The orchestra builds, each section entering in turn with that rhythm, then moving to the countermelody as the next entrant arrives. Underneath it, a sea begins to surge, breaking into triplets: on its waves the theme rises and rises, from simple idea to overwhelming obsession. The woodwind and brass transform it into a fanfare, and the drums come into play, to unsettling effect. The entire orchestra is united in proclaiming this fundamental truth and its elaboration, with everyone contributing part of an idea, pulling together, which is the only way a revolution can take place.

A contrast: a clarinet melody like a hymn, singing perhaps of idealism and hope; other voices shadow it while the rhythm treads on beneath. An interruption, a blockage; what next? Back comes the countermelody, this time with another countertheme in semiquavers, while the fundamental motif is almost buried under the complications it has spawned. The strings bicker, while the woodwind keep a trajectory of beauty and eloquence. And into a fugue – how Luigi loves his fugues. Now back soars the original idea, stronger than ever, together with its ideal-world transformation and an argument, a war between major and minor: a continuing struggle, with nobody ready to give in. The initial rhythm retreats into a corner – on hushed upper woodwind, passing down, whispered, suppressed, through the lower registers until it reaches pizzicato, going underground. It seems to have lost the battle, but that doesn't change its truth. At last a resurgence is promised, but left dangling in mid-air. The second movement of Beethoven's Symphony No. 7 ends as it began, on the same poised chord, waiting. After all that has passed, the human condition is the same; injustice remains injustice.

The orchestra on the platform is framed by three tall, arched windows. I can see Schuppanzigh in the leader's chair, his rotund form in his frock coat leaning towards Beethoven, attuned to his every move. Behind him among the violinists, the Roman-nosed profile of Louis Spohr, concentrating with all his might; leading the double basses, the lanky, slope-shouldered virtuoso Domenico Dragonetti, who is visiting from England and cannot resist taking part in this event; and in the cellos the celebrated Mauro Giuliani, who is really a guitarist. This orchestra of maestri are watching Luigi conduct, as if a saint is before them, albeit a confusing and unreliable one, and sometimes an amusing one, too, as his erratic gestures find him flinging his arms wide for the loudest passages, or jumping up and down for the sforzandi. When the players complained at the first rehearsal that the piece was too difficult, he'd had the temerity to say they should take their parts home and practise. Incredibly, they obeyed; now at the concert they can play the right notes, and the sound is like the opening of heaven's gates.

Silence. An intake of breath – then applause that will not stop. I gaze at the onlookers. The students crammed in at the sides shuffle their feet and shout their enthusiasm. The dignitaries – sashes, medals, swallow-tailed coats – stand and cheer. Women's begloved hands move like a flock of birds that cannot settle. Eyes shine with revelation as their owners understand, perhaps for the first time, what remarkable communications can be carried in the art of wordless music; others brim with tears yet to be shed. Snow is falling all around on our devastated city; many of the audience still wear their overcoats or shawls. Yet we feel the warming ray of our togetherness and open to it as if to a form of divine grace.

Beethoven gives in: instead of pressing on with the scherzo, they play the allegretto again. Luigi's music is tunnelling into my being, turning me inside out and reflecting everything back to me so that I can suffer the relief of tears. I weep for my beloved friend Marianna and her sister Antonia, who have both fallen into death's icy embrace. And I weep for my sister, at home a few minutes' walk away, with her seventh child: an eight-month-old baby girl, dark-eyed, dark-haired and with an enchanting smile in her strong little jaw.

We came back to Vienna from Hacking in September 1812. Pepi sat in the corner of the coach, green and nauseous; now and then she had to lean out to be sick.

'Mama,' said Viky beside her, holding her hand.

'I must have eaten something...'

'Don't be silly.' Viky knew her mother better than Pepi thought.

At home, Pepi took to wearing voluminous dresses and two layers of shawls to conceal her swelling form, essential since she must deal daily with museum visitors, many of whom would know that Stackelberg had not been seen in Vienna since June. News travels fast in a city full of cafés and booksellers – the establishments in which he spent two-thirds of his waking hours.

We must carry on as if nothing had changed. The only practical difference was that I was now simultaneously governess and permanent manager of the museum. Sauer stayed for a few weeks after we returned. I saw him staring at Pepi with curiosity; days later he told us he was leaving for Naples, with no idea when he might return.

'What about Mother?' said Pepi. 'What about Franz and Lotti? We must tell them nothing until Christoph comes back.'

'*Will* Christoph come back?' A note had arrived from Reval, having taken weeks to reach us. It contained little more than an acknowledgement of Pepi's plea.

'And Luigi? Where is he?' I demanded. Everything had gone much too quiet.

'Linz. He is visiting his brother Johann. He wants to – I don't know, perhaps clear the air.'

'It is possibly as well that he is away.'

'I don't know. I can't live more than one day at a time at the moment.'

'Pips – does he *know*?'

'I have not told him. I dare not write down a word of it.'

I feared that the longer ago their encounter was – despite its results – the more difficult it would be to resume that relationship and the more factors would crowd in to prevent it.

I was not wrong.

A commotion by the museum entrance. An all too familiar figure, pounding up the stairs, pulling a Russian fur hat from his fair hair.

The scent of rosemary eau de Cologne drifted towards us from the sitting room doorway: he stood there, staring at us.

'Josephine,' said Stackelberg.

I had been reading to the children. Distress crossed Viky's face. Pepi sat motionless, holding Theophile on her lap, concealing the swell of pregnancy. Her gaze level across the top of Theo's head, she quietly said: 'Hello, Christoph.'

I motioned the Deym children up and out, fast. Then I slid away to my office – and waited.

Pepi, Stackelberg and I had one thing in common: we all lived first in our dreams and in the real world only second. Then again, dreams are crucial if we are to keep our spirits whole and filled with hope.

'Therese, dear sister.' Stackelberg accosted me brightly in the morning. 'It strikes me that to restore us all to the happiness in which we once existed, Pepi and I could return to the places that filled us with joy: the Italian journey, Pisa, Florence, Rome. What do you think?'

I stopped myself from asking if Pepi were fit to travel. 'It's a wonderful idea. I could take the children to Marton-vásár and tutor them…' This plan would remove Pepi from Beethoven's city, ease Laura back into the family fold (for she was still with her foster mother), and get me well away from Stackelberg.

He seemed not to doubt that the child was his and due in March. For a while he and Pepi researched places and means to live simply and frugally in Pisa, for what do people need besides one outfit to wear and a basic, nourishing meal per day? Franz supported my suggestion eagerly from Hungary; Viky declared she could not wait to get started. This time, perhaps our optimism would triumph. Yet every time I passed the Pasqualati House my heart threatened to choke me: whether with pity, guilt or despair, I could not have said.

Travelling nevertheless requires practicality, good sense and, in particular, money. There was none; moreover the city, tenser by the day, was preoccupied with war.

We in Austria were now forced to fight *for* Napoleon – or our sons, brothers, fathers, uncles and nephews were. Walking past the Stephansdom, watching my fellow citizens, I would note exhaustion, and traces of tears, on the faces of women while vendors yelled the headlines. 'Seventy thousand dead and injured!' 'Napoleon takes Moscow – city abandoned!' By winter, what French soldiers remained – and what Austrian conscripts – were in retreat, maimed, terrified and freezing to death in the cruel blizzards. Russia was triumphant and Napoleon defeated for the first time, our land with him.

In the Palais, we soon had our own battlefield. There was no reason a marriage once stormy and violent should become anything else. In my sister, though, I noticed a new core of strength, despite all. She was learning a lesson I had tackled years before: self-reliance. Perhaps it supported her to know that the man she loved, and whose child she was carrying, loved her as fervently as she loved him, if from a distance.

As Pepi had told me, Luigi was in Linz to visit his brother Johann, the pharmacy manager, with a sorry and, under the circumstances, rather ironic task in mind. Johann had become involved with his own housekeeper – unfortunately named Therese – and wanted to marry her. Luigi intended to persuade them to part, for the shame that this dubious woman would bring to the family: she had an illegitimate daughter, who was five. It struck me that his drive for respectability might concern his continual hope that Pepi would somehow become free and that his family must be cleaner than the snow on Mont Cenis if she were to be per-suaded to marry him. A strange fantasy for this troubled man to entertain. Johann and Therese, however, had no inten-tion of separating, and Luigi spent much of his visit ill in bed. I do not know if this ailment was physical or psycho-logical, since word must have reached him that Stackelberg was back and reunited with his oh-so-happy family; any one of his Vienna friends could have mentioned it, in all inno-cence, or possibly even Franz, who had not – yet – any idea of the truth. If Luigi had had a plan, this was not part of it.

One afternoon I spotted four familiar figures munching their way with gusto through double portions of poppyseed cake in the Café Imperial: Schuppanzigh with his string quartet, unwinding after a long morning of rehearsal. They greeted me with the news that Beethoven was back in town at last. 'Just yesterday I saw him purchasing what looked like enough bottles of ink to write a new symphony,' Schuppanzigh confided.

'No word of this must touch any page that might fall in front of the wrong eyes,' Pepi insisted, when I told her in private that we must now face him with the news – all of it. How innocuous the incident of the *An die Hoffnung* dedication seemed now.

Someone had to go and see him. Do you wonder who it would be?

I made the twenty-minute walk in the rain to the Pasqualati House, bronzed and blackening autumn leaves dank beneath my feet. The load in my heart grew heavier with each step up towards his door. I could hear the sound of the piano behind it.

At the last twist in the staircase, I stopped short, and not only for lack of breath. On the threshold was the figure of a middle-aged man, sitting on the step with his head in his hands. It took me a moment to recognise him.

'Your Highness?' I ventured. 'It's me, Therese Brunsvik. Is everything all right?'

'Countess Therese?' Prince Lichnowsky gazed at me, his eyes rich with sorrow. I knew that he and Princess Christiane had moved to modest quarters, all but ruined by the inflation. 'You've caught me in the act,' he said in a whisper. 'Believe it or not, I am here quite often, just like this.'

'But why?'

'He won't let me in. He won't speak to me. I've stopped asking. I just want to hear him play.'

'He doesn't still hold a grudge, does he? *That* was years ago.' I thought of Luigi marching away in fury through the rain.

'He does not forget or forgive. That is all right – I don't blame him. He doesn't know I come here, at least I don't think he does. You go in, Countess Therese – don't mind me. I will hide round the corner until you are admitted.'

The prince and I shook hands, he the humblest I had yet seen him, and I the most bemused.

'Luigi...' I perched on the edge of his sofa. 'I have some news.'

'I know.'

I looked straight into his eyes, then spoke into his ear trumpet. 'She said she hadn't contacted you.'

A flicker of pain crossed his otherwise calm face. 'I'm quite capable of doing addition, Tesi. I have had an endless stream of visitors since my return and they are all full of gossip. Clearly she is in town, yet nobody has seen her. This means she is not going out, even with the children; and there must be a good reason, because Pepi loves to go out. And suddenly she has taken *him* back. She would not do that without some good reason, which for me is very easy to guess. As for the pain it causes me...'

The great irony was that, more than anything, Luigi wanted to be a father. To have a normal family life, like any other man. Was that asking too much?

'A child,' he mumbled, staring at his shoes. I wondered if he were fighting actual tears; if so, he would never let me see. 'Are you sure, Tesi? Is *she* sure it is not Stackelberg's?'

There was no question that Stackelberg had left in June, and unless Pepi had already been a month pregnant when she went to Prague...

'She *seems* sure.'

'I might have to leave Vienna. He may challenge me. I am no dueller.'

'But then he'd have to admit that the child is not his. It might suit him better to pretend. He's a man who cares more about what society thinks than about his own wife's feelings.'

'I'd feel sorry for any child who looked like me.'

'Pepi is dark too.' Laura and Theophile both took after Stackelberg, fair and long-limbed.

'But – *him*.' He could not bring himself to say Stackelberg's name. 'He will send everything to ruin.'

'He will. And yet we must find a way to carry on, and to do what's best for the children. The future belongs to them.'


March arrived, then advanced. The bank account was draining faster than ever. Each evening Stackelberg asked if we needed to send for a midwife. We did not, Pepi assured him. He would give a grunt and disappear back to his books.

'He is late,' he said.

'It might be a girl, dear.'

'Deflecting again. Josephine, you are not near your time yet. Are you?'

'Christoph, there are anxious days ahead, but beautiful, happy ones too…'

But he was beginning to suspect. It had taken him a while.

I went the next day to Stackelberg's favourite bookseller to request they order for me some English texts by a young poet: a revolutionary atheist, anti-monarchist and anti-war writer named Percy Bysshe Shelley. Whether such volumes would be allowed into Vienna I had no idea, but it was worth trying. The shop was busy, yet when I walked in, where there had been motion there now was stillness; where customers had been poring over pages or engaging in conversation, they fell silent, glaring. This had not happened a week earlier. Something had changed my fellow book-buyers, moving them against me – or against us.

The proprietor had known me for years before Stackelberg entered our lives. 'I will gladly place an order for you, countess,' was all that he said now, 'but please do not allow your sister to collect the parcel.'

My hands turned icy. A reputation, once lost, is gone for good. A husband briefing against his own wife in the bookshops of Vienna, and she in the last stages of pregnancy? Any tolerance I had restored for Stackelberg evaporated at once.

On my way up the Palais stairs I heard their voices, high and agonised. Pepi was ablaze with righteous fury. 'If you believe me to have transgressed against you, then challenge the man you suspect!'

That would be the public admission she, Luigi and I dreaded.

'Tell me who he is and I shall.'

'If you do not know his identity, you cannot accuse me.'

'I believe you to be very popular with the gentlemen. How am I to choose just one?'

'How dare you?' Pepi hissed.

'You have turned your back on God and on me, your husband, and become a wanton, depraved slut!'

I could not let this go: I must rescue her. I opened the door at exactly the wrong moment, for as it swung outward, a saucer was hurtling through the air and I walked straight into its path; it struck me on the temple.

In a way this did rescue Pepi. She had to attend to the mild shock I received, and her own distress at having hurt the person upon whom she most relied. Stackelberg made himself scarce.

Viky heard the commotion and ran to help. I told Pepi
to leave the two of us alone. My knees had turned to jelly.
My niece bathed my wound and spoke soothing words. I
hugged her.

'One day, darling, we will go together to Hungary and
found the best school for girls that has ever existed,' I said.
'Would you like that?'

'I will go any time you want to.'

We sat together, my precious Viky and I, building castles
in the air – far away from Vienna and Stackelberg. But by
the time we had both regained our equilibrium, the slam of
a door had indicated Stackelberg's departure.

'What happened?' I asked Pepi.

'I don't know, I don't care and I never want to see him
again.'

The note he sent rhymed with last year's: a variation. He
had taken a room across town and was praying. He wished
to start a new life devoted to the service of God. 'At least,' I
remarked, 'he can't physically damage the Almighty.'

Pepi lay down on the sofa, her pregnancy huge above her.
Perhaps she, too, was praying – that this latest news might
finally bring her freedom.


On 8 April in the late afternoon, Magda burst into my office.
'Madame, the baby is coming…' I rushed out to seek a midwife Pepi knew, close to the Kärthnertor.

Pepi's body, adept at the process of childbirth, was making
rapid progress when I returned – this would be quick. I sent
Viky and Fritz downstairs to close the museum and watch
out for the woman I had summoned.

'No sign,' Viky reported.

The sun sank in the spring evening. Pepi's contractions

were frequent and she was giving way to shouts of pain. My skin prickled: had the woman failed to arrive because she was detained elsewhere? Or had a rumour that Baroness Stackelberg's child was not her husband's induced her to stay away?

'I don't care,' Pepi muttered from her bed, struggling for breath. 'I hate those wretched women anyway. I know what to do – but Tesi, you're going to have to help me. Where's Magda?'

'I sent her to chase up the midwife. Quick, tell me what you need.'

'Hot water in a basin. Towels and cloths. A pair of scissors – and hold the blades in the stove for a few seconds first. And please – oh, Tesi…'

'I'm here, Pips. I'm with you.' I swallowed my rising gorge and my sensation of panic. If I was anxious, how must Pepi feel?

'Hold my hand for a bit?' Her dark eyes were huge and frightened. Her fingers shook when they were not clutching mine.

I drew upon my memories of her with Lotti, years ago. I breathed with her, spoke words of encouragement, wiped her brow, massaged her exposed belly. I told myself it would be over soon. I tried to detach my emotions. This was a natural process; we had to pass through it, but at the end there would be a new child to love. Pepi was six times a mother; all her children had survived and so had she. Perhaps there is something magic about a seventh child…

'*Now*…' Her whole body was in contraction.

Fighting my own reactions and the dim light that made it difficult to see in the bloodied forest of stretching organs, I reached out and felt the smooth crown of a tiny head in motion. A long, high shriek from Pepi, and my hands grasped a warm little slimy creature and with a sudden last convulsion the child slithered forth, followed by its afterbirth. And there came the first cry of a new voice.

'There, Pips!' I tried to steady myself. 'You've done it. Come along, little one, let's give you a wash...' I took the scissors and snipped away the cord, then whisked the bloodied baby over to the basin.

'Tesi?'

I was wiping down the infant, who looked most bemused by this strange development. I couldn't take my eyes off her.

'*Tesi.* Is it a boy or a girl?'

'Oh. A girl.'

'Fair or dark?'

'Dark.'

'Give her to me?'

I wrapped the baby in a towel and placed her in her mother's outstretched arms. Together, we gazed down at her. Tiny, azure-veined eyelids. Perfect rosy toes. Broad little hands.

'She's so beautiful,' whispered Pepi. 'She's perfect. Don't you think she's more beautiful than the others were?'

I was searching the shape of the baby's face, the jawline, the forehead and temples, the dark curls she already had, the beady round eyes.

'You can't tell yet who she'll look like – they change so fast in the first days.'

'Yes, Pepi.'

An hour later, the bedroom was spotless, Pepi was sleeping and the baby was dressed and safely in her cradle. Finally the midwife arrived. 'What a little character,' she said to the infant. 'She's a beauty and all.'

I reached into the cradle and my new niece curled a tight miniature fist around my finger.

## 21

My dear,

That might have sounded like a picture-perfect arrival for a new baby girl. By morning everything was different.

Pepi's health, as you know, was no longer robust. Her breasts, so full of nourishment when she suckled Viky, were now painful and weak; the milk production did not appear to be happening. A solution had to be found, fast. I set off to the Fleischmarkt at dawn, covering my nose and mouth against the stink; there I surveyed the stallholders who dealt in live animals, and hired a nanny goat. It trotted home behind me on a string leash. We received some strange looks from the guards at the Rotenturmtor.

'What's *that*?' Poor Magda was less than thrilled at the prospect of an animal taking up residence in the kitchen yard. I assured her it would only be for a little while, until we either found a wet-nurse or had weaned the baby. Magda moved the cradle into my room beside my bed and covered the floor with suitable material. Here we brought and milked the compliant goat; I soaked the end of a cloth in the milk and gave it to the infant to suck.

'What's her name?' asked Magda, as enchanted by the little one as I was.

You know her name, my dear. Maria Theresia Selma Arria Cornelia Minona. A reason for every one of them. Do you remember Goethe's wraith, the poetry reading in the story of *Werther*? We called her simply Minona.


Beethoven was in Heiligenstadt; I sent a well-sealed envelope containing a message intelligible to none but him. Stackelberg had left, offering no information on his whereabouts. At least they would not be able to fight a duel.

It was Pepi who should have written – but for all her determination, she was suffering. Whether it was her inability to feed her baby, or the pressures piling upon her, or that black malaise that so often besets women after giving birth, I could not say. She would not venture outside; some days she did not bother getting out of bed. May was soon blazing upon the rest of Vienna, but in her wall-oppressed house she lived only in shadow.

Remembering that my garden at Martonvásár had pulled me through my mourning after Father died, I had an idea: Pepi, not I, should take the children home to Hungary, at least for the summer, perhaps longer. Mother, though harsh with us, was less strict with her grandchildren; Pepi would be well supported, need not worry about money, and might recover her strength. Viky would be her aide, the boys would learn about farming from Uncle Franz, and I would stay in Vienna, keeping Minona (and the goat) with me. We would not have to explain, yet, why the new baby looked so very different from her sisters.

A look swept over Pepi of such relief that I knew I had found a solution.

The house was quiet without them, but I was free to spend the summer months as I chose. I was safe with 'my' baby from the travails of the bigger children, and the headache of sorting out the debris that, however much I loved her, Pepi tended to leave in her wake. I had never felt so free in all my life. How intoxicating it was to wake on a summer morning, even in a hot, smelly, empty city, and face a day of pure peace.

I talked constantly to Minona, who learned to smile and laugh. When she was hungry, I fed her; when she needed changing, I changed her. Soon she slept through the night. I grew quite fond of our little goat as well. But I had in mind one special journey for which there could be no substitute – and which I saw no reason to agree in advance with my sister.

For one florin, you could take a pleasure trip on a special, extra-capacious coach into the countryside – notably to Heiligenstadt. The ride was not even two hours long. My fellow passengers made a tremendous fuss of Minona. What a pretty, bright little thing! Look at those beady eyes! Isn't she good? I am just her doting aunt and future governess, I explained.

We alighted in the tiny square by the Heiligenstadt church, uphill from which Beethoven had lodged during the crisis of 1802. There I wound Minona securely into a blanket that I could fasten around my shoulders, forming a type of sling in which she could ride, leaving my arms free. Our travelling companions marvelled at this invention and waved us a cheery goodbye.

The midday sun was intense, but we were heading for the

woodland shade, where sheltering foliage softened the light and whispered in the summer breeze. The damp ground beside the brooklet emitted a welcome earthy smell and a red squirrel bounded across the path in front of us. We walked, as we had been advised, for about fifteen minutes – I sang the *Pastoral Symphony*'s second movement to Minona as we went; then the trees thinned and we spotted our land-mark, a group of three lindens and a tempting patch of grass overlooking the water. Here I unwrapped the baby, who had been wriggling and kicking, and we sat down to wait.

A moving shadow, broad and heavy; a strong step; frag-mented humming and singing, perhaps unconscious. His shadow fell across us. Less welcome: an unwashed, unshaven, reddened face; half-disintegrating boots; a whiff of wine on the breath. My expression must have betrayed my distress, because he mumbled, 'I'm sorry,' as he lumbered down beside me.

We did not speak for a few minutes, because there was little to say. I lifted Minona: beside the raddled spectacle of the man on my right, she was as delicate as a woodland lily. Given his current state, I wondered if it was safe to let him hold her.

His arms ventured towards me, half in readiness, half in plea. I leaned towards his left ear. 'Be very careful,' I said, in my extra-loud talking-to-Beethoven voice, 'and support her head.' He obeyed, holding her at arm's length. I expected her to cry at a stranger's touch, but by some miracle, she did not.

His gaze softened. 'She's just like her mother.'

'I think she may also be just like her father.'

He turned with such an abrupt movement that I had to grab the baby back from him. 'How can I be sure she's really mine?'

I faltered. 'Pepi has told me so and she is not a wanton woman.'

'I sense she *should* be my child, but is that only because her mother *should have been* my wife? How can we ever *know*?'

'Since Stackelberg had been gone a month by the time Pepi went to Prague, and this baby was born exactly nine months after her visit, and all Pepi's infants enjoyed punctual arrivals, I would say there is a strong likelihood that Minona is your daughter,' I recited, rather too fast.

'Dear God.' He turned away.

'Don't reject her out of hand.'

'If I hold her more, I will love her – but she can never be truly mine, so what is the point?'

'Luigi, bitterness will solve nothing.'

'I'm not bitter. I want to die.'

This was not what I'd expected.

'I thought about claiming her,' he said, 'and what it would take to do so.'

'It would be an act of great courage.'

'It would be a great act, but entail tremendous sacrifice – not only for me. It would be pure selfishness on my part, a terrible business for Pepi, and hasn't she has suffered enough already? Stackelberg would challenge me and kill me, for I have no appetite to kill him. The day you sent word to me of her birth I considered I might have to leave Vienna immediately. No, the sacrifice must be mine alone: to see my child grow up without me.'

I stared down at my niece in my lap. This tiny girl, her dark eyes watching the birds pass by overhead, could destroy every adult who had a hand in her existence, including myself. Dear God, forgive me – I had been the one to persuade Pepi to give him up, all those years ago. If only I could prostrate myself before Beethoven to beg his forgiveness. He would be the first to say it was too late for regrets.

'Look. Take this. Please give it to her.' With shaking hand, he reached into an inner pocket and brought out an envelope. At first I thought it was a very long letter. Closer examination proved that it was filled with banknotes. 'She needs it more than I do.'

'You know she is in Hungary? She's at Martonvásár with Mother, Franz and the other children.'

'I gathered as much. Keep this for when she returns. I want so much to comfort her... How has she been, Tesi?'

'Pepi is all right, but it won't surprise you to hear that she has been better in both health and spirits than she is now.'

'And... *him?*'

'*He* plans to devote his life to God.'

'Will he return, do you think?'

I pondered. 'Knowing their behaviour in the past, I fear he may.'

'At Martonvásár, they will know if she receives a letter from me – but do they know about this? I cannot imagine how Franz regards this business.'

'Hopefully he knows nothing. They will think your, er, friendship passed and finished. So you could perhaps write Franz letters and he may show them to Pepi...'

His face brightened. 'Yes, they will be as much for her as for him, if suitably veiled. And Tesi, *please* take this for her. Nobody need know.'

'Forgive me, Luigi, but you look as if you should not spare your money. You need new boots, for a start. What's going on? What of your princes and your stipend?'

'They can go to hell. Kinsky is dead – he fell off his horse, so he probably already has. Poor man, he was thirty... Lobkowitz is bankrupt and has fled Vienna to escape his creditors. The archduke is the best of them – he is faithful. But of course, it was all arranged in Bancozettel. So now, other than a few good friends like Brentano, who has lent me some money, I can only rely on myself.'

I thought of telling him that Pepi had reached the same conclusion on her own account, but he needed little prompting that they were often of one mind.

'I'll find people to commission works and pay me for them,' he said. 'It is the one honest way to live. The aristocracy – forgive me, "Countess" Tesi, but you are different – care nothing for those they tread upon in their urge for pleasure and power.' He gave his best bitter laugh, with an exhalation of cheap wine. 'I am hoist with my own petard – many times over.'

The envelope lurked between us, awaiting a decision.

'Can you tell me in all honesty that she does not need money? That oaf of a baron…'

'He gives not a fig for the children's well-being or hers.'

'If there is no other way I can be a father, I can at least send her some help.' He turned towards me and now I saw the wildness in his eye, the loss, the despair. 'It's just that I can't believe it. A child – *my* child?'

Minona was gurgling on my lap. He reached down and lifted her to his heart. As I watched, a tear dropped from his eye into the soft curls on the crown of her head.

It was only a few days after Minona was born that Luigi's brother Kasper Karl put Luigi's name into his will as co-guardian to his son, jointly with his wife, Johanna. Though relations between the brothers were not ideal, it seemed a sensible enough move. The *Josephinische Gesetzbuch*, the legal reforms of 1787 – though this had just been superseded in 1812 by the ABGB, the General Civil Code – had given the father the right to appoint in his will a co-guardian for the child of a surviving widow. A co-guardian for a widow was obligatory in any case; the person would have to be approved by the guardianship authority, normally the paternal grandfather, and should preferably be a relative. Luigi, as the eldest brother, their father being deceased, was the natural choice. Nobody thought twice about it at the time.

Luigi had never valued money for its own sake, and was hopeless at managing it. If he had not sent it to Pepi, someone else would have filched it from him – one of his endless succession of servants, or a copyist who read him too well, or some hanger-on of a musician sponging off him. He should have had enough to continue renting the apartment in the Pasqualati House, but with the consortium of princes in shreds, it proved impossible. He moved out to live somewhere smaller, somewhere darker, somewhere that would be affordable even if he were to give away most of what he had.

Under the censorious gaze of jealous Vienna, all he could do for Pepi beyond the envelopes I sometimes ferried for him was to try to help with the Palais. He had for a while been friendly with the 'Court Mechanician' Johann Nepomuk Mälzel, whose creations included his ear trumpet. Mälzel's most celebrated invention was the metronome: a box with an adjustable pendulum that could create audible beats to exactly the desired number per minute, thereby setting a tempo for a piece of music. Beethoven was as mesmerised by the notion as I was; what sort of ingenious mind could have dreamed up such a thing? In a form of creative matchmaking, he sent Mälzel to the Palais to see if the inventor might lease the place and its automatons from Pepi. The well-intentioned plan came to nothing; Mälzel decided it would mean too much work and expense, which from my own experience seemed a fair assessment. By the time Pepi returned, with the approach of winter, we were facing blank days, wondering how to manage the place, ourselves, the children and food. Mother had given Pepi some money; it was up to us to make it last.

As the months ran away, Minona was growing fast: wriggling became crawling and we could anticipate the time when she would begin to stand up. Her siblings clamoured to help feed her, clothe her and play with her. Sephine prayed for her. Theophile and the newly integrated Laura were proprietorial, thinking her *their* real sister. Minona regarded the lot with sparkling dark eyes and her little jaw square and determined; and if I held her on my lap at the piano, she would bash the keys, thrilled at being able to make so much noise.

Pepi confided in me as the little one's first birthday came and went. 'Every day I dread that Christoph may return,' she said. 'I am more content, alone with my family, than I could have imagined, despite our hardships, and I know *he* is here, near us. Even if I never set eyes upon him, or only from a window, that knowledge makes me happy. Where I am, he is with me; where he is, I am with him.'

I do not know if she ever met him without telling me. I do not know what they wrote to each other, even if sometimes I carried a sealed envelope between them myself. But then came the resuscitation of *Fidelio* – and the prospect of missing it was more than Pepi could bear.

That evening, 23 May, we made our cautious way up to the Guicciardis' box in the Kärnthnertortheater. Our dear Aunt Susanna had died six months earlier; Uncle Francesco retained their box, but rarely used it, giving us more or less free rein therein. Behind me, Pepi sat in the shadows. She wore a hat with a veil; as only our vestibule was behind her, she need not remove it. A glitter of excess diamonds across the auditorium indicated Julie and Gallenberg, who were guests of the intendant. Gallenberg was ballet director at the opera house in Naples, and had wangled matters so that tonight he could serve as its representative.

Two seats in our box remained empty, although hundreds of people outside were clamouring for places. 'We should find someone to use them,' Pepi said, 'though I'd prefer it not to be anyone who knows us, obviously...'

'Perhaps just one person, then – I'll offer it to a student,' I suggested.

Outside the doors, I could hardly believe the contrast of this atmosphere with that of the opera's other premiere in front of all those jeering French occupiers. Of course we were now in peacetime, of sorts; but Beethoven's fame had grown to such a degree that there was nobody in Vienna (other than Uncle Francesco) who did not want to be there that night. A hubbub of young men, students and even schoolboys crowded the cobbled street by the entrance, some clutching signs reading 'Suche' – looking for a ticket – and others yelling, 'I only need one place...'

Among them I noticed a curly-haired lad whom I at first thought about twelve years old. He was adding to the general rumpus with shouted pleas for a seat: 'I sold my books to be here!' His round, slightly pudgy face held such a desperate expression that I caught his eye and beckoned. He had small but bright blue eyes, protected by a pair of tiny round spectacles. A few questions revealed him to be seventeen, though small for his age. 'You sold your schoolbooks to afford a ticket?' I said.

He nodded, suddenly shy, fumbling in his pocket for the banknotes.

'Don't be silly. Come with me. We've got a spare seat and it is yours.'

His mouth fell open in astonishment and he followed me in without another word.

Once we had swung through the padded leather door into the box, my new young friend, tongue-tied, grateful and deferential, spoke only when spoken to; he was too shy even to say his name when I introduced him to Pepi. But now Beethoven took his place in front of the orchestra – aided, to my distress, by a musician I recognised as Michael Umlauf as a second conductor, lest the composer's hearing let him down – and our young companion leaned over the ledge to drink in our Master's every move while the new overture progressed.

'I'm afraid it can be a painful sight,' I whispered to him, when it became evident that Umlauf's beat, rather than Beethoven's, was guiding the players.

'It's cruel. Unbearably cruel.' Beneath that unprepossessing teenaged exterior lurked a startling degree of intensity. What *was* it about him?

Luigi had overhauled the opera, but its core was just as I remembered. When the quartet began – '*Mir ist so wunderbar*', that celestial moment of reflection – I felt tears welling up and could not stop them, for I had not expected to be fortunate enough ever to encounter it again. And now here was a theatre crammed full, soaking up its marvels, yet its composer could not hear it; someone else had to conduct it for him.

The scene arrived when Leonore, disguised as Fidelio, persuades Rocco to let her unlock the prison cells and bring the inmates out for a moment of sunshine. She hopes to discover among them her missing husband. They emerge and sing a hushed, grateful chorus to the beauty of the open air – '*O welche Lust, in freier Luft...*' Oh, what joy, to breathe freely again! I remembered it mesmerising me before. Our young friend glanced at me, interested.

'Listen – this is very special,' I told him. He answered with a soft intake of breath.

'Shush!' came a reprimand from the next box. For as the prisoners sang, a preternatural silence was settling upon the entire theatre. Gone was the usual undertow of rustle, murmur and low-grade conversation that attended nights at the opera; nobody was willing to miss one note. I saw the boy's mouth open with wonder; down in the stalls, every listener seemed to be sitting up and forward, as if reaching out physically for the spiritual sustenance this music could bring them. In the orchestra the players breathed as one, in fixed concentration, united with Luigi – the focal point of it all, his movements shadowed by Umlauf. I wondered if he could at least sense the wondrous hush behind him.

Was it as good as I remembered? Far, far better. At the end of the first half, I glanced across the theatre to see Julie dabbing her eyes with a handkerchief. Behind me, Pepi was sobbing softly into her veil. Our student friend, who had gathered his senses again, was craning out, surveying the audience. 'Every musician in Vienna must be here tonight. Salieri's down there.' He pointed.

'You know him?'

'He's my composition teacher.' The boy gave a cheeky grin. 'I can't wait to tell him I was up in an actual box with two countesses!'

The second half powered us towards Leonore and Florestan's triumph – and Luigi's. He had changed Florestan's big aria at the start of this act. '*Gott! welch' Dunkel hier,*' cries the prisoner – 'God! What darkness here…' He dreams of Leonore hastening to save him: '*ein Engel, Leonoren.*' An angel – the term he, Beethoven, who perhaps was really Florestan, often used to address Pepi; and now – or was I imagining it? – the name was sung to a variant of Pepi's motif. Perhaps I should not have been surprised, yet it can be difficult, at such moments, to believe one's own ears.

Anna Milder was singing Leonore again, but now she was a star, with a good decade of experience behind her and all Vienna at her feet. Her tenor strove to match her, and the energy from the audience carried them both. Every soul in the theatre was singing with them of their nameless joy.

The opera's final chord sounded; the audience rose as one to its feet – except for our young friend, who sat still as if trying to preserve this sublime moment for as long as possible. Pepi hid in the shadows at the back of the box. I elected to be unladylike by cheering aloud.

'Come and meet him,' I said to the boy.

'I couldn't. Really. I'd die.'

'No, you wouldn't. You're a composition student and he would take an interest in your work. He knows Salieri doesn't accept just anyone. And though he looks like a grizzly bear, he is the kindest of men.'

'I appreciate your thoughtfulness, Madame, but I'd be too shy.' Beethoven was on stage, pressing Anna Milder's hand to his lips and acknowledging the applause with gruff gestures of thanks. The boy watched him as if seeing the Archangel Gabriel. Then he bent to scoop up his hat from under his chair. 'I must go. My father will be wondering where I am.'

'What does your father do?'

'He's a schoolmaster. I'm training to be one too – though my heart belongs to music.'

'Teaching is an admirable vocation,' I assured him. 'I, too, am a teacher, so we have that in common. Let me know if you ever change your mind and want to meet Beethoven. You can find us at the Palais Deym, where the Müller Museum is.'

'Thank you, Countess Brunsvik.' He was preparing not so much to leave as to flee for his life.

'Wait! Remind me, what's your name again? Where are you from?'

He turned in the doorway, his curls silhouetted against the candlelight. 'I live in Alsergrund. My name is Franz Schubert.' And then he was gone.

So was Pepi. My sister had disappeared, as if with the music itself.

I could guess her intent. How could she bear not to see him? That was why she had worn the veiled hat – not for distance, but for nearness. I longed to join her, to see him too, but thought it best to leave her to her task.

In the loggia foyer, I spotted a familiar figure in pale silk coming towards me, diamonds glittering at her throat. It was many years since I had last seen Julie. She was unchanged, even if Gallenberg, just behind her, had gained a considerable paunch. Nevertheless, her face was etched with telltale lines of sorrow, for she was mourning her mother.

'I miss her every moment of every day,' she told me, her eyes brimming. I shared her grief, for I had adored Aunt Susanna; thus I uttered a warm, cousinly invitation: 'Why don't you come and spend a few days with us at the Palais?'

It seemed a splendid idea. We could have a dinner party for them, our first in years; catch up on the news of life on the beautiful Bay of Naples; and Pepi's children could become properly acquainted with their well-connected relatives. 'That would be wonderful,' Julie said, taking her husband's arm.

I like to think well of people. I prefer to give them the benefit of the doubt for as long as possible. I always believe that most people act for the best, as they see it, even Stackelberg. Not for one moment would I have anticipated the effect that this visit was to have upon all our lives.

And Pepi? She would be dashing down the furthest stairs to the pass door at the side of the parterre, navigating her way backstage among the oil lamps and dust and discarded coffee cups and music stands and disrobing chorus, to find him. It was unbearable to think he might go unembraced by one who truly loved him after such a triumph.

I waited by the pass door. When she emerged her eyes behind her net veil were too bright.

'Did you find him?'

She nodded. 'Let's go. Quickly.'

## 22

My dear,

Do you retain, somewhere, the impression of a scent that could make your head swim with cool lavender and warm cloves? If a whiff of it passes your nose, do you see again the curve of that neck wreathed in diamonds, hear the swish of her rose-coloured skirts, or the ringing laugh that could convey, without a word, the exact degree of sensuality, contempt, grandeur and, yes, vanity, that lay coiled within her soul? If you do not, so much the better, because there was one person who did retain these memories, and for a long time.

When 'Countess Vanity' sauntered up the Palais staircase, the opulence of her figure, the depth of her violet-blue eyes, the curls of her dark brown hair and the full-cream complexion nourished with luxurious lotions made the children's eyes light up with amazement. They arrayed themselves in a line to greet their cousins, Viky at the head and Theophile at the end; the gentle Sephine held Minona's hands to keep her upright on her one-year-old feet.

'Goodness, what a fine family!' Julie cried, probably faking delight. She had not brought her own daughter to Vienna.

'Viky? I remember when you were learning to walk, and our friend Beethoven was writing his piano sonatas at Martonvásár. And Fritz – all grown up and *what* a handsome young man, ready to take on the world...' And so she passed down the row, so much like royalty that when she reached Laura, the confused child stared up at her and bobbed a curtsey.

We had scrubbed the dining room from floor to picture rail and I had been overseeing preparations for the meal. 'I need to lie down for a bit,' said Pepi, who was coughing and had run a slight temperature since our night at the opera.

'Don't worry, Mama, we will give our cousins a tour of the museum and show them to their rooms,' Fritz declared, his eyes following Julie's every move.

'Your children will be excellent guides.' The portly Gallenberg smiled down at Minona and waggled his fingers at her. She waggled back in confident response.

Julie paused in her tracks and surveyed her. 'What a striking child. The image of... someone. Lotti, perhaps.'

'Possibly,' I said. Pepi's hem vanished round the corner towards the back stairs.

All through dinner – Julie's favourite Danube trout, for which we had paid an agonising price to please her – our cousin felt the need to tell Gallenberg all about our memories: the time we climbed the pillars at Lake Balaton and naughty Tesi left her petticoats behind a tree, and how Beethoven had given her his most beautiful sonata and ate apples while lying in her lap. I could feel a governessly expression setting into my lips.

'Could we not have invited Beethoven tonight?' Julie pleaded. 'How I would love to see him again.'

'He doesn't like parties,' I said. 'He can't hear and he feels awkward about it, so he would not have accepted. I am sure you could visit him – he is not wholly unsociable.'

'Where does he live?' Gallenberg asked. I told them.

'But that is outside the city walls.' Julie was horrified. 'Virtually a slum.'

'You'd be visiting him, not his apartment.'

Pepi, who had been making an heroic effort to mimic the bright self she had been at twenty, said quietly that she felt feverish and excused herself.

'We should definitely take *Fidelio* to Naples,' Gallenberg said, and for the next ten minutes he talked non-stop about the practicalities, the singers, the work's special challenges. I appreciated his sensitivity.

On the third afternoon of the visit, when everyone had gone their separate ways for a quiet hour or two, I padded to the study to catch up on paperwork. I could hear a trickle of piano music: Viky practising. Pepi was in bed, asleep or pretending to be, with Minona napping in a cot next to her. From Gallenberg's bedroom emanated a snore that could travel beyond the city walls unaided. Magda had taken the other children out for a walk. Julie was nowhere to be found; I assumed she had gone to her room to rest.

I welcomed the peace and quiet. I feared I was becoming less sociable with my advancing years, though perhaps it was both natural and right that I should loathe Julie for saying the word 'Beethoven' in front of Pepi. What did she know? Anything? If it was so difficult to keep a secret in Vienna, why did the whole city not already recognise Beethoven as Minona's father? We must have done better than usual at concealment.

Magda glanced in. 'Madame, we are back.'

'Excellent. A good time?'

'Of course. They are such angels.' And they trooped past my door: Carl, Sephine, Laura, Theophile.

'Where's Fritz?'

'Oh, he stayed home. He said he had schoolwork to do.'

To the best of my knowledge, Fritz had never once prioritised schoolwork over a good run on the Glacis. Something was wrong. I don't know what Cassandra instinct it was that set a chill over me, making me run to the back stairs and up to the top floor where the children's bedrooms were. The little girls were already in Sephine's room, making a racket, so I heard nothing until it was too late. Fritz's door was shut, and without bothering to knock, I pushed it wide open.

The curtains were drawn, but a narrow shaft of sunlight illuminated, atop the coverlet, the back view of my cousin, magnificent and naked: Julie of the Beautiful Buttocks, her hair cascading around her wax-pale shoulders – and beside her a smaller figure, disrobed, hands moving in entranced wonder across the gleaming female physique arrayed before him. I stood there, trying to force myself to awaken and find it was all a bad dream, which it was not.

'What in the name of Nemesis—?' I heard myself boom.

Julie glanced over one shoulder at me. Her face betrayed only mild amusement. 'Oh *dear*,' she said. 'Fritz, darling, we've been rumbled.'

There was no ceremony. Hysterics, yes – and if mine were severe, Pepi's were half deranged. I can still hear the howl with which she pitched herself into Julie's room, where she grabbed the half-packed trunk, which should have been much too heavy for her to carry – and Julie running in her dressing gown in time to see Pepi sending all her silk stockings, dancing shoes, many-coloured shawls and pantaloons bouncing away down the stone stairs.

'Pepi!' I tried in vain to calm her. 'Please – the neighbours, the servants…'

'Darling, darling, why are you so upset?' Julie begged, genuinely (I think) contrite, but level-tempered as ever. 'Fritz is of a certain age now. Would you not prefer him to be *educated* by a responsible woman concerned for his well-being, rather than a common prostitute, which would be the usual procedure?'

The sleepy Gallenberg came wandering out just then, making exclamations of astonishment and confusion. He had slumbered throughout the rumpus and we could hardly tell him what had happened, so I took his arm and led him to the study to give him a carefully shortened version.

'But she is mad,' the impresario opined, staring after the wild-haired, red-faced Pepi in horror. 'How can she make us leave the house at a moment's notice? Whatever will people say?'

'Just for now, please believe me, dear cousin, that it will be for the best if you do as Pepi asks and remove yourselves to your father-in-law's house. It will make life much easier and pleasanter for you both.'

Oddly, Gallenberg complied without much argument. I wondered how many times before he had discovered his wife with company – and taken it as a compliment that no man, or boy, could resist her charms, since she still belonged, ostensibly, to him.

I left Pepi to give her son the ferocious admonishments he was due. Later I spotted him snuffling into a handkerchief in a corner window seat. Poor lad, I reflected; he was only thirteen and must wonder what on earth had hit him today.

'He needs a man's hand,' Pepi mused later, wrung out

with misery. I disliked this notion. Why could a tender mother and an intelligent aunt not do a better job of bringing up children than some lying, philistine father who happened to be male? But even if we understood that theory, perhaps the children did not.

Neither would our neighbours. Vienna was still Vienna. A screaming row involving flung luggage and unscheduled departures would be prime gossip in every palace salon before you could say 'Prince Lichnowsky'.

How long it took for letters to reach Reval and responses to be written and returned I am not precisely sure. How long it would take to travel from Estonia to Vienna, across war-ravaged land through Lithuania, Poland, Silesia and Moravia I could scarcely imagine; it was a distance greater than one and a half thousand kilometres. Yet correspondence must have been sent, horrors imagined, situations worsened through words interpreted and reinterpreted; carriages loaded, horses harnessed and whips cracked, until finally a letter found its way to a silver tray in Magda's hand, being delivered to Pepi.

Magda's face betrayed her alarm. The missive was in familiar writing with concave lower loops.

'Who brought it?' Pepi demanded.

'A servant, Madame. He said Baron von Stackelberg wants him to return for an answer in the morning.'

'Thanks, Magda. And don't *worry*.' Pepi gave her a bright smile, then retreated to her sitting room to see what Stackelberg was throwing at her now. I gave her some minutes of solitude, then went in to investigate.

Pepi was holding the crumpled letter in one fist; standing

by the window, she was staring out at the night sky above the city wall. 'He wants us to go with him to Reval.'

'Heavens – Estonia?'

'He's inherited some land from one of his elder brothers who has died. I suppose it would be fair enough, were we still properly married, and if he showed any concern for my well-being and the children's, and if I were willing to be separated from my family and… those I love the most.'

'Don't do it.' I went over and hugged her.

'I won't. I'll never go. Especially not when he speaks to me like this.'

I untwisted the letter. Reading it, I tried to extrapolate any possible good. He was trying to sort out some of the mess over the Witschapp estate; he was in touch with Lotti's husband, Emerich, over this, asking for recommendations of lawyers. More disturbing was an undertone that insinuated nefarious goings-on under our roof, developments that might in due course affect the well-being not only of his own daughters, but of the Deym children as well.

'How dare he?' Pepi fumed. 'How can he say such things? As if my children would…'

'"Countess Vanity".'

'But alleging they might *do things together*? The siblings? My God, what a man to believe such depravity…'

Pepi scribbled an ice-cold reply, thanking him and declaring that she and the children preferred to stay in Vienna, where they had friends, family and responsibilities. I wrote him a letter of my own. In the morning Magda handed both documents to Stackelberg's servant. We thought that would be the last of it.

Nobody could have imagined the revenge that Stackelberg was planning.

We were in the sitting room together, as we often were: Pepi on the sofa with Minona on her lap, Laura and Theophile playing a game with their dolls at her feet. I was swotting for the next day's lessons: learning ancient Greek is an endless process. The boys were upstairs doing schoolwork, and Sephine and Viky were in the music room together, practising the piano. Hooves and a carriage sounded beneath the window; a cry of alarm from the manservant downstairs; then steps – many men in strong boots tramping up the stairs.

I leapt to my feet, but before I could move Stackelberg was there, striding towards Pepi and the children, and the doorway was blocked by a bevy of policemen – six, as I discovered when I tried to push past and saw their backups on the landing.

Pepi was speechless with shock.

'What are you doing?' I yelled at Stackelberg. I swear I have never seen such an intense expression of pure evil on any man's face.

'Laura. Theophile. Come with me,' he said.

'Where are we going?' Laura asked.

'Home to Estonia.'

'But *this* is home,' Laura protested. The poor darling had only just become used to living here. Theophile began to howl.

'And the little one.' Stackelberg swung towards Pepi and the infant on her lap. 'Josephine, give her to me.' He swooped down to grab Minona out of her mother's arms.

Pepi, trapped by her own sofa, let out a shriek. Stackelberg pinned her down with one knee while two of the policemen tried to prise her grip away from the terrified, whimpering toddler.

'Do what you like to me, but leave me my children!' Pepi pleaded from this ignominious position. 'I live for my children!'

'You can keep the others,' Stackelberg smirked. 'You have plenty. Though I should take them too – from what I hear, their moral well-being is far from safe in this godforsaken house.'

Pepi's mistake was that she had given Stackelberg too much of herself. He knew her greatest weakness: the perennial terror that her children would be taken from her. So he would take them – not because he wanted them, not because he believed it in their best interests, but because it would cause his wife the greatest pain she could imagine. Julie was not the cause; she had simply provided the perfect excuse.

I flew across the room and slapped his face so hard that he staggered back, reeling and swearing. The coward. The weakling. The pathetic bully. He could not even take the attack of a misshapen woman of nearly forty. Powerful hands seized my shoulders. However forceful my rage, the brawn of two policemen was more than I could fend off.

Stackelberg stood upright. Minona was in his arms, scarlet-faced, open-mouthed and screaming. There was no way, looking at the pair of them, that anybody in their right mind could have imagined Stackelberg her actual father. He addressed Laura and Theophile. 'Come on. We're off.'

Three policemen escorted the party of cursing baron and three tiny children; the remaining officers were charged with preventing Pepi and me from giving chase.

'Kidnap!' Pepi shouted. 'Abduction! Why are you, the Viennese police, helping this man steal my children?'

'Orders, Madame.' The policeman who had planted himself in the sitting room doorway pulled an official document from a pocket and handed it to her. 'Not for us to judge. Just doing as we was told.'

'This is morally indefensible.' I was still struggling against my two minders. They had evidently decided I was the greater danger, though a mere aunt. 'Ripping a one-year-old child from her mother's arms! How dare you? Don't you have children of your own?'

'Don't *you*?' One of them leered into my face. I restrained myself from biting him.

'We'd doubtless do the same,' said the other, with a yawn. 'A father's rights must be guarded.'

I longed to say that Stackelberg had no father's rights over Minona – but that would unleash problems of a different kind. I tried to focus, to say a prayer, to find guidance, yet sensed only a fearful emptiness. Minona's cries were fading into the distance as Stackelberg carried her away down the stairs.

Speed must have been Stackelberg's priority, for no time seemed to elapse before we, imprisoned, heard the sickening clop and rattle of a two-horse carriage echoing back at us, amplified by the city wall opposite.

'The girls will need their clothes,' I said.

'The gentleman will send a servant for them in the morning. Don't you worry, miss. You can pack for them, picnic and all. They're going on a long, long journey.' The last policemen released my arm and then, to my horror, patted my behind.

A minute later, all was eerie silence.

Pepi, shaking with fright, had in her hand a new document in Stackelberg's writing. We read it together.

*'The Trauttmansdorff business is only property,'* he wrote. *'But here, we are dealing with sacred matters. To answer your dishon-*

*est claptrap ... would be like trying to wash a Negro white ...*
*Believe me, Josephine, that you are clueless; believe me, Therese,*
*that you are insane; believe me, you will be pilloried, and one day*
*you will both shed tears of blood.'*

'Oh God, my God,' cried Pepi. She dropped the letter and
fled towards the back stairs. I made my unsteady way to the
music room to find the Deym children, who were huddling
together there, waiting for someone to rescue them.

In the sitting room, a slip of material lay abandoned on
the floor by the sofa: the little linen bib that had fallen from
around Minona's neck. Sephine lifted it and pressed it to her
heart.

## 23

My dear niece,

With the first frosts of 1814 came the first dignitaries, their carriages bowling into town and through the Hofburg's courtyards, ready for the Congress of Vienna. The city was abubble with anticipation.

The aim was to resolve the division of European territories once and for all. They were coming to Vienna – the kings, princes and ambassadors and their wives, mistresses and entourages – the whole boiling lot, for what length of time nobody yet knew. During the day they would decide the fate of the little people in their lands. In the evening, they would require entertainment. Beethoven would provide some of it, in the form of a grand concert in the Hofburg's Grosser Redoutensaal, the great hall used for royal dinners, balls and, naturally, symphonies.

More than two years had gone by since the Prague encounter. Our darling Minona – wherever she was now – would be eighteen months old. I imagined her speaking her first words. After the abduction, I insisted to Pepi that we must not neglect our care for the children still present through anguish over those who were not. I went through the motions of teaching, and they of learning. Pepi took to her bed. Grief grew like silvery mould across our minds.

No communication came from Stackelberg: no news of the girls, no report on their well-being, no postbag containing Laura's drawings or Theophile's first writing. If we ever saw them again, perhaps they would speak only Russian or Estonian. As for Minona...

I had had to make my sorry way to that apartment – the notion of which had so horrified Julie – to face its occupant. Pepi dared not go herself. Two copyists were at the table, working on a large score that I presumed was a symphony, but for once I did not stop to ask. I had to find honeyed words, persuasive explanations and finally desperate pleas to achieve some privacy with him. He turned from his desk in the window, his gaze burning with immediate recognition that something serious was afoot.

When the copyists had agreed to leave early and the servant had slipped away as bidden, I motioned to Luigi to sit down. Then I knelt at his feet, took his hand in mine for a moment and begged him not to interrupt while I wrote out, in chalk on an erasable slate, the events that had brought me to him today. As he followed the words, his fingers tautened their grip on the arm of the chair. By the time the story was complete, he had lowered his head to his wrists, his shoulders heaving with sobs. I faltered.

'We will find a way to get her back,' I wrote. 'We have to. It is a kidnap.'

'My poor Pepi. My poor darling girl. And I can do nothing. Nothing to protect them or comfort them or save them. Oh, if I had only taken that brave step I considered, this would not have happened.'

'We don't know that. He might have killed you, or you him, and that would have done no good either.'

'The odds are so heavily slanted towards *him*... Pepi has no rights. I have even fewer. He will win everything.'

'We *can't* see this as the end. We have to keep hoping and we have to find a way to get Minona back. And Luigi, do you not think that now, after such disgrace, he might see fit to divorce Pepi?'

Without that, Pepi could never be free to marry again. If any semblance of an affair between her and Luigi was continuing, I did not want to know; but I saw no signs of it. He dared not visit our house; and Pepi, traumatised and depressed, scarcely went out. For Luigi, this enduring, overwhelming passion for her had to be his whole life, or nothing. Not many years before, he had been courting Therese Malfatti, flirting with Bettina Brentano, eyeing up pretty girls; he hungered for stability, family, normal life. He had dressed smartly, shaved regularly, bathed often enough – one friend reported that Beethoven had received him while in the bath and had then jumped out, gone to open the window and wondered why the street urchins outside were pointing and laughing. Now everything was different.

In my black dress and veiled hat, I, unlike Pepi, was not afraid to slip through the shadows in the grey and ochre side streets to his latest dwelling – for now he would never settle properly anywhere. After breaking the news of Minona's abduction, I tried to see him once a week. Often he was ill; his colic could confine him to bed for days on end. I doubted his state of mind would have been much better than Pepi's, but for one thing: he had music to write.

'You must stop this isolation,' I told him, finding him hard at work in a set of dark, chilly rooms which smelled as if nobody had cleaned them in months. 'Try and be sociable. Either you must take a risk with Pepi or you must find someone else.'

'Tesi.' Beethoven thumped down his pen and glared at me. 'I don't want to go out. I don't want to be sociable. And I don't want to find someone else. I know she is trapped by *him*, but unless I can marry her I do not want to continue with her, or even to see her, because it is painful for me and unfair to her. If I cannot marry *her*, then I shall not marry. Even if I never possess her fully, I want no other. All those well-meaning ideas can go to hell.'

Normally I could stand up to Luigi in a bad mood. This was different. 'Well, then... I will leave you in peace to work.'

He took up his pen and dipped it in what liquid remained in the inkpot after what looked like a serious spillage over the piano. 'You will like the result. It's a piano sonata.'

'Not a symphony?'

'Too many ceremonial things to write for the bloody Congress. This sonata is my light relief – some real art. Now... I must work. My copyists are arriving at any moment.' The sonata turned eventually into his Op. 90, one of my cherished favourites.


Outside, the city had sprung to life. The tailors were ordering extra supplies of the finest merino. The confectioners and pharmacists on the Graben were building additional shelves. Restaurants changed their menus to include Russian koulibiac, French coq au vin, Danish roast pork with red cabbage. In the music shops the latest, most expensive models of fortepiano were on display, their keyboards open in toothy grins. The influx of the Congress's participants – and their extreme wealth – was more than any merchant could resist. Besides, while the borders were shifted and the continent sliced up, Vienna would exhume and dust down its old, pre-Napoleonic self to indulge in party after party.

'Will we be invited to anything?' Pepi gloomed.

'Everything, if I have my way.'

My sister needed a chance, for once, to have some fun. I made a plan and sat down to write letters: Prince Lobkowitz, Count Razumovsky, Schuppanzigh, the Bigots, Countess Marie Erdödy, Zmeskall, every aristocratic patron I could think of, their dear wives and the tragically widowed Princess Kinsky. '*Dear Princess Caroline, it is so long since we last saw you; supposing we find a time to meet soon? My sister has not been well, but her health is improving and she is playing the piano once again. Do you remember how you used to love her performances at your salon? How wonderful it would be to encourage her back to her former glory…*'

I sent off the letters and waited.

A few days later, envelopes began to arrive. One invitation was to a musical soirée at Prince Lobkowitz's: Carl Maria von Weber would perform on the piano and Anna Milder would sing arias by a young Italian composer, Gioachino Rossini, whose *opera buffa* was captivating the pleasure-hungry city. Another was for a masked ball at Count Razumovsky's palace, that Arcadian paradise full of Canovas, Van Eycks and Stradivarius violins.

Some of my contacts seemed willing to help us sidle back into the circuit of the Viennese season. Others did not. I kept quiet about those.

'How did you do that?' Pepi asked. 'I thought nobody would speak to us.'

'A bit of creative wording.'

'Show-off.' Pepi could be as grumpy and bearlike as Beethoven when she wanted to be.

'You don't have to go unless you want to.' But soon the prospect of the Razumovsky ball was putting a spring in her step.

There was the small matter of what to wear. It was years since we had last attended a ball and we could not justify spending money on new dresses. We retrieved our musty old gowns from their wardrobes in our walk-in dressing rooms, where the moths, mercifully, had not eaten them all. Perhaps we could ask a dressmaker to update their styles. Pepi selected her white and pink satin with silver and cherry-red trimmings.

'I shall wear black,' I said.

'Don't be silly.' Pepi pointed at a pastel lilac dress I had last worn a decade ago. 'We can put some gold lace on that...'

A few days later I stared at myself in the mirror while the seamstress chattered over her measuring tapes and pins. Give or take the kink of my spine, I did not look as bad as I expected. Fashions had changed. Elegance meant simplicity; everything was about shape. Necklines scooped downward, exposing a certain amount of décolletage, and close-fitted sleeves were edged with satin or ruffled with lace below the elbow. Above her pale satin, Pepi's collarbones protruded like garden rakes. It was hard to believe such a fragile-looking woman could have given birth to seven healthy children.

'Masks.' The dressmaker winked up at me from her hemming. 'Do order yourselves some fine masks. Because at a masked ball, anybody can be... anybody.'

When we were alone again, Pepi turned to me. 'Tesi, do we have any jewels left?'

We had fewer than we used to – but we would wear them all to Count Razumovsky's.

Carriage after carriage rolled up the icy streets towards the great park, the horses' breaths forming clouds of steam in the night air. Razumovsky was a chief negotiator at the Congress and the whole gathering was invited: the smiling King of Denmark and tight-lipped King of Bavaria; the blond-haired, energetic figure of Talleyrand; Razumovsky's successor as Russian ambassador, who happened to be a Count Stackelberg distantly related to Christoph. All the staff, the civil servants, the wives and daughters and sisters and brothers, Schuppanzigh and his string quartet (I suspected he had helped to wangle our invitation): everyone would meet that night in the count's vast marbled galleries. Some said the place was an attempt to show the Habsburgs that not they but the Russians were the richest, most powerful nation of our time. Razumovsky – re-employed as a plenipotentiary, since he was too good for the tsar to lose – had built the finest palace in Vienna, employed the best string quartet, assembled the most impressive art collection and helped to support the most celebrated composer, Beethoven. And his nation had vanquished Napoleon.

Clad in our old fur wraps, yet still shivering inside our carriage, we planned our strategy.

'Hopefully there will be so many guests that we won't have to speak to anybody for too long,' Pepi reflected. 'I am so out of practice…'

'Oh, Pips – look!'

The palace had come into view. Flaming torches blazed bronze and gold, lighting up the pale stone of the mansion; through the grounds, an English-style park in which the count's guests could roam in the summer months, the dark ribbon of the Donaukanal wound its way; and while we were unhanded from the carriage and ascended a floating staircase to the first of the reception halls, music reached us: a plangent violin, the pulse of a waltz. Later there would be dancing.

The first person we recognised, to my chagrin, was Julie Gallenberg. She must have spotted our hesitant figures and zigzagged through the crowd to meet us, her arms extended. We had not seen her since what Pepi now termed 'the business'. Julie ran the risk that if she did not come up to us first, we would cut her dead, so by greeting us as the family we were, as if nothing had ever gone wrong, she left us no choice. 'Darlings… how wonderful that you are back amongst us again! My husband will be delighted to see you. Therese, you look spectacular in this unusual colour.'

I did not bother answering as she rattled on, every sentence an insult veiled within a compliment. She and Gallenberg, staying in Vienna for the excitement of the Congress, had lost no time ingratiating themselves with the count – and Julie's celebrated beauty was proving quite an asset to her husband while he sought potential sponsors.

Pepi hung back, fighting tears. 'I'm not sure I can cope.'

'Be strong, Pips. It's going to be fine.' We had to stand our ground; if we did not, we would never leave our own four walls again.

'Julie, dear!' I linked my arm through hers, rather to her surprise. 'Why don't we go and explore this incredible place?'

My dress felt tight around my ribs, the lace was scratchy on my shoulders and the reflected shine of satin felt too bright amid the thousands of candles that made the mirrors gleam and twinkle around us. I wondered how long it had taken Razumovsky's servants to light them all. It was startlingly warm, too – more than just the effect of naked candle flames. 'He has installed a French heating system,' Julie said. 'Don't ask me how it works, but it is rather wonderful. One forgets, in the south, how frightfully cold Vienna can be.'

Pepi, on my other side, was looking about at the women in many-jewelled tiaras: the wives, sisters or mistresses of Congress delegates, flaunting their wealth and beauty, while every detail of their private lives was being openly discussed yet left no scratch of scandal upon them in this palace of fantasies – the idealised, larger-than-life vision of a Russian count who had far more money than he knew what to do with. 'He has a private income from his estates in Ukraine,' Julie said dismissively.

I let Julie chatter. One useful thing about spending time among children is that you learn to listen to several different conversations at once. Pepi was talking to a woman I vaguely recognised. 'Yes, my three youngest are staying with their father in Reval,' Pepi was saying, smiling and gracious. 'I have so many responsibilities in Vienna, otherwise I too would be enjoying the beauties of the Baltic... yes, the ambassador is a relation, though I cannot say whether second cousin once removed or...'

The ringing of a handbell summoned everyone to the opposite wing for the recital. Fifteen minutes later we were seated among at least five hundred guests in a hall of mirrors worthy of Versailles, in which Schuppanzigh and his quartet performed some Haydn followed by the first work of Beethoven's Op. 59 set. Julie yawned. 'I was hoping he would have a performance by the Russian Ballet. He's done that before. We can hear Beethoven quartets *any* time. The least Luigi could have done is show up and play to us himself.'

Razumovsky had invited him. He was probably the only person in Vienna who had refused. 'He'd hate it,' Pepi whispered, reading my mind. 'These noisy crowds would be a living hell for him.'

Luxury, luxury – what is it *for*? I gazed around while Beethoven's marvels rippled out from the quartet. Such an array of statues of naked Greek gods, friezes of cherubs and nymphs, Pan with his horns and hooves, cypresses and laurels, lilies with half-opened blooms and drooping leaves, set in stone yet seeming freshly plucked from Mount Olympus: they must have taken a platoon of stonemasons years to carve. The flooring, inlaid with intricate swirls and curlicues: whatever did this cost? It was hard enough to keep up the polish on the museum's plain parquet. Was Razumovsky's intention to assert that Russians could be more European than the Europeans? Or was he simply building the palace of his dreams because he *could* – thanks to the broken backs and shortened lives of a hundred thousand serfs who worked upon his Ukrainian estate?

After the concert Razumovsky himself waylaid me in his deep bass tones and kissed my hand. 'Dear Countess Therese.'

'Count Razumovsky, I am overwhelmed,' I said. 'What are you seeking to create in this paradise of yours?'

'Precisely paradise. It is best we can be – any of us – and to share with as many friends as possible. You approve?' He tucked my arm through his: 'Come and see paintings.'

We strolled through room after room, doorway opening upon doorway in a long stream of parallel lines stretching far ahead. Through his gallery the Van Eycks were arrayed in rows up towards the ceiling, along with more Dutch portraits and interiors – florid gold frames cradling dark backgrounds, cream lace sleeves, brown beards and knowing grey eyes, still lifes of hanging partridges ready to cook, rosy apples, purple-brown plums and grapes in bronze-gold bowls. The count pointed out his favourites, telling me where he had bought them – Amsterdam, Utrecht, Cologne, Milan – and in some cases how much they had cost. 'This is my favourite Rembrandt.' He came to a halt by a self-portrait: the artist's crimson-tinged, bulbous nose, curly grey hair, anxious and penetrating eyes, everything filtered through deep gold-green candlelight.

'Amazing. How I wish I could paint like that.'

'I would show you Canova statues, but you will have supper among them soon. And afterwards: masked ball! Please, you reserve dance for me, "worthy Therese". It is delight to talk with one so respected yet so elusive.'

I had never thought of myself that way, nor suspected that others might. Did I trust Razumovsky? It was hard not to warm to him, to be enthused by his joy in his acquisitions, to be drawn into his world, as Beethoven was.

Supper was announced. Pepi and I were on a table in, sure enough, the Canova Hall. Did the count remember exactly where every one of his five hundred guests was to be seated? I wouldn't put it past him.

Beneath the plinths that supported the perfect marble forms, I found my place: Gallenberg was on my right and a personable Dane to my left. Pepi was between a French Duc de Zumzingk-or-Other and a youthful Italian, whom she proceeded to mother throughout the meal. But to call this a meal would be like calling Beethoven's Seventh Symphony a 'piece'. While I alternated between Gallenberg's ponderings of trends in ballet music and attempting some words in my Danish companion's language, the pronunciation of which seemed to be missing the concept of consonants, we munched our way through oysters from the Holland coast, bizarrely fresh given the distance they had travelled, full of the scent of unformed pearls; caviar from Russian sturgeons, purple-black and posing a threat to the teeth for the rest of the evening; partridge with black truffles from France; velvety meat cooked in fine red wine; and slices of the most peculiar fruit I had ever seen: elongated prickly objects with spiny leaves like unruly hair, brought from far across the western seas. They had been reassembled after their dissection so we could see how they looked before we ate them. Inside, the flesh was bright yellow, stringy, sweet and slightly sour.

'What *is* this?' Pepi said through her first mouthful. 'It's astonishing!'

'It's called a pineapple,' her young Italian told us.

'They expect one to dance after such a banquet? I shall find a quiet corner to sleep until it is digested.' Gallenberg sat back, well contented, with his hands folded over his paunch. Julie, across the table, gave him a broad smile in which her eyes did not participate.

But dancing there was, in yet another wing: a vast ballroom under a ceiling painted with clouds, sunbursts, cherubs and Greek goddesses with exposed breasts. A bevy of trumpeters issued a fanfare and now masks were donned – black cat-like forms and white weeping Pierrots, gold and green Orientals and pale, floral mystery women – and from this moment on nobody was exactly who you thought they were; and time, though sounded by the occasional clock, was forgotten, along with the work the Congress had done all day and must return to in the morning.

I had feared nobody would dance with us, but soon we were circling the ballroom in the grand polonaise that opens every self-respecting ball: my arms crossed to hold the hands of the French Duke, while a flash of pink and white going by showed Pepi, silver-lace mask strapped around her eyes, dancing with Schuppanzigh, who did not bother masquerading since his figure was unmistakable. Soon music was taking us over while our heads lightened and brightened in the weird warm winter night.

I had been whirling round the room with the young Italian in an écossaise, and we had stopped to catch breath, when someone tapped my dancing partner on the shoulder: a friend who knew him despite, or maybe because of, his raven-feathered mask. Behind the gold and black visage of a Mandarin, the stranger's voice suggested they were of similar years. Then he turned to me. 'Madame, may I have the pleasure of the next dance? Lilac is my favourite colour – associated with the blooms of wisdom in Russian lore.'

'I know your accent.' I surveyed him from behind my mask, which transformed me into a black and white cat.

'I am Chinese!' The Mandarin laughed.

'Ah, but I suspect you are Hungarian.'

'In part, yes. And you, o fair feline?'

I smiled despite myself. 'I, too, am Hungarian.'

'How excellent, then, that I have found you in time for a waltz.'

'I'm not very good at waltzes,' I confided, while the orchestra struck up the introduction; couples were taking their places in the centre of the room. I did not want to admit that when I had learned to dance, the waltz did not exist; it might show how old I was.

'Don't worry,' he said. 'I'll hold you if you fall.'

His hand on my waist was warm and welcome; heat spread through my back beneath it. His other hand, gently holding mine to one side, was pleasing, inspiring trust. I watched Princess Bagration glide past with Tsar Alexander. As the strange Mandarin and I spun through the room I saw the graceful pose of the women leaning back upon the supportive arms of their partners, and tried to emulate it. But was every woman with someone she should not be with? It was impossible to escape the Congress gossip: the king of a German state had been seen with a mysterious young girl in the dark passages near the Esterházykeller, each count had a non-countess to his side, every baroness an illicit lover. This Congress might not solve the future of Europe, but perhaps not all its participants were there primarily to do so. Any love affair one had ever dreamed of could take place here in the city's gilded palaces, and nobody was going to stop their protagonists, because they were so wealthy and powerful that nothing could touch them except another individual with the same attributes, seeking sex.

Yet these people had shunned Pepi for her misfortunes, which they considered 'immorality'. How many women had our unmarried brother Franz slept with over the past two decades? How many love affairs would my young dancing partner have already enjoyed, despite his tender years? Anyone and everyone could have affairs and get away with it, uninterrupted and uncensored – except, it seemed, my sister.

'What's the matter?' my Mandarin asked. 'You are tense. Relax, dear kitty, and let me stroke your silken ears.' He spoke with such spirit that I laughed aloud. Perhaps I should jettison my habitual black more often.

'My sister has been unwell and I must ensure she is enjoying herself and does not need my aid.'

'If she does, she will look for you, or send someone to find you.' That sounded sensible enough. The waltz was ending and we sank to the finish, I in a curtsey, he in a deep bow that showed me the top of his head. Gold-brown curls without a hint of thinning. How young *was* he?

'Stay with me, little kitty? Another dance, and then maybe another?'

'Miaow,' I heard myself say. And we polkaed, our steps in easy and thoughtless unison. I knew only that with his hand curled around mine, I felt comfortable, secure and ridiculously happy.

Pepi galloped by in the arms of a minor Russian royal. Her old sparkle shone from her dark eyes. Whirling, giddy, beautified and taken up in the thrill of dancing, we stepped away from our daily selves – and Razumovsky stood to one side with arms folded and wide-set eyes smiling as he relished the splendours he had created for us all to enjoy.

We came to a halt, parched. 'Drink?' suggested my Mandarin.

I took his offered arm; we strolled to a side room set with ice buckets bearing champagne, lemonade and ice cream.

'Champagne.' He bounded forward; I watched him. He could not be more than twenty-four or twenty-five. Whatever was he going to say when he learned who I was, and my age?

Our glasses filled, we wandered to a quieter room where nests of velvet chairs and sofas were dotted about beneath paintings by Titian and Canaletto and between vast windows overlooking the park. Moonlight etched out the frosty branches of the oaks and lindens. Never in my life had I seen such a beautiful winter night.

We took the most distant and private group of chairs and sat opposite one another.

'Won't you tell me who you are?' I said.

'I will, if you will.'

'You first.'

'No, you!'

'Masks off – together,' I decided. 'One, two, three…'

A swift motion and we were no longer cat and mandarin – and the sweetest, brightest brown eyes I had ever seen gazed back at me, astonished.

'I expect I'm not who you thought.' I bolstered myself for his disappointment.

'But I know you! You are Countess Therese Brunsvik, are you not? I have seen your portrait. My name is Migazzi – Count Louis Migazzi. I work at the Hungarian Court Chancellery and I have had occasion to see portraits from many great Hungarian families. Your image stayed with me, beyond any other, for the wisdom in your eyes and the pride in your bearing. Others seek to be Aphrodite or Hera, but you are Athena.'

'I'm older than you expected.'

'I saw and felt only – *you*. That is the wonder of a masquerade. You dance not with who you see, but who you sense. This is much better, don't you think?'

'Tell me about yourself?'

He bowed his head. 'I am half Italian, half Hungarian. You may know my family name from my kinsman, who was once Archbishop of Vienna.'

His choice of an archaic word for his famous relative intrigued me. 'You sound as if you are fond of literature?'

Louis Migazzi's eyes lit up. He reminded me of a puppy whose big paws indicated that his full magnificence was yet to come. 'My favourite is Shakespeare. I have read all his plays in chronological order, to see how he develops.'

'In which language?'

'English! The only way.'

The floor beneath my feet evaporated. 'I couldn't agree more.'

Pepi came up to us just then, curious and smiling. I introduced my new acquaintance; he fetched her a drink. When he returned he mentioned a book he had been reading which I was hoping to read too, and I told him of our friendship with Schuppanzigh, and it turned out Migazzi was a keen violinist, and soon Pepi excused herself to take a turn around the ballroom with the Dane from our dinner table. The moon rose higher over the gleaming Donaukanal. Rumour had it, Migazzi said, that a mass sleigh ride to Schönbrunn was planned for later in the winter, ending there with a grand masked ball.

We went to stand at the window, gazing over Razumovsky's magical domain.

'May I call on you tomorrow, after work?' he asked. 'We can welcome in the new year.'

'Of course.' I told him where we could be found.

'I wonder what 1815 will have in store for us all.'

'Whatever it is,' I mused, 'it will not be what we expect.'

It must have been past four o'clock in the morning when Pepi and I made our exhausted, exhilarated way down Razumovsky's floating staircase to fetch our furs and summon our coachman.

'I hope the children are warm enough at home,' Pepi remarked as the icy air struck our noses.

'They'll be fine. Oh, Pips, do you think Migazzi will come to call?'

'He is smitten, Tesi. Make the most of it.'

'But I must be fifteen years older than him!'

So chattering, we climbed into our carriage. The horses began a brisk trot through the park, towards the distant gateway.

After some minutes I noticed strange sounds behind us.

What was that? Shouting? We quietened. The carriage was slowing down.

'Stefan,' Pepi called up to the coachman, 'what's going on?'

He stopped the carriage. A long minute of silence went by before his anxious face appeared in the window.

'Mesdames, it's not good. It seems something has happened at the palace.'

The rising tide of noise was now urgent and unmistakable. I threw open the door and jumped down into the night. Pepi followed. Together we took in the small signals of the vast catastrophe unfolding far behind. Smoke pricked in our nostrils; the crisp air was beginning to blur with its first billows. 'Stefan, can we go back to see what has transpired?' Pepi asked.

Rounding a bend in the road, we acquired a sudden and devastating view of the whole. The wing of the palace in which we had been eating oysters, truffles and pineapple not eight hours earlier was in conflagration. Its windows, emptied of glass, were vomiting fire. The beams that held up the roof above the Canova gallery were naked and black against the blaze. While we watched, they began to shift as if on an axis and slowly, block after block, splinter after splinter, their edifice imploded. The sound of the crashes reached us a moment later.

In the smoke, outlined against the voracious red, darkened figures were scuttling and scattering – servants trying to save what they could.

'The Canovas,' I said. 'The Stradivaris.'

'Where's Schuppanzigh?'

'I don't know. Oh, Pepi – how is this *possible?*'

We picked up our skirts and began to run towards the inferno that the palace had become. A moment later we encountered Julie and Gallenberg, whose carriage was a little way behind ours; beside it the impresario was holding and comforting his wife, who for once had given way to tears on his shoulder. I was pleased to feel glad they were safe.

'Schuppanzigh!' Pepi shouted. 'Ignaz Schuppanzigh! Where are you?'

'Louis!' was the first name that came to my lips. 'Louis Migazzi!' He had left when we left – hadn't he? With fresh horror, I remembered Toni and his terrible fate among the millions of slaughtered men sacrificed to Napoleon's megalomania.

Footsteps and a yell behind us: 'Therese! Thank God!' He was there, a tall, lithe figure running towards us – he engulfed us both within his wide wingspan. He, too, had rushed back to try to help.

'It must already have started when we left,' he said. 'It was probably burning for a long time, somewhere unseen...'

The heat on our faces grew fierce. Incandescent sparks whirled past our temples. Pepi in her fur wrap was shivering more with fright than with cold.

Louis dashed ahead and managed to waylay a terrified servant, who was trying to muster the courage to go back and save some paintings.

'He thinks it might be that fancy heating system,' he reported, coughing against the smoke. 'It's fired up from the wooden extension. That's a silly place for anything involving flame...'

From the second floor windows objects were flying to earth – underclothes, coats, trousers, waistcoats. A Chinese Ming vase appeared at the end of a pair of arms; a moment later it was in splinters on the ground. From another room, leather-bound books were being flung from a great height, mahogany and gilt doors plummeted down, dark against the fire, and the gleam of a silver tray soared through the air.

'The vultures will be out for this lot.' Louis was almost in tears. 'Oh God, the Rembrandt...'

Out of the crowd of terrified onlookers, a podgy figure clutching three instrument cases in his arms was stumbling towards us. 'Schuppanzigh! Thank heavens,' cried Pepi.

The violinist sank to his knees, gasping for breath. 'It's the Apocalypse,' he said. 'There's a whole orchestra of Italian instruments in there, burning. Everybody is saving the silverware instead. They'll steal the lot – think they can sell it – oh, the morons, the philistines, they don't know the real value of anything! Oh, Josephine, Therese – all is vanity, nothing but vanity. This is the truth. This is the city of hell.'

'Come on, Schuppanzigh.' Pepi crouched beside him. 'You're safe now and that's what matters. Your wife will be so worried, and so relieved.'

'I know, I know...' He was weeping where he knelt, clasping his beloved violins. 'But how are we to live? That is my *job*, going up in flames.' For seven years Razumovsky had fully employed his quartet; for seven years he and his three colleagues had not had a moment's worry about income, despite the financial chaos all around.

Silently, Louis touched my arm and pointed. There beneath a huge oak, hidden in the shadow, was a tall figure in a dark cloak, clutching the tree trunk and shaking with sobs. Razumovsky, his treasures lost and his Arcadian dream smashed to pieces, was alone in the dark, weeping for his shattered world.

# 24

My dear,

We thought everything that could destroy us had already taken place. I would urge anybody who believes such a thing to think again.

The trouble that Louis Migazzi and I could not foresee for the year ahead, in those blessed hours before the fire, had begun innocently enough in the autumn of 1814, when Fritz sat down for a serious talk with his mother and me about his future.

'I want to become a soldier,' he said.

Pepi, like me, had developed a horror of the military. Austria had lost several hundred thousand men to Napoleon's campaigns, whether fighting against him or for him; as for those alive but horrifically injured, we were accustomed to seeing them, destitute and sometimes deranged, begging on the streets of Vienna.

'You are much too young even to think of such a thing,' she snapped.

'But Mama, this is what I want to do. I am old enough to know that.' Fritz was developing fast, as Julie had surmised. He was tall for his age, with a gait not unlike that of his late father, and a fuzz of incipient moustache was showing above his lip.

'But *why?*' Pepi demanded. 'To be killed or left wrecked for life? To kill and maim others? I will *never* let you do that, either you or your brother!'

To me, it was obvious why. A military career did not require schoolwork. It did not demand a university degree and the memorisation of difficult texts and Latin terms, unlike law or medicine. It did not take talent, unlike music or art. Physical strength, discipline, a fondness for guns and a hatred of foreigners were, as far as I could tell, the principal requirements. Some of the military, like my unfortunate Toni, undertook army careers because their families demanded it. Ours was the opposite.

'It will suit me and I could do well,' said Fritz.

'He could,' Carl asserted, 'and so could I.' His voice was not yet near breaking.

Pepi ran weeping from the room.

'You must realise that she is afraid for you and does not wish your lives to be endangered,' I said to the distressed lads. 'I concur entirely.'

They exchanged grimaces.

I found Pepi at her writing table, still quivering with anger. She was addressing a letter to Pestalozzi. We had had no contact with him since matters turned bad with Stackelberg.

'It is just as I feared,' she said. 'They need a man's hand – they will not listen to me. Or to you. I must find them a tutor.'

In the end, we found a solution closer to home than Pestalozzi: a few local enquiries brought Eduard, Baron von Andrian-Werburg into our lives. He was a personable widower, my junior by a couple of years, and an experienced professor of history and mathematics; he taught at the Theresianum and seemed to us a paragon of virtue, with the gravitas to bring our incipiently wild youths under control. The boys liked him at once. So did we.

'A man's life falls into three phases,' Andrian noted when we interviewed him. 'First, education; next, responsibility to others; finally, once the virility of youth is behind us, we may take care of ourselves.'

'It is thus, too, with women,' I suggested.

'Not entirely. A woman never quite takes care of herself – nor should she have to.'

'Why not move into the Palais with us?' Pepi suggested. 'There is plenty of room.'

As with a musical motif, events do not have to be identical in order to rhyme.


Up in the hills, yet with the red roofs and yellow ochre glow of Vienna visible on the horizon, Döbling offered the fresh air and long walking trails that Luigi craved. In winter he would make two circuits of Vienna's city walls in double-quick time every afternoon, no matter the weather. In summer, countryside hikes beckoned. That summer, in Döbling – as I discovered, leafing through her appointment book – Pepi intended to meet him. She said nothing to me. She simply wrote '*Döbling. Beeth.*'

She travelled there for a few weeks, alone, under a false name. She refused my company and revealed few details later – but occasionally let slip a word about walks above the vineyards, or the wondrous view of the city and the gleam of the Danube in the distance, or the joy of a picnic lunch, something she would never do alone. I pretended to know nothing.

Andrian was taking the boys away for a summer of catch-up coaching in maths, history and outdoor sports. Viky had made a decision to leave us. She told Pepi that it was in order to spare us expense: she would live with her aunt Victoria Golz in Prague and, for the summer, Nemischl. To me, she confided something different.

Andrian, she said, had come into her room while she was studying her Greek, then encouraged her to set it aside and to let him teach her something that would be more valuable for a young woman's prosperous future. Standing behind her, he placed his hands over hers and, pressing, closed the book. By this gesture, his arms folded around her body.

'I pushed him off.' Viky's cheeks were carmine with distress. 'I was so scared – and he looked surprised – I think he didn't expect me to object.'

'You got away?'

'I ran. I hid in the museum. It was quite busy, so I felt safe there.'

Safe, among Deym's pornographic sculptures? My poor darling Viky, growing at fourteen into the Fair Sleeper? Not if I had anything to do with it. Agonising though it was to consider losing her, her safety was paramount. I promised to organise at once for her to travel to Prague.

A chill ran over me at the thought of Sephine – who was only eleven, but would soon grow to womanhood too. Would she be safe from the monster Pepi had admitted into our home? For the summer, I sought the haven of Martonvásár and took the little girl with me. There, sitting by my monument to the grandfather she had never known, she confided that she longed to go to the Institute of Mary's seminary and eventually to take holy orders. When an eleven-year-old girl elects to leave the family home of her own accord, you can be certain that not all is well around her. 'It's a very good idea,' I assured her. 'I will make sure your mother agrees.'

If Pepi were meeting Luigi, I could see no point in trying to separate them now. All possible damage had already been done. She was not strong; her illness recurred often and I was beginning to fear that the intense flame of her life was flickering and might soon be extinguished. Why deny her and Luigi the rare solace of companionship, even if it could be no more than that?

There was another reason not to disturb them. Pepi was six months pregnant.

I would not have wished to witness Luigi's anguish when he understood. If I thought my sister was an idiot to be snared yet again, telling her so would not help; but I could hardly believe she was going through all this once more, out of wedlock for the third time. If the child were Luigi's, I would have found a measure of hope in the situation – but it was not.

Pepi had welcomed Andrian with such warmth, encouraged him to stay with such enthusiasm, that it was no wonder if he thought her favourably disposed towards him. Again she was too pleased to have a man in the house. Again, I did not warn her away soon or strongly enough, being preoccupied with other matters – this time, Louis Migazzi; and with an open heart of my own, I must somehow have considered that an open heart in others was nothing to be ashamed of.

When we arrived home from the tragic night at Razumovsky's, Pepi was weeping with exhaustion and shock and I was fixated on Louis Migazzi, my emotions imploding like the palace's roof. So when the servants came out to meet us, and Andrian appeared in his dressing gown to hear the terrible news, Pepi probably needed comforting, but I went straight to my room without noticing what everyone else did. A fairy-tale night, a catastrophe, overwrought emotions and a seemingly sympathetic man ready to pounce – I should have seen the likely outcome from a great distance. I fear I was too close to it to recognise the pattern.

Pepi was all bone and sinews now, but for her swelling abdomen. It was a pregnancy too far, for all of us. If Beethoven were depressed and unproductive, I could not be surprised. At intervals through 1814, 1815 and 1816 he wrote a series of atrocious things commissioned either for the Congress or by participants who came looking for him while in Vienna; ceremonial pieces, nationalistic twiddles and jingoistic bang-crash-wallops that were likely to vanish into their patrons' storerooms after a single hearing.

As for the family, word would out. Minona could be passed off, to Mother and Franz, as Stackelberg's, at least for the moment; but this pregnancy could not, for Stackelberg was long gone. Franz was ablaze with fury – even as he galloped over the Danube bridge towards Pest and its finest brothel.

'*Please tell Pepi to take care of herself*,' wrote Lotti, to me, but not to her. '*I hope all will go well.*'

'You should go to Hungary and live with Mother,' I told Pepi.

'Do you want them to kill me?' she said.

Mother sent money; she always did. Franz was less kind: '*She shall have no more cash from me. No sister of mine would prostitute herself this way.*'

If only Pepi had left the boys at Pestalozzi's institute back in 1809, none of this would have happened. When September arrived, Pepi disappeared into the countryside and would not let me accompany her. She returned several weeks later with a baby daughter in her arms.

I reached out a finger for my new niece to hold. Pepi snatched her away, her gaze upon me furious – as if it were all my fault.

'Stop it,' she said. 'Her name is Emilie. I don't much love her, I don't want her and I don't want anything to do with her.'

'But I could…'

'You stay away from her. *He* will take her and raise her as his "ward". Better he should take her now than kidnap her later.'

'Pips, let me help you,' I pleaded.

'Stop it. Just stop it.' Pepi deposited her tiny bundle of baby on the sofa, then crumpled down next to her. 'I'm sending Magda to hire a wet-nurse. Or a goat. Or anything, until *he* can get out and take her with him.'

'Is she baptised?'

'Of course. I found a priest who recorded her as legitimate, for a small fee, and her godmother is Therese Busch.'

'What? As in – plants in the Vienna Woods?' I tried to laugh, but Pepi was in no laughing mood. 'You are not yourself, darling. Let me get you something to eat…'

'Leave me alone,' said Pepi into her hands. 'You will poison me.'


Andrian packed his trunk plus a parcel of baby clothes from Pepi's armoire, then took his leave, promising to write regarding Emilie's well-being. He kept in touch with the boys, who bade him a sorrowful farewell. Word came two years later that Emilie had contracted measles and died. The innocent child passed away before she was old enough to know how unfortunate she was.

I do not want to blame Pepi for her misfortunes. I cannot bear to think of her illness and her gradual loss of grasp on reality. But if she had not allowed herself to be taken in by Andrian, might she not have reasserted the strength of her relationship with Luigi? He must have taken this extraordinary turn of events as a betrayal of his love – for so it was. Yet I believe he must have found in his heart the capacity to forgive her. I do not know the full truth, though, either because Pepi would no longer confide in me, or perhaps because I was too addle-headed at the time to hear what she was trying to say.

'I could be your mother.'

I was with Louis in the small sitting room of his apartment, set in a crumbling palace building owned by the Hungarian Chancellery, just across the road from the Minoritenplatz. It was a more amenable setting for our meetings than Pepi's home.

'You'd have had to be a very young mother.' Louis was lying with his stockinged feet up on the arm of the sofa and his head in my lap. The fingers of my right hand seemed to have acquired a life of their own, twisting through his gold-brown curls.

'I'm forty. You're twenty-three.'

'You'd have had to be seventeen.' A contented smile. 'I don't care. Life is short. We should live it to the full, while we can.'

'And there is but one chance to please God.'

On this, Louis disagreed. He was inclining to what at first seemed an insane if somewhat beautiful idea: reincarnation, karma, enlightenment. Not a European Enlightenment, but a spiritual, Eastern one. As a student he had acquired, out of curiosity, a copy of the *Bhagavad Gita*. 'The greatest revelation of my life,' he told me, placing a copy of Friedrich Majer's German translation in my hands.

'You haven't had much of your life yet.'

He ignored that. 'You must read it. You won't find poetry, legends or philosophies to touch it. It makes our Western writings look like clodhopping bumbles.'

He was amassing a collection of Indian writings, some of it shipped all the way from Delhi. He had an English contact, a former fellow student whom he'd met in Leipzig, who was now an officer in Bengal with the East India Company, as captivated by the country's life as Louis was by its literature.

'The British soldiers are always being warned not to "go native",' he remarked, while I marvelled over the latest arrivals, with their silky-fine paper on which was printed text in an unfathomable script. 'Sanskrit. I am determined to learn it. It's a gateway to another world. My friend, Captain Dalrymple, says India brings a different way of thinking about every aspect of life. And a lot of British soldiers are falling in love with the Indian girls.'

'What if a British woman were to fall in love with an Indian man?'

'And if a man of forty falls in love with a girl of twenty-three, all is acceptable...'

'But here...'

'It only matters if we *make* it matter.'

'Would your family hear of it?'

'I don't intend to ask them.'

'Nor need you, since I have no intention of marrying you or anybody, ever.'

'You haven't?' Louis swung himself upright. I put out a hand to caress his cheek; he leaned catlike into my palm.

'I took a vow,' I said.

A mischievous gleam. 'I haven't proposed to you in any case. Come back here...'


'Come back,' I said to the other Louis, Luigi or Ludwig, the names interchangeable in the multinational melting pot of what remained of the Empire. 'Please come and play for us at the Palais.'

Louis and I were planning a musical soirée – after numerous discussions, calculations and promises to Pepi that she would not have to foot the bill. The salon stood cold and dark. We longed to inject a little life force into a place that felt drained of it.

Schuppanzigh provided the perfect excuse. He was leaving the country. After the Razumovsky fire, his quartet had gone their separate ways, of necessity; now the count, financially and psychologically half ruined, had helped to find the violinist a position at court in St Petersburg. Our soirée would be our old friend's farewell to Vienna. His former cellist, Joseph Linke, volunteered to play the 'Archduke' Trio with him – and its composer. Pepi's piano was neglected, hideously out of tune and with pedals that threatened to fall off; Nanette Streicher had offered to lend us an instrument from her piano firm for the occasion, on condition that her old friend Beethoven agreed, for once, to play.

I had also sent a messenger to Alsergrund to look for our young composer friend and ask him to attend, with his latest songs. The city's leading baritone, Johann Michael Vogl, who had sung Pizarro in *Fidelio*, promised to perform them.

We wondered whether anybody would actually turn up. Pepi watched from the Palais windows, like an anxious child, for the first carriages.

'Those who truly love us will be here,' Luigi said to her from the newly delivered piano, where he was warming up. She gave him a bittersweet smile.

I watched them, my face turned half away so they would not see how flummoxed I was. Pepi and Luigi, here, together, in the same room – and in the same harmony. Had the vast betrayal of the Andrian affair left nothing unchanged between them? From Luigi, no hint of bitterness. From Pepi, only the love that shone through her gaze upon him. *How?*

The servants had polished the tarnished silver trays with spirits of ammonia and turpentine, washed the dust off the disused china and cleaned the crystal glasses with fuller's earth. They prepared platters of refreshments and ice buckets for Sekt. Pepi, energised by Beethoven's presence, was presenting a good semblance of her old bustling, excitable self. Occasionally she went over to the rehearsing musicians and stood for a while behind her loved one's left shoulder, turning the pages for him.

While they were in full flow, the door creaked open and a diminutive figure tiptoed into the shadows. His companion, the affable Stephan von Breuning, motioned him forward; they listened in awed silence. At the end I rose to welcome them.

'Herr Schubert, excellent to see you again!' I put a hand on his shoulder to propel him towards Beethoven, because if I had not, he would have fled the room.

Beethoven turned from the keyboard and extended a

hand and a warm smile to the youth, who was too scared to utter anything but a gruff 'Master.'

'Herr Schubert has brought some of his compositions,' I scribbled for Luigi.

'May I see?' He held out his bear-paw to take the music. Schubert flushed, shoved them towards him, then turned and hurried out. He could not look on while Beethoven examined his work. Louis, on his way in, smiled after him, then came up to be introduced.

'Ludwig, meet Ludwig,' I wrote.

'Ah, the Orientalist! I've heard much about you,' Beethoven said, too loudly. 'We must talk matters Indian. I'd love some reading recommendations.'

An hour later, the room was populated by loyal friends – and some less loyal – who could not resist the chance to be at Schuppanzigh's last Viennese performance. Beethoven's protégé Carl Czerny, a brilliant young pianist, arrived with both his parents, his trousers dotted with gobbets of cat hair. 'How many cats did you say you had?' I asked him.

Czerny had the grace to blush. 'Sixteen.'

Terrible emptinesses reminded us of those friends we would never see again. Marianna and Antonia, dead of consumption; Prince Kinsky, killed by his fall; Prince Lichnowsky, felled by a stroke, would haunt Beethoven's stairs no longer; and Prince Lobkowitz, bankrupted by the war, had never come back.

Vogl, whom I judged somewhat too aware of his own grandeur, strode up to sing Schubert's settings of poems by Goethe. '*Who rides so late through night so wild? It is the father with his child…*'

Alongside this opulent voice, Schubert at the piano

seemed to be giving way to a peculiar type of insanity. His right hand was pounding at repeated octaves with such violence that I feared he would wreck the instrument. The song, *Erlkönig*, was full of shifts between major and minor, eerie spirit voices, the terrified child's interjections, the horse's hooves galloping until, in the devastating last line, the child is dead in his father's arms. There was a silence as we all tried to get our breath. Then tumultuous applause.

Beethoven could not hear much of it, but he could see the effect it made and he could read the music. 'This is remarkable,' he said to me. 'You must watch this young man – he has a divine spark in him.'

I fumbled for my paper and pencil. 'I wish he would come out of his shell,' I wrote. 'He's too shy to talk to patrons and will make no impression at all.'

'He will find his way via his music. Tell him I said so.'

Pepi slid into a chair beside us; I saw their hands brush for a moment. Schubert, at the piano, had started a bouncy accompaniment. *Heidenröslein* had the deceptive guise of a folk song. A boy finds a rose on the heath. He wants to pluck her. She won't be plucked. He says he will take her by force. Then my thorns shall prick you, she says. Both are as good as their word. 'So true,' Pepi mumbled.

Finally Vogl invited Anna Milder to take his place. Our Leonore, the toast of the Vienna opera, was gracing us with a rare presence. Schubert's accompaniment set up the rhythm of a spinning wheel; Anna sang Goethe's Gretchen. '*My peace is gone, my heart is sore, I shall find it never, never more…*'

The poet's words struck home; and I sensed all of us in our isolated selves sharing myriad emotions through the same music: Pepi and Beethoven's past, Goethe's wisdom, Schubert's future, and goodness only knew what would become of me and Louis…

'That's what music is *for*,' he said, when I confided my thoughts during the applause. Watching Schuppanzigh and Linke tuning up for the trio, it struck me that I had never thought of music being *for* anything other than itself.

The violinist and cellist were generous to their composer as the trio progressed; it was self-evident that they might never perform together again. Their rehearsal earlier now counted for little: Beethoven could not hear what he or his colleagues were doing. He crashed through the loud passages, but could no better judge the soft ones, pressing the keys too little so that clutches of notes did not sound at all.

Everyone understood. Nobody could have listened to this without praying for the largest quotient of tact the Almighty could endow. Luigi must have realised the moment he had dreaded for years had arrived: he could no longer perform his own music. I sensed Pepi beside me crumbling, trying to conceal her sorrow.

The music over, the guests flocked around our star singers beside the platters and ice buckets. Schubert made a quiet escape down the back stairs. I lost track of Luigi. I could imagine why he might want to disappear, but his absence bothered me. His hat was still on top of the cupboard by the door. Across the main landing, the museum entrance was slightly ajar.

I found Luigi standing in front of one of Deym's Etruscan urns, lost in contemplation.

'They are impressive, aren't they?' I said, hand on his arm.

'An art that lasts for millennia, undefiled. But I wasn't

looking at them particularly. I was wondering how I used to play as I did – ever.'

I linked my arm through his and pressed. There was nothing I could say.

'And Pepi.' His voice was choked with emotion.

'You forgave her?' I scribbled.

'There's nothing to forgive. I know what it is to be lonely… No, Tesi, it concerns me more that now there is nowhere to go. We are lost, both of us. What should I do? How can I live through this?'

'Trust to God. Leave it in the hands of the omniscient one. And, Luigi, please try not to put yourself into a situation where you might feel weakened and give way to an injustice that is not worthy of you.' I still feared that Luigi's famous temper might yet turn upon my sister.

'And you… will look after her? Promise me?'

'I give you my word of honour.'

'Your devotion deserves never to be forgotten. I know there can never be any benefit to me from that,' he added, 'but it all springs from goodness. I've always known the goodness of your heart, Tesi, and I always will.'

We wandered back to the salon; a handful of guests were still there, staying until the small hours, like old times. But the farewells from some would perhaps be forever.

'I *will* come back,' Schuppanzigh insisted, cloak over his shoulders and violin case in his hand. 'I am not sure when, but…'

'Goodbye, dear Schuppanzigh. Go well,' I said. This once, as old friends taking a long leave, we hugged one another. He swallowed one last chocolate in a gulp, beamed his familiar fleshy grin towards us, then disappeared into the night.

Beethoven went to Pepi and bowed low before her. Then he whispered to her – but I could read his lips.

'Goodnight, my angel.'

## 25

My dear,

A small boy is sitting at Beethoven's table, pencilling doodles on a creased sheet of paper. Now and then his little hand slows and he stares into space.

'This is Karl,' says Luigi from the shadows. 'My nephew.'

This was no place for a child. Beethoven's latest abode, on the Sailerstätte, was his least pleasant yet. A musty, mouldy smell hung in the air; the window seemed unopenable; and under the piano an unemptied chamber pot awaited attention.

'Luigi,' I said into his ear trumpet, '*what are you doing?*'

'Trying to write. It's no good.' He would scarcely hear me; but he knew me well enough to anticipate my words.

'Where are your servants?'

'I dismissed them both.'

Perhaps they felt their work should not include child-minding. I turned to Karl, who looked up at me with big, solemn eyes. 'What about you? What's the story, little one?'

'Uncle Ludwig says I must stay with him because my Papa died,' Karl mumbled.

'That's one reason I wanted to see you, Tesi.' Beethoven

lumbered across the room and slapped a protective paw down on Karl's shoulder. The lad shrank away. 'Tell me about Pestalozzi.'

Since Luigi's brother Kasper Karl had died – the one he had wrestled with in the Heiligenstadt street – Luigi, officially the lad's co-guardian, had been trying to take sole custody. Naturally Johanna, his sister-in-law, was incensed with fury. Luigi thought her wanton, frivolous, dishonest. I should add that Johanna had been tried, convicted and imprisoned for theft; it seemed natural that Luigi would wish to remove his likely heir from a proven criminal and give him instead the best possible start in life. The problem was that he had not the first idea how to do it, let alone how to contend with his inevitable communication problem. Lawyers became involved.

'And you, Karl?' I asked. 'How do *you* feel?'

'I miss my Mama. Uncle Ludwig doesn't let me see her very often.'

'Isn't Uncle Ludwig good to you?'

'Oh, he is. He really is. But... he doesn't hear me if I say anything, so I just sit here.'

'You ought to be in school.'

How were Luigi and I supposed to converse freely in front of poor Karl? Complying, since there was no conflict-free alternative, I began to scribble some notes about Pestalozzi's teaching methods and where a tutor or specialist school might be found. I had nevertheless come round to tell him something quite different: namely, that we were, at least for now, leaving the Palais.

Louis shone into our lives like the Christmas star above

Bethlehem. When he had first come to us, he bounded pup-pylike into the Palais and roared with laughter at Ferdinand IV and the Fair Sleeper; later, since he was as good as family, he surveyed the rooms and the paperwork. 'You could let your own living quarters for good money,' he noted. 'But the place is falling down. You must move out, fix it up, then cash in. If you like, I will try and find you a loan for the costs and somewhere suitable you can live in the interim.'

He knew of a large apartment on the Minoritenplatz that was currently empty; he argued our case and secured it for us at a pittance. I could step out of the door and go straight into the Minoritenkirche for my morning prayer. I loved this church for its austere atmosphere – plain glass, charcoal-grey pillars and high Gothic arches, rather than the fancy baroque confections of the Peterskirche, or the Stephans-dom, which was more a social centre than a place of wor-ship. Alone there, before dawn, I could experience a state of meditative grace that made the day ahead bearable until I could see Louis again. Another advantage of living here was that his lodgings were over the road.

I would walk each morning to the museum, before most of Vienna had woken. Trying not to say 'Leave it to me,' I decided to stay in the stinking cesspit that the city became in midsummer despite its supposedly modern sewers. Someone had to manage the repairs, which must be done before the place came back to life in September. The balconies needed resurfacing. The stone eagles above the portico posed a dan-ger to those passing below – I received a police order that they must come down before they fell. Pocks, chips and missing chunks spattered the stonework after Napoleon's shelling. The museum, with the public tramping in and out, needed endless maintenance, which cost more than the place could ever generate.

Pepi, with heavy heart, capitulated. She was too weak to do anything more. She sent the boys away to cadet school and Sephine to her longed-for seminary; she accepted the loan Louis organised, paid for the repairs and lived on three florins a day. 'It's your fault,' she accused me. 'You don't have to spend that much on the place.'

'Did you *read* this?' I waved the police order under her nose.

'We're ruined, and you're ruining us.'

I ate once a day: nuts, broth, vegetables. Sometimes Louis had given me dinner. Now he had gone to his family estate for two months.

I raided what remained of the Palais coffers and brought Pepi a folder of paper ducats. 'Go and take a cure,' I advised – it would be an economy if it improved her health.

She needed no second bidding. Using her old name, Countess Deym, she applied for a passport: a document to prove one's identity, as if this bizarre new world's expectation was that nobody would really be who they said they were. Without this, one now could not go even as far as Baden, which was no distance at all. She requested it for six months. Eventually the authorities sent one for half that time, objecting that the passport of 'Countess Deym' actually belonged to 'Baroness von Stackelberg'. Finally she set off, alone. Beethoven, too, was in Baden again – the country retreat he loved the most.

During the summer of 1816 the sun did not shine. The blue skies above the Vienna Woods turned black, an unnatural, terrifying darkness, full of tainted air that reminded me of the tragic night at Razumovsky's palace. No wind arrived to blow these smoke-like clouds away. Near Lake Geneva, a group of English writers I admired – Lord Byron, John Polidori, Percy Bysshe Shelley and his young wife Mary, daughter of my heroine Mary Wollstonecraft – were trying to take a holiday. They set themselves the challenge of writing ghost stories instead.

Across the world, on an Indonesian island called Sumbawa, a volcano, Mount Tambora, had undergone a violent eruption as long ago as the previous April. What we were experiencing now was not divine retribution, but smoke and ash, debris from the moment when the innermost core of what felt like half our planet roared out molten into the heavens. Over the intervening months this mass of horror had blown all the way to Europe, and now it spread over us like a fatal suffocating pillow. The temperature plummeted; rain and torrents followed, bringing down ash in the water; everywhere the crops failed. Yet in Baden, Beethoven would accept the challenge of the elements and maintain his routine in defiance. Perhaps, when the rain stopped, Pepi might be at his side, and Karl trotting along behind, wondering who this strange, frail woman was with whom Uncle Ludwig walked arm in arm, silent under the cold charcoal skies.

How would she have found him? Fussing over clean handkerchiefs for his confused and unhappy nephew. And a new set of songs on the table. A mini-opera, for one singer and piano, lasting about fifteen minutes – an invention of his own. 'Call it a "*Liederkreis*",' he suggested. A circle, or cycle, of songs.

My dear, you will often read that Beethoven did not like to write songs. Yet during these straitened times, he was composing more in this genre than in any other. Upon discovering that a young medical student he met by chance was a fine amateur poet, he pounced on a set of his poems and decided to put them to music when a suitable commission gave him the chance.

The title was *An die ferne Geliebte*. 'To the Distant Beloved.' He had dreamed up a new genre especially for it, these verses addressed to someone far away, longed for across the valleys, among the trees, flowers and birds – and finally united through the power of song.

The medical student, Alois Jeitteles from Brünn, was twenty-two, even younger than my Louis; he had published a few poems in literary journals. Luigi became animated as he spoke of him: to Jeitteles, he told me, music, writing and medicine were linked at a profound spiritual level. He could no more divide one from another than he could choose between his limbs. His forefathers in the eighteenth-century Jewish Enlightenment had understood this well, he claimed: in Vilna, a venerated sage known as the Gaon promulgated scientific learning and the art of music as virtually one and the same. Surprisingly to some, Luigi was unfazed upon learning that Jeitteles was Jewish.

'He's a bright, principled young man and his writing has the ring of truth to it,' he remarked.

'You are a healer too, through music.'

'Antonie Brentano says something similar.' He gave one of those unfathomable private smiles. It crossed my mind that perhaps Antonie Brentano meant more to him than he admitted. He had played to her continually when she was ill and depressed in Vienna. Now the family was back in Frankfurt, her husband sent Luigi money and letters full of valuable advice regarding the legal situation over poor little Karl; and Luigi, in turn, sent them music. Several years earlier he had dedicated a song to Antonie called *To the Beloved* – though had he addressed this to Pepi, it would have been regarded as compromising. Antonie could freely commission it from him, with guitar accompaniment which she could play. Why must there be one rule for a wealthy, settled, married woman with five children and a sickly infant – Antonie's youngest son was born three weeks before Minona – and another for a widowed countess whose misfortunes had long ago turned her mind in catastrophic directions?

He dedicated the new 'song cycle' to Prince Lobkowitz, not to Antonie and certainly not to Pepi (and, alas, the good prince died before he had a chance to hear it). With hindsight, I cannot help noticing that it is called not 'To the Immortal Beloved', but 'To the *Distant* Beloved'. But Pepi was more distant than she was immortal, and 'her' theme is everywhere in it. I think of them in the country, walking side by side: is this his gesture of forgiveness? You could see unity through music as the thin end of the wedge. You could also see it as a comfort, a way to reassure her and find resolution within himself.

'*Take them then, these songs that I have sung for you...*' Listen to that melody in the first song that returns in the last: Pepi's theme, reincarnated again, this time in a chromatic variant, but still rhyming. The *Andante favori*, the F minor String Quartet, the E flat minuet, *Ich denke dein*, Florestan's cry for his angel Leonore. The fixed idea, the obsession, the immovable one: my sister, Pepi.


'Don't be stupid,' Pepi protested from her bed. She was back from the country; its curative effects had been short-lived. I was playing the song cycle obsessively, insisting it held *her* theme.

'You're the one who spotted it first. *You* said he was setting your name.'

Pepi – who had started to find anger more motivating than happiness, sympathy or enthusiasm – sat up, fighting her cough. Her gaze was furious.

'The motifs are different.' Her tone seemed to accuse me – of what? Idiocy? Madness? 'Just sing them. They are *not* the same.'

I obeyed. The outline was obvious – at least, to me.

'They are not identical, but they are too similar not to notice,' I said.

'But that's just *how he writes.* It's everywhere in his music, because that's his language. It's nothing to do with me.'

'So why is he writing songs to a distant beloved where this, of all things, is the centre of it? Why is Luigi writing songs at all?'

'Maybe he saw Schubert's and wanted to try some himself. Luigi was telling me how impressed he was…'

'So you *did* see him in Baden?'

'Oh, Tesi, *of course* I saw him. What does it matter? What does any of it matter? It's too late. It's all squandered. It's all gone.'


I made my escape. It was late in the evening and in his rooms Louis would be taking off his boots, stretching his shoulders after a long day at the desk, and enjoying a warm brandy and perhaps some bread and herring or cheese. Veiled, I padded along the dark Minoritenplatz, under the archways beside the church, and over the road; here I crossed the courtyard, then climbed the flight of shallow stairs I had come to know so well.

He let me in without a word and embraced me.

'Good evening, my Socrates,' I said.

'Greetings, my Diotima.'

He was just as I had expected: in shirtsleeves on the sofa, a half-drunk snifter of brandy and crumb-sprinkled plate on the table beside an oil lamp and his downturned book. 'What's the matter?' he asked, having called his servant to bring me refreshments. 'Something is bothering you very much. Is it me?'

'You could not trouble me if you tried to.' I stroked his curls away from his broad forehead. 'You'll laugh, but it is a piece of music that will not leave me alone. A series of songs Beethoven has written, which I know is for my sister – though she rejects it.'

'We will have it, then, at our next soirée, and you shall choose the singer. Then we'll see. And we will ask Schubert to bring more of his plentiful efforts. They say he even scribbles them on the back of tavern receipts if he happens to dream one up over his beer.'

'Perhaps I should "adopt" him too. I should adopt a whole family of young men.'

'Don't you dare! I'm keeping you all to myself.'

We sat side by side and sipped, the warmth seeping through us. After a minute he put one long arm around me and I leaned my head on his shoulder. The pull between us was too strong and he tipped my face upwards to press his lips to mine.

I still could not believe that a man's lips were so soft, or his skin so tender. Perhaps it was only that he was so young, rather like a girl himself.

'Don't go. Stay with me tonight.'

'I can't.'

'Of course you can. Anyone who saw you will assume the worst in any case. You might as well give them something to gossip about!'

I smiled despite myself. 'I made a vow…'

'I won't ask you for something you are not ready to give. I just want you to be here, with me, asleep in my arms.'

I would not know how to sleep in someone's arms. Yet this longing – infinite longing – seemed like the surge of a tide beneath a cliff or the revolutions of the moon in the heavens.

I need to rise above this. I need to resist. I cannot be taken by the physical demands of a body that is mine, but is not my self.

'Louis, I can't stay.'

'Tesi… Why is this wonderful thing between us so terrible to you?'

'I don't want you to desire me like any common woman. Our bond is spiritual and intellectual, and I want it always to be that way.'

'And so it will – but that needn't exclude love.'

At last I was beginning to understand what had conquered my sister, but with that arrived a further comprehension: when a physical drive takes over a relationship, it is halfway to destruction. Once it is consummated, you can never go back. Then all is lost. Pepi was the proof.

'You are so precious to me – I don't want to ruin everything.'

Louis laughed. 'But you *couldn't*.'

How could I admit my fears: that my body might rebel at the last minute, or some element of my womanly form would not work as it was meant to; or that I was forty and a virgin and had no idea what to do; or that I might, like Pepi, become pregnant out of wedlock…

'I have to go, Louis.'

Defeated, he stood and placed my cloak around my shoulders. 'Dearest Diotima – may I *hope*?'

I expect he could read the answer that was swimming in my eyes.

I struggled in vain for sleep that night. Just as in Plato's *Symposium* Socrates had the friendship of the seer and priestess Diotima to direct him in the philosophy of love, so Louis would have the best I could give him from my spirit and my learning. Plato affirms that the beauty of the beloved inspires us to seek spiritual beauty – and through this, to love divinity. Why contaminate that with a body that was deficient and could only disappoint?

What was happening to me anyway? Why this obsession with the beauty of a young man? I could have married the unspellable count to whom Franz had introduced me; he wrote regularly to renew his proposal. I could have had an easy life with him, an 'arrangement', and a lover – Louis – sneaking in on the side. I did not want an easy life; I wanted to make my mark and found my school, as soon as Viky was old enough to be my partner in the venture. But if I looked away from my work, the sensation of his hair under my hand and the sound of his laughter would fill my being. I would have a hard task to force myself out of my dream.

Was my physicality playing a trick on me? Did it know something that I, its owner, rejected: that its demand for fertility, independent from my mind and my will, must soon be spent? Was Louis my body's plot against my spirit?

I will not give way. I shall sing myself silently into a stupor, thinking of my own distant beloved, just across the road...

'*Take them then, these songs which I have sung for you. Sing them always in the evening, to the sweet strains of the lute. As the sun sets towards the azure lake, and its last rays glow then fade behind the mountain heights, and you sing what I sing, with overflowing heart – without display, aware only of your longing – then through these songs, the distance between us shall dissolve, and a loving heart shall be touched by that which a loving heart has consecrated.'*

## 26

My dear niece,

Where does change begin? Where does splendour begin its turn to destruction, excess to depravity, or love to confusion and thence to hatred? Thinking back on interlocking chains of event and counter-event, it is tempting to blame the stars, the planets, the cyclic forces of nature. How else to explain the horrific sequence of Napoleon's return from Elba and his easy marshalling of a new army, followed by the catastrophe of the year without a summer? Who could have imagined that the extravagance of Razumovsky's last ball would give way so soon to penury, famine and pestilence throughout Europe?

The disastrous summer of 1816 and its failed harvests extended from Ireland to Ukraine; the inflation that followed the financial collapse sent the price of grain in the Habsburg Empire up to seventeen times what it had been three years before. I cannot imagine what the speculators did to worsen others' hardship at this gruesome time; the evil of man's cruelty and selfishness shows most clearly at moments of catastrophe. All this occurred just when the continent had been depleted of its most capable young men, slaughtered in the new, unanticipated Napoleonic wars. Crisis led to unemployment, to destitution, to riots and looting. They termed 1817 the Year of the Beggars.

Then there seeped in, with the vermin and lice and hunger, something still worse: unstoppable typhus, felling the war-weakened population across the continent. Lotti wrote from Siebenbürgen that the mountain folk of Wallachia were reduced to eating bark; that one could not travel for an hour without encountering the rotting corpse of one who had succumbed to the illness or starved to death. It was as if an Old Testament plague were being visited upon us.

We cowered in the Palais, but even here we were not safe from our personal plague: an unexpected demand, via an envoy from Stackelberg, for money to support Pepi's three girls. Presumably, wherever they were was as severely hit as anywhere else. Stackelberg sent word that he would be coming to Vienna soon and expected to spend time with his wife. Pepi did the unthinkable: she borrowed as much money as she could in order to fulfil his demand. We had no idea whether it ever did benefit the children.

If Luigi wrote little during that year of horrors, I can scarcely blame him. If others suffered hardship and scarcity, so would he. If he were depressed, who would not be?


I found Pepi lying fully clad on her bed, dry-eyed, staring motionless at the canopy above her. We sent for Dr Malfatti, who was Luigi's preferred physician and the uncle of Therese Malfatti to whom he had once paid court. A knot of fear had tightened under my ribcage: I insisted we must consult only the best.

Pepi accepted the small bottle of potion that Malfatti gave her. 'I should tell you the truth,' she said. 'My body is only expressing my spirit – that is where the real pain is. I long for light… for air… I feel as if I'm suffocating.'

'You are much too thin,' Malfatti noted. 'You are poorly nourished. What are you eating?'

'I've no appetite and no money to buy nutritious food. The creditors are chasing me the whole time.' The money she had sent to Stackelberg was just the latest cause. 'The world is eating my body and my soul.'

'Have confidence,' Malfatti told her gently. 'Be hopeful. The medicine can help you a little, but please, try to rouse yourself to pleasurable activities. See your friends. Have at least one hot meal every day. And play your piano. Music is the best cure.'

Perhaps Beethoven considered them united when she played his music – but now she never did. She was past all that. Be hopeful? Unless Stackelberg divorced her, she was his prisoner – and he knew it, and he would not. Pepi's lung congestion befitted her state of mind: a slow suffocation, the air closed off, window by window. Without breath, without hope, her connection with the man she loved was beginning to die.

Luigi was meanwhile being reduced to a public scandal, through pursuing the strangest of lawsuits.

Just as I regard you, my niece, as the dearest person to me, so Luigi had decided his nephew must be the closest being to him. I could not be a mother at all, and have devoted many years to the children of others, so perhaps I understand something of what was in his heart: unable to be a father to his natural child, he sought, fervently, to do some good in place of it. Karl was a sweet lad, with the dark eyes and strong brows of his uncle, but a longer, oval face and softer, weaker chin. He was no musician – his uncle sent him for piano lessons with Czerny, who declared him utterly devoid of talent – and he resisted, sullen, the great man's attempts to persuade him to practise.

I made enquiries and found a suitable institute in which Luigi could enrol Karl: a boarding school run by Cajetan Giannattasio del Rio. Luigi, having succeeded in his first application to become Karl's sole guardian, had packed him off there at once; it must have been in January 1816. Johanna, as a widow, had few rights – the judges could have used a much slighter excuse than the existing one to take Karl away – yet she remained determined to bring him home. She and Luigi, like the women before King Solomon, virtually sliced the poor child in two rather than concede defeat; but now nobody would give way for the sake of the boy's well-being. It did not seem to occur to Luigi that while Pepi's obsession was her fear of losing custody of her children, he himself was now trying to remove a child from its mother – and Johanna lacked nothing in motherly instinct, even if she also had a criminal record.

Next Luigi obtained a directive from the Landrecht to prevent Johanna from visiting Karl at school; she was forced to meet him only outside the place and only with Luigi's permission. I cannot imagine for whom this was worse, the furious mother or her troubled little son. Luigi himself visited the school often and developed a friendship with Giannattasio, whose teenage daughter took rather a liking to him (if you think Luigi was a wholly unappealing character, you are quite wrong. Young people admired him, were fascinated by him and became devoted to him – the girls as much as the boys.)

As we have noted, legal matters eat paper as bitterness eats the soul. Luigi struggled with this lawsuit for five years or more. Five years of obsession, frustration, fury: when he should have been writing music, he was spitting brimstone over legal texts instead. The law can do many things if you know how to map its inner game of chess, but it can never provide emotional release, which was, I suspect, what he really wanted. Moreover, the law has laws of its own – and here in Vienna, two legal institutions had two sets of different laws: one for aristocrats and another for everybody else.

Luigi had taken his case to the Landrecht. During one of the hearings, he let slip that the Theresianum in Vienna would have been an appropriate school *if Karl had been* of noble birth. What? said the judge. This is the aristocratic court. If you are not of the nobility, your case cannot be heard here. Off you go to the magistracy.

It was all over Vienna within a day. Shock revelation: Ludwig *van* Beethoven is a commoner! Vienna's greatest composer is no better than a grocer or a servant. Vienna's celebrated, foreign genius is worthy of nothing but a Flemish beetroot field. To me the surprise was first that Luigi had been importunate enough to approach the upper court in the first place; secondly, that they accepted him; and thirdly, that anybody could ever have believed him a nobleman at all. On the other hand, popular rumour had it that he was the illegitimate son of the King of Prussia. I never cease to wonder at humankind's capacity to believe in the most obvious and extreme idiocies.

The spirit can recover, as long as it has something to recover for. One must have tasks, dreams, plans, longings. One must have hope. I had my daily duties, my dreams for my future school, and a man I adored who wanted to become my lover. Pepi's loss of hope was appalling to witness; such tenacity and determination, smothered and starved to oblivion. How could she live without something to live for?

Luigi was struggling, but working, slowly, painfully, upon new creations. He had made important contacts during the Congress, especially from London. Salomon, who had invited Haydn to England in the 1790s, was a vital link; Ferdinand Ries was now living there – he and Luigi were friends again; and Luigi hoped that an organisation called the Royal Philharmonic Society would commission three symphonies. Its director had written to invite him to London as their guest. 'I should go,' he said to me. 'You and Pepi should come too. We should all go.'

I daydreamed, wandering back to the Palais in a mist of imagination: Pepi and Beethoven, Louis and I, at the prow of a boat approaching the island shore, then walking arm in arm through St Paul's Cathedral, listening to Luigi's works being performed in Westminster Abbey…

'We could travel,' I told Pepi, who was half asleep in bed. 'Italy. Or further – South America, Brazil – or we could go to London with Beethoven. Plans. Dreams. Hopes. We could do anything, darling, if you would only get up and motivate yourself!'

'London? With Luigi? Don't be silly.' Pepi turned over and closed her eyes.


After his public humiliation at the Landrecht, Beethoven too crashed into a bout of ill health – his usual stomach problems were worsening. I wondered if something he liked to eat or drink provoked such a reaction, or perhaps the strain he was continually under. Still, I had resisted visiting him until I could trust myself not to accuse him of bringing his troubles upon his own head. He had come to believe his own fiction; like the public, like Pepi, he had shown a remarkable capacity for self-deceit. He truly thought his art had ennobled him.

As always, his solution must lie in music. His next triumph must cancel out these disasters. This, therefore, was what I told him, to bring comfort when I visited his latest apartment on the Landstrasse Hauptstrasse, some way into the gloom beyond the city ramparts. 'You will blast the naysayers out of existence,' I declared. 'The fuss will be forgotten in no time.'

I was pleased to find him alone; nowadays it was a rare phenomenon. Usually the place would be heaving with copyists, secretary, musicians, deliveries, continual visitors wanting things of him, and Luigi still trying to write, his deafness occasionally proving worthwhile against would-be distractors.

'You can't trust anybody,' he grumbled. 'They're scoundrels, top to bottom. Nobody keeps his word unless it is in writing.'

'Sometimes not even then,' I remarked, from foul experience.

'I hate this city. I always have.'

It is strange to think, looking back, that he spent more than thirty years in Vienna, yet all his life he missed Bonn, its straight-talking inhabitants, its open riverscapes. In claustrophobic Vienna he arrived as a stranger; and that is how he stayed.

He ranted on. 'They expect a man to work hard, but then pay him as if they were beggars...' The Congress still rankled. For that great concert in the Redoutensaal he had been so excited beforehand that he invited Franz to come from Hungary to attend it; but when the princes paid their admission tickets and, as was expected, added a little extra for

Luigi, only the Tsar of Russia presented two hundred ducats. The King of Prussia – who was not Luigi's father – gave ten.

'Luigi, try to forget it, and have a look at this.' I rummaged in my holdall for the volume I had brought.

I had amassed a large number of books. Stackelberg had not bothered to remove many of his purchases, and combined with my own acquisitions and access to my father's collection in Hungary, I could pride myself on quite a library. Word had spread and by now I was familiar enough with Viennese borrowing habits to make notes of who took which books away on which date, so that I could if necessary demand their return.

I handed him a slender volume on which Louis had pounced; now so did Luigi, his fine-tipped fingers handling the pages with the care they once used upon the piano keys. It was a translation of a play, *Shakuntala*, by the ancient Sanskrit poet Kālidāsa, which Herder had published; this version had emerged through translations via other languages, notably English. 'It's a wonderful tale,' I told Luigi. 'It is a beautiful love story from one of the most ancient and richest collections in literature anywhere in the world, the *Mahābhārata*. Your friend Goethe is among its admirers. You will find in it his model for the prologue of *Faust*, no less.'

'Goethe is hardly my friend,' Luigi growled.

The play is about an innocent princess, abandoned by her parents, who grows up, marries and is given a ring by her husband, the king Dushyanta. He goes away to his court; she must join him later, showing the ring to claim her place at his side. A visiting sage, angered by her lack of attention to him, bewitches Dushyanta and makes him forget his bride. When she arrives he has no memory of her. She must show him the ring – but she has lost it during her journey.

Abandoned again, she gives birth to a son. Dushyanta comes upon the boy by chance and realises the child is his. The family is reunited.

Luigi located, at the back of the book, a folded envelope addressed to him in Pepi's writing. He cast me a quick look. I pretended not to notice. 'It's an immortal love story,' I assured him, while he tucked the paper beneath his shirt.

A few weeks later, he returned the book when I called in. 'It would make a wonderful opera,' I encouraged him. 'Don't you think so?'

'Apparently Salieri has a student who has been working on one for years already,' he returned. 'And Schubert is interested in it – "the little mushroom", they call him…'

'That shouldn't stop *you*. You could adapt it. Call it something else.'

'Such as?' Luigi glowered. '*Fidelio* instead of *Leonore?*'

'Something clear and immediate. What about *The Ring?*'

'Writing an opera is far too much trouble. It is a gigantic task – and worse, you have to please the singers.'

'Gioachino Rossini is churning out three a year.'

Everybody adored Rossini, who was sociable, garrulous and enthusiastic – and when not writing music could be found in his kitchen, whizzing up fabulous Italian food for his friends with his own hands. 'Devil of a fellow,' Luigi said, smiling. 'He's welcome to it. I appreciate you trying to inspire me, Tesi, but I think I can say more with music that does not have to have words. Thank you for the book – it is certainly fascinating.'

He handed it to me. Something was padding out the back cover; a fat envelope addressed to Pepi.

'Make sure she eats,' was all he said.

After Luigi returned books to me with such insertions, Pepi and I could eat properly for a fortnight.

'What news of the children?'

'They have all gone. They write – the Deyms do, anyway. They're living their own lives as best they can.'

'They are too young, and it is so hard for her to be parted from them...'

It seemed a moment to change the subject. Something else had caught my eye as soon as I walked into the room.

A strange contraption had appeared on top of the piano: a three-sided metal box, like a hood, above the keyboard. 'Luigi, whatever is that?'

'Try it. Put your head into the box and then play.'

I tried. The sound exploded upon my ears like Napoleon's howitzers. 'Not a miracle, but a useful object,' Beethoven said, watching my reaction with amusement. 'You are over-whelmed. I can just about hear a little something. Here's another thing.' He waved at me a slim wooden stick. 'I shall demonstrate.' Taking my place at the keyboard, he set one end of the stick against the instrument; the other end he inserted between his teeth. From this bizarre position, he began to play.

'If I place the stick there, or against my jawbone, or behind one ear, the vibrations travel to my head and I can gain some idea of what the hell I am doing,' he said finally.

The piano, too, was a recent arrival: longer and wider than most. Above the keys was emblazoned the name BROADWOOD. The London firm had sent him this gigantic instrument as a gift; it took a year to reach him.

'Was that a new sonata you were playing?' I scribbled.

'A trifle. But my three-legged friend here has been a good incentive to finish it.' He patted the piano as if it were a favourite horse. 'Ries even now is trying to sell the piece in

London. I've told him not to worry about the order of the movements – it is quite big, as trifles go, and they can leave one out if it's too long, or just take the last two, whatever they like.'

'They should be ashamed if they do not print every note exactly as you have written it.'

'They might. God knows what they will pay. I expect they shall consider this worth "a ha'penny and a farthing".'

'Luigi, won't you play me the rest?'

'As long as you don't mind that I am a clumsy goat.'

The next instant the house was shaking with what felt like the eruption of the Sumbawa volcano. The speed was insane, and Luigi ploughed through fistfuls of wrong notes, but as the piece went on – a wild, shining allegro, then a scherzo full of abrupt gestures and violent outbursts – my fascination grew. Its extremity reminded me of the *Eroica* Symphony when we first heard it, when Luigi had said he was seeking a new path. Now that path was too small. Was this the rejection of *any* path – in favour, instead, of flight?

The adagio must have lasted twenty minutes; in it there seemed to speak every sorrow known to mankind. A cleansing interlude followed, one I would have thought improvised were it not written down. Abruptly, then, an explosive trill – and Luigi launched into a fugue that could almost wake Bach from his grave: through its gigantic span he handled every technical device at his disposal the way Kant could articulate a philosophical argument or Shakespeare the plot of a play. There was nothing he could not do; no moment in which he did not burn human limitations to a frazzle. Dear Lord, if only Pepi could hear this.

'There,' said Luigi into my stunned silence at the end. 'I don't imagine anyone will actually wish to *play* it, but if they do, here it is.'

That was my first encounter with the Sonata in B flat major, Op. 106, which was published as *Große Sonate für das Hammerklavier*. With his increasing dislike of Italian terms, Luigi had found a different, German name for his new piano. Art *should* be difficult, he insisted; we should need to work on it, whether to understand it or to perform it, for then the reward is worthwhile. If art is easy, if it talks down to its recipients, it is compromised, false and without integrity. Yet I never heard the *Hammerklavier* again in his lifetime. Nobody played it in public. Nobody dared to – until your acquaintance, Franz Liszt.

I had feared that Luigi was destroying himself, through agony over Pepi, fury at his deafness, and his inner fire running aground upon his obsession with his nephew. But here he was, flaming back into life like a hibernating dragon awakening to unfurl immense black wings against the night sky, an unimaginable power harnessed and sent out to do its work. It would burn us to purity and let us be born anew – and its composer with it. He had always had the gift of healing by capturing his listener's psyche and reflecting it back in music. Perhaps here he had done the same, for himself.

## 27

My dear niece,

There you were, the three of you, cowering beside the doorway, holding hands: two thin, solemn, golden-haired little girls, and a dark, stocky, alert child, smaller but much more confident. There had been no warning, no missive to say 'expect your children on Thursday' – indeed, no communication whatsoever since Stackelberg's vague expression of intent to visit Vienna this year. I could only thank and tip the messenger tasked with bringing them to us.

You were the first to step forward.

'Which one is our mother?' you said.

Pepi crouched and held out her arms. Laura and Theophile huddled together and did not move. You stared straight at me. 'That's funny,' you mused, 'I thought it was *you*.'

'Darling, I am your Aunt Therese and you can call me Auntie Tesi. Come inside properly, all of you, and say hello to your mother…'

'Come on, you two,' you instructed your elder sisters. You marched up to Pepi and extended a small hand. 'Hello,

Mother. I am Minona. I am six and my sisters are nine and ten.'

If *Werther* and Ossian's plaintive, singing spirits had been in Pepi's mind when she named this child, nothing could be less suited to this vivid little person with her curly hair and strong stumpy legs. Ironic that it would probably be Laura and Theophile, etiolated blondes like their father, who would someday be considered the beauties.

My poor sister: if one thing is worse than having your children removed, perhaps it is having them returned with no recollection of you. Pepi's voice quavered. 'Don't you remember me at all?'

The bigger girls inched forward. 'I *think* I do,' said Laura.

'And Auntie Tesi... was teaching us something?' Theophile ventured.

'It was Ancient Greek, dear, like your name.'

Pepi slumped onto the nearest chair and burst into tears.

You looked on, typically unimpressed. 'But we're your daughters. Papa said you'd be *pleased* to see us.'


Stackelberg had decided, without consultation, to bring the girls to Pepi for six months and thought himself magnanimous in doing so. The timing could not have been worse. Pepi was in no condition to be their mother, and my roles as sister, daughter and administrator periodically threatened to drown me.

In Ofen, Mother was starting to suffer the effects of her age, at least physically. She remained as ferocious as ever. 'Tesi, I need you,' she would insist. 'My arthritis is making life a misery and the estate needs your strong hand. *Why* won't you come back?'

Her exhortations would have been easier to manage, had I

ever felt in my youth that she wanted my actual company. It was more difficult, however, to deny her assistance that she genuinely needed. I must find a way, once again, to divide my time between her and Pepi.

Taking Pepi and the little girls to Hungary would have simplified matters, but she would not budge. 'No! You will poison me,' she wept from her bed. 'You want me to die.' No sensible argument I tried would sway her fragmenting spirit.

Stackelberg, who I cannot deny was stricken with conscience at the sight of her wasted form and distracted gaze, knelt beside her bed. 'Dearest, come to Reval,' he pleaded. 'We can look after you properly there. My mother and sisters are longing to have you. We can be a real family again.'

'Never. You will kill me.' It was true that in her state she could not have survived that journey.

'Somewhere nearer, then. Somewhere we can make a fresh start. Berlin is a wonderful city…'

'I will not leave my home for a man who has brought destruction upon me.'

Stackelberg, defeated, trailed away. I found him sitting in the museum, sobbing and helpless. For the only time in my life, I hugged him.

Finally he departed sooner than planned, taking you and your sisters with him. As I waved you away, watching your stern little face pressed to the carriage window as the coach swung through the arch of the Rotenturmtor, I wondered if I would ever see you again.


I cannot deny that a spell at Martonvásár provided me with a personal respite. I slept solidly for three days after arrival, then set about structuring my time.

'I thought you'd enjoy this,' Franz remarked, placing in front of me a volume by Immanuel Kant. 'You can't get it in Vienna – it's banned.' I settled down in the library with it.

'*Two things fill me anew with increasing awe and wonder: the starry sky above me and the moral law within me,*' I read. The images unlocked closed gates, stealing my breath with what lay beyond. I knew someone else who would appreciate the awe of the heavens and their mirror in the heart of humanity, macrocosm and microcosm together – similar to his favourite Christian Christoph Sturm poetry.

Franz had befriended the director of the Ofen Planetarium, Dr Littrow, who was overwhelmed by the marvels of this philosopher and had written a newspaper article containing that same quote. 'Don't give Luigi the book – it will get him into trouble,' Franz advised, amazed to find me hard at work copying out the entire volume, but guessing my purpose at once. 'I'll get Littrow to send us a copy of his article and you can pass that on instead.' When I returned to Vienna, I took it with me, for Beethoven.

By now, both my nephews were away, Fritz training for the military and Carl at agricultural college. Fritz was even wilder than his uncle Franz. God alone knew how he ran through so much money, how many whores he visited in the city brothels, or how he could consume such quantities of alcohol and live to send us the bills. I found a pile of them, ripped and scrunched, in Pepi's waste-paper basket. The danger was that Carl, who had a gentler nature and was ever in his brother's shadow, might begin to emulate him. Viky was with Victoria, Sephine at her seminary. Lotti and Emerich wanted to send me Blanka and Emma to teach – two exceptionally bright girls, they declared – but how could I take them when each morning I awoke wondering if we would live to see the sunset? Pepi's soul had a shattered wheel and we would all be dragged behind as her carriage veered out of control.

I made one decision that was mine to make. I could not leave my family duties, so could not even consider marriage to Louis, but that did not mean I must give him up. I would never ask him who else he saw, how he unwound, what outlets he found when we were not together; I knew I had not the right. While another year slunk away, I stared out at the wall that blocked any vestige of brightness and beauty from the house and goaded myself onwards. Every morning, after the servant knocked on the door to wake me, I would think hard for five minutes to invent another way that Louis and I could live together.

'You are my Diotima, first in my heart, and that cannot and will not change,' Louis insisted.

'I could marry the count, Franz's friend. As it would be a marriage of convenience, you could live with us and we could talk for hours every day.'

'Tesi...'

'*You* could get married. You could have a bride and a family, I could be governess to your children and we could talk for hours every day.'

'For heaven's sake!'

'We could have different apartments in the same building, and...'

'Any more hare-brained schemes up your sleeve, Tesi?'

'It keeps me distracted,' I admitted. Louis, of all people, knew that my sister was dying both spiritually and physically and there was nothing I could do to prevent it.

The human heart is strong: think what it withstands. You can go through multiple bereavements, the sacking of your city by a foreign power, the abduction of your children or the loss of the sense upon which your vocation depends, and still come out with that organ pulsing away undimmed. It takes a great deal to make someone die of a broken heart. That does not mean it doesn't happen. As the dread disease that killed our father reached out its arms to Pepi, her ruined spirit opened the door to welcome it in.

Franz had cut off his contact with Pepi when she asked once too often for money, after the Andrian debacle. He was past forty; he was thinking of settling down, should he find the right bride; how could he acknowledge his sister as a wanton, fallen woman? 'Depraved,' he said. She would bring disgrace upon us all. And she always, always needed cash. He refused. I called him unbrotherly. He called her unsisterly. He said she was out of her mind. 'The devil has got her!'

Mother? 'Pepi sinned against God,' she said, months later. 'I always knew she would. Her death is for the best.'

Oh, dear God, what a family – provincial, mean-spirited, cruel beyond cruelty. Oh, dear God – my sweet sister, destroyed by the same qualities for which everybody loved her.

I cooked her a broth, easy to swallow, full of healthy sustenance – meat, vegetables, warming peppers. She repulsed me with barely a gesture.

'You must eat, Pips. You need to build your strength to get better.'

'Go away. I don't want your food.'

I stood my ground. 'When did you last eat properly?'

'Who knows? Who cares?'

I stared at her sharpening cheekbones, at the eye sockets blue and white around her mahogany-dark eyes, the trails of her hair, once so lavish but now thinning and silvering. I reached for her hand. Cold as snow. She pulled it from my grasp.

Seeking privacy in my room, I wept. If my sister were determined to starve herself to death, how could I stop her?

On a blustery March afternoon I found a roomful of people with Luigi in his Landstrasse apartment. Besides the two copyists, here was the Archduke Rudolph, who was now Archbishop of Olmütz; the bulky personage of Vogl the baritone; and young Karl, who was growing up now, possibly too fast. He was moving to an institute I had recommended, a boarding school run by Joseph Blöchlinger, a follower of Pestalozzi. Among them sat Schubert, listening more than he talked. He, too, was growing up, but his terrible shyness was unchanged; today he scarcely dared speak one word to the good, kind archduke. In Luigi's presence he remained star-struck and monosyllabic. On the desk I spotted an unruly stack of musical sketches, topped with a scrawled title: SYMPHONY NO. 9, with a semi-legible sentence that appeared to involve Friedrich Schiller.

Luigi saw me and held out one arm. 'Vogl is going to sing us Schubert's latest,' he barked, motioning me to come and sit beside him.

'This is not a new song,' said Schubert in the veiled tones of some anxious wood-sprite, making hesitant progress towards the piano, 'but it is one I'm pleased with.'

Bleak chords spread over the room. While Vogl sang, Beethoven read a copy of the manuscript on his lap, holding it so that I could follow it too.

The poem was by Matthias Claudius. Death comes to a maiden as a friend, as a lover. She begs him to go away: she is young and afraid of his touch. I am not wild, he tells her. You will sleep softly in my arms. Such was Schubert's intensity that his notes, invested with the bleakness inside his heart, could not help but be infected. A chill as if from the gaping grave possessed me.

Nobody else seemed thus affected. While I sat still, collecting myself, they were assembling at the table, congratulating Vogl and Schubert, ready to enjoy the refreshments that Luigi's new maidservant had prepared. Luigi himself glowered at the head of the table; the teenaged Karl sat at the far end, twisting his fingers together, ignoring the conversation about the challenges of setting poetry to music.

Then there came a battering upon the door. It was almost as if I had known it would happen. Soon the frazzled maid was hastening to my side.

'Countess Brunsvik, your servant is here. He says it is extremely urgent.'

A look at his pallid face told me everything. I retrieved my shawl and slipped out of the door, grateful that Beethoven could not hear the word 'Josephine'.


She was lying still, pale and shrunken. Any breath she could muster caught and rattled in her throat. Magda was sitting beside her, trying to coax her to drink some broth, but to no avail. On the bedside cabinet was a red heap that for a moment I mistook for a small bunch of roses. It was a pile of rags, soaked with blood. Pepi had suffered a haemorrhage.

'Oh, Magda,' I faltered.

Our poor maid, overcome by tears, stood and embraced me. I did my best to comfort her – but what comfort can there be in the face of a slow suicide unfurling day after darkening night?

'Pepi.' I sat on the bed and reached forward to stroke her

hair, expecting a fight back, accusation, rejection, now her habitual attitude to me. Instead, she gazed out, mute, her dark eyes pleading in the silence from her self-made prison.

'What can I give you, darling?' I whispered. 'What do you want? The children? Shall I ask them to come home?' She had never once summoned them while the slope beneath her feet propelled her ever further down its treacherous shingle, towards the lightless lake beneath. Fritz and Carl could be there in time; the girls, at their greater distance, possibly not...

The smallest shake of her head. A hand, half lifting in a gesture that spoke of her shattered body, of not wanting them to see her in this state.

'Pips. Shall I get Luigi? I know he will come if you want him to.'

Her eyes filled. She closed them and turned away.

After a day and two nights, everything is over.

I sit beside the body of my sister. The motionless air, the house frozen in sympathy. As if when the spirit departs, traces of the soul leave those objects that held them. The wooden washstand with its jug and basin, the armoire where she had kept the children's baby clothes, the dressing room with its row of useless gowns, now fodder for the fire, if I can ever move from my chair again, which I doubt. I seem unable to gather what shards of my mind remain.

In death, her cheekbones press against the stretched skin. Her eyelashes are coal-dark on her waxen face; I have closed her eyes myself, and her mouth too, for at the last she was staring upwards in the struggle for air that her lungs refused her. The cause of death will be recorded as consumption. I alone know that she wanted to die and to this end has starved herself. Nobody will ever think to consider this a suicide, except me.

I take from her bedside cabinet the same scissors with which I cut Minona's umbilical cord. I snip off a lock of her hair to keep with me forever.

So this is how it ends. The passion, the music, the fights, the exquisite body that brought forth eight children after being worshipped, possessed or violated by four different men. The waltzes, the satin and the Sekt; the chiming cough and the steadfast stance; falling out of the boat, running up the stairs, practising the semiquavers slowly, singing with me *Ich denke dein*, I think of you. For years I have stood by her, sat next to her, sustaining her, tied to her, body and soul. For what? For *this*? Is this all there is?

'Madame.' Magda was in the doorway, tearful. 'Please let me bring you something to drink. You have been sitting here for two hours.'

'I appreciate that, Magda – thank you.'

It struck me that we never really thanked Magda. She had given Pepi her best years. She could have married and had children; she had not. She simply looked after us, with all our foibles, for board, lodging and what small salary we could give her. How were we ever worth it?

'Magda,' I said, 'I don't know what we would do without you.' But she had already gone down to the kitchen.

What of Brahma, the life cycles and 'karma' of the Indian literature that Louis and I devoured, which might carry us through to the next incarnation? Perhaps even now Pepi's delicate spirit was entering the body of an eagle, like the one she had drawn for Luigi? Her empty shell would let me believe neither that, nor the theory of heaven and salvation. All that moralising. How could a woman like Pepi ever be saved? How could a woman like Pepi ever *not* be saved?

I downed the hot, reviving wine. There would be much to organise. Now I must fall back on my technique.

Once I started, I could not stop. Notes to send, arrangements to make, paperwork and numbers to assess – oh God, how were we to afford her funeral? I had to write to Viky, to the boys at their colleges and a long letter to Sephine – her seminary was too far away and she would not come back. I had to tell Franz. Lotti. Mother. Stackelberg and the three girls. Would they even respond?

And now I must tell Luigi.

I grabbed a shawl against the cold March wind and plunged out of the Palais into the busy streets. The noise of hooves, rattling carriages and shouting vendors cut through me. I covered my ears. I must, I supposed, be tired. I couldn't remember when I had last slept.

Out of the centre, leaving the churches and the Graben behind, marching southeast through windswept, bullet-damaged streets, through and beyond the ramparts towards Landstrasse. Long terraces, crammed apartments, dark pelmets fronting bleak little courtyards and snaking, bare stone staircases. Down to the house; up to the apartment.

Alone, lit by a slanting ray of early evening sun, Luigi was at his desk, pen in hand. I could hear the scratching of nib on paper. Of course he did not notice me come in, so I went to stand beside him to announce my presence. With one look the understanding seemed to strike him, his calm gaze holding disbelief, longing and horror all at once: a moment in which there surged over me a wave of unanswerable questions – the slicing away of a lifetime's dream and my part in it that could not be unpicked. I thought he might shout, or howl or throw something in despair. Instead he set down the pen and stood, holding out his arms to me. Convention dissolved in our grief; he did not speak and I could not, for no words could encompass all that I longed to say to him, filled too late with inexpressible guilt and regret.

For once, the brother of my soul and I must share our grief unencumbered. While we embraced and wept together, I think one of his copyists tried to sidle in. There came the soft clunk of the closing door as he thought better of it.

I have no recollection of reaching the street, but I was outside, half walking, half running, dodging people, carriages and piles of dung, my hat falling off in the wind. It might be faster to circle the city by the walls, for the road was less clogged. Tears grew chilly in my eyes and against my skin. If I went back to the Palais I must face it all again.

The end of the day was upon us, the bells ringing out for Mass, when I found myself crossing the courtyard towards Louis's apartment. Continual knocking on his door proved fruitless; he was out. I sat on the step and pressed my forehead onto my knees. Perhaps if I believed hard enough in the darkness, I could disappear into it.

Footsteps approaching from the street; his soft touch on my shoulder; his warm hand closing around mine. 'Is it Pepi?'

I nodded. For my second Ludwig, my voice failed me. I followed him inside and allowed him to pour me first some water, then a fierce pálinka that half burned my throat.

Too much feeling, unexpressed, is bound to erupt when finally released. So I told myself later. Over the years of struggle, my relationship with Louis had settled into friendship alone; sometimes he pushed me away, and often I neglected him for the sake of my duties, but we could return to one another as a constant: a family that was not a family, lovers who never made love.

I was so exhausted that my knees were buckling. 'When did you last eat?' Louis demanded.

'I don't know.'

'When did you last sleep?'

'There's too much to do…'

'Lie down and rest, Tesi. I'll find you some food.'

A minute later I was flat on Louis's modest bed. The pillow smelled of the pomade he used to smooth his curls.

'Here. You have to eat.' Bread, cheese and honey: I must somehow sit up, but my head was muzzy with exhaustion, so he propped me against him and fed me mouthfuls as if I were a baby. I imagined that the honey would flow into my veins. The warmth of his shoulder was as welcome as a blaze of sunset. I turned and let both my arms encircle him. 'Louis.'

He pulled away; he fled the room. Maybe I'd gone too far. No matter… I would breathe his scent from his sheets and content myself with a moment to close my eyes in a place that was not the Palais.

A moment later I felt his fingers at the lace around my throat, looking for the buttons. He had been sending his servant out for the evening.

'I should go back,' I mumbled. 'They'll need me.'

'Don't be silly.' My dress slid to the floor.

I could say that I didn't know what I was doing, because I didn't. If my body were still playing tricks on me, so be it. We will all end as an empty husk, we do not know where our spirits will go, and to reject love for the sake of the stories our worlds have invented to stop it, at such moments seems nothing short of idiocy. After all those years, the fear, anxiety and avoidance, it did not seem difficult, or

distressing, or embarrassing, or anything other than where
we should have been all along. I wept throughout, but not
with pain.

Later, we lay close, arms around each other, dropping an
occasional kiss on a shoulder, an ear or the hollow at the base
of the neck. '*Now* marry me, Tesi,' said Louis.

I turned onto my side and drank in the beauty of his soft
skin gleaming golden beneath our candle; the bright eyes
searching for hope in mine; the attitude that told me he had
waited for me all this time, and at last, here we were. I had
to tell him the truth.

'I love you, Louis, and I give myself freely to you, equal
to equal – but I do not want to belong to you by law. Now
that Pepi is dead, I must seek my freedom and my fulfilment.
I cannot belong to one person, because I wish to belong to
the whole world.'

Louis lay back, turning his face away. I watched his left
hand clenching into a fist. It took me a moment to understand that he was trying not to shed tears in front of me.


In Pepi's empty study I began to hunt through the contents
of her writing table. It did not take long to find what
I wanted: her diary. Anguish, in her lavish script, spread
before me. Words that accused me of causing her suffering
by overspending on the museum, or of trying to kill her by
sending her to Hungary, away from everything she loved.
Sentences of a fury, a madness, that she rarely expressed –
like a nightmare in which you scream, but no sound comes
out.

The diary included drafts of letters that she had made
before writing out a final copy to send. A date on one caught
my eye: 8 April. It was surrounded by entries from spring

1818. Minona's fifth birthday, then – a day I now knew the little one and her half-sisters had spent in Bohemia, not Russia, because the truth was that Stackelberg had initially dumped the girls there with a governess and gone back to Reval alone. He did not want to take them to his family; he only wanted to take them away from Pepi.

I read Pepi's words, transfixed. There was no mistaking the target.

'... *I cannot begin to tell you how I feel when I see you. We do not know what we do, what we say, what we are – the universe within every person's heart, and therefore in our own, is the starry sky, where these conditions are the same immeasurable distances – as in the stars. It seems to break the axis in us, dissolved, torn from the hinges, we stand – opposite each other... for what we have destroyed in each other and in ourselves, we see within. You ... deaf ... busy, with a stern expression, and so calm – serene – partly in a state of negative happiness. The Book of Memories has many shades – you have often leafed through it, focused – and examined before the Highest the jewel you have found...*

*We can only meld into one when we have melded with eternity – with true intimacy, this pure desire, the purer it becomes – only this is union – forever...*'

The moral law within, the starry sky above. Or something more extreme: the two of them can only be united as pure spirit, beyond death. Pepi had melded into the Immortal; there, she would wait for him to join her.

## 28

My dear Minona,

By the time Luigi published his last three piano sonatas in 1822, I had moved back to Hungary, to take care of Mother and try to repair bridges with my brother and remaining sister. Lotti brought Blanka and Emma to Martonvásár. Their younger brother, Miki, was away at school. Bright, intellectually hungry young women, dark as Turks and strong as Magyár warriors, the girls gasped with joy on seeing our library. Blanka was losing herself in Mary Shelley's *Frankenstein*, and Emma in E. T. A. Hoffmann's fantastical tales; her favourite was *The Sandman*, in which the sinister Dr Coppelius forges terrifying glass eyes that send the hero mad. Lotti's beautiful black hair had turned snow white. At least her mother-in-law was dead.

Beethoven's sonatas Opp. 109, 110 and 111 should have been finished earlier, but 1821 had conspired against him. Op. 109 was complete, but the other two barely drafted when that year of calamity began. Luigi suffered an attack of jaundice – a presage of the disease that would later kill him; when he felt well enough to work, he would bury himself alive in the all-consuming demands of his Missa

Solemnis. He was trying to raise funds for it by subscription, approaching princes including the archduke, who wanted the dedication, or the Russian Prince Galitzin, who wanted the premiere in St Petersburg. Luigi sold ten subscriptions and promised each patron a signed, handwritten manuscript. The battles over Karl continued. Pepi died.

Franz heard a story on the grapevine, which he told me with great relish. Early in the autumn a university professor and his colleagues were enjoying some fresh *Sturm* at a *Heuriger* near the canal when a policeman on horseback clattered in, requesting that he help identify a tramp.

'This man,' Franz related, 'unshaven and uncouth, his boots falling to pieces, a felt hat set well back on his head, had been peering into people's houses and failing to respond when anyone called to him. When they apprehended him, he declared he was Ludwig van Beethoven and they must release him at once.'

'It really was him,' I surmised.

'The chief of police didn't want to believe it. He insisted Beethoven did not look like this! He'd be well dressed, well spoken – if Germanic – and a civilised person who would never go around pressing his nose against strangers' windows. But the tramp was making so much noise about being Beethoven that they decided to check. The professor went with them to the cell and found Luigi beside himself with anger. The police released him, and the professor helped to find him a room for the night, plus a good dinner; he had not eaten all day.'

'But whatever was he doing?'

'Going for a walk on the towpath. It was a beautiful day, silver sun on golden leaves, and every time he thought he might turn back, he decided to go just a little further, to see what was round the next bend. Somehow he lost track of time. Night fell; he had no idea where he was, how long he had been walking or how long it would take him to return.'

So it is in the late sonatas, the quartets, the last choral pieces. Every time you think he might turn back, he does not. He keeps exploring, deeper and further, through the onset of night. Here no prison cell awaits him, but unity with the infinite, melding together.

I met him once more by chance before I left Vienna. At the Währing Cemetery I wanted to tend Pepi's grave, for I had no idea when I might see it again. As I approached the distant grove where we had laid her to rest, I saw the figure of a man standing there, head bowed, hat in hand. He seemed deep in prayer. It was some time before he turned and noticed me. He held out an arm; I went to him. We stood side by side, gazing together down at the earth.

I have no doubt about what held up his work on those sonatas, or why they emerged as they did. Now and then, I try to play them.

Op. 109's elusive first movement is full of subtleties, intimacy, improvisational flights; then its brief span gives way to a demoniac scherzo. The finale is a set of variations on a sarabande; it reminds me significantly of the Bach *Goldberg Variations*. Yet the theme contains a motif I recognise. It is different, it is a variant, but it rhymes with the *Andante favori* and its companions. Then in the first variation there's a strange gesture: a reaching octave followed by Pepi's motif, as I think of it. That same octave gesture appears in *An die ferne Geliebte*. What is he *doing*?

I mutter to myself over my practising. It is difficult – and becomes harder as it goes along, finishing with a welter of trills and cascades, like comets diving across the heavens and silver light pulsating in the constellations.

What of the dedication? To Maximiliane, daughter of Antonie and Franz Brentano. Perhaps Brentano was still helping him out financially – though without Pepi, Luigi might now be able to keep more of his resources. Perhaps there was some link with Antonie of which I knew nothing – for love is simple up to a point, beyond which it can become extremely complicated. But I am convinced that the music is more important than the words at its head; for Luigi, words were always inadequate.

The other two sonatas were written after Pepi's death. The A flat major, Op. 110, is less technically ferocious than its siblings, though by no means easy. An exquisite, quiet opening sings to me: the rhythm rhyming with Pepi's, its melody varied again – then the lightest of halos glimmering from the top of the keyboard to the bottom and back again, as if he has set her among the heavens.

But that is only the beginning. After a terse little scherzo something new begins, ushered in by a peculiar improvisatory passage, as if setting the scene for Florestan in his dungeon. An anguished lament sounds out over dense, pulsing chords, in A flat minor; what a key for a tragedy. Yet now a single line begins in the tenor range, a new idea that climbs towards the sky; and soon he is saving himself, and us, with a fugue, gathering energy, returning to life – until, approaching its climax, the music collapses. The tragedy has gone; nothing is left but bleak despair. The lament returns, but broken, reset in a blank G minor; it can scarcely speak for exhaustion. But deep in its heart, the darkest moment is lifted by the switch of a single note: minor to major. The sonority sinks into the piano, then rises out of it; the fugue is back, but upside down, melting, transfigured in transparency – and finally he sets it free. There it goes, flying out like a soul released from bodily captivity, an apotheosis, liberation exploding into unity. We rise, we rise, we rise once again, it sings to me. Rise once again.

'Tesi, dear,' called Mother's querulous voice, 'can't you play something else? I think I know how that one goes now.'

She couldn't say she hadn't asked for it. I turned the page and faced Op. 111.

I didn't know this would be his last sonata. How does he do it, this process of continual growth, preserving his essence while coaxing from his piano something so new? The opening plunge announces a type of French overture, a towering crag portending fury before the storm breaks, roaring through the ensuing allegro, with only a moment of sunshine – another version of Pepi's motif, perhaps – gleaming here and there. By the end the thundercloud has blown itself out; all passion is spent. There are two movements: the unity of opposites. The second is a set of variations, the theme perhaps a ghost of a sarabande – or, still and hushed, of Pepi's favourite sonata, Op. 31, No. 3. Two variations increase the energy, until the third is a whirlwind, full of crazed syncopations. I turned cross-eyed trying to read it. But then... one is tired from this exertion and sleep begins to encroach – or is it death? Dreams – or hope of new life? A long, sustained harmony beneath lulls you; then the planets glimmer overhead and you begin to fly up towards them. Gradually the music travels further into the beyond, into the untold wonders of this firmament, until the final variation is so soft, so distant, that you can scarcely glimpse the face hidden behind the veil in its ineffable paradise. As the variations unfurl all the worlds cocooned inside their theme, so are we reborn. A final rope ladder of notes carries us back towards earth and with a quiet C major chord Beethoven's ultimate sonata is over.

All or nothing. Wholly with you, or not at all. Pepi and Luigi are wholly together, in the peculiar spirit realm of this music. Louis and I, though, were not at all. I could not persuade him that I must be free, that marriage would have made me his property, to which I would never consent. It was as I feared: once a physical relationship intruded, our fragile balance was overturned and nothing could restore it. I do not regret my night of weakness, for never have I so needed the comfort of another human body; and I shall not die without having tasted the life force that rules many of us, my sister included. But our precious friendship was gone forever.

He arrived to bid me farewell when my trunks were packed for my move to Ofen, once the Palais was sold and its contents were being dispersed. We stood at the top of the stairs and shook hands.

'Tesi,' he said, 'you will live always in my heart.'

'And you in mine.'

'I know you will achieve all that you wish to do, and more. I'm sorry not to be part of it. Goodbye, my Diotima.'

I tried to speak, but no words would emerge. I watched in silence as he turned away and descended to the street, to stride out to the city wall, pivot left and vanish from sight. Louis – or Ludwig – Migazzi was indeed the only man I have ever loved.

Fritz officially inherited the Palais, but he wanted as little to do with it now as I did. Arm in arm with our cousin Julie, who was present without her husband, he consented to the sale: he preferred the money to the museum. Now everyone had what they wanted.

Outside, the movers were taking away the waxworks. There went the clockwork nightingale, the Fair Dreamer, the Aphrodite mirrors, my old friend Ferdinand IV. Gone – as if they had never been there at all.

From Ofen, the distance to Vienna pained me. I sent letter after letter to Luigi. Sometimes a scrawl came back; now and then, a new piece of music. He was writing string quartets, he told me: five of them, commissioned by Prince Galitzin in St Petersburg. E flat major, Op. 127, with an opening rhythm that took me several playthroughs to grasp. A work in C sharp minor, Op. 131 – a thorny, aromatic garland, seven movements played without a break. The A major Quartet, Op. 132, involving a profound prayer of thanksgiving after recovery from illness. And two more…

Schuppanzigh was back in Vienna after seven years in Russia. He had re-established his quartet with some old and some new members – his second violin was now the youthful Karl Holz, who was in thrall to the Master, as young musicians tended to be. With Schuppanzigh's devotion undimmed, along with his appetite, his energy and his endless fount of anecdotes about Russian life, he and Galitzin were bringing the impetus to Luigi's quartets that the Broadwood had brought the piano music.

Yet I was missing all of this in Hungary? Was it only because I must aid my cantankerous mother and educate two young women who in a just world should have been training for high-level professions? Alas, no. My dear niece, I have something terrible to tell you, which I beg you not to divulge beyond your four walls.

The run of horror in our family began with Pepi's death. A few months later came news that an epidemic had struck the Institute of Mary at Lilienhof, where Sephine was a student. My poor little angel, determined to devote her life to God, had been taken to him in person. I prayed that now she was with her mother again.

Viky, who was preparing to move to Ofen to join me, had been helping with preparations for our school, honing her skills as a teacher and investigating financial systems to underpin our new institution. We corresponded every day. We ruminated on whether it was more sensible to train teenagers or small children, girls alone or both the sexes, those of all backgrounds or those from poverty, and whether a daily institution or a boarding school would be most workable. How much money could we raise through educational associations? If we had a boarding school for, say, twenty children, what would it cost to feed and care for them? How many teachers must we hire? And so the discussions continued.

Until, that is, one day in January 1823 when no letter arrived from Viky. Nor the next day, nor the next, only a terrifying silence. Finally Victoria wrote to break the news. An outbreak of scarlet fever had carried off the person I loved best in all the world. By the time I read her last letter, it was too late for me even to attend her funeral.

My Viky! My own beloved girl! Blanka and Emma stepped forward: they wanted to help me themselves. But – forgive me, dear, for I know you are fond of Blanka – Viky was so different, more like her mother, with an appealing delicacy and humour alongside her brilliance that is somewhat absent from the indomitable Transylvanian sisters. Blanka was a natural artist, in any case; she must go to

Paris to study painting. Emma, proud and generous, longed for travel. I would never divert them from their dreams. But how, how, how could I manage without my Viky? Everything must be shelved; my grief-stricken soul was too numb and exhausted to find the energy the project required.

Then there came a visitor who shall remain nameless. I do not want you to know her, dear, lest you rebuke her too much for what her news did to me. I shall write it, fast, and we must put it behind us, if we can.

Scarlet fever is a lethal disease and highly infectious. Therefore its victims must be buried fast. The body of the beautiful twenty-two-year-old Viky was laid to rest in a sarcophagus in the Deym family vault, my 'friend' related. The crypt, with its locked iron gate, thereafter was unattended for some weeks. The chaplain who next attempted to enter faced a horrific scene. The heavy stone lid of the coffin had been slid aside. On the steps leading up to the gate lay the body of my sweet niece.

For a minute I misunderstood as that cursed visitor chattered away at me. Tomb robbers? 'Oh no, dear,' she answered. 'The poor girl was buried alive and had tried to escape...'

Waking, in a coffin? Alone in the crypt, nobody to hear her, nobody to free her, surrounded by the foul air of the grave; my darling girl, starving to a second death, attacked perhaps by vermin –

I passed out. I am not given to fainting. But for three years I could not sleep, haunted to the point of derangement by that clinging image. I became too ill to leave Ofen even if I wished to.

While I mourned my nieces, there came more devastating news from Vienna.

Karl van Beethoven was a young man of limited talents. He was a decent linguist and showed signs of a good business sense, to which end he enrolled at university; but, like Pepi's son, he found the allure of military glamour all too tempting. His uncle reacted to this declared aim just as Pepi had with Fritz: Beethoven, though, expressed his fury in far more violent and distressing terms.

Karl could take no more. Loss of hope can overwhelm us when there is no greater dream to follow and no vocation that demands fulfilment. We know now what the death of hope can do.

He took a coach to Baden, where he had spent his happiest childhood moments, walking in the Helenental with his uncle. It was a hot summer day. He hiked through the valley, then turned up the mountainside to where the ruins of Rauhenstein Castle sprout from the rock face and the rustling woodland. Here he, like Werther, drew two pistols and fired one of them at his own head. He missed. With the second gunshot he injured himself in the temple: a graze, but enough to knock him unconscious. The next day a passer-by found him and ran down to the village to fetch not a doctor but the police – suicide was legally an offence against the church. Roused at last, the injured youth asked to be taken not to his uncle's house, but his mother Johanna's. When questioned, he blamed Beethoven. 'I grew worse,' he said, 'because my uncle wanted me to be better.'

Six months later, Luigi was dead.


There is life after death, and I have found it in Beethoven's last works.

Looking back towards Vienna, along the Danube from

our house in the city I now term Buda, thanks to the rising predominance of the Hungarian language, the distance seemed greater every day. But sometimes Franz and his wife, Sidonie, a fabulous pianist who won his love by playing Beethoven, held musical soirées at which Franz convened his string quartet. They made a valiant attempt at some of those last pieces that crowned Luigi's works before his body gave way to liver disease. Sometimes we attended, in Pest's Church of the Blessed Virgin Mary, performances of the vast masterpiece of faith and humanity in which he absorbed himself after Pepi's death and which bound him once again to life: the Missa Solemnis, a musical cathedral with the giant dome of the credo at its summit.

We attended, too, his Ninth Symphony on the rare occasions it could be heard: most precious for the shattering moment when the music breaks free from everything we had thought a symphony was and becomes instead a choral extravaganza. At last he had found a way to set his favourite Schiller poem, *An die Freude*, the Ode to Joy, after some twenty-five years of trying. It was much adapted, with an eye on the audience, the poem's craziest excesses stripped away, but retaining the verses of pure idealism. The symphony was the only survivor of his commissions for London's Royal Philharmonic Society, but proved significant enough for ten works, never mind three.

Franz and Sidonie travelled to Vienna for the premiere in 1824. 'A triumph, but ghastly,' said Franz. 'Poor Luigi couldn't hear a note.'

I teach my schoolchildren to sing it. All people shall be brothers, says the poem. And sisters, too, I remind my 'garden of angels'. We shall be brothers and sisters together. We shall be *people* before we are aristocrats or paupers, masters or servants, princes or composers: one people, united, not divided.

Blanka almost gave her life for this ideal. She spent ten years in a Hungarian dungeon after her revolutionary activities in 1848, as did her partner, who happened to be another woman. I remain sadly convinced that their prison sentences were doubled due to this. Blanka, together with her pupils at the girls' school she founded in our city in 1846, was the first to petition for equal rights for women in Hungary, from the right to vote to the right to a university education – indeed, the right for women to be people. If she could only have seen the divisions that had cleft her family, that destroyed the aunt who supported her mother as she struggled to give birth to her, she would see the worth of her actions confirmed. I like to think that perhaps I had some influence in shaping this extraordinary woman. Blanka is all I would have been had I lived one generation later, and had I only had the same degree of courage.

I find in Beethoven's late music a process that can be contained in no other form, unless it be life itself. It is of transfiguration: nothing stays the same, everything is varied, in constant flux. It was what he had been seeking all along. The *Eroica* Symphony was the self-making of a hero – not Napoleon, but Luigi himself; and though he unfurled that symphony as a new path, he had in some ways been exploring the same idea when we first played his variations on that little Righini aria. He never stopped writing variations, even when it did not occur to us that he was, so entirely had he absorbed the principle into his larger forms.

I cannot believe that Beethoven died with broken spirit, yet the gunshots of Karl's suicide attempt, casting the blame upon him, perhaps did the uncle more harm than they did the nephew. His liver gave out. Perhaps an infection took him. Perhaps it was too much drink, like his father – though I never considered Luigi an alcoholic, even if his experiences could have driven anyone to seek oblivion. They say he expired during a thunderstorm, shaking his fist at the heavens. I am not sure I believe that. They also say that just before he died, news arrived that the publishing firm of Schott's, based in Mainz, had sent him a case of the fine Rhineland wine he loved; he could only lament, 'Too late.' This is easier to believe.

It was impossible to accept that I had not been able to see him while he was suffering his last illness; unthinkable that he was gone; more difficult still to grasp that such a vast spirit had ever been alive.

I arrived in Vienna just in time for his funeral – joining twenty thousand others. At the steps of the Holy Trinity Church in Alsergrund, beneath its twin onion-domed towers, I had to batter my way to the front of the crowd with my umbrella, shouting that I was a countess and a pupil of the Master and must be admitted. In the end I slipped in when the usher was looking the other way. When the coffin arrived and was carried up the aisle, I spotted among the torchbearers the diminutive figures of Carl Czerny and Franz Schubert.

After the ceremony, the black carriage and its tragic load swept through the city towards Währing Cemetery, where his friends had decided to bury him because he liked to walk and linger there. I remembered my last glimpse of him beside Pepi's grave – and understood. At least they would rest near one another now.

If every person who ran onto the streets to gawp had contributed one florin to Beethoven's stipend every year, they could have helped to support him in creating the music that sustains our spirits. They did not. They cared just enough to stare and point. And if they had ceased their gossiping, their rush to judgment, their censorious, supercilious hypocrisy, Pepi and he could have been together. They were made for one another. Imagine what he could have become with her as his wife; both could have been alive today, with you beside them as their daughter.

Do you believe that an artist can only create fine work in misery, adversity and solitude? Once upon a time, so did I. After all, I insisted on remaining single in order to belong to the world and accomplish my aims. But I am a woman; and this course of action was my own choice. For an artist, a man, a Beethoven? Turn that traditional assumption on its head, my dear: we use the myth of the lonely, embattled creator for our own ends, to excuse the deplorable conditions in which we allow our artists to exist – as if it is for their own good. We have the music of a struggling Beethoven. Just imagine what he could have written for us in happiness.

At least at a funeral the bitterest tears are welcome. I could sit there in the darkness, gazing at the coffin, listening to Franz Grillparzer's oration, praying uselessly, and recognise that in the chain of cause and effect the oppression that destroyed my sister had also contributed to killing the man she loved. We cannot simply stand in front of a situation knowing that it is wrong and remain silent. We have to do something to change it. *I* have to do something to change it.

Two months later, in the full, shining spring of 1827, I set off on a lengthy stagecoach journey to the Teleki castle beyond the three rivers of Siebenbürgen. I had not been back since Blanka was born. Now, as Lotti's carriage brought me up the drive and the dusky green distance spread out below the hilltop, I remembered it: Lotti running out, pregnant; Emerich with his dogs; the chill of religious disapproval. While the coachman unloaded my trunk I felt the sunshine on my face and smelled the fragrant air, honeyed with cherry blossom. Perhaps the countess had taken the ice away with her when she died.

There seemed to be nobody around. A breeze sighed across the castle and the calls of soaring birds of prey reached me from high above. Then the distant patter of hooves. The sound came nearer; for a moment I expected a posse of Napoleonic soldiers to burst out of the woods and charge towards me, alone with my trunk in a strange land. But no: a lone figure, riding a large black horse was approaching through a halo of dust. A woman in a blue dress – Lotti? No, because her hair was dark, long and curly, unleashed to the freedom of the wind. And she was only a young girl, no more than fourteen…

'Minona?'

You uttered an instruction to your steed and pulled on the reins. He came to a halt, nostrils flared, skin steaming; you must have had a long and vigorous excursion. You swung yourself down from the saddle in one smooth move and bounded forward to give me a strong hug. 'Auntie Tesi! I'm so glad you are here.'

'Minona, let me look at you…'

There you were: the dark brows, the snub nose, the forth-right gaze, somewhat forbidding even from a teenaged girl.

'Have I changed? I'm sure I haven't.' You flashed a white-toothed smile that put me in mind of another that I used to know.

'You've certainly grown. But you're right – people don't

change very much. They just grow older. Where *is* every-one, darling?'

'Oh, somewhere.' You shrugged, turning back to your horse and petting his mane.

'They let you go out riding on your own, at your age?'

'Auntie Tesi, you should hear yourself.' You laughed, then swept your hair back from your face and shouted: 'Auntie Lotti! Uncle Emy! Come and see who's here.'

Dearest Minona, at your age I would have had to fight for the right to ride alone through the hills and forests; my father would never have granted it. You probably never asked. You could have been an elfin figure from a Grimm fairy tale, authored by the relations of Bettina von Arnim; a mysterious horsewoman from a Sir Walter Scott novel; a changeling, a wood-nymph, or a semi-goddess in training, fathered by a demi-god.

'We ride for hours and hours.' You threw your arms open to the horizon. 'I love being in the woods, alone with nature all around us.'

'But... aren't there bears? And I remember hearing wolves...'

'They're more scared of us than we are of them. Besides, I love them. They wouldn't hurt me.'

'Don't you get lost?'

You kissed your horse on the nose. '*He* knows the way home.'


I had ample time to settle in while Lotti, plump in middle age, sat and talked to me. You went to drag Emerich out of his library, from the depths of which he had not heard my arrival. Theophile and Laura were in Estonia with their father; it must have taken some negotiation between

Emerich and Stackelberg to have you dispatched to Siebenbürgen for a lengthy stay. It wasn't so difficult, you said: 'I
like to spend several hours each day practising the piano, and
Papa does not like that. But I will not stop, and so we argue
a great deal. Here I may practise all day long, when I am not
out riding.'

After dinner – rich meat-stuffed cabbage and a glass of
dark local wine – Emerich looked over the candlesticks at
me. 'Therese, I sense there's something you want to tell us.'

'I do. My dears, you know that our Beethoven is dead.'

The pair glanced at each other, then at you; you looked
stricken.

'He's my favourite composer,' you said. 'I've been learning
some of his pieces. You *know* him?'

'Where to begin? He was... our dearest friend. In spirit,
he was my brother. Minona, dear, I have some things that
belonged to him. I would like to give them to you.'


I am in the Schwarzspanierhaus, in the apartment where he
died, the day after the funeral. A tall, bespectacled young
man with a convex nose and hatchet-shaped jaw introduces
himself to me: 'Anton Schindler, devoted secretary to the
Master.' His air is that of a minor civil servant who considers
himself distinguished – a type not uncommon around
Vienna. Schuppanzigh's young second violinist, Karl Holz,
is there with him: he too had become a secretary to the Master, who as I later learned couldn't stand Schindler.

These devotees have found among his effects my Greek-
priestess portrait, given to him eighteen years ago, and two
miniatures of young women. They ask me who they are.
I gaze with sorrow at the images of Julie (he kept that?
Really?) – and of Pepi, young, fresh and beautiful in a white

Empire-line dress. Some instinct tells me not to let Schindler get his paws on my sister's memory. Rarely have I taken such a dislike to anybody at first sight: he is buzzing around Beethoven's possessions like an insect hoping to snatch a mandibleful of blood. To judge from the state of the apartment, he has already taken away plenty of stuff that does not belong to him. 'The first is Countess Julie Guicciardi. The other – I'm not sure, but I think that's his great friend Countess Marie Erdödy,' I tell them.

'Please, Countess Therese, take something to remember him by,' Holz says. As if I could ever forget him. I locate a few books on the shelf that are already mine, unreturned; then I request some sheets of manuscript in his hand and one of his silver-tipped walking sticks. A presentiment, brought about by the increasingly pronounced curve of my spine, tells me the stick will have a practical use someday. Oh, and Pepi's eagle drawing, if they can find it. That is easy: it is still on the piano.

Luigi has left everything financial to his nephew. I question Holz.

'You are certain: everything?'

'Why do you ask?'

'I'm being nosy.' I smile. 'But are you *sure*?'

'A change was made in the will shortly before he died.' Holz shifts his feet, looking uncomfortable. 'Stephan von Breuning made the alteration for him – he was insistent. It was essential, you see, that Karl's mother would not receive any monies, should something untoward take place, so they created a trust for Karl, from which he will have the income during his lifetime. The reversion was to be to Beethoven's "legitimate" heirs, but he – weak, dying, with trembling hand as he signed his name – insisted that the word "legitimate" be changed to "natural".'

'Do you mean he has... another heir, who is... natural?'

'Dear Countess, I would never presume to consider such a thing.'

His estate had been valued at 9,885 florins and 13 kroner. My preoccupation you will have guessed: should there be money for you? If so, would you ever see it? I knew, my dear, how desperately unlikely that was, and deep is my regret that I could not make the difference necessary to gain your benefit. I judged that even if I told them the full story, they would not accept it. I did not know then about the 'Immortal Beloved' letter; and though I now realise Schindler must already have found it, he said nothing, for reasons of his own. Still, I believe Beethoven wished, as he lay dying, to make some gesture towards you – his only 'natural' heir.


'This is a drawing your mother made for him.' I pushed the eagle across the table to you. 'Here is a manuscript page of sketches, in his handwriting. When you are older, I have some letters to give you too.'

You took the papers with your fingertips, as if afraid to handle them.

'There's so much to tell you, my dear...'

But you did not want to listen. You were, after all, still a young girl, and you wanted to talk. You wanted to tell me about the castle, the gardens, the neighbours – some miles away – whose children were becoming your friends. You wanted to talk about Laura and Theophile who were so dear, but so terribly pale and droopy. You would not stop chattering. What a wonderful girl you were, and how very unlike your Stackelberg sisters. You would seize fate by the throat every morning if you had to.

We kissed you goodnight. The room turned too quiet after you had gone up to bed.

'She is remarkable.' Emerich's eyes were gentle with fondness. 'We both love her to pieces. She's a little like Blanka, in her own way, but softer, more open – more like Josephine.'

'Sometimes,' said Lotti, 'I think she will be the strongest of us all.'


I was with Blanka and Emma in the Martonvásár library, working on our English – we were reading Jane Austen's novel *Sense and Sensibility*, about two sisters, one ruled by her head, the other by her heart – when Franz's corpulent figure waddled in. 'Tesi, forgive the interruption, but come and look at this. Luigi, may he rest in peace, must finally have lost his mind.'

In the music room, he and his three companions, instruments at the ready, were puzzling over a string quartet.

'Keeping time is proving difficult,' Franz said. 'It may be that this thing is unplayable, but if you would *conduct* us, perhaps we can gain some idea of it.'

A full score sat on the floor between their music stands. I took it up. It was headed 'GROSSE FUGE, Op. 133'. Great Fugue. Another one? In B flat again? It seemed redolent of that vast piano sonata Op. 106. That had been possible, so this would be too. Why be intimidated?

The fugue had originally belonged to his quartet, Op. 130, but his publishers found it a step too far ('For heaven's sake, bring us something people can actually play, or nobody will buy it!'). You would expect Luigi to refuse to compromise, but he did not. Perhaps it was thanks to his fondness for his substitute nephew, Karl Holz, who was charged with persuading him – but it's possible, too, that he had no energy left to fight. He agreed, rather meekly, and wrote a new finale: less interesting, but relatively straight-forward. The fugue would stand alone. Those who wished to tackle it were free to try.

Soon I, too, was wondering if Luigi had gone over the edge.

'What does he *want*?' Franz grumbled. 'Are those notes tied or re-sounded? If they're tied, why didn't he just write a flaming crotchet? And those semiquavers – first they're together, then they're against triplets, then against quavers and semiquavers – do we play the rhythm the same way all the way through, or change according to the context?'

I attempted to keep time and to cue in each player at the right moments. Some extraordinary eloquence flowered out, and some intense passages in unison, but mostly this music seemed to be mathematical exactitude from deep within the brain of someone who had disconnected from the outside world in order to travel beyond it. Could he have written such a thing without the sonic solitude of deafness, which protected him from malign influences and turned him inward, towards a universe that existed only within the spirit? I was beginning to grant such ideas more currency than I had while my friend lived.

We reached the last bar. Silence fell while we all stared at the music, completely stumped.

'Hopeless,' said the violist. 'We'll have to *practise* it.'

'I think we all deserve a drink,' said the first violinist.

'Yes, and then onward,' said Franz. 'There's only one more quartet: let's try it. Op. 135. It can't be any crazier.'

'Do you want me to conduct this too?'

'No, no.' Franz was tuning his cello. 'But stay and listen.'

Luigi rarely made 'programmes' for his works explicit. Schindler said that a narrative existed for each of the piano sonatas, but the composer had never got round to writing them down. Now, for the last movement of the last quartet, there came a title: '*Der schwer gefasste Entschluss*' – the difficult decision. A slow introduction, with discordant harmonies: '*Muss es sein?*'; then a reply, joyous and accepting: '*Es muss sein!*'. Must it be? It must be. He has made his decision. He has chosen to live.

No trace here of Pepi's theme. But I have the late piano pieces with me, including the *33 Variations in C on a Waltz by Diabelli* and some sets of tiny pieces entitled Bagatelles. The *Diabelli Variations* approaches its conclusion with a giant fugue, yet one more variation follows: a minuet, poised, graceful, to be danced, maybe in a pearly-gated ballroom, by one who far preferred it to a waltz. As for the last bagatelle, it opens with a furious few bars that sound like a coda; then comes a meditative song, fragmented, distilled, Pepi's motif at its purest. She is still with him. Now only the music is left.

The year after Luigi died, I sold the house I owned in Buda. I sold my remaining jewels. I cashed in my investments. I put everything I had into the founding of my first educational association, designed to support the development of the first school in Hungary for very young girls – my garden of angels, or, as they now call it, a kindergarten. My final duty to my sister was over. Now it was time to belong to the world.

My dearest Minona, please accept with this letter the truth of your heritage. I am sending you today the documents I promised you, which I found among your mother's effects after her death: letters from your real father, the man she loved and who loved her, steadfast and unshakeable, for the rest of his life. Guard them well; preserve them for posterity. I have done all I can to concur with your uncle Franz's determination to conceal the truth, but it cannot be forever. I am the last of my generation and may not have long to live. You are the last of yours; the early deaths of your sisters were each a tragedy, and your brothers died too young, though at least were granted the bliss of children of their own. It is as if you, the daughter of my sister's true love, were the only one destined for a long life. May you be the keeper of your father's flame. God bless you.

Your aunt,
Therese.

My letter today is to myself alone: a memo. For my niece has responded to my missive as only she could.

The candles were burning low, and I was wondering whether to summon a medicinal cognac nightcap, when there was a commotion outside my door. My maid appeared in some agitation.

'Madame, your niece is here.'

'Who? Blanka?'

'No, Madame, it's Baroness Stackelberg. I should warn you, Madame, she seems rather upset.'

She was still a Stackelberg to all intents and purposes. The aristocratic title had ensured her a good post with Countess Bánffy. The splendid horsewoman, the brave young girl with her passion for nature, was forty-six years old and, to my mind, more like Luigi every day.

She strode in past the maid. 'I have not brought it with me.' She kept her voice low, as if to avoid eavesdroppers. 'But if I had, I would slap it down on your desk and ask what the meaning of this is.'

I was lost for words, which is unlike me.

'Aunt Therese, you are saying that I am an illegitimate child.'

That is one logical conclusion, I suppose.

'It is outrageous,' she hissed. 'To think my own aunt could accuse me of such a thing!'

'It's not an "accusation", Minona. It's not your fault. Have you not heard the rumours in the family?'

'That is gossip. You are asserting it as fact. Why? Why would you want to put me through this?'

'Because...' I looked at Minona's fist, clenched white with fury as she leaned on my desk. 'I want you to understand your mother. She suffered endless torment, and...'

'You are making it worse. You say Beethoven was my father. How dare you?'

'I expected you to be *pleased* to be Beethoven's daughter, especially since music is your own calling.'

'Can you prove it? Of course not. You can't prove anything.'

I had written her a lengthy letter aiming to do exactly that.

'It proves nothing. You are surmising. You are using vague, subjective, circumstantial evidence, not *fact*.'

'You're saying it wouldn't stand up in court.' I smiled, more to myself than her. My best Beethovenian smile. 'As if courts were the answer.'

'And why should I believe a word you say? Your memory is going. You're eighty-four, Aunt Therese – and you can't remember where people were when, or even what you witnessed or did not. You were in Buda with Grandmother when Aunt Lotti was living with my mother in Hietzing – you were running a music festival, doing dramatic declamations and drawing great praise from the King of Naples – no wonder you had such a fixation on that wax sculpture.

And you and my mother *were not at* the Congress of Vienna!
I don't doubt that you heard about the fire at Count Razumovsky's, but you cannot have been there yourselves.'

'You were not even two years old. How would you
know?'

'I found letters from you to Aunt Lotti, written that year
and sent from Buda. I looked through them as soon as I read
that fairy-tale description of something you never even saw.
You and Mama were in Buda with Grandmother, trying to
make ends meet.'

My mind flattened like a sunless sea. Yes, Pepi went home
to Hungary so that she could be properly fed. I remember
I was there at some point, but when exactly... I went back
and forth so many times... but I remember the ball as if it
were yesterday. Meeting Louis.

Or did I? Palace courtyards, Grecian porticos, twisting
stone stairways, it all melts into one...

'And it is absolute bunkum about Viky. That horror story
about her death. What nonsense! She was dead for two days
before they buried her and it was never in a crypt at all.
Fritz's widow told me. Whoever gave you that little tale was
setting out deliberately to upset you.'

I fought a lump in my throat. 'She succeeded, then. I was
nearly mad for three years.'

'Aunt Therese, you are, by your own admission, quite
disconnected from reality. All this Greek philosophy and
Hindu literature, and that vow of yours. What really happened to "Toni"? Who on earth was he? Where was he
killed?'

I swallowed and took a breath. 'He wasn't, dear. I thought
for a long time that he was dead. He just... went away. Perhaps he was a cad and a bounder, or he decided against his

courtship, or his family objected. Possibly all three. It caused me some pain, which I prefer to forget.'

'I see.' Minona glared. 'You just didn't fancy setting it out for me. But what about the way you treated Louis Migazzi? The poor man must have taken years to recover.'

'He was fine,' I snapped. 'He married at forty; he had a family; he did not suffer any longer from my foolishness.'

'It's as if...' She was breathing hard, hunting for words through her seething emotions; I shrank back in my chair. 'It's as if you could only love a man if you either worshipped him as your father or as a hero – like Beethoven – or else, if you made him worship you as a mother – like Migazzi. There's something insane about it, something unhealthy...'

I parried her attack with calm. 'I could have married. I didn't want to. I have done other things instead.'

'I would have married, if I could, but I cannot. That's because there are too many rumours that I am not my father's daughter, and too little money to support my dowry. Uncle Franz and Aunt Sidonie would not help, and my father – Baron Stackelberg – has played little part in my life. You have merely confirmed the worst. If you really loved me, you would write another document, declaring that I am indubitably the daughter of Baron Christoph von Stackelberg – so help you, God.'

Perhaps she had a point. Through decades of dedication to my schools, and the politics that dogged the associations as the network grew and men started wanting to take my success for themselves, I had paid scant attention to anything else. I lived for a while in Munich, further still from Minona's life in Estonia; I knew nothing of her innermost heart or romantic attachments. She nursed her sister Theophile when she died too young; after Stackelberg's death in 1841 she and Laura went to the Telekis, where

Minona then ended up nursing both her last sister and her beloved aunt Lotti in their final illnesses. She stayed with the ageing Emerich as his housekeeper and librarian until he, too, departed this world, for by then Emma and Blanka were far away.

I had thought Minona now had a good life as a paid companion, with her own apartment in her employer's beautiful Viennese palais. She mixed with the cream of society and met all the best musicians. She gave piano lessons and played well; occasionally she composed pieces of her own. Yet perhaps I had misjudged her...

I rang the bell and summoned two cognacs. We were both overwrought; it might calm us.

Instead, the tawny liquid jolted something in my mind.

'Have you read the letters I gave you?'

'Yes.'

'Where are they now?'

Minona set her jaw. Her developing jowls were acquiring a distinctive and familiar downward curve. 'I have burned them.'

Thank goodness that, with a little foresight, I had kept back a handful, just in case.

'He may have called her his undying love, immortal beloved or whatever you like,' she said, 'but the sooner we wipe poor Mama's memory away from the family, the better for everybody.'

'Everybody except them.'

'They've been dead for decades.'

'Not to me, they haven't.'

That made her pause. She could see how upset I was. 'I'm sorry, Aunt Tesi. I should simply have brought the letters back to you.'

'It's all right, Minona. It's too late. Now only the music matters.'

The fury was dwindling, the attack dissipating. We sat together in the last of the candlelight. Near my chair the tip of my walking stick – Luigi's – gleamed silver.

'It's my fault,' I said. 'I'm a silly old fool. I understand, my dear, and I've done all I can to keep your mother's name and ours clear of public notoriety. Franz spreads word, with the help of gullible Schindler, that the "Immortal Beloved" was our cousin Julie. Marie Hrussoczky will write a book telling the world that it is me, which will add a pleasing dose of obfuscation to the issue – after all, I never married anybody, unlike my sister – and should anyone find my diary once I am gone, they will see many references to a certain "Louis"… But there is the small matter of the truth.'

Minona reached for my hand and pressed it. 'Is it too late in the evening for me to play your piano?'

She went to the new Bechstein grand that the hotel had allowed me to hire during my stay – an instrument with several times the power of Beethoven's old Broadwood. I wonder what he would have written for this one, given the chance.

'I want to play you something,' she said. 'It's by Robert Schumann.'

Under her strong hands, broad of palm with fine-tipped fingers, a cascade of music streamed out. A flood of ideas, surging by at high speed like a dream, filled with incandescent passion. Minona's face shone, transfigured, as the music passed through her to my ears. Finally it subsided – and coalesced into a familiar theme.

'From *An die ferne Geliebte*,' she said, without stopping. 'A direct quote. He was in love with a young pianist – you know Clara Schumann…'

'Yes, yes, I know Clara Schumann, I've met her... This was for her?'

The music came to rest. 'He took the message from the song cycle – "When you sing what I have sung, then our spirits are united" – and he sent it in music to her while they were forbidden to meet. So... the truth was in Beethoven's music, and now it's in Schumann's Fantasie in C major. Reincarnated, if you like.'

A new rhyme, a developing variation: here lies true immortality.

Perhaps Minona was right: I expected too much of her, just as I used to expect too much of everybody, including myself. We are all variations on our own themes and it is up to us – to some degree – whether we finish as a great fugue or a simple minuet. No matter. It is too late for regrets. Today I can look back over my achievements, and I think my father might be proud of me.

# Coda

**Therese Brunsvik** in 1828 founded a pioneering school for children aged three to six in Buda, the first of its kind to open in central Europe. She went on to establish kindergartens across Hungary and beyond, focusing not only on education for girls, but for children from impoverished backgrounds. Her memory is revered in this field. She died in 1861, aged eighty-six.

**Anton Schindler**'s biography of Beethoven was published in 1840. It revealed the 'Immortal Beloved' letter and declared 'Giulietta' Guicciardi its intended recipient. Schindler's book has been widely discredited; he has been accused of falsifying and indeed destroying some of the 'conversation books' with which Beethoven had communicated. None survive from 1821, the year of Josephine's death. While it is possible Schindler did not know about Josephine's relationship with Beethoven, it also seems likely that his friendship with Franz Brunsvik led him to conceal her under cover of her cousin.

**Franz Brunsvik** became the manager of the Pest Theatre in 1819 and married a celebrated Hungarian pianist, Sidonie Justh (who was not of noble birth, but became a countess upon marriage to him), in 1823. They were in the audience when the violinist Joseph Joachim made his debut as a seven-year-old child prodigy in Pest in 1838. In 1850 a Brunsvik genealogical book was published that did not mention Josephine's name. Franz died in Vienna in 1849.

Josephine's son **Fritz** – Friedrich Deym, Count von Střítež – became a politician and political writer. His first wife, Pauline Seignan de Casteras, died aged only twenty in 1825. His second marriage was to Maria Longueval von Buquoy and the couple had three children. He died in Vienna in 1853.

**Julie Gallenberg**, née Guicciardi, is famous as the dedicatee of Beethoven's Piano Sonata Op. 27, No. 2, the 'Moonlight'. Her husband, Count Wenzel Robert von Gallenberg, wrote music for around fifty ballets, and held posts at both the opera house in Naples and at the Kärntnerthortheater in Vienna, which he leased from 1829 to 1830. Gallenberg died in 1839 and Julie in 1856.

**Minona Stackelberg** died in 1897 and is buried in Vienna not far from Beethoven's grave. Surviving photographs of her suggest a striking likeness to him and his mother. An opera has been written about her life by the Estonian composer Jüri Reinvere, premiered in Regensburg in 2020.

**Blanka Teleki**, after her release from prison, spent the last years of her life in Paris. She died there in 1862.

**Marianna Martines** (1744–1812) was a remarkable musician and composer whose works were long forgotten. Her story is told in Anna Beer's book *Sounds and Sweet Airs*, an exploration of seven female composers' lives.

**Ignaz Schuppanzigh**, the revered violinist and lifelong

friend of Beethoven, died in Vienna in 1830. His ensemble was the world's first professional string quartet.

**Franz Schubert** died in 1828, aged thirty-one. His prolific musical output needs no introduction. It also included sketches for an opera, *Shakuntala*. Elements of this same story can be found in Richard Wagner's *Götterdämmerung*, the last (though the first planned) opera of his *Ring* tetralogy.

**Marie Hrussoczy**, writing as 'Mariam Tenger', published her book about Therese only in 1890. Full of anecdotes supposedly related by the countess, it provided a powerful red herring, suggesting Therese was the 'Immortal Beloved' and had been secretly engaged to Beethoven until the latter broke off the relationship. The book is widely assumed to be a fabrication, though whether purely by Hrussoczy or with the actual encouragement of Therese is not certain.

*A note on place names*: Ofen and Pest are modern-day Budapest. Siebenbürgen is Transylvania. Pressburg is Bratislava, Brünn is Brno, Karlsbad is the popular spa town of Karlovy Vary, Franzensbad is Františkovy Lázně, Znaim is Znojmo and Teplitz is Teplice. Stackelberg's hometown, Reval, is Tallinn, Estonia. The Donaukanal is not an actual canal, but a branch of the River Danube.

# Author's Note

The story told in *Immortal* is not new. It has been well known in a corner of Beethoven research for many years, but for complex reasons has been slow to achieve wide recognition. This book is not an academic study, but a novel, and offers its interpretation not as a definitive solution, but as a possible one.

Numerous theories still abound regarding the identity of the 'Immortal Beloved'; as none are supported by more than circumstantial evidence, one must weigh up how convincing that circumstantial evidence is in each case. To me, there seems no contest, but I appreciate that others can and will disagree. This is partly why I decided to tackle the tale as fiction: in many ways it always will be.

My aims are, first, to bring the mystery out into the daylight for general readers who love Beethoven's music; and secondly, to tell the story from the perspective of its female characters. The pioneering educationalist and feminist Countess Therese Brunsvik von Korompa, the closest confidante of her sister Josephine, presented herself as the ideal narrator – whether she is reliable or otherwise.

While sticking closely to the facts as far as they are

known, I have occasionally employed what used to be called
'artistic licence' in order to dramatise and interpret events. I
crave the reader's indulgence and good sense at such points.
Examples include Franz's visit to Beethoven in Heiligenstadt, and the scene in which Josephine arrives back, dis-
traught, from Prague; it is not known exactly how she and
Beethoven encountered one another there (nor is it even
certain that they did), so the scenario she describes is a possibility rather than an actuality. Then there is the *Fidelio* premiere at which Schubert enters the story. He did sell his
schoolbooks to buy a ticket, but in real life was probably not
swept up into the Brunsvik sisters' box. Marianna Martines's
friendship with Therese is imaginary, but far from impossible. Therese's 'Toni' is real, but his exact identity remains
mysterious. The characters of Takács the coachman and his
daughter Magda, Pepi's maid, are fictional, as is the outing
to Lake Balaton.

At certain moments I have placed Therese in Vienna, so
that she can observe her sister at first hand, when actually she
was in Hungary (for example, in 1816). Also, little is known
of Louis Migazzi and his strange relationship with Therese;
I have therefore attempted to 'create' him in a way that
reflects the idealised memories of the ageing countess. The
scene describing Minona in Transylvania is likewise idealised; she was probably in Estonia with Stackelberg at this
time. According to Therese's memoirs, however, Minona
lived with the Telekis after Stackelberg's death in 1841,
and one could consider that she might earlier have built a
relationship with her aunt and uncle. As for Fritz and his
teenage misdemeanours, he chronicled these in his memoirs,
which are reported (in an article by Rita Steblin) to reveal
an affair with Julie in 1821. Fritz's wild behaviour at thirteen

appears to be what prompted Stackelberg to abduct his own daughters.

I encourage readers to explore the other theories of the 'Immortal Beloved' – including Antonie Brentano (a case built by the scholars Maynard Solomon and Susan Lund, among others) and even Bettina Brentano – and make up their own minds. The only possible proof, or otherwise, of the Josephine theory would be a DNA test on the skeletons of Ludwig van Beethoven and Minona Stackelberg. While the idea has sometimes been mooted, appetite for such a move is unsurprisingly scarce.

# Acknowledgements

I am deeply indebted to the articles of the late Rita Steblin, whose sterling research is published in numerous musicological journals, notably in the series of *Bonn Beethoven Studies*, *Österreichische Musikzeitschrift* and *The Musical Times:* the latter's summer 2019 edition included her crucial article, 'New evidence for Josephine as the "Immortal Beloved" involving Beethoven and England in 1818'.

Marie-Elisabeth Tellenbach's *Beethoven und seine 'unsterbliche Geliebte' Josephine Brunswick* (1983) was a seminal work, especially as regards 'traces' of Josephine in Beethoven's music. Jean and Brigitte Massin's 1955 biography of Beethoven also explores these musical traces. Tellenbach's book is available in English translation by the late John E. Klapproth. A zealous devotee of Josephine as Immortal Beloved, Klapproth wrote *The Immortal Beloved Compendium* and translated a number of books on the topic, also including *All About Beethoven's Immortal Beloved* by Harry Goldschmidt and *Beethoven and the Brunsviks* by Ida Maria Lipsius, 'La Mara' (1909). I found further important material in a detailed online article by Michael Lorenz entitled *The Exhumation of Josephine Countess von Deym*.

Of prime importance is the collection of letters held at the Beethoven-Haus in Bonn, the most precious resource for Beethoven researchers on location and, in digitised form, the world over. Where extracts of letters appear in the novel, these are my attempts at rendering them from the German. Any mistakes – there or elsewhere – are entirely mine.

The draft of the letter that Josephine wrote on Minona's fifth birthday is in Marie-Elisabeth Tellenbach's book, as is Stackelberg's shocking letter to his wife. Toni's warning to Therese and the latter's persuasive words to Princess Kinsky, however, are fictional.

There is naturally no shortage of literature about Beethoven and his world. Recommended reading includes Alexander Thayer's *Life of Beethoven*, Romain Rolland's *Beethoven the Creator*, Jan Swafford's *Beethoven: Anguish and Triumph*, *The Letters of Beethoven* collected and translated by Emily Anderson, Jan Caeyers' *Beethoven: A Life*, Laura Tunbridge's *Beethoven: A Life in Nine Pieces*, John Suchet's *Beethoven: The Man Revealed*, Oscar Sonneck's *Beethoven: Impressions by his Contemporaries*, William S. Newman's *Beethoven on Beethoven*, Edward Dusinberre's *Beethoven for a Later Age*, Eric Hobsbawm's *The Age of Revolution*, David King's *Vienna, 1814* and Rachel Hewitt's *A Revolution of Feeling*. This list could continue for many pages: my apologies for not listing everything here.

The people I must thank are innumerable, and again I apologise for any omissions. Dr Malte Boecker, director of the Beethoven-Haus, kindly confirmed to me that the vast majority of Beethoven scholars now accept Josephine as the most likely 'Immortal Beloved'. Alexander Freiherr von dem Bottlenberg's insights into the Austrian aristocracy have been invaluable and he kindly connected me with Dr

Eric Heinke and his office in Vienna, who provided substantial information regarding the workings of the law there in the late eighteenth and early nineteenth centuries. Murray Perahia's Henle Urtext edition of the Sonata Op. 27, No. 2 (the 'Moonlight') inspired an important episode of the novel. And without Eric Wen's encouragement I might not have written anything at all. For many and varied reasons, my warmest thanks also to Marios Papadopoulos, Marin Alsop, Daniel Hope, Vladimir Jurowski, Richard Bratby, Roxanna Panufnik, Julian Rushton, Kathryn Stott, Nicky Thomas, Rachel Tregenza, Hugh Mather, John Gilhooly, Mishka Rushdie Momen and Viv McLean. Deep gratitude to John Mitchinson, Anna Simpson, Julia Koppitz, Sadie Mayne, Elodie Olson-Coons, Xander Cansell and the whole wonderful team at Unbound, and of course to my husband Thomas Eisner for putting up heroically with my regular disappearances into the nineteenth century.

Last but not least, my profound thanks to all the subscribers who have contributed so generously to the funding of this book. Beethoven himself would have recognised this model.

Unbound is the world's first crowdfunding publisher, established in 2011.

We believe that wonderful things can happen when you clear a path for people who share a passion. That's why we've built a platform that brings together readers and authors to crowdfund books they believe in – and give fresh ideas that don't fit the traditional mould the chance they deserve.

This book is in your hands because readers made it possible. Everyone who pledged their support is listed at the front of the book and below. Join them by visiting unbound.com and supporting a book today.

Rebekah Drury
Leslie East
Susan Elkin
Tom Ellett
Yvonne Frindle
Sophie Fuller
Malcolm Gibson
Helen H
Ben Hogwood
Claire Jackson
Norman Jacobs
Robin Jacobs
Mary Jordan-Smith
Tim Lund Jorgensen
Sascha Kelly
Fozia Khanam
Marjan and Jane Kiepura
Dan Kieran
Helene Kreysa
Steven Ledbetter
Peter Marks
Douglas McFarland
Erin McGann
Hannes Minnaar
John Mitchinson

Mishka Momen
Fiona Moncur
Margarida Mota-Bull
Rhel ná DecVandé
Carlo Navato
Dilys Page
Melis Peykoğlu
Jenny Pichierri
Justin Pollard
Rhian Heulwen Price
Danielle Salamon
Heather Sharp
Sue Shorter
David Singerman
Clare Slator
Henriette B. Stavis
Clare Stevens
Galina Tanney
Ina Tullo
Beverly Usher
Angelo Villani
Jo W
Andrew Wales
SJ Wanta
Philip Ward